A Time to Rise

Books by Nadine Brandes

Out of Time series

A Time to Die | BOOK ONE

A Time to Speak | BOOK TWO

A Time to Rise | BOOK THREE

Fawkes

Romanov

Wishtress

A Time to Rise

The Out of Time Series:

Book Three

Nadine Brandes

A Time to Rise
Copyright © 2016 by Nadine Brandes

Published by Enclave Publishing, an imprint of Oasis Family Media.

Carol Stream, Illinois, USA.
www.enclavepublishing.com

ISBN: 978-1-68370-046-3 (printed softcover)
ISBN: 978-1-68370-047-0 (eBook)

Cover designed by Kirk DouPonce, www.DogEaredDesign.com
Interior designed by Beth Shagene

Printed in the United States of America.

This book is dedicated to
my beloved husband, Daylen:
the greatest supporter of my writing
and constant example of shalom.
Let's exalt His name together.

And also to my readers.
I make you cry, then you make me cry . . .
and somehow we're all smiling.
Thank you.

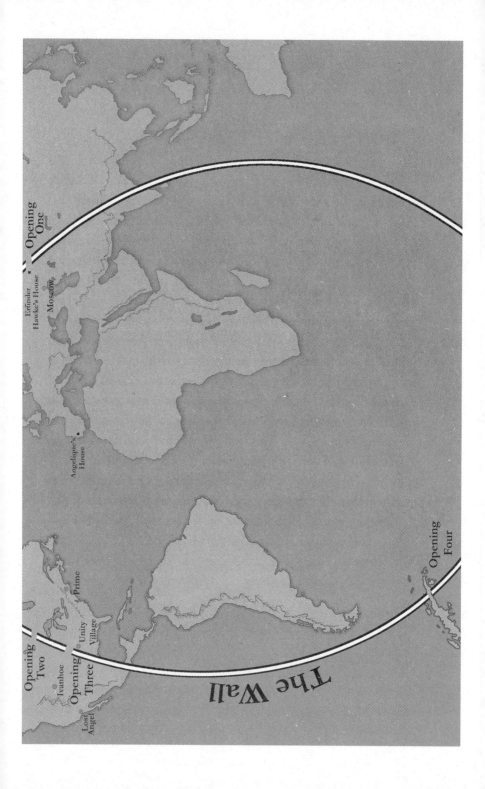

1

I wake in a coffin.

The beep of my own flatline is fresh in my memory. What's going on? Where am I? Why am I . . . not dead?

My arms press against walls of wood. My hot breath rebounds off the underside of the coffin lid, hitting my face. Flashes. Glimpses of memories. I can't remember. Something happened to me—something traumatic. Something powerful. My emotions are drained, but I can't pinpoint why I'm here.

ARISE.

I start. Nothing wakes me more than that voice. *His* voice.

"God, where are you?" I open my eyes wide, meeting only darkness. "Where am *I*?"

Dying.

I am *dying* right now . . . in this coffin. My very breaths tremble. Why can't I remember details?

Another burst of breath. My chest seizes. What woke me? I feel . . . startled. Is it because I'm suffocating?

I'm suffocating!

The beat of my heart is frantic, like a trapped bird. My next inhale is thin. There's not much oxygen left in the casket. How long have I been in here?

How . . .

. . . am I . . .

. . . alive?

I flail and push against the coffin lid with my hand and stump. It groans like a slave beneath the weight of a hundred shackles. The cold seeps through the thin walls, through my clothing, and the creak of wood tells me I'm underground.

Deep underground.

My elbows and knees knock wood and bruise. I'm lost in my mind. Lost in a coffin. Who would bury me? *Alive?*

"Help!"

My own voice startles me, rebounding around my ears in this death box.

What do I do? *God, what do I do?*

ARISE.

The calm that floods my heart brings with it a distant recollection. The last time I lay in His peace, beneath the umbrella of His voice, I was dying. But He's woken me. For . . . something. A last prayer, maybe?

Then they come, like a marching troop—memories parading across my mind:

I broke down a chunk of the Wall.

I helped free people from the United States of the East.

The Council captured me—*us*. Us . . . Solomon, Elm, Frenchie, Kaphtor, Cap, Gabbie.

I am Parvin Blackwater.

Where is Skelley Chase, the Council member who helped kill me? Where is Solomon? Did he escape? He can't possibly know the Council buried me alive.

I'm alive.

With this thought comes a rerun of the emotions that abducted my heart the last time I was awake. Hope that my friends escaped. Peace in the sacrifice of my life for their sakes.

"I'm alive!" I laugh and then clap my lips shut. There goes

more oxygen, but I'm not afraid. I should be dead, which means God had different plans. And *that* means . . .

I'm escaping this coffin.

This is the second time in my life I've willingly embraced death, and both times God responded with, NOT YET. Giddy excitement fills my heaving chest with a thousand mini bubbles. What does He have in store for me?

I squirm in the space. It's roomy—not made for me. My feet hit something lumpy. Ugh, not another body! No, it's too small to be a body.

How does one escape a buried box? I don't have a nanobook to send a message for help. Besides, I have no idea *where* I'm buried. Help would be too late, NAB or not. I'm not strong enough to lift the dirt, but the Council probably buried me with haste to get rid of the evidence, so they might not have buried me down all six feet.

The Council. They think I'm dead. Once I escape, I'll be invisible to them.

I kick the lump at my feet again, snag it with my heels, and scoot it toward my torso. I need light! This darkness threatens to replace my shaky peace with fear. My knees hit the underside of the coffin, barely bent, but it's enough. I squirm to one side, reaching with my right hand—my only hand—for the lump. Fingers brush canvas.

My shoulder pack.

The Council had it searched and practically emptied when putting me in the cell. Yet here it is. All evidence is buried with me—at least, that must have been their plan. Good thing they didn't cremate me.

If Solomon managed to escape with the others, he's still out there spreading truth. My heart squeaks.

Solomon.

He thinks I'm dead.

He was so brave in accepting my choice to succumb to the Council's torture. For a moment, I allow myself to create a vision of the last time I saw his face. He was crying. Resigned. I mentally wipe the tears from his light skin, turn his squinted, teal eyes into open ones filled with hope and surprise.

I must find him. The man I love.

ARISE.

God. His voice. His presence in my mind reminds me why I'm here. I'm alive and fully His. *I'm fully Yours.* My agenda doesn't matter. I focus on obeying. Arising.

I hold my breath and reach, pressing my face and shoulder against the rough coffin wood. It creaks as I wrap my fingers around the pack strap. This coffin isn't Father's handiwork. It smells old and breakable. That's a plus.

The minus is that if it breaks, the dirt will cave in on me. I'll be suffocated before I can move. I'm already weak and light-headed. My chest aches.

I yank the pack up the side of the coffin until it's on my chest. The air grows thinner and my breaths more frequent. I'm tempted to panic, but then I remember why I'm awake.

I'M NOT DONE WITH YOU YET.

I smile and fumble with the pack straps. They're tied tight. Without a left hand, it takes me twice as long to get them untangled. I can't angle my head to bite the knot where I need to. There must be *something* in here to help me escape.

The darkness presses on my eyes, mocking me. I'd laugh back in its face, but oxygen is too precious. I'm dizzy. Or I might be suffocating. Maybe there are still matches in my pack.

Oh! Silly me. I search for the thread-thin metal cord around my left wrist that's causing so much havoc in the United States of the East right now—the Clock telling me the day I'm supposed to die.

It's secure, but so light I barely feel it. With my thumb and forefinger, I press the thickest portion of the wire. A blue screen reveals my underground prison. The projected red Numbers that used to mean so much to me click down, virtually, second by second:

031.014.17.02.44
Parvin Brielle Blackwater
OVERRIDDEN

That's supposed to be the day I'll die. Thirty-one years, fourteen days, seventeen hours, blah, blah, blah. I don't believe a second of it. Besides, the word glowing beneath my ticking Numbers is what matters: *OVERRIDDEN*

That's why there's chaos in the USE. These new Clock inventions—stolen from Jude by the Council—have a glitch. They don't tell me my future. What the Numbers *do* tell me is that I was with the Council just over two hours ago.

I died as they tested my Clock.

The Council was afraid of that—I've proven their new system is flawed. They're going to have to admit it to the public eventually . . . and pay the consequences.

If I was buried within the last two hours, the dirt above me will be fresh and loose. I hold my illuminated stump aloft, taking a good look at my situation. I look long at my healed wrist, no longer feeling heart pain because of my missing hand. Funny how a single year can change my perspective.

The lid of the coffin is bowed from the weight. Best to figure out an escape plan before I run out of oxygen. My stomach lurches. Maybe . . . maybe God *will* let me die this time.

I fiddle with the pack flap again. My breathing accelerates and I close my eyes to steady my lungs. *Be calm.*

One flap comes loose. I thrust my hand into the pack and search. My fingers encounter fabric and fur—the skirt Mother made me. Within its folds, I find a small length of wood—the whistle Jude gave me before he died. Useless, but still sentimental.

I blow it, its calm *toot!* too gentle. No one above ground will hear. As if anyone's up there waiting for me.

Next, my fingers brush over my thick Bible. The pages were waterlogged once, but now they're dried and still readable. The Council didn't know quality when they saw it, searching my pack. Too bad for them. They left me with the one tool that will make me stronger than the most powerful member of the Council—who is, hands-down, Skelley Chase . . . followed closely by Elan Brickbat.

I continue the blind search and pass over my sentra—the camera-like contraption that takes emotigraphs—my last gift from Reid. Next, my fingers find *The Daily Hemisphere* electro-sheet. Despite my curiosity at what the Council might be reporting regarding my "death" and the destruction of a Wall chunk, I move it aside and keep searching.

Nothing. Nothing else. Traitorous tears burn my eyes. What did I expect to find? A NAB to signal Solomon for help?

Among the nothingness is a realization that all my emotigraphs are gone—the thin snapshots of emotions taken during my travels to and from Antarctica, leading the people to freedom. Maybe Skelley or Brickbat will feel one of those emotigraphs and come one step closer to understanding my passion and calling toward shalom.

I pull out my Bible and let it rest on my chest. My pounding heartbeat bumps against it, hitting the palm of my hand as if reminding me I'm still alive and to not give up yet. My thumb flips the pages of the Bible in rhythm with my thoughts. The short *whoosh* of pages sends a breath of wind against my face, as if God is whispering to me: *FEAR NOT.*

"For You are with me." My thumb catches on a chunk of pages. I tilt my head and open the Bible to that section. I raise my wrist-Clock to see better by its glow. In between the pages, like a bookmark, rests a small silver square about the size and thickness of a matchbook. I pull it out with my thumb and forefinger. On the face of the silver square is a stick figure flexing his muscles.

"No way."

It's one of Wilbur Sherrod's shrunken enhanced outfits—the Brawn suit. I could kiss that silly Irish man for his amazing tech brain!

Didn't Solomon say that he'd snuck an outfit into my pack? I'd assumed the Enforcers found and took it. But no . . . because of Wilbur's new addition of shrinking the suits to small squares, the Brawn outfit took refuge between the pages of my Bible—something no Enforcer will touch.

Their carelessness—and God's sneakiness—is going to save my life.

I laugh now. Loudly. Joyfully. At this point, I care not how much oxygen I use. The Brawn suit enables me to lift thousands of pounds. The moment it's on, escaping this coffin will be like climbing through six feet of cotton.

I set the matchbook on my sternum and press it, despite the achy twinge in my chest. Smooth material slithers across my body, spreading like the world's thinnest—yet most powerful—blanket. Super-strength, here I come.

The suit takes less than a second to cover me. It's secure over my body. With a twist, I roll onto my stomach, loop my left arm around my pack and then push my back against the underside of the coffin lid. It snaps and the foot of the coffin caves in.

Dirt pours into my space and I suck in a gasp of dust. I hold my breath against a cough and grip the strap of my shoulder pack.

I'm buried.

I'm suffocating.

But I'm in the Brawn suit.

I yank the collar of my undershirt over my nose and mouth. Should have done *that* earlier. The breath I take is small, but clean. I cough.

One more inhale, then I launch to a standing position. The movement disturbs the dirt—though I don't feel any resistance because of the Brawn suit. The dirt fills the coffin, giving me a small pocket of air to breathe before more falls around me.

I reach my left arm up. My right still holds my pack tight against my side. The stump of my left hand breaks through to the surface. I move it in circular motions, loosening up the dirt and claw myself free. The moment my head pops out, I wipe my face with my elbow and allow the coughing to take over.

I must be a sight. A handless, famous, "dead" Radical crawling out of a fresh grave. I scan my surroundings. Deep shadows stretch from tree trunks and gravestones onto the manicured grass around me. It's nighttime. No one is here. The only light comes from the Clock on my wrist. My tombstone is in front of my face. Blank.

How touching.

After catching my breath, I crawl the rest of the way out. I'm careful not to move too much. The medibot inside me has a tracker chip and I'm willing to bet Skelley Chase is watching the tracking screen, even two hours after my "death."

The dirt around me is still dark from fresh digging. I consider smoothing it out so it doesn't look like I escaped, but the two-foot depression from my collapsed coffin *might* just give me away.

I flop back on the ground and stare at the stars for a long time. Where do I begin with my thoughts? This is a new life. A new me. I died . . . and now I'm alive again.

How am I alive?

Why am I alive?

The answer isn't a word or explanation. It's a feeling—a sensation of deep purpose so far beyond my understanding, yet pressed upon my heart.

God has woken me. I am fully and freely His, invisible to the enemy. I have a mission. My own desires barely tug my heart when set beside His calling. In fact, my desires start to parallel His calling. This is what it's like to truly surrender to Him.

Where do I go? I'm here. Send me.

"I knew you wouldn't die." I jump at the man's voice, mere feet away.

I launch into a sitting position and my wrist Clock illuminates two Enforcers resting against a thick Maple trunk. Long black cloaks concealed them in the shadows, but now I make out the backward E tattoos on their left temples. One is asleep. The other—the buzzed redhead with the prominent Adam's apple who, I think, helped Solomon escape—stares at me, eyes wide like mini moons. He straightens, as though trying to be brave, but he's trembling.

My eyes flick to the sleeping Enforcer.

"Don't worry about him," the Adam's-apple Enforcer says. "I can't wake him up. Yet *I* can't fall asleep. I figured it was because I was meant to see something." He gestures to me. "You."

What can I say? The Council placed guards at my grave. But the guards aren't hauling me off to the Council. That's a start.

"My name's Zeke, by the way."

"Hi," I croak. How to respond? He's an *Enforcer*, but he was in the room when I died. *God, am I supposed to give him a special message or something?*

Zeke readjusts against the tree. "Do you . . . remember anything that's happened recently?"

It's like he knows about my struggle in the coffin to find my memories. "It came back slowly, but I think it's all there now. I . . . The Council killed me, and my friends . . . escaped?" Please say it's true.

"Strange." He shakes his head. "You remember things *and* . . . you're not dead. Why is that?"

He didn't deny that Solomon and the others escaped. That's good enough hope for me. I shrug. "God still has things for me to do." I think of last time something miraculous happened—when the wound on my right hand healed over the course of a day in Antarctica. "And . . . I have a medibot in me."

"What do you think He has for you?"

I died in front of the Council because I needed to. My death proved to them the Clocks weren't accurate. Jude made sure of that when he tweaked the invention. But now . . . what is my purpose? God's only woken me. I have no other direction. *Should* I go find Solomon? He's probably safer without me. My medibot is a tracker. I can't move.

"I'm still deciding." I'm just your everyday girl, crawling out of a grave and not sure whether to go save the world or take a nap. "But my medibot is tracking me. Skelley can see wherever I go. That's a problem."

"Oh." Zeke scratches his *E* tattoo and glances at the stars. "I don't think your medibot is tracking you anymore." He tilts his head. "This makes a little more sense now."

"What does?" My medibot's not a problem? Is the Council disbanded?

"Your medibot probably restarted your heart after neutralizing the pirate chip toxin. The higher-tech medibots are programmed to expel their last energy to restart one's heart. So it's dead, tracker and all."

Could he be right? Or might this be a trick? I lift my illuminated Clock. "I overrode my Clock, so . . . I guess you're right. I must have died."

"You definitely died." His voice is tight. "I've never seen Council member Chase so silent."

Victory. "Wow, God," I whisper.

Zeke maintains my gaze. "I don't understand it—this God thing of yours." He runs a hand through his hair. "But . . . I want to."

"Then you know Who to seek." I quirk a smile. "*My* 'God

thing' started with a desperate prayer on a hospital floor, asking Him to do something with my life." Now look at me.

Zeke nods. I close my eyes and take deep, freeing breaths. It is astonishing where God's taken me since then. When I open my eyes, Zeke's head rests against the trunk of the tree, eyes closed and breathing deeply.

"Uh . . . Zeke?"

I guess he fell asleep. I bite my knuckle, then spit because it's covered in dirt. I crawl closer and give his shoulder a shake. No response other than a half-snore. Weird. Kind of creepy. *Uh . . . God?* This is my sign that it's time to go.

I don't know if Zeke'll end up reporting me or not. But I suspect that this moment will change his life forever. My death sowed doubt into the minds of the Council. Now my life sows doubt in the minds of the Council's lackeys. Skelley was worried about what my death would mean. Now they know they've set up all of the United States of the East with faulty Clocks.

The Council caused its own downfall.

Here I am. A ghost. They think I'm dead, but I'm only just starting to live. I have a calling to fulfill. We broke down one part of the Wall, but now it's time to take it all down. No more barriers across our land. No more captivity.

That is my only goal. I will succeed because God pulled me out of a coffin to do it. Deep inside I know Zeke was right. The medibot is dead. I need not fear.

And through her faith, though she died, she still speaks. Those were my last thoughts before I succumbed to the pirate chip's toxin—my own version of Hebrews 11:4 and the verse of the week from the underground church in Prime.

That means their meeting is on Wednesday at 11:40pm.

Tonight.

I search the Enforcers until I find a watch and a NAB. I

steal both. I hope that's okay. After a moment, I take the other Enforcer's coat. Black is good cover at night.

According to the watch, it's 10pm. According to the NAB, I'm on the outskirts of Prime. Only an hour's walk away from the underground church. I rest, torn. Should I go to Solomon or continue on my own?

God?

GO.

A grin steals over my face. Solomon thinks I'm dead and, if he succeeded in escape, he's sure to be at that meeting. At last, instead of taking things from him, I can give something back.

I can give him me.

I sit up and brush the dirt off my face. Then, with my pack on my shoulder and my confidence dancing in God's hands, I arise.

Resurrected.

2

I lurk in the dark corner of the underground church. I'm early. Fight and Idris arrived about an hour ago. My Brawn suit is in my pocket and I'm dressed in my white Council prison clothes, Mother's skirt, and the black Enforcer coat.

No one has seen me yet. I don't reveal myself. I want my first eye contact to be with Solomon.

But what if he doesn't come?

What if he goes straight to the orphanage to rescue Willow? That's something he would do. He thinks I'm dead. But he would come here, too. This is his next family. He would at least bring Cap, Gabbie, Frenchie, Kaphtor, and Elm here for safety . . . unless he took them back to Unity Village.

I clamp my hand over my eyes. These questions push me to doubt, and I will *not* doubt. Not tonight.

The smell of earth on my clothes reminds me why doubt is a threat. The old Parvin Blackwater was the doubter. But I'm new. I'm strong. I'm God's.

He knows I want Solomon here with me, but if Solomon doesn't come then I'll be on my own. And that's okay. That's my sign that I'm to continue alone. Me and God. I like the sound of that. Uninterrupted devotion.

"Crazy about the Wall, huh?" Fight—the young redhead dude who leads the underground church meetings—stares at an electrosheet. His voice echoes against the cement of the abandoned factory basement. "People are still going through. Even though Enforcers are fighting them, Radicals are escaping to the West. Crazy."

Idris, Fight's fancy blond girlfriend, sits on the ground, her knees up high and her elbows resting on them. Her hair is twisted back from her face with metal skulls and butterflies holding it in place. She stares at the floor. "Yeah." Her voice is soft. "Crazy."

"Do you think they'll be here tonight?" Fight toys with his spiked red hair and adjusts the belt around his head that's holding it up.

She laughs once through her nose, only there's no mirth in her expression. She looks up. "Really, Fight? You think they'll be here? The Council was *at the Wall* when Parvin destroyed that big chunk. Solomon, Parvin, and the others are probably dead."

She shakes her head and returns her gaze to the ground. I feel cruel eavesdropping on them, not revealing my survival. As if I'm observing my own funeral.

"But their plan worked, right? The video that Parvin made helped people cross over to safety. I bet people are *still* going over."

"I wish *we'd* gone," she whispers. "We could still go."

He turns off the electrosheet and the glow leaves his face. "Come on, Idris. We've gone over this. We can't desert the people here in Prime."

"They're *choosing* to stay in bondage here! I want freedom, Fight. Parvin took that Wall down because she knew we wanted a free place to gather and study and worship and *live*. She probably died for that, and we didn't even take the chance to cross over. That might have been our *only* chance."

She's right—her comments about wanting a free place to worship *did* instigate my desire to tear down the Wall, but it was never just for her. It was for all people oppressed by the Council and the Clocks. And every day, that number grows.

A few other people arrive, but not the same amount as when I attended with Solomon two months ago.

"Nobody's coming." Fight voices my thoughts.

"Because they're *gone*. They crossed the Wall." Idris launches to her feet. "Or they're scared." She embraces a young woman who descends the concrete steps. "We're all scared. We saw that Dusten boy's body in Parvin's video. He was clearly dead and his Clock was still ticking. This changes so much."

Yes, it does. Smart girl.

And that's not all that's going to change. The break in the stone Wall was a start. I'm going to tear it all down. I'm going to find the control system behind the *projected* Wall and destroy it.

In breaking down the barriers, I will help build a new world.

Idris toys with the metal Clock band on her wrist. So, she forked out a hundred specie for a new Clock. Her old, stylish Clock that used to project from one of her many belts is gone. Looks like the Council took away the glamorous High City Clocks. Now everyone's the same.

"I heard that someone else died in Prime before their Clock was up," says the lady who just entered.

"Someone outlived their Clock in Neos," another chimes in. "They tried to get a new one, but it showed only zeroes, their name, and said *OVERRIDDEN*."

Idris crosses her arms tight over her stomach. "This isn't good! The Enforcers destroyed my old Clock. The one on my wrist has the same Numbers but . . . what if they're wrong?" She sounds on the verge of tears.

"If Solomon comes tonight"—Fight wraps his arms around her—"we'll ask him."

She hits his hands away. "He's dead!"

Just then a door slams from above. I freeze. Fight and Idris instantly slink into a shadow. People don't slam doors if they're coming here. The moment an Enforcer finds out about the secret church meeting, where we talk about topics forbidden by law, people will be punished.

Stealth is of the essence.

My heart pounds a warning—*Skelley Chase! Elan Brickbat! Enforcers!* —but in an odd, strong way, for which I can claim no credit—I'm not afraid. If anything, the pounding is instigated by the greater and more emotional nervousness of revealing myself to the man I love.

A woman's voice hisses something from the top of the concrete stairs. A male responds in like. I don't recognize their voices, but then, whispers are hard to decipher.

The first form to walk in is tall, with dark blond hair and multiple scars on the left side of his face from where the Enforcers carved off his tattoo. His bright teal eyes catch a flash of light—and in them I see hollowness.

Solomon Hawke.

My Solomon.

Behind him are Gabbie, the black reporter who helped me make a video revealing the Council's treachery, and Cap, the milkman from Unity Village. His saggy face is as grouchy as ever, probably because he hasn't returned to his goats yet. Then comes Frenchie, half draped over tall Kaphtor's shoulders. Where is Elm? Did he go after Willow on his own?

All five of my friends look weary and weathered. Solomon most of all.

I want to run to him, but Idris gets there first.

She launches into a hug. "You're alive!" She leans back and hugs the others. Gabbie receives the embrace with raised eyebrows and a relieved smile. Cap reels away, as if physical touch will kill him.

Idris doesn't try hugging Kaphtor or Frenchie—they look on the verge of collapse. My worries cease when Elm, my teenage albino friend with an eye patch, walks through the door last. Alert. Strong.

"Where's Parvin?" Idris leans around Solomon, peering at the door as though I'll walk through after them. My throat constricts. This was a bad idea. I don't want all these people here, watching as I step forward. I just want . . . Solomon.

Idris looks at his face. His jaw works furiously, but it doesn't stop the well of tears in his eyes. "Oh, Solomon."

"She . . . she gave herself to the Council. So we could"—he chokes—"escape."

I can't handle it. For some reason, I'm more terrified of revealing myself to him in this moment than I've ever been of anything else. I shouldn't have done it this way. I shouldn't have even *come*. When I look at Solomon, all I desire is escape. With him. To a calm life of rest.

But that's not today's calling.

My words come out in a dusty croak. "Solomon, I'm . . . I'm here." I step out of the shadow.

Solomon's head snaps up. He searches the enormous space until his eyes land on me. My knees tremble and I'm sure I'll fall. This moment—this prolonged stare where his mind could be swirling with any amount of questions—almost kills me.

Then he's running.

I can't move.

He stumbles on the bottom two steps, but that doesn't stop him. The space between the stairs and me closes faster than a snap of fingers.

I'm in his arms. Crushed. Suffocating in the best possible way.

My arms are tight around his neck, his around my waist, and I'm pretty sure we're both crying. My feet don't touch the ground.

Someday, when I finally step into heaven, I imagine I will run into God's arms like this. I can't fathom what it will feel like, because in this moment, I can barely survive the onslaught of happiness and hope.

Solomon mumbles something into my shoulder.

"What?"

He just shakes his head. There are no words. I can't imagine how he must have felt, thinking I was dead. We were forced to bid each other good-bye. Forced to accept that we'd be together only through death.

My ears tune back into the sounds around us. Clapping. Laughing. Even Cap is smiling—something I don't think I've ever seen him fully do. Solomon sets me back down on my feet.

I look up into his eyes and he takes my face in his hands, leaning his forehead against mine. "How?"

I shake my head, at a loss. "God."

He laughs, then sniffs. "Of course."

Fight lets out a whoop, but Idris socks him in the stomach. "Keep it down!"

"I *love* stuff like this," he says in an exaggerated whisper. "God's so cool."

That's one way to put it. Idris turns to me, hands on hips. "Have you been here the whole time?"

"Sorry." Now I feel like an eavesdropper. "I . . . had a lot on my mind."

Idris gives an impish grin. "Like I care. I'm just glad you're alive. Sneaky."

I step back from Solomon and meet his gaze. As much as I want to relish this reunion . . . "There are things I need to do."

He nods once. "Willow."

And then the projected Wall. But it sounds too ominous to start our reunion with, "Yes, and we're going to break down the Council's entire system and free the world."

I step past Solomon and walk up to Elm. We don't hug. We don't greet each other at all, really, which is pretty normal for us.

He's taller than I am now, and only four years younger, yet I still see him as a boy, despite his claims of strength and manhood. "We're getting her back, Elm. That's the first thing we'll do."

For a moment, I imagine he's still as brick-wall confident as always, but a muscle twitches in his jaw and something in his hardened gaze falters.

"What about your tracker?" Cap slides to the ground against a pillar. "You're gonna bring the whole Council down upon us again!" Frenchie's blond head snaps up and she looks at Kaphtor. They stop midway down the stairs, as if ready to turn around and flee.

"It's dead. It restarted my heart in the coffin as a last action." A tiny pocket of emotion twinges when I think of the small metal spider I used to despise.

"You were in a coffin?" Solomon slides his hand down my arm and then pinches a piece of the coat fabric as if just realizing I'm wearing an Enforcer coat. "That explains the dirt smell."

"I'll get into details later." I want to tell him about Enforcer Zeke, about my fresh confidence in God. There's so much. But first, I address the small group of gathered Believers. "I'm stepping out."

The muttering and celebration stop and we refocus. Before telling them what I plan to do, I start with the story of what I've already done. I tell them how the Council sent all the Low City Radicals—even some non-Radicals—to Antarctica as slaves, to go through the Wall and perish. I tell them how Solomon and I destroyed the projected Wall temporarily to escape on the cargo ship. I tell them of our trek across the West from Lost Angel to Ivanhoe to the Wall.

Much of this story was included in the video we sent out to the public before the destruction of the Wall, but not everything. Not the uglier details.

I have no trouble speaking now. I'm not nervous. It's like I view life differently. There's no time to be hindered by nervousness. In the end, it doesn't matter what others think of my story or my delivery of it. A wall has been broken down—not just the physical Wall, but a spiritual wall. A new anchor dropped into the sea of God's confidence and strength.

"The Council put a terminating pirate chip in my skull." As if urged on by the memory, a spot at the base of my cranium twinges. I rub my hand over the puncture wound.

"Wait . . . and you remember things?" Solomon steps closer. "You remember everything?"

How can I know if I remember everything? "I . . . I think so." Zeke asked me the same thing, yet the only time I was confused and lost was when I first woke.

"How'd you survive?" Fight asks.

I look at Solomon as if he'll have the answer, but he raises an eyebrow. I look back at Fight. "I can only guess that God used the medibot to keep me in and out of death, like a bobber, until it finally restarted my heart inside the coffin. It combated the toxins."

I picture the medibot as a mini army, fighting the toxin warriors to its last breath. Then, finally, sacrificing itself for me. How ironic that the man who has tried to kill me countless times is the one who put the medibot in me.

"Skelley Chase didn't know what he was doing when he put that in your body." Solomon takes my hand away from my neck and holds it tight.

His words aren't right. Skelley always knows what he's doing. That's what makes him so intimidating. Did he think of the medibot when Elan Brickbat used the pirate chip on me?

He couldn't have. I saw a tear on his cheek—a tear on the skin of the devil's servant. It didn't fit. It made him human. His sorrow tells me he thought I'd die.

"So what's your step out?" Idris asks.

"First"—I squeeze Solomon's hand, inwardly praying he will join me on my list of missions—"I'm going to save Willow from the orphanage." My tug to destroy the projected Wall is stronger, but I promised Elm. I promised Willow. I will not abandon her.

"They still have her?" Idris asks, aghast.

My thoughts exactly.

Elm growls low in his throat. "Not for long." He'll find his sweet grafting partner. And I'll help where I can.

"It's perfect timing. Elan Brickbat and the other Council members think I'm dead, and they're distracted by the hole in the Wall." Then, in order to get them back home . . . "I'm going to destroy the rest of the Wall. For good."

Fight rolls his eyes and plays with the Clock band on his wrist. "Didn't you just *do* that? I mean, you totally broke down a chunk like a female Samson. Besides . . . that's a *lot* of stone."

"The gap we created is already guarded by Enforcers. The Council is probably sending more to secure it." I really need to read my *Daily Hemisphere* electrosheet.

I step into the midst of them. The closeness makes me feel like my words will hit home harder. "I'm not going after the stone Wall this time. If I can permanently destroy the *projection*, something *Solomon's great-grandfather* invented"—I point to Solomon—"then the Wall will be open. The projection covers all sections of water. Once it's down, people can cross *anywhere* on the ocean."

I meet Idris's eyes. "You can finally go somewhere to study and worship God without hiding. There are no bans on Scripture topics in the West. There are no laws against teaching children under eighteen about God. There's no punishment for meeting to pray."

And there is an albino village that wants a spiritual teacher. Idris might be the perfect match to help Ash and Black understand the Bible.

Fight plops onto a cement pedestal that used to have some sort of statue on it. "And *how* are you going to do this?"

I smile and shake my head. "The *how* isn't my job to figure out. I just know this is what I'm *supposed* to do." They don't seem convinced, but their belief isn't my priority. "So . . . who wants to come?"

I've never heard a louder silence.

Alone. I'm okay trying to free the world on my own, if that's what it takes. Solomon squeezes my hand, and my tension vanishes. That's his "yes." He doesn't need to verbalize it. We're a team.

Cap grumbles something about his goats, and that's fine with me.

"Of course I'll come." Idris folds her arms.

"You can't go!" Fight lowers his voice at someone's hushing. "It's . . . it's . . . you could get caught! And what if your Clock *isn't* accurate and you die?"

Idris quirks an eyebrow. "I can't let risks dictate my life, Fight. We've played this believer thing pretty safe. I'm ready to step out. Come with."

"Not until I know the plan." He shoves the belt around his red hair a little higher.

Frankly, I'm not sure I want Fight to come. He seems overreactive and fickle—two qualities that make me wonder why he's the leader of this gathering. Is it only because he swallowed a Bible cap?

Then again, God used me to lead and I was an impulsive life-waster.

He can use anyone.

Gabbie toys with the burn scabs on her head from when the Council bombed the *Ivanhoe Independent*. "I'm not going, Parvin. I need to . . . think through some things." Her smile lacks its usual lightness. "But if you want to make another video, I'll pick up a

NAB from my home . . . if home still exists. Just send it to me and I'll get it out there."

Another video. That's an idea. It will be nice having that option.

"I am going 'ome." Even in her exhausted state, Frenchie looks exhilarated. "To *la France*."

Kaphtor, the tall, black ex-Enforcer, says nothing.

"So, what's the plan?" Fight asks me.

I turn to Solomon. "Do you think we could go to your father's house? You said he lives near the orphanage, right?" Not to mention he's another generation closer to Erfinder Hawke, the inventor of the projected Wall.

"Of course."

A slam comes from above us. Everyone's voices and breathing go mute. "Fight! Idris!" a woman calls from above. Her voice is shrill and shaky, like she's being chased. I think I know this voice.

Everyone in the basement seems to recognize the panic in her call. They scatter to the shadows, some clawing for the stairs. I press myself against Solomon's side.

"They're coming!" Through the doorway flies a dainty blond girl with soft features, who knows how to wring my heart with her words.

Tawny Blackwater. My sister-in-law.

She slams against the rail at the top of the stairs and leans over. "Enforcers are coming! The Council knows about you!"

3

The Council knows about *me?* Or does she mean the meeting in general? In a gust of doubt, I wonder if my medibot *isn't* dead and whether or not Enforcer Zeke lied. But then Tawny's perfect blue eyes alight on me, and she jerks back. "Parvin?"

It's not about me. The Council's coming after the church.

"Let's go." Solomon pulls me after him, up the stairs. I stumble, still weak from *dying* a couple of hours ago. He slows and we're the last on the stairs. People clamber up, letting loose cries of terror. Why aren't they being quieter?

I am not afraid. Should I be?

FEAR NOT.

Okay.

By the time we reach the top of the stairs, only Tawny is there. "We're going to my dad's house," Solomon pants. "Come with us."

Tawny looks wary. She stares at me. All the animosity and confusion that usually rests between us isn't there—at least not for me. I pull her into a hug, giving her a kiss on the cheek. "I'm so glad you're safe."

She's stiff as a corpse, then gives a firm squeeze. Solomon doesn't give us any more than that before he yanks us after the others to the back door. This floor is dark, but moonlight through stained windows catches the floating dust. We dodge around a metal beam. "How far are they, Tawny?"

"I'm surprised they're not here yet—"

We're through the back just as the front door on the other side of the room bursts open. Our door closes. I don't think they saw us, but I'm not waiting to find out. We run, slipping into pockets of shadow and imitating Solomon's every move.

He still holds my hand.

We hunker down in an alley behind some wooden crates. Sometimes running is more of a giveaway than hiding. Our breathing is hitched and loud. I try to calm it. A door opens and a rush of footsteps head toward us. Enforcers. A flashlight beam sweeps the road leading to our alley.

Tawny squeaks, but Solomon rests his other hand on her knee.

The beam comes closer. Then a voice—Skelley Chase's voice. "They won't be this close; go deeper into the city."

The lights cut off and Enforcers sprint past us, not even glancing toward our shadowy corner. A single set of softer footsteps follow them. Slowly. Meandering. Skelley comes into view. The scent of lemon meets my nose. His avocado-green fedora rests at a jaunt on his head. His goatee is a bit shaggier than usual.

I await the rush of hatred that should come when I see my brother's murderer. But all I remember is the tear sliding down his cheek as he watched me die. I study what I can see of his face beneath the moonlight. I have no fear of him finding us. He's not looking . . . for anyone. The lines around his eyes and a frown convey a mind preoccupied. He stops, releases a sigh, and rubs a hand down his face.

Something about him seems . . . broken.

Then, with a deep breath, he lifts his chin in an action that reminds me oddly of myself, and *clip-clip-clips* out of view.

He still thinks I'm dead.

We wait for several minutes until the silence prompts us to creep into the next alley.

It's not empty.

"Parvin," Frenchie hisses. She crouches in the deepest shadow of the alley with Kaphtor, Elm, Idris, and Fight. Now that we're all together, we're a human beacon.

"Where are Cap and Gabbie?" I mouth.

They all shrug. Great. I hope they're safe.

Solomon takes charge, guiding us with hand motions and Enforcer-like leadership. In only a minute, we've reached a busy hub of Prime. Sidewalks are crowded with people, even though it's past midnight, and projected advertisements light our way more than a full moon. We climb into a taxi with bench seats. Solomon lifts the skin flap on his wrist to scan it, but Idris grabs his shoulder. "No. You're a watched man."

She scans her own wrist while he punches in an address. We glide along the road, drifting in with the programmed traffic. Instead of staring out the window as I did my first time in Prime, I lean my head back and stare at the ceiling of the taxi.

Here we go again. We're back in the action. My time in the coffin was, weirdly, a much-needed reprieve, even though I was unconscious for most of it. Now the anxiety and fast-paced scrambling returns.

"Phew!" Idris wipes her palms on her belt skirt. Elm adjusts his eye patch and looks no worse for wear after the close encounter. He must have expert hiding skills since he escaped notice with his albino skin and glowing white hair.

"We're going straight to the train station." Solomon looks at each person—he still hasn't let go of my hand. I'm not sure I'll let him. Ever.

"I've got to go home first," Idris says. "But I live near the station. Give me your dad's address, and I'll meet you there."

Fight puts his arm around her. "I'm coming with you."

She shrugs him off. "Okay, but you're gross and sweaty. Yuck."

Tawny remains uncharacteristically quiet. Then, "How did

they find us?" Her gaze goes straight to me. "How did they know where we were meeting?"

Idris and Solomon follow her gaze. My hand drifts up to my left shoulder where the dead medibot would be. "Maybe . . . maybe my medibot is still tracking me." But then Skelley would have been sending the Enforcers to find *me*. No, they think I'm dead.

"Or maybe"—Solomon squeezes my hand—"they got the information from the pirate chip."

I'd forgotten about that. My neck twinges. That must be it, but if that's so . . . what else did they take from my mind? I don't feel like I've forgotten anything, but how would I know? "Wouldn't I have forgotten that information, then? If they stole it?"

He holds my gaze for a long moment. "Somehow . . . you remember. I think God preserved your memory."

We all get out at the train station. Idris approaches the ticket counter and returns with a ticket for each of us. "See you soon."

That phrase jolts the memory of Jude's last words before he died. I swallow hard. "S-see you soon."

During the train ride I keep expecting to see Skelley or Brickbat. Part of me *wants* to reveal my survival to them, to show them how strong God is—He resurrected me.

But it's not time yet.

The Council will know eventually.

Frenchie and Kaphtor fall asleep, her head on his shoulder and his head rested on hers. It looks cozy. It looks . . . strange. He once lugged her away as a convict. He once lugged *me* away as a convict. And now they're . . . what? Boyfriend and girlfriend? Buddies? Soul mates?

Who cares? They're cute. In a weird way.

Tawny sits three rows ahead of me. I want to talk to her, but there are a few strangers on the train, and this isn't the time to make a scene. I'd hate to upset Tawny and then have everyone notice me—the famous handless Radical who broke down the Wall.

We'll wait to create chaos until we're in Mr. Hawke's home. Besides, I want to talk to Solomon more.

Since it's past midnight, no one else on the train even opens their eyes long enough to register who I am. I don't think my whispering will bother them. I turn my head to speak in Solomon's ear, but find him already staring at me.

He smiles and tiny crinkles mark the corners of his eyes. Some day, when he's an old man, those will be my favorite feature on him. Despite the sorrow we've seen, I think we'll both end up with smile wrinkles.

I sit straighter at the thought. Here I am, imagining us . . . *old*. And surviving. I've never imagined myself old before. It'd be nice to live long enough to get wrinkly, saggy, and grey-haired.

"I was selfish." Solomon's words rise, barely, over the hum of the High City train. His voice breaks.

My thoughts about old Grandma Parvin hiccup to a halt. "What do you mean?"

His eyes glass over, briefly, and his jaw works, but he seems to get himself under control. "I prayed that you'd survive."

"That's not selfish. That's . . . human."

He lifts his hand and moves my hair behind my ear. "Since the moment I saw you alive at the Bible meeting, I've been praying something else now, too. Another selfish thing."

My heart dances inside me. "What?" What has this strong, wonderful man been asking God for?

"That next time . . . He'll take us both. Together."

Not quite the romantic prayer I was expecting. "That would be nice."

I imagine both of us strapped to a chair in front of the Council, holding hands. Brickbat gives us each a pirate chip and we fade away together.

There was another time I wished that I would die with some-one else—with my brother Reid. I wanted us to zero-out at the same time. A cold dread worms its way through me. God allowed Reid—and Jude—to die without me. Will He allow the same thing with Solomon?

The dread is crushed as I remember where I am, what He's done, and why. God still had—*has*—a calling for me. He'll answer our prayers in a way that glorifies Him the most. That's all I want.

Death's just a temporary separation.

I focus on our current mission. "Do you think I'll be able to ask your dad about Jude? Would he mind?"

Perhaps I shouldn't have mentioned Solomon's dead brother—the man I claimed to first love. Now that I'm with Solomon, though, I'm not sure what I felt with Jude. I cared for him greatly, but it was different—a discovery of love. Not an understanding of it. With Solomon, I have more understanding of what love looks like day-to-day.

"Dad won't mind, though I don't know what answers you think you'll find. I talked to him already, and he doesn't know what Jude did to the Clocks."

"But maybe he'll know things about the projected Wall and how to destroy it. After all, *his* grandfather invented it."

"We'll think about it when we get there, okay?"

Frost gathers in the corners of the train window. I stare at the crystals, wanting to press my finger against them and melt my thumbprint among their art.

Solomon leans forward into my line of sight. "I thought you were gone, Parvin." He looks at our clasped hands. "For good."

"I know. I'm sorry." What else could I have done?

His smile is weak. "Don't be. You did what you felt was needed. I'm so . . . proud of you. I was ready to do what God asked of me. I was ready to follow your example, but it wasn't easy. Feeling alone."

My example. I've never thought of setting an example before. I guess I never thought I'd *do* anything that anyone would want to emulate.

Solomon had the harder role of the two. It's easier to leave people behind and die. But continuing on with strength through sorrow . . . how did Solomon do it? I guess the same way I did it after losing Jude and Reid. "Solomon, how did you escape?"

He slips a little matchbook suit from his pocket. "Wilbur's Armor suit was pretty amazing. It allowed me to reach my arm through the cell's projected door and fiddle with the control panel."

My jaw drops. "It didn't burn up your arm?"

He rotates his right arm as though to show off. "Nope. Got pretty hot after about thirty seconds, so it wasn't a permanent fix. But after I deactivated the door, I went for the others. Ran into an Enforcer with red hair—"

"Zeke! I knew he'd help you!"

Solomon uses his free hand to pull his arm sleeve back down so it's covering our hands. He wraps his free hand around my stump. It's cold in this train. "Well, he didn't *stop* us. I didn't know if he'd go tell the Council members. I guess he didn't."

"He only reported that you'd escaped."

Solomon nods, but his blink is heavy. He's exhausted. *I'm* exhausted. I tuck my stump arm into the crook of his. "Let's close our eyes a bit, hmm? We're back together now."

"You go ahead. I'll watch for the correct stop."

I shake my head, but he chuckles and tucks it against his shoulder. Oh, all right. It's cruel to leave him alone . . . having to stay awake and wait for the right stop. But if he insists.

"Can't imagine why you're tired, though." I hear the wink in his voice and close my eyes with a grin.

"Thanks." *Even though it was only a few hours . . . I missed you.*

"Welks."

It's good that I rested on the train. We arrive at the stop and it's as rural as Unity Village. No taxis, no . . . anything. Solomon could call for transportation, but it's too risky. We have to walk to Mr. Hawke's house, and it's over a mile away. Frenchie looks like she's about to faint.

Kaphtor hoists her onto his back, piggyback style. Frenchie cries out and clenches her fingers into his shoulders. Her cracked ribs are still fairly fresh. "I'm sorry, Angelique."

Kaphtor looks dead on his feet. Only now do I understand how much he cares for her. He moves gently, even with his leg still healing from a gunshot wound, and falls in line after Solomon. Elm takes up the rear like a glowing sentry in the early morning darkness. Tawny weaves a few feet in front of him, her eyes half closed.

I join Solomon.

I can't make out anything—no trees, no houses, no moon. But Solomon knows the way. He stumbles a few times, but I think it's because he's falling asleep as he walks.

"Could you get the *Daily Hemisphere* electrosheet from my pack?" Maybe a job will give him an extra boost of wakefulness.

He seems grateful for the distraction and rummages in my shoulder pack as we walk. He hands me the small scroll. I unfurl it with a swipe of my hand. For a moment I'm annoyed with the thing because I can't hold his hand if I'm holding the electrosheet. But on impulse I step to his other side and link my stump through his arm. I swallow hard, trying not to feel embarrassed or self-conscious. He places his free hand over my forearm and gives it a squeeze.

I look at the dimmed glow of the electrosheet. What new headlines of chaos are to be found?

Council Sends Extra Enforcers to Guard the Broken Wall

We expected that. The pictures and a scan of the article tell me that no more Radicals are getting through. I'm thankful for those who *did* escape the Council's forced Clock-matching.

I share the news with Solomon, talking as animatedly as possible to keep him awake. He stumbles fewer times. Every so often I glance over my shoulder to make sure the others are there.

Elm is invincible, walking tall and focused. Kaphtor looks like a turtle, hunched over with Frenchie—limp and moaning—over his shoulders. Tawny drags her feet with squinted eyes, one hand on her lower back. She's probably not used to such traveling.

"Here we are." Those three words from Solomon wake everyone up. Through the darkness looms a modest-sized house made of neatly stained wood slats with a wrap-around porch. It's two stories high, from what I can tell in the dark.

No lights are on. "Are you sure he's home?"

Solomon shrugs. "Maybe he's not. I didn't alert him with our NAB because I wasn't sure if the Council had targeted him yet." We ascend the three steps to the porch, and Solomon opens the door.

I'd expected him to knock. The inside is so dark. The blackness too thick. I tighten my arm around his elbow. "Solomon." My voice is a hiss.

He flicks a switch on the wall and three electric lights illuminate a wood-furnished living room. The tightness in my chest crumbles to the floor. Ah, the beauty of light.

Elm surveys the house with narrowed eyes, lingering on the woodwork for a while, but he says nothing. Things may have changed in his village, but he's still adjusting to seeing carved wood everywhere. Kaphtor and Frenchie come in and, without so much as a "May I?" Frenchie sinks onto the cowhide sofa and rests her face in her hands. Tawny follows suit.

"Dad?"

We all jump at Solomon's call. He gives an apologetic grin. "It's best to just announce our presence. Otherwise he'll hear something and might try to shoot us."

Shoot us? What sort of man is Mr. Hawke?

A mid-range, youngish voice comes from the top of the stairs. "I thought I heard something."

My heart leaps to my throat. That voice.

It sounds almost like . . . Jude.

4

But it's not.

It's not Jude and I almost cry. Which is odd, because Jude being alive would be . . . too much. Too confusing. Then I feel guilty that part of me is happy it's not Jude.

I run a hand over my face. Goodness, I'm tired.

The man descending the stairs has many of Jude's features, only they're older. Weathered. Tired. His skin is naturally tanned beneath a crop of dark brown hair. He has a narrow chin and raspberry-chocolate eyes that land first on Solomon. Severe eye crinkles reveal his weakness for smiling.

"Sol!" He stumbles down the last four steps and embraces his adopted son. My arm is still looped through Solomon's, so I'm jerked forward. Mr. Hawke barely gives me a glance before pulling me in with his other arm. I soak it in, as though I'm giving Jude a hug.

He steps back with a hand on each of our shoulders and shakes his head with a grin. "You two . . ." His gaze lands on me. "Miss Blackwater . . . I have no idea how you're alive right now, but *wow.*" He shakes his head again.

How did he know I was *dead?* His eyes turn squinty and move back to Solomon. He hugs his son a second time. Maybe Solomon told him I'd died. What did that message look like?

"The rest of you, get upstairs. Sol can show you the guest

rooms. Introductions, food, explanations and the like . . . tomorrow." Mr. Hawke just became everyone's favorite. Frenchie even kisses him on the cheek on her way past.

"There are two more coming, Dad." Solomon leads us upstairs. "Also, be on guard for Enforcers or the Council. We escaped from them, but if they put two-and-two together, they'll come looking for me here eventually."

"I'll put the projections up."

"Make sure Fight and Idris get through, first."

Projections? Is that something similar to the projected Wall tech? Whatever he means, I'm sure I'll like it.

There are three rooms with large beds set in wood frames. Tawny and I claim one while Kaphtor and Elm take another. Solomon opens the door to the third. "Angelique, you take this bed and Idris will join you when she gets here. Fight can take the couch downstairs."

Mr. Hawke grabs a thick blanket from a linen closet. "Sol, go bed down in my room. I'll stay up until the other two get here." Solomon opens his mouth, but Mr. Hawke pushes him out the bedroom door. "No arguing or you're grounded." He winks at me.

Solomon hesitates at the top of the stairs, looking at me as though to fix me in his memory. "Good night, Parvin."

It's then that I realize I'm still holding on to his hand. I don't want to let go. What if something happens tonight and we're separated again? Perhaps he senses my hesitation because he steps close and kisses me on the forehead. "It's okay. I'll see you in the morning."

I swallow hard and nod, then slide my hand away. "Good night."

Everyone retreats to their rooms, but I step forward and give Mr. Hawke a kiss on the cheek. "Thank you."

"You're welcome, Miss Blackwater. You're always welcome." I turn away, but he touches my arm. He tilts his head toward the bedroom Solomon went into. "That boy loves you. He loves you deeply."

That boy. The true sign of a father—his kids will always be kids. "Solomon loves all things deeply," I respond.

"You . . . you're different."

I'm different. This time in my life, that statement means something positive. The words warm me.

"Be kind to him." Mr. Hawke plods downstairs with his blanket.

"I will," I whisper, but my stomach frosts over with guilt. I think of all the times I've deserted him, all the decisions I've made that almost cost him his life. *Can* I be the type of woman he needs?

Stop.

My sleep-deprived brain is latching onto strange fears. I'll go to bed, and in the morning I'll be back to normal. But as I drift off, I catch the distant sounds of weeping. I tiptoe out of bed. The sound comes from behind one of the closed doors. I shouldn't eavesdrop—it could be any one of my friends—but something in my gut tells me it's Solomon.

My heart withers. I press my ear against the door and hear him croak words between sobs. "Thank you. God . . . thank you. *Thank you.*"

It takes me hours to fall asleep.

My first thought upon waking: *Why am I so comfortable?*

The amount of *rest* wrapping my body like a cocoon feels deceptive. I think it's because I haven't woken in a *bed* for . . . for . . .

I lift my right fist and try counting on my fingers. Last night, I woke in a coffin. Before that, I woke on the floor of a Council prison chamber. Prior to *that* we were sleeping in the forest, traveling with the albinos to destroy the Wall.

When *was* the last time I slept in a bed? Was it the night before the *Ivanhoe Independent* blew up? My stomach gurgles loudly enough to wake Tawny, but she doesn't move.

Hmm . . . when was the last time I *ate?*

I swing my legs over the edge of the bed. Tawny's face is buried beneath the edge of the quilted blanket, like a little ostrich. I hope she's breathing okay. The plank floor is ice, and I pull my feet back with a hiss. I look around for a solution—slippers, socks, anything. My socks from yesterday are so disgusting that I'd rather go barefoot.

Turning wimpy, I climb back under the covers but remain in a sitting position. A flutter of white paper catches my eye from the bedside table. A note. From Tawny, maybe? I open it.

> *Just because we're not in a boxcar doesn't mean I won't pester you with notes. This morning, I woke up thanking God that you are faithful and brave enough to give your life for Him. But I thanked Him even more that He was gracious enough to give you back to me.*
>
> *Good sunrise, Parvin.*

I think of what I heard last night—Solomon broken before God. It's humbling, but my entire body warms. His tears were of thankfulness and, for some reason, that doesn't distress me.

He left me a note this morning. He crept in here while I was sleeping and probably saw me drooling, yet *still* left me a beautiful note. I'll put it in my Bible.

I undo the buckles of my pack as quietly as possible. My fingers crunch the delicate pages of my Bible before I pull it out. I open it to the crunched section—the book of Isaiah—and smooth out the crinkles. In the center lies the whistle Jude carved for me. I set it on the nightstand and replace it with Solomon's note.

In my hand is a note from the man I love more than anyone. On my lap is a book of notes from the One who loves *me* more than anyone else could.

So much shalom.

As the pages of my Bible unfurl, so does my heart, sucking in a deep breath of comfort. Such power in a single book. My eyes find the beginning of a chapter and stop, brought up short by a single word:

Arise. That's what God whispered to me in the coffin! I read the first verse.

Arise, shine, for your light has come, and the glory of the Lord has risen upon you.

It's a command, and it clamps onto my mind as though shouted into my ears. I've risen from my supposed death and now I'm a beacon for Him. That's a weighty calling. Am I ready for it?

Then again, have I ever been ready for His plans?

I'm not sure what it means to arise *today.* I've already crawled from a grave, but I'll chew on the word . . . while I chew on breakfast. My stomach growls again. I throw off the covers, prep myself for touchdown, and squeal. Then I tiptoe to the dresser in the room and find some man socks in the top drawer. I'm sure Mr. Hawke won't mind.

I wrap a throw-blanket around my shoulders and ease out of the bedroom. My white prison pants and tank smell like dirt and coffin. It can't be helped, I suppose. I tie on Mother's skirt for extra warmth over the pants.

The stairs lead down into the living room, where Fight is curled on the sofa in front of a now-crackling fire. His flame hair doesn't look quite so suave all rat-nested against the pillow.

Now that light streams through the many windows, I see the abode of an inventor family. Stacks of electrosheets and some old NABs sit on the entry table. Every surface that could be called a table has gears, papers with scribbles, charts, gadgets, and hybrid electronics. Aside from those, the house is very well kept. Floors are swept, blankets are folded. The mixture is rather comical.

Voices come from my right. A door is cracked, leading to the kitchen. As I approach, I glimpse Solomon, Elm, and Mr. Hawke with a sketchpad at the kitchen table. So much of my life has been spent in conversation around a kitchen table—it's a safe place to ideate.

I knock and then push the door all the way open. "I hope I'm not interrupting." If it had been only Mr. Hawke and Solomon, I would have left them alone. Even though men don't admit it, father-son time is just as precious as mother-daughter time. But since Elm is with them, I'm okay barging in; I'm hungry.

Solomon's face lights up and my stomach leaps. I'm one lucky Radical girl. "Good mid-morn, Parvin. Oh, and happy New Year."

"New Year?" No way. All that chaos at the Wall, my torture, and *dying* happened . . . yesterday?

New Year. New life.

"What better time to plan eradicating the Clocks and the Wall than on their anniversaries?" Mr. Hawke says.

Yeah, 2150 is a big year. Clocks have been around for one hundred years and the Wall for fifty. "Happy New Year."

"Scrambled eggs are in the pan over there." Mr. Hawke gestures with a pencil to the stovetop. "They're probably cold, but you can zap them."

The very idea of food causes my knees to shake. None of us has had a decent meal in several days. My stomach whines. I must tame the starving little beast.

I grab a bowl, but in doing so let go of the blanket around my shoulders. It falls to the ground. "Sorry," I mutter to no one in particular. I reach down to pick it up, but if I do, how will I get eggs? I could loop the blanket over my stump arm.

"I've got it." There he is, my breakfast hero. Solomon scoops two generous servings of eggs into a small glass bowl and sets it in front of the open seat at the kitchen table.

I sit down, warm in the face. "Thanks." I want to thank him for the note, but not in front of the others.

"Welks." He forgot to "zap" them, as Mr. Hawke mentioned—whatever that means—but I don't bring it up. I've had cold eggs plenty of times and they're just as tasty.

Forkful number one. Solomon takes his seat. "We were talking about how to get Willow out of the orphanage."

Forkful number two. "I will go in." Elm's frown wrinkles catch on the edge of his eye patch.

Forkful number three. "We need to think this through as a team." Mr. Hawke sketches what look like floor plans on the notebook of blank paper in his hands. "It's not just about getting her out, it's about where you go next. Do you come back here? What if there are Enforcers here? Do you go to the Wall? How do you get through? It's not a one-man job, Elm."

Forkful number four. Solomon slides my bowl away from me. "Take it easy. I know you're hungry, but eat too fast and you'll feel sick."

Give me back my eggs.

"Sol and I know the orphanage best, Elm. You'd do well to follow us instead of doing it on your own." Mr. Hawke's pencil makes soft hissing noises over the page. "When I finish, this sketch will help you with the layout."

"I'm coming, too." I slide my hand across the table for my bowl of eggs. Solomon slides it even farther out of my reach. Oh it's a game now, is it? I lunge, but he's a step ahead of me and lifts it in the air. I giggle. "Thief."

He curls the arm with the eggs around me and sets the bowl on the table on my other side. I try to eat slower for risk of being denied breakfast again. I internally sigh. Here I am, alive, empowered, fed, with Solomon's arm around me. I am content. Amazing. God brings contentedness even during turmoil.

"When do we plan to go?" I'm ready to get Willow back, once and for all. How will she be? The Council threatened to harm and torture her if I didn't cooperate with them. What have they done to her? *God, she's been entrusted into Your hands. I trust You to care for her.*

"Tonight." Mr. Hawke tosses the sketchpad in front of Elm. "*Late* tonight. So it's everyone's duty to rest as much as possible today." He points at the layout. "Study that."

The conversation hits a lull. I chew my eggs slowly, waiting for an opportunity. Or waiting for the courage to take it. "Mr. Hawke?"

"The name's Christian."

That would be like calling my own father, Oliver. Weird. But if he insists . . . "Christian. Um . . . would you mind if we . . . talked about Jude's invention?"

The lines on his face harden, but he gives a stiff nod. "I don't think I'll have much for you."

"Did you know that he was altering his Clock-matching invention?"

He leans back on two legs of his chair. "He was always tweaking things, inventing things, doing new tests. The year before he went through the Wall, he was living in Prime, so I didn't see him much."

"He seemed to think, just before dying, that Solomon could answer my questions." I glance at Solomon, but he stares at the table. I would hate to be in his position—to feel like I'm letting my brother down because I don't have the answers.

Back and forth, back and forth Christian rocks. "Well, what was your question?" He asks matter-of-factly, like we're discussing a science project. Maybe, to him, it is.

"I asked him why." The scene is sharp in my memory. Jude bending over me with seconds left, his tear dropping on my cheek, his kiss touching my skin. "Why did he give the assassin his information? Why did he let the assassin kill him?"

Mr. Hawke raises an eyebrow. "And he responded . . .?"

"*Ask Solomon.*" Solomon looks up. "That's what he said—ask

me. But he never explained his inventions to me! I don't know how they work." His dark blond hair falls near his eyes and he brushes it away, revealing lines of torment on his face.

Christian clunks his chair back to all fours. "Maybe it's not about exact answers, Sol. You knew him better than anyone. What do you know about him that could *lead* us to an answer? He wouldn't give Parvin hope if there wasn't any."

I never thought of it this way. I figured if Solomon didn't know, then there was no answer. But this . . . this is simply a mystery. And Solomon is our first clue. "Maybe he wrote everything down, in a notebook somewhere."

"That boy hated paper." Christian grins. "He was obsessed with all things electronic—never took up a normal hobby."

That's not totally true—he carved wood when we were together. But maybe he took up that hobby only once he crossed into the West, seeing how little access to electronics there was. "Did he have an extra NAB, where he might have written it down? Maybe in his old bedroom?"

Christian shakes his head. "He wouldn't just leave that lying around."

"Testimony Log?" I'm grasping at straws.

"Jude and Sol put together false scenes on their Testimony Logs to send the Council on the wrong trail."

Solomon removes his arm from around my shoulders, the playful flirting long gone. "Why do we even need to know?" He lowers his head into his hands. "Why do we need to know what Jude did to the Clocks? Why do we *always* want to know?"

I raise my eyebrows. "What do you mean?" Doesn't *he* want to know?

He glances up and shakes his head at us. "That's how all of this started. Some inventor wanted to know when we'd die. So he devoted his life to creating the Clocks. Look where that got us.

48

Now that we're in the process of undoing that, *we* want to know why the Clocks aren't working."

Elm watches the three of us discuss this, his cheek resting on one hand. Something in his good eye looks . . . amused. Like we're arguing about something childish. This must seem so foreign to him. He's been on our side of the Wall for only a couple of days.

"There's nothing wrong with a healthy thirst for knowledge, Sol."

He huffs through his nose. "Tell that to Adam and Eve."

Is he right? Should we leave this mystery alone? The Clock system is collapsing on itself already—something we wanted. The moment any one of us learns the *why* behind it, that knowledge can be stolen from our minds with a pirate chip.

I slide my fingers into Solomon's—they close around mine. "Adam and Eve's downfall was because of their disobedience. *But*"—I surge on before he can argue—"you're right. We should pursue only what God wants us to pursue. Do you think this is a mystery He wants us to solve?"

Solomon shakes his head. "I don't know. I don't know what He wants." He meets my eyes. "Do you?"

"Sometimes. Not today." My curiosity scrapes its fingernails down the inside of my skin. I want to know. I want to know what Jude did to the Clocks. "If we find the answer to these Clocks, then we can prove to the Council they're faulty. Then the Council will stop forcing them on people."

"We've already done that. *You* did that, Parvin, by dying at their hands. They know the new Clocks are faulty. Besides, if we know what's wrong with the Clocks, then the Council will know where to start trying to repair them."

Why must this be so complicated? "We can find the evidence and destroy it, then. The fact remains, Jude pointed me to you because there's something for us to find. It exists and if the Council gets the answers first, we're in trouble. If anything, we need to find this journal or NAB or source of answers that Jude used and burn it. "

After I take a peek, of course.

"But anything we put in our heads can be stolen with a pirate chip." Solomon clunks his forearms on the table.

It's not a matter of figuring out the Clock mystery for me. It's not the simple thirst for knowledge. I need to know . . . why Jude gave his life. Because right now, the evidence points to the fact that he was trying to save me. And I can't bear to believe that he betrayed the entire USE just to save my life.

Then again, his Clock glitch is freeing people. But . . . I need to be free of this everlasting swirl of questions. Jude said Solomon would have the answers. And the people of the USE expect *me* to have them.

We'll find them.

"What about Willow?" Elm speaks for the first time since we started this discussion.

Solomon, with seemingly no trouble, switches topics. "Yes, what time do we want to head to the orphanage?"

Christian leans over the sketch and points, but my head tumbles down a hill of questions and confusion. Ugh. *Give me insight!* And peace. "I'm going to go . . . read." I rise from the table. I didn't finish my eggs but, as Solomon predicted, my stomach squirms from eating too fast.

No one protests my departure.

Tawny is still asleep in our room. I pick up Jude's whistle from the nightstand, wanting to blow it and hear its soft sound, but Tawny is sleeping. I rub my thumb over it, scraping the plug of sap on the end. The wood tube is smooth. Flawless.

I grab my Bible and crack it open. I need guidance. My muscles surrender and I hunch over the book. The first verse my eyes fall on while I toy with the whistle says, *You will seek me and find me, when you seek me with all your heart.* I scan the surrounding verses, still unsure when the Old Testament verses are allowed to apply to my life. The most I figure out is that it's God speaking to His people. Well . . . I'm His, aren't I?

Am I seeking Him with all my heart? Am I putting Him first with this Jude-thing? Is that what it means to *arise* like in that Isaiah chapter?

My thumb worries faster and faster over the smooth wood, as if trying to start a fire. *Take this from me. Take this curiosity, this worry, this lack of peace away from me.* My eyes are closed and I step instantly into His presence. A long breath snakes out of my lungs. Here I am again. Where I'm supposed to be. *Hello, God.*

I WILL BE FOUND BY YOU.

I lie back on the bed. Softly. Relishing our time, almost as if I'm back in the coffin with only Him. *And I will seek You.* He resurrected me, and I'm already getting distracted.

A snap in my hand jolts me upright.

Jude's whistle lays in two pieces. "No." My plea is choked.

I broke it. I broke the only gift Jude ever gave to me. Is this because God's displeased? Is He trying to free me from this part of my past?

I grip the two pieces of wood and hold my fist to my forehead, my eyes closed tight. *Okay. Okay . . . I'll let go.*

I don't want to. But I must. Despite my own wants, I want God more.

I open my fist and allow the two pieces to roll out onto the blanket. During their tumble, something falls onto my lap from inside one of the halves. Something small, curved, and clear.

A set of Testimony Log contact lenses.

5

I fly down the stairs, blinded by my shock. My legs can't keep up and I trip the last two steps. I throw my arms out to brace for the fall, but Solomon is there. He catches me with one arm, lurching backward a few steps. "Whoa, are you okay?"

I look into his wide eyes and hold up my fist. "I found it! I found the answer!" He rights me to a standing position, his arm still around my waist as if unsure whether I'm sane enough to keep myself up.

"Jude hid a Testimony Log in the whistle he carved for me!" The words rush out. "I was in bed, praying, and the whistle snapped in half . . ."

His eyes drift to my fist and, trancelike, he reaches up with an open palm. I drop the contacts into his hand, turning solemn. "We don't have to watch them, Solomon. I'm giving them to you and, if you want, you can destroy them without telling anyone else."

It sounds like this was my plan all along, but the decision arose the moment I saw his surprise. Solomon is struggling with this more than anyone. I want it to be his choice. Why is this so hard? There's something more behind his hesitance than just conviction.

He closes his fingers around them. His knuckles turn white, as if he might crush the lenses. "Of course we'll watch them. They were obviously important to Jude."

If they were so important, why didn't Jude tell me the Testimony Log was in the whistle? Maybe he knew that I wouldn't know what to do with it. Maybe he knew the Council would search me or ask me questions.

Maybe he didn't trust me.

"Come on, let's get Dad."

It takes a moment for me to explain everything to Christian, but he seems used to surprises. He takes the contacts and gathers a box of metal chunks and cords. "I haven't used this in a while."

"It's a way to view the Testimony Logs," Solomon explains to me. "Jude had little trust in the Testimony Banks, so he invented a way to watch the footage at home."

In other words, he cheated the system again and this is probably illegal. Not that I care.

Idris and Kaphtor both wake by the time Christian gets the projector working. The six of us scoot the chairs together so they're facing the blank wall. As the machinery starts up with a clack and Christian slips the contact lenses in, my gut startles like a frightened squirrel.

I don't think I want to watch this.

No, I'm certain I don't.

I get my feet under me to stand up when a whirlwind of color and earth swirls on the wall. Then it settles with a tremble or two, and Jude is looking at me. He's perfect. His dark brown eyes are still carefree and excited, free of the brooding torment that overtook him in the last couple of months we were together.

Next to me, Solomon tenses. Only our shoulders touch, nothing else. He's not holding my hand, and I wonder if it's because it's too strange touching me when he knows that Jude and I did the same thing.

I don't want Solomon to feel jealous. I want him to be confident in my affection for him. But why does my heart pitch with longing at the very sight of Jude's face?

"Hello, hello," Jude says in an upbeat greeting, "And welcome to the Jude Hawke show!"

The explosion of his voice on my memories is almost too much. Idris bursts into tears, pulling her knees up to her chest. Perhaps it's her breakdown that keeps me together. I'll let her cry for the both of us. I need to be strong. For Solomon. For me.

"Today's program is particularly special because I have secrets to share!" Jude throws his arms wide, but the camera is too close, so we see only the jerk of his shoulders. He leans close to the contact lens until it's almost comical. "Sol, pay attention. You've got to carry on my legacy of awesomeness, brother."

I want Jude to be serious. It's foolish, because he probably filmed this before he even knew me, but his goofiness doesn't match our mood.

As if he heard my thoughts, his voice loses its jubilance. "Okay, I'll cut to the chase. I'm going through the Wall in a couple of days. We've got it all set up, you and me—all the fake scenes so you can stay an Enforcer and keep an eye on things. But, Sol, I've gone behind your back."

He grins that quirky, one-sided grin that I so desperately craved but rarely received. "You know me—I can't help it. Secretive, mysterious Jude. Well, after the Council did what they did"—he swallows hard—"and I realized I couldn't give them my Clock invention . . . that wasn't enough for me. I can't just hide the invention. You know the Council—Brickbat and Chase are schemers. They'll probably catch me, even when I'm over the Wall, so I've made a plan."

He taps his head. "Gonna burn out some of my brain cells, Sol. I've been working on the Clocks, tweaking them." He glances around as if nervous someone might overhear him. "*Changing* them so that if the Council gets my information, it will be flawed."

His head jerks around and, in a flash, the screen goes black.

The next time it starts up again, we're not looking at him; we're in his eyes. He's tromping through forest—forest that I know. He's on the other side of the Wall.

When he speaks, it's between gusts of air. "We did it, Sol. I'm through and I'm alive. It's so cool over here. Wish you could be adventuring with me. I miss you. I mean, you think we'll see each other again, but I hate to break it to you . . . we won't."

Solomon's face is in his hands.

"There's a reason I never let you know which of my little Clock contraptions was the real one. But . . . I'll get to that later. Not sure how I'll get this Testimony Log to you, but I'll find a way. You know me. I always do."

Another cut. Another scene.

Ivanhoe. The lenses shake like Jude's walking, but then he stops. "Look at this place, Sol. Just . . . look at it. It's another world. It's the main hub here, which means the Council's probably sent some assassins to wait for me there. Man, I want to go. You'll just have to visit for me someday."

Cut.

He's in the albino village and a smaller, more carefree Willow waves at the screen.

Cut.

He's on a tightrope over the Dregs. "Look what I can do!"

Cut.

"It's lonely here, Sol."

Every cut of the scene is a cut to my heart.

With the next one, he's back in the forest. "Hate to admit it, Sol, but the NAB notes aren't enough for me. So, I'm going to pretend that you're here, tromping along with me—exhausted and sweaty, I might add, because I'm in better shape than you—and we can chat without your Enforcer Testimony Logs peering over our shoulders."

He laughs and pushes through some overhanging branches. "Don't get me wrong, I'm really impressed with all the messages you're able to send me while you're being watched. But don't be too careless. If the Council catches you, they'll strip your Enforcerhoo—"

A distant *pop* sound comes from Jude's side of the screen. I know that sound—he just got a NAB message. His NAB is smaller than mine was and he flips it open. There's a message. I think I see my name in the message—*my* name!—before Jude drops his arm and breaks into a sprint.

The next fifteen minutes have him running. Panting. Pushing himself. I grow tired watching him and my heart pounds harder as though *I'm* the one running. At one point, as he jumps over a stream, he gasps, "I don't know . . . if I'll make it, Sol." That confession seems to urge him faster. "I'm . . . trying."

Then screaming enters the picture. Wild, desperate screams for help . . .

. . . in my voice.

I want to plug my ears, block out the memory. It sends chills down my body, even though I know what's coming and I've already lived through it.

Jude ducks under a low hanging branch, and then the albino huts come into view with their stone walls and animal-hide doors. Up on a knoll beneath the blooming, pink dogwood tree is a group of albinos. Alder has his axe raised over a human stretched out on the ground—

Jude sucks in what sounds like a painful breath. "Alder, stop!" He reaches out with a hand.

But the axe swings down. I shut my eyes, and a shriek rips from my own throat, echoing in the kitchen. I hear the *thunk* of the axe in the sandbag, but then Solomon's arms are around me and he's pulling my head to his chest, where I bury my face.

My left arm burns where my hand used to be. I can feel Black's fingers tight around my wrist, stretching me out against my will.

I'm drowning under anger, fury, *hatred* over the injustice done to me.

But then I resurface. I suck in deep breaths and pull away from Solomon. The Log of Jude is still rolling, only we're in a different scene. But everyone in the kitchen is focused on me.

"Parvin?" Solomon's voice is tender.

"I'm fine." My voice is harsh. I'm not fine. I want to be invisible right now. I gesture to the projector. "We better pay attention."

This time it's facing Jude again, and he's no longer carefree. His eyes are sunken and dirt coats his forehead. Weeks have passed. It's dusk, and the red glow of the sunset makes him look almost wild.

"She left me, Sol."

I didn't think my stomach could plummet any further, but now it's crawling down through my feet and into the tile below them to hide.

"She left me because I hit her." His fists clench and press against his temples. "Me . . . the guy who loves kids and wants to protect orphans. I *hit* her! I was angry about her journal entries informing the assassin of our location. And now she's angry at me."

His eyes flick to the lenses, then away. "And *you're* probably angry because I'm not looking after her like you asked. I'm betraying you, Sol. Parvin's making me go crazy, and I'm betraying my own brother . . . because I don't just want to protect her."

He can't seem to make eye contact. His jaw muscle pulses, and he gives his head a sharp shake. "I want to *love* her. I want her to be mine. Not yours."

Looking at him like this is the last straw. I start to cry—stupid, sniffing-choked crying. Was I such a monster to Jude? Did I truly cause such grief and jealousy and betrayal?

"Jude-man?" Willow's soft, light voice comes from far off. I spin around in my seat before I realize she's in Jude's recording, not in the kitchen.

Jude's hand shoots forward and turns off the Testimony Log.

Willow. We're getting her back today. I need to keep it together. I want this Log to be *over*.

Tawny stands in the doorway, watching me. I wipe my eyes and try to look strong, but no one's fooled.

The rest of Jude's video is a daze, like he's not interested in giving any more answers or baring his soul. Just a few updates here and there that hold little weight. Then comes the one we've been searching for. The one I've waited through emotional hell for.

He's in the healing hut in the albino village, and we're basically looking up into his nostrils, which tells me the contact lenses are on his lap. He adjusts them a bit so it's not such a strange view.

"Well, Sol, looks like you're going to win. After all, you've got the upper hand now." He lifts both his arms and grimaces. His right arm is amputated above the elbow.

He flops his head back against the pillow. "That was sort of a joke. Truth is, I think the assassin's going to find us. He saw us in Ivanhoe, he knows we're trying to leave. He'll put two-and-two together with the help of the Council, and he'll find us. But you've got to know some things about the Clocks . . . while I remember them."

He lowers his voice, even though no one else is in the hut. Every word seems to suck strength out of him. "I'm not going to explain how it all works because we all know *I'm* the tech brain. Besides, if the Council gets this Log, then at least they won't have the details. But before I crossed the Wall, I did some new . . . tests. I've been researching strength of will—that unexplainable force that empowers a mom to lift a car off her baby, or someone to recover from an incurable disease. We don't see it as often nowadays because people just roll over and accept the Numbers their Clocks give them."

Jude shakes his head. "Did you know that the guy who invented the Clocks didn't even know how he did it? Even *I* can't break them down to find the original setup. It's weird, Sol. Weird. But anyway . . ."

He takes several breaths, running his tongue over his dry, cracked lips. "I think I've harnessed that . . . the strength of will. It's closely connected with faith. Don't ask me how I harnessed it 'cause I won't—*can't*—tell. But let me just say I found some powerful emotigraphs. It still needs to be tested. I guess I'm no better than the original Clock inventor. But now when the Council Clock-matches people, the fighters, the doubters, the people who resist . . . should be able to override their Clocks. Like my orphans." His voice cracks.

"This can go both ways . . . at least I hope it can. People can die before their Numbers, or they can outlive them." His eyes droop. "That's the plan, anyway. I still haven't tested it. How do you test that, you know? Ask someone to try and die early? I didn't have enough time. My only hope is that *I'll* be able to test it."

Here, his eyes lock onto the lenses, boring deep into each of us. "Solomon, my real Numbers have me zeroing-out on October first."

A collective gasp runs through the kitchen. Jude died on September twenty-fifth—Solomon's birthday. So *that's* why he gave in to the assassin . . . to test his new Clock invention.

And it worked.

"See, I had Dad destroy the brain cells that contain all the equations and how-tos of the Clock-invention." Jude's eyes are closed now.

Solomon's head snaps sideways, his gaze locking on Christian. "You never told me this. You said the doctor was a family friend."

Christian shrugs. "I promised Jude I wouldn't tell."

"We couldn't get all of it. That's complicated surgery, you know." Still with eyes closed, Jude grins. "But Dad's the best." His grin spreads, wider and wider, until he laughs. It's a little maniacal, considering the circumstances. "Get it, Sol? Do you see? The

Council will be stealing an invention that will, ultimately, destroy them . . . if it works." His last three words are a whisper.

His thin form is pale from lack of blood. The laughter fades from his lips. I couldn't have done what Jude did. He was so strong. His breathing turns labored and with a last wink, he says, "I'll miss you two . . . more than anyone. If I'm able to keep her alive . . . take care of her, Sol."

The Log goes blank.

"Oh Jude . . ." Idris's broken whisper speaks for us all.

I don't want to encounter the aftermath of this video. I need to be away. Alone. I can't look at Solomon.

"But . . . the Council used a pirate chip on him, I thought." Tawny moves from the doorway. "Wouldn't they have this information?"

I don't want to talk about it.

Solomon shakes his head. "Pirate chips are programmed with focus words. Unless the Council had the correct focus words, they might not have gotten this extra side of Jude's story." He sounds so stoic. Detached.

Trying to appear calm and contemplative—not desperate to flee—I rise from my chair. "I'm going to go . . . think."

I walk out of the kitchen, pretending I don't hear Solomon's, "Parvin?" behind me.

Fight is rising from the couch in the living room. Perfect— he'll go in there and everyone will have to update him. Or replay the video. Meanwhile, I'll be in my room.

I lay down on the rumpled bed, not bothering to smooth out the blankets. I stare at the painted, peaked ceiling. God wanted me to find those lenses. He revealed them to me after I'd just sur- rendered to Him. Will I still surrender to Him? Surrender Jude? Surrender my doubts? Surrender myself? *I don't even know what to think now, Lord.*

An hour ticks by. Two. I think I fall asleep at some point.

I wake to a weight on the mattress. Tawny sits beside me, clutching a thick, rumpled book to her chest. "I'm sorry about Jude."

I stare at her. What do I say? Thanks?

She looks at the book in her hands, and that's when I recognize it. Reid's journal. "You know, I wasn't always this . . . unpleasant. Reid really liked who I was."

"I'm sure he did." Obviously he liked her—he married her.

"I've just been . . . grieving. I blamed you a lot, Parvin. Even though you'd lost your brother, I thought you couldn't understand what I'd gone through. I lost my husband."

I think I hear an apology coming. And it makes me feel guilty because I haven't thought kindly of Tawny.

"But now I understand a little more. And . . . I'm sorry that you couldn't be with Jude."

I put my hand on her arm. "It really was for the best, Tawny."

A tear drips from her eyelashes. "How can you say that?"

Something tugs at me—the command to rise above this hurt and this history. I hoist myself upward so I'm leaning back on my elbows. "Because not everything's about romantic love. Jude died for the sake of . . . all of us. He died to save me from the assassin. He died to save all of us from the Council's schemes. That's exactly what Christ did for us, and Jude couldn't have asked for anything more than to represent Him in his death."

The words purge the dark emotions chaining me to the bed. "And in the end, I get to be with Solomon. I liked Solomon from the start, but I picked Jude because I thought I'd never see Solomon again. Yet here I am. God knew who I needed. We all have different purposes in our lives . . . some roads are shorter than others."

I glimpse movement by the doorframe. Black clothing. Is that Solomon? Listening in?

Tawny rubs the Clock thread around her wrist. "So how long is my road?"

"I don't know." Did she see all of Jude's video? Or did she come in too late? "Don't think about how long or short it might be. Focus instead on the *now*."

This seems to irk her. She stands abruptly. "Sometimes we *need* to think about the future! There are things to prepare for, life adjustments. We can't always live day-to-day like you, ready to die on a whim."

She slams Reid's journal on the bedside table, turns on her heel, and opens the door. "I came up here to tell you that they're planning the rescue mission. You're needed."

Despite the outburst, I think that conversation went rather well for us.

I stare at Reid's journal. She put it beside me. Is that because she wants me to read it? I've been through it briefly. Every entry I read shattered or challenged my view of life.

I crack the cover open and fan the pages.

There's more writing than before. I open the journal the rest of the way. Tawny's been deciphering the smudges, writing words over the smears. Resting between the pages is what looks like a square magnifying glass, with a black frame. I hold it over one of the words she wrote out—*travel*—and the typed word TRAVEL shows up in red inside the glass. I move it over a black smudge and the glass blinks *Deciphering . . . Assessing imprints . . .* then a list of word options pop up:

OUTDOORS

OUTWARD

OUTBOUND

This little piece of glass is a decoder. Reid's journal isn't completely ruined after all. How did Tawny *find* a piece of tech like this?

"Parvin!" she calls.

I head downstairs, significantly cheered. Sometimes it takes a moment of reflecting on God to align one's emotions.

Everyone is gathered in the living room, sitting on a mixture of chairs—wooden kitchen chairs; bendy, black desk chairs; and the sofa. Solomon stands at the edge of the circle. He tries to smile at me. I wish he felt comfortable enough to show his sorrow. But maybe it's different in front of his dad. I join him and slip my hand into his. My stomach lurches—nervous. Hesitant.

He squeezes my hand as if it's a lifeline. When I look in his face, I think about what we've been through together—what *he's* had to endure. Only yesterday, he thought I was dead.

"We're talking about where we'll go once we get Willow out." Christian looks up from his sketched diagram of the orphanage.

"Back through the Wall." Elm crosses his arms and glares with his good eye.

Kaphtor tosses a *Daily Hemisphere* electrosheet onto the table. "Not possible."

We all lean forward. A video shows hundreds of Enforcers guarding the giant gap we made in the Wall. People are fighting with them, trying to get through. Instead, the Enforcers mow them down with bullets. Other Enforcers are building tall pillars and directing helicopters that lift the pillars to the top of the Wall. Are they trying to repair it? Rebuild the stone? They'll never succeed.

"We'll go to the Opening." Elm runs a hand through his choppy, multi-length hair. "Parvin has the Brawn suit. We smash through the Opening door, go through the tunnel, and escape on the other side. The Council is not watching that area."

Christian gropes for words.

"Or," Elm continues, "in Canada, like the Jude-man did. The Council has no power there. We go through *that* Opening. It is closer."

How is it that all the young albinos I know are born leaders? Survivors? Geniuses? Even eleven-year-old Willow.

"That's an excellent idea." Christian scans the room. "Who would like to go through the Wall?"

It won't be that easy. Does he realize this? Besides, if we have a way through the Wall like that, we need to let other Radicals know.

His eyes land on Tawny. "I'm assuming you will. Solomon told me your family is over there."

Her eyes widen. "Me? No!"

"Why not?" And here I thought we'd made headway earlier. "Don't you want to be with Mother and Father?"

"Well, yes . . ." She grips the arm of the couch. "But not yet."

Idris narrows her eyes. "This isn't a vacation, Tawny. You may have only one chance to cross."

"Why is everyone looking at *me?*" Tawny glares right back. "I can take care of myself—I can make my own decisions."

I try not to sound accusatory. "Yes, but what's keeping you here?" Maybe she has family in Florida. Or maybe she wants to be rid of us Blackwaters. I hope it's not that. I think that we could become friends with enough time and freedom.

I want her to be safe.

Her mouth works, as if chewing on a confession. Her gaze lands on me like the blow of a hammer. Whatever she has to say, it's going to impact me.

"Because . . . I'm pregnant."

6

"What does being pregnant have to do with escaping to freedom?" Idris demands without a blink of surprise.

I'm glad she asked, because I'm still choking on my own shock. Tawny's *pregnant?*

Tawny leaps to her feet. "I will *not* give birth to a baby in the *forest!* I have a Clock with plenty of time to get me care in the hospital. What's available in the West? A tree nook?"

She's pregnant.

"Ivanhoe has medical tech," Elm says.

She's going to have a *baby.*

"The train was bombed, remember?" Kaphtor says.

How? How is she pregnant? Reid's been dead for almost three months.

"My village is very skilled with birthing." Elm yawns. "Or she could walk to Ivanhoe."

My eyes land on her belly. It doesn't look any bigger. Then again, she's wearing a sweater.

"Oh sure, make a pregnant woman *walk* for three weeks in the wild?" She barks a laugh.

"Is it Reid's?" It's the stupidest thing I could have said. So stupid, in fact, I hold my breath and wish I could suffocate into unconsciousness before I see her response.

But her response is not visual. It's not a look of shock. It's a

65

slap. A hard, sharp, very-much-deserved slap across my face. Then she's gone, up the stairs.

No one looks at me. I just ruined any headway Tawny and I made during our talk. And everyone watched me do it. "That was dumb. I don't know why I asked."

"Well, she didn't exactly answer the question." Fight seems amused by the whole thing. Idris elbows him in the ribs.

Of course it's Reid's baby. Maybe they . . . you know . . . tried getting pregnant since he knew he was going to die. But being a lone mother seems depressing to me.

Christian heads up the stairs after Tawny. He's some type of doctor, isn't he? That's what Jude once told me. Maybe he'll talk some sense into her. After all, if *he* crosses the Wall, then he could deliver her baby. For time's sake, *I* delivered Ash's baby in the albino village!

There are options. Why is Tawny so hesitant?

"We're heading to the orphanage at two in the morning." Solomon squeezes my hand. His forced focus on the mission makes me feel even worse, though I know he's trying to divert the attention away from my stupidity.

"I still don't see why we're doing this the sneaky way." Idris crosses one leg over the other and leans back against the couch.

Fight drapes his arm over her shoulders. "We're kidnapping an orphan, Idris. It's a sneaky job."

"We're *rescuing* a *captive*. Get the terms right. But don't you think we could pull it off during daytime? A few people go in, act like visitors, find Willow, and sneak her out. That would get us inside, no problem."

Solomon shakes his head. "Then staff at the orphanage would know *we* did it. Not to mention we don't know where they're keeping Willow. And sneaking her away during the daytime makes it harder to hide. Besides, it's New Year's. They're probably having celebrations all day."

"They'll have cameras either way that'll catch our faces." Idris snuggles closer to Fight. Why does she date him? They seem so unmatched.

"At night we can cover our faces and blend into the shadows. Black clothing."

Idris smirks. "I've got a lot of that." I survey her. Black leggings, black belt-skirt, black vest over a sheer, black, long-sleeved shirt. She'll be invisible. She catches my eye. "I'll lend you some, Parvin."

Frenchie's eyes are still puffy from lack of sleep, but her energy level seems higher. "Eez eet really safe for Parvin to come?"

I recoil at the thought of waiting in this house while everyone else goes to find Willow. "Of course I'm going!"

"But ze Council doesn't know you are alive. I think you should stay 'ere and plan what you are going to do next."

"I agree." Sure, take *her* side, Kaphtor.

"Besides"—Fight gestures to my stump—"you're missing a hand."

And you're missing a brain!

"Parvin is perfectly capable of helping," Solomon says. "She'd probably be the greatest asset to the mission."

Thank you. Thank you very much.

He turns to me. "But I do think it'd be best if you stay behind—both for your safety and for planning purposes. The Council is after us, and if they see you everything will change. Remember, they think you're dead."

My pride flares, and I want to point my finger and remind them that *all of us* are enemies of the Council. But I trust Solomon, and I want him to know I trust him. If he thinks I shouldn't go . . . then I won't. "You said Enforcers will probably show up here soon. This isn't any safer."

"*Monsieur* Hawke mentioned a tunnel." Frenchie bites her lower lip.

"There are projected walls around this house—the same ones that make the Wall over the ocean. No one can get in—"

"—or out," I finish for him. A cage. That's what this would be.

"False." Solomon holds up a finger. "There's a tunnel from our cellar out to the forest. It was Jude's plan. That's where a lot of his old inventions are kept. I'll show it to you so you can escape if need be."

"We'll need someone here as a lookout anyway." Christian descends the stairs, with Tawny a few steps behind him. She doesn't look at any of us. "We can't risk coming back without knowing if the Enforcers are watching the house." His gaze lands on me. "Parvin, you and Tawny can stay here and keep an eye out. If Enforcers show up, meet us at the end of the tunnel to warn us."

Me and Tawny. She glares at the ground. The potential alone time sends a jerk of dread against my gut, but we need this. And I like that I'll be here to protect her.

I give a firm nod.

All day I've seen small barricades and walls popping up in my relationships or thinking. I think I'm getting the hang of what God means when he says to arise. It's a daily choice to rise above the despair, the doubt, or the attack from the Enemy.

I have a feeling this is only the beginning.

We spend the rest of the day planning, eating, resting, and—for me—glancing out the window for Enforcers. During one of my naps, when I have the bedroom all to myself, I snag Reid's journal again. I didn't read it as much as I should have when he first gave it to me. It's a source of guilt that will never fully go away.

But now I have another chance.

09.17.2148 Time: 23:15

I'm cruel. I took Tawny out for dinner and still haven't told her that my time is short. We haven't talked about Clocks yet. Am I the only one avoiding the topic or is she avoiding it, too? Maybe her Clock is also short.

I don't really want to read about Tawny, but these sections have the most deciphering, so I continue.

Everything is different with her. It's not like the girls from Unity—those finicky daters who flirt like airheads. If I were honest, I'd admit I like the flirting to an extent.

What? Reid's always been the perfect gentleman and I used to pride myself on having a brother who didn't flirt. All this time . . . I guess he *was* human. I grin.

But I like realness more. It's just so . . . rare. Tawny has it.

I haven't seen what Reid saw in Tawny. Instead of realness, Tawny gives sarcasm and sass. There must be so much more to her. She just hasn't opened up to me yet. Maybe there's hope for us as sisters.

09.24.2148 Time: 9:03
I haven't seen Tawny for a week. It might as well have been a year. I'm such a sap.

I laugh and it comes out choked. All this took place only a few weeks before he came home for his One Year Assessment. I skim down to those entries. Tawny hasn't put as much effort into deciphering them, or maybe she's simply not finished.

10.05.2148 Time: 15:11
I've decid _____ o leave. Tawny's life is _____ _____ _____ so _____ _____ _____ rror. Ab _____ e father, ver_lly a _____ ve mother, alone. I can't _____ _____ _____ hope _____ a _____ _____ with me wh _____ die in a year.
I don't _____ nt _____ o die _____ a ye_. There's so

much _____ life I haven't _____ _____ _____ _____ yet.
Yet . . . I don't _____ _____ Par _____ n to die either.

"What are you doing?" My head pops up. Tawny stands in the doorway.

Guilt makes my palm sweat and I set the journal aside. "Reading Reid's journal."

"Christian wants to show you the tunnels." She doesn't mention the journal. Doesn't snap at me. Doesn't ask any more questions.

For some reason, that makes me feel even guiltier. I hop out of bed and meet Christian at the base of the stairs.

"Ready?" He smiles, then leads me through the kitchen. The frigid cellar is deep beneath the house and smells of moist dirt— the kind that holds worms and beetles. Across from the cellar stairs is a crate of onions wrapped in newspapers. Christian shoves the crate aside, then removes a loose brick from the wall to reveal a small screen.

"The code is *5R69N45R*." He types it in and a wooden slat slides away into the floor, revealing a shimmery, aqua-colored projection across the face of a square hole leading to steps—the entrance of the tunnel. "Now be careful not to touch that. It will destroy whatever part of the body tries to cross it. There's another code here." He punches in *81WK5*.

I take note of both codes, putting my memory skills to the test. They seem so random, but random is good, right? "Quite the safety measures."

"Jude was always cautious." Christian leads me down into the tunnel where twenty coats hang in a line along one wall. "His ultimate plan was to get all the orphans out someday and hide them in here."

The tunnel is deep underground and made of concrete that chills right through my boots. Christian turns a silver knob in the wall and air seeps in—warm air. He lights a torch that rests in a wall sconce. "This is the only time Jude didn't want to rely too much on electricity. Darkness can be a harsher enemy than any human."

He stands in the center of the tunnel, staring into the stretch of black for a long time. I lay my hand on his shoulder. "I'm so sorry about Jude."

"Thank you, Parvin. But we'll see him again soon. He had a passion for the epic . . . like my grandfather."

"Erfinder?"

He chuckles. "He hated that name. I called him Opa Fin."

"Opa?"

He pulls out the torch and leads me down the tunnel. "It means *Grandpa* in German."

I stay close to him so the darkness doesn't press too hard on me. This tunnel is even narrower than the Wall Opening. Where was Jude going to keep the orphans?

Christian knocks on a metal door to his left as we pass it. "Food supplies." We pass another door to our right. "Sleeping supplies." He stops. "Follow this to the end and there will be an exit. Same codes to get out. Got it?"

I nod. We turn around and head back. Hawke blood flows through the soil and structure of this home—everything is about inventions. "Christian?"

"Hmm?" We reach the beginning, and he sets the torch back in its bracket.

"You use a lot of projections around your house. Does that mean that you would know how to shut down the projected Wall?" It's probably a dumb question and I jumped right into it, but I must know. Can he help me on my quest?

He turns off the heater and we climb the stairs out, back into the frigid cellar. "*I* can't help you. Jude was trying to figure out Opa Fin's invention but never finished." He points at the codes.

Test time. I kneel down and enter the first one: *81WK5*. The projection zaps back into place, and then I enter the next code. I pride myself on getting both right the first time. Despite pirate-chip toxin, my super-memory still works. The wood slats slide back into place. "What do you mean he was trying to figure it out?"

A grin slithers over Christian's face. "If you hadn't noticed yet, the Hawke men like to be secretive."

"Tell me about it." Jude and his secret invention, his secret death, his secret plan to get the pirate chip out of his arm, his secret Testimony Log. "So your . . . opa didn't share how to create the projected Wall?"

"Like how Jude didn't tell the Council how to create his Clock invention. Opa Fin showed it to the world, trained only a handful of technicians, and then retired in a little cabin in Russia."

"Russia? But . . . aren't you German?"

"I'm also odd." He grins and places the brick back in the wall. "Oddness runs in the Hawke bloodline. Don't ask me why Opa Fin moved to Russia. Jude was convinced it was to hide the secrets to his inventions—I think that's why Jude made the Testimony Log you found. He liked hidden messages."

Russia. The name carries the same draw that Ivanhoe did when I first heard about it. *Maybe Erfinder Hawke made Testimony Logs about his invention.*

I want to press Christian further, but his attention is already switched to the upcoming rescue mission.

I'll wait.

"We'll be back with Willow," Solomon assures me as they head to the cellar.

It's night and my eyes are grainy. We spent the past hour hang-ing black cloths in front of the windows and lighting only a few candles throughout the house. The less people can see inside, the better.

I stand by the cellar, ready to use the codes and close the doors after them.

It's not right. I should be going! I open my mouth, but a pained look from Solomon stops me. He understands. Of *course* he understands. I left him behind again and again when he wanted to join me—like when I blackmailed the Council.

Ugh! God! This isn't . . . what? Isn't fair? Isn't fun? Isn't what I want? My prayer turns into a grumble. But I give up the desire to argue. *Fine. I'll stay.*

I didn't manage a nap—my grouchy prayer is proof enough of that—but it doesn't matter much since I'm not joining in on the rescue. Everyone's packed, with their belongings on their backs. Solomon wears the Armor suit and Elm wears my Brawn suit. Solomon has his NAB, and I have the one I stole from Zeke at the gravesite.

At least we can communicate.

It's eerie staying behind with Tawny, who hasn't spoken to me since the journal. The longer we go on with the silent treatment, the harder it will be to break it.

Solomon reaches out and squeezes my arm. "Send us a message if anything happens."

If anything happens. Like, if Enforcers show up or if the Council bombs the house. "You too."

Before he descends out of view, he whispers, "And thank you for what you said earlier to Tawny. I was . . . I was afraid maybe you wished Jude was still . . ." He looks down. "Anyway, thank you."

So he *was* listening in. I'm glad. "It's all truth, Solomon."

They enter the tunnel, and I double-check the codes and projections once they're gone. I don't want to turn my back on the cellar. It's too final. *God, please keep them safe. Please rescue Willow and bring her back to us. And . . . sorry I griped at You.*

Such a weak prayer for such a desperate time.

When I return to the living room, Tawny's on the couch flipping through Reid's journal. A single candle flickers from the end table. Maybe she never intended for me to read his journal. Or maybe she's just angry and took it back.

I sit beside her, sucking in heavy breaths under the weight of my shame. From one ball of stomach nerves to the next. "I'm so sorry, Tawny." Admitting it is as pleasant as chewing on horseradish. "It was a stupid thing for me to say. I'm . . . I'm really excited for you and your baby."

"Sure you are." She turns a page. Her handwriting mixes with the blurred scribbles of Reid's.

"I saw that you're deciphering Reid's journal."

"Only because I have to."

She might as well have slapped me again. I stand. "I'll leave you to it, then."

She smacks her hands down on the pages. "You're always walking away! Always escaping, Parvin. Will you ever stick anything out?"

Me? Walking away? I came back for her! I came back from the West for her, from the *dead* for her. My self-control shatters. "You don't know me, Tawny!"

She rises slowly. "And you don't seem to *want* to know me. You're so focused on *your* goals, *your* mission, *your* survival, you, you, *you!*"

"How can you say any of that? I *died* yesterday for others." My voice rises to a scream, but the words are sour on my tongue. She's wrong. "You're wrong! You . . . you . . ." Forget this.

I throw my hand in the air and Tawny flinches so hard I fear I might have nicked her with a fingernail. But no, her eyes are squeezed shut and her shoulders hunch forward with her arms around her belly. Like she's waiting for a blow.

That's when I realize . . . she's been hit before.

I *don't* know her.

For the first time, I imagine things through her eyes. She's alone. Reid, the one person who knew and loved her deeply, died. And now she's afraid because she has to care for a baby . . . alone.

My voice comes out soft. "Tawny . . . I don't like fighting." Her eyes crack open. I forge on, my anger subsiding. "I want you to know." And I want her to know I'd never *ever* hit her. I want to know about her past, but now doesn't seem like the right time to ask.

Maybe the reason God is making me stay here is to mend my relationship with Tawny. After all, who knows if the future will bring us together again after we go our separate ways?

"I understand why you don't want to cross the Wall yet." If I was the one pregnant, I'd probably prefer safe medical care over the idea of giving birth in a forest. "I'm just thinking of your safety."

She swivels toward me, her blond hair whipping across her face. "Why do you even want me with your family, Parvin? Even *they* don't want me."

"Of course they do! You were there for Mother during all the chaos with the Wall. She needs you." A lump of coal lodges in my throat as Mother's burned face wavers into view. "She needs you, Tawny."

I'm not trying to convince her anymore; the words float up from my soul. "I can't be there for her." My chin quivers, and I bite my lip to stop it. "I've never been there for her, and now she's hurt . . . because of me."

Tawny's face puckers in a dainty frown. "Hurt?"

She doesn't know. Of course she doesn't know! Father wasn't with her to tell her. "Mother was injured during a train explosion. The Council attacked us on the *Ivanhoe Independent*, and Mother got wounded. Her face . . ." Blood. Peeling skin. Charred cells. " . . . she . . . she got burned. Badly. Ash has been taking care of her in the albino village and says Mother will live but"—I clench my nails against the couch leather—"she needs us."

Tawny stares at her hands in her lap. "I haven't told them, Parvin."

I look up, taking deep breaths as though my emotions have my heart sprinting. "That you're pregnant?"

She shakes her head. "I was afraid they'd react . . . like you did."

"I didn't mean to—"

"Don't say you didn't *mean* it! Speaking is a choice and you *chose* to let those words out."

"For time's sake, I said I'm sorry!" No one in my family was ever a shouter . . . except me. It's the main thing I hate about myself. I take a deep breath.

Tawny lodges Reid's journal under her arm. "I'm going to bed."

I want to tell her that's ridiculous, but it *is* almost three in the morning. Still . . . we need to be on our toes. We need to be ready for a change in plans. I grab her free wrist. "Please wait."

She hesitates with her back to me, but yanks her arm from my grasp.

We're sisters; we *have* to make this work. She's family and, as little as we get along, I still don't want to lose her. She said she wasn't always this way, and I believe her. I imagine her being sweet, giggling with Reid and dreaming of a future. Sorrow affects everyone differently, and it's my job to push past the fact that we don't react the same.

"Tawny, what if you stayed with Christian Hawke until the baby comes? He's a doctor. He can take care of you. When is the baby due?"

"June."

My eyes drop to her stomach. I still don't see a bump. Is there really a baby in there? A little mini Reid? Or a mini Tawny? Admittedly, I like the mini-Reid idea more. "Then when you have the baby, you two can cross the Wall."

"You make it sound so easy."

I shrug one shoulder. Why doesn't she turn around? "Hopefully by then, more of the Wall will be down." It's barely the start of change in the USE. And this change is big.

"Parvin . . ."

"I really think it's possible, Tawny." Jude was smart; if he thought Erfinder Hawke hid information about his invention in his home in Russia, then it's probably there. God has pushed me into breaking down this barrier and, in doing so, revealed clues. The answer lies in Russia, in Erfinder's house.

I'll find it. I'll get everyone to freedom.

"Parvin . . ." Tawny takes a step back toward me, her voice quaking and her spine stiff.

Something's wrong. "Is it the baby?" I reach for her.

She shakes her head and inches behind me. "Enforcers are outside."

7

My first impulse is to tackle Tawny to the ground, but then logic raps on the inside of my skull. *She's pregnant, you idiot!*

I blow out the candle on the end table. "How do you know?"

Her fingers latch onto my bicep. "I saw movement outside, passing under the moonlight."

She *saw* movement? The windows are covered, with only a few cracks here and there. "Are you sure it's not Solomon and the others returning?" I know better. They wouldn't return through the front of the house. But I see *nothing*. There's a blanket in front of the window, *and* it's dark.

"Of course I'm not sure!" she squeals.

"Shh!" Okay, so talking logic with Tawny isn't the way to go right now. Physically, my heart shreds the restraint behind my panic, but I need to remain firm. I am not afraid. I need to be the leader.

I wish Solomon were here.

"Let's head to the cellar," I say.

"But . . . my things are upstairs."

Of course they would be. *My* pack is by my feet at the base of the couch, but I'm not about to point that out. I snag the brown throw blanket from the back of the couch. "Wrap this around your shoulders so your clothes don't catch their attention."

She sets Reid's journal on the ground and obeys, trembling. A stab of compassion hits me straight in the chest—more powerful and more painful than when the medibot restarted my heart. I hate turning my back to the windows where the Enforcers are, but I do it anyway and wrap Tawny in as tight a hug as I can muster. "Be brave, Tawny. It's going to be okay. Christian has the projected walls up, we'll head to the cellar, and they don't ever have to know we're here. They can't see in." It's a half-truth. If she saw *them*, they probably saw our candle go out. And since the projected walls are up, they probably know people are hiding inside. "I'll go get your bag, okay?"

"Don't leave." She sinks her fingers into my arms like iron claws.

There's no way I'm taking her with me. "Give me sixty seconds. Start counting." I give her a firm squeeze with my good hand and then creep in a crouch toward the stairs.

"One, two, three, four . . ." Her voice breaks the eerie silence like a creepy ghost-Clock.

I make it up the stairs at *thirteen* and into the bedroom at *nineteen*. That gives me at least twenty seconds to assess the situation from the upstairs window. It's not covered with cloth, so I inch my eyes and nose over the sill.

I see nothing. And I mean, *nothing*. A stretch of grass, the black poles that supposedly project the protective wall around the house, some trees . . . did Tawny lie? Is she just paranoid?

Something flashes under the slivered moonlight and my gaze holds that spot. Then I see one black lump . . . huddled with another black lump. It's like spotting a herd of deer—first you see one and then you pull back your focus and realize there are fifty.

Enforcers carpet the outer lawn of the house. The black cloaks part and there's a silver silhouette—a Brawn suit wearing a fedora. I don't need a beam of moonlight to tell me the fedora's green.

Skelley Chase is here.

But the real question is . . . does he know *I'm* here? He can't

79

possibly know I'm even *alive* unless Enforcer Zeke from the gravesite told him. Skelley must be here hunting Solomon and the others. Solomon said it was only a matter of time, hence the projected walls and the tunnel.

I back away from the window, throw Tawny's bag over my shoulder, and tiptoe out of the room. At the top of the stairs I run into a human. I suck in a gasp and reel backward. The other human squeals.

"Tawny!"

"You said sixty seconds! That was twenty seconds ago."

"It was a *guesstimate*, for time's sake! Let's go to the cellar. And keep that blanket around your shoulders."

I'll assume she nods, though I can't see it. "I have your pack."

Thank heaven she did something helpful. "Thank you." I don't tell her I saw Skelley.

We crawl from the bottom of the stairs toward the kitchen. We reach the edge of the living room and just touch the kitchen door when Skelley's voice sounds from a megaphone. It might as well be right over my shoulder from the startle it gives me. "Mr. Christian Hawke, this is Skelley Chase from the Citizen Welfare Development Council. I'd like a word, if you please."

I have a feeling his "word" will be spoken with a bullet. No one asks for a chat at four in the morning.

Tawny pauses in her crawl. "Skelley . . . Chase?"

"Keep going." I push her ahead of me.

"Shouldn't we listen to what he says?"

No we shouldn't. *That man shot your husband, remember?* "Tawny, he—"

"Killed Reid, I know." Her breaths come in gasps. I press my hand over hers and find it trembling. Maybe she *can't* move. I don't blame her for being afraid of the man who claims he can do anything.

"I won't let him hurt you."

"You can't promise that."

I close my eyes. I can't promise it, but something in me is confident he won't *touch* Tawny. I think he'd listen to me if given the chance, if only to hear *how* I'm alive.

God pulled me from the grave and brought me here. Despite the mistakes and harsh words I've let slip out, I do not fear that man or his Enforcers. Skelley has murdered, blackmailed, and betrayed . . . but I still see him as human. I can't explain it. In fact, I'm almost guilt-ridden because of it, but God droppered a single bead of compassion onto my heart for Skelley, starting with the tear I saw on his cheek at my death.

"Mister Hawke, we'll wait here until you come out. You are not in danger; these Enforcers are a precaution in the chance that you are harboring your son and other fugitives from the law." If Skelley is here, that means he doesn't know Solomon and the others are trying to rescue Willow right now.

"We have to get to the cellar *now*." The Council controls the projected Wall. What if Skelley has a way to get past the projection around the Hawke house?

I push Tawny forward. She resumes her crawl, which is unnecessary once we're in the kitchen, but I imitate—well, knee-crawl since I can't put pressure on my left arm—if only to help her feel calmer.

We enter the pantry, open the blended door in the floor, and descend into the icy cellar.

"It's freezing!"

"There are blankets inside the tunnel." I close the door behind us and then move ahead of her, taking her by the hand as we work our way across the room by feel. I don't dare light a candle.

We reach the corner and I sweep my hand over the wall in search of the special brick and code screen. The cellar is clean and spotless. This way, if anyone comes down here to look for the trap door, they won't see marks in the dust.

My fingers find the brick. I remove it and a blue glow illuminates my face. I punch in the code: *5R69N45R*, then *81WK5*, and we're inside. I close both doors before lighting the first tunnel torch. It's almost too bright and, despite the fact we're deep underground, my heart lurches at the fear that Skelley might see something.

Tawny breathes for what seems like the first time.

I turn the heater dial and a blast of air comes in, morphing from icy to warm. "Let's go deeper and find more blankets. Then I need to send a message to Solomon."

Will this interrupt their rescue mission? Will he stop things because Skelley is so near?

I take the torch with us until we're at the doors Christian pointed out. Inside one room are several sets of bunk beds, each with a pillow and folded blanket at the foot. Tawny clutches her blanket around herself, pulling folds free of my pack straps.

"Thank you for grabbing my pack." I set the torch in an empty bracket and then take my pack from her. The NAB lights up the room even more than the torch does. Tawny sinks onto a bed, sliding the pillow to the head of the mattress.

I speak a message to the NAB instead of typing.

>*Solomon, it's not safe to return to the house. Skelley has come in a Brawn suit and brought Enforcers with him. He thinks you and your dad are here. Don't come back. Where should Tawny and I meet you?*

Send.

I don't ask how the rescue mission is going.

God, get Willow out of there safely. I imagine her emaciated and distant, scarred from Council experiments. Brickbat threatened to torture her, but I entrusted her to God. I have to believe He's protected her.

"You sound so calm." Tawny leans against the cold concrete wall. "It's eerie."

I lower the NAB to my lap, fighting the old-Parvin hesitance to share. "Ever since I woke in that coffin, I've had this odd confidence in God. It's like . . . nothing else matters. Twice, I've been ready to die. I've readily accepted the idea of leaving this Earth. It was oddly freeing knowing that, in mere seconds, I'd be with God, who understands every aspect of this twisted world. He knows what's going on, what needs to happen. He knows the ending. And twice He's chosen for me to stay here and continue on. How can I fear after that?"

Tawny picks at a loose string on the blanket around her shoulders. "Reid used to talk like that."

Reid. The first flash that blinds my mental vision is of him folding to the ground after Skelley shot him. Why that? Why does *that* come to mind? Why can't I think of his laugh as he showered me with gifts of ribbons? Or his grin whenever he thought up a mischievous prank? Or his big-brother anger when he took out the bullies picking on me?

"He'd get these bouts of confidence, completely content with dying." She blows out a long breath. "And even as he talked about it, he'd be . . . *happy*. I mean, I *get* it. I get that we're going to heaven. I love God in my own way, but the idea of dying doesn't make me joyful. Is that . . . wrong?"

The comparison does more than she probably intended. She compared us . . . Reid and me. For the first time, someone compared us and came away calling us similar. Equal. I'm no longer the lesser triplet.

"It's not wrong, Tawny." At least, I don't think it is. "It's not that dying made me joyful. It's in the *moments* when I was dying that I let go of any fear or doubts. I finally saw in those seconds how God could be the number one, the only purpose, the King of my life. There's this strange peace in that. I think Reid was exceptional in that he could have that peace early on and . . . all the time. For me, it's only after I've almost died twice that I have that peace."

Will it last? It's been one full day and already I've wavered. *God, don't take it away. Being confident in You is so . . . freeing.*

It's shalom.

The NAB in my lap pops a message alert. "It's from Solomon."

~Parvin, stay in the tunnel, it should be safe enough.
We've encountered some things we didn't expect. Still in the
orphanage. I'll send another message soon.

Things they didn't expect? Like what? Willow's okay, isn't she? Is Elm getting out of hand with his desperation to save her? I repeat the message to Tawny.

"Does Chase know you're alive, Parvin?"

I shake my head. "Not as far as I know." I don't want him to know. I want him to know. I don't. I do.

I want him to see God's power.

I pull out the *Daily Hemisphere* electrosheet. The front page shows some replaying videos at the hole in the Wall. "Tawny, look."

I join her on her bed, holding the electrosheet toward her, and we both watch the video. Helicopters deliver giant batches of Enforcers who gun down anyone trying to get through the Wall. A mass of people crowd by the gap, shouting things at the Enforcers. They seem hesitant to get violent, but they want through.

They want freedom.

One helicopter lands too near the people and they mob it. It tries to take off again, but people get inside. It veers through the hole in the Wall and then crashes in a mini explosion that illuminates the night scene even more in the forest beyond the flats.

They were free for ten seconds.

Now they're dead. All because the Council wants to keep us locked on this side of the USE.

No Enforcers go after the burning helicopter. Instead, they increase their frenzy of assembling metal poles and sending them to other workers on the top of the Wall. Those poles look familiar. Tall, slender, black. "They're setting up a projection."

They're not trying to rebuild the stone. They're going to replace it with Erfinder Hawke's invention. Now, more than ever, I want to figure out a way to overcome the projection invention for good. I'll go all the way to Erfinder's house in Russia if I have to.

"I wish Reid could see what you've done." Tawny leans against her pillow.

What I've done? At first I think it's an accusation, but then I realize she meant it as a compliment. "Me too." He'd be so proud. He'd be so fired up and part of the adventure. Would Tawny have joined him in that zeal? It's hard to imagine.

"Tawny?"

"Mmm?"

Maybe I shouldn't start this, but maybe I'll never have another chance. And this will help pass the time. "Will you tell me about yourself? About your life?" Despite her fire, she always seems afraid. Nervous. Now I know why. She's been hit in her past. I want her to feel safe with me.

She sniffs. "There's not much to tell."

That just means there's not much *good* to tell. I put the *Daily Hemisphere* away and give her my full focus. "I'll listen to whatever you want to tell me."

"You sound like a therapist."

I clamp down the urge to give up, and I try being funny instead. I lean forward and use a deep, mysterious voice. "Tell me your deepest and darkest secrets, young one."

She snorts, then fights a grin. "I have a confession."

"Tell me." Still in the deep voice.

"I'm . . . addicted . . . to strawberries."

I chuckle. This is a good start. Tawny's grin fades, but she still tries to insert lightness in her next words. "I always wanted to see a therapist."

"Why would you want *that?*" I picture sitting across from Trevor Rain, my old Mentor, and baring my soul. No thanks.

"They hear your story. They don't judge. They try and help. I just . . . wanted someone to know about my life." She grips Reid's journal tight in both hands until her knuckles turn white.

I place my hand over hers. "Who hurt you, Tawny?"

"My dad." She speaks through clenched teeth. "He visited from Prime only three times a year." Her eyes flick to me, nervous, like she's holding something back. "My mom wasn't much better."

"She hit you, too?" How could any mother do that?

"Fists aren't the only things that cause harm."

I don't know what to say. No wonder she wanted away from there. No wonder she and Reid married so quickly. He could help her. He was probably the first person to love her. To *know* her. "I'm sorry if I ever hurt you."

Do I have anyone in my life who really knows *me?*

"You're fine, Parvin. I can be tough."

"Yeah, but you shouldn't need to be tough with me."

Her hands relax against the journal. "Thank you."

We rest in silence for a few minutes. I'm not sure where to go from here—I want to know more details, probe more and show her that I can be trusted.

She speaks first. "So we are just waiting here for them to return?" Torchlight illuminates one side of her face, flickering and bouncing off her skin.

"No, we're waiting for Solomon to tell us what's going on. He said they ran into some complications."

She yawns deeply. Maybe, with any luck, she'll fall asleep through this chaos. "Are you sure it's safe down here?"

No. "Jude made it. We'll be fine. Besides, no one even knows about—"

An explosion jars our teeth and rains cement dust down on our heads. Tawny screams and a crack bursts in the ceiling. "What was that?" She jerks away from the wall.

The shudders recede, and I'm gripping the bunk bed post so tight I get slivers. "I . . . I think . . . it was some sort of . . . bomb."

Tawny's the world's worst runner. I blame it on the pregnancy.

We sprint to the end of the tunnel, which takes longer than I'd expected. The torch flickers against the wind from our movement, but doesn't go out. There hasn't been another explosion, but I want us to be near the door if there's a cave-in. Why is Skelley bombing the house? Does he really believe that Christian is inside? And if he does, why is he trying to *kill* him?

It's got to be some sort of scare tactic. Or perhaps it's his attempt at breaking down the projected wall so they can get to the house. Is the house even standing anymore? Did he find out I'm in here?

"Where does this tunnel lead?" Tawny places her hands on her lower back and catches her breath.

"Christian said it leads into the forest." I fumble with the NAB, balancing it on my stump, and speak a quick message to Solomon.

-There was an explosion. I think Skelley bombed the house. We're near the exit, waiting to hear from you.

Tawny bounces on her toes, looking up the tunnel, at the ceiling, at the door, and then at me. "Has he responded yet?"

The NAB is blank. Black. Lonely and silent. "No."

"What should we do?" She's a follower, an easy role to fill when Reid was around. I was always a follower, too . . . until I no longer had him. Then I had to become a leader—a leader of myself, which then bled into becoming a leader of others.

Tawny, however, clings to the leaders. I wish she were stronger, only because I don't want to lead in this moment. I don't know the answers, and that's the worst situation for leadership.

Pop! Solomon replied.

-Stay put.

Tawny leans over my shoulder. I move the torch away so it doesn't catch in her hair. "That's all he writes?"

"I guess." I stare at the two words, wishing for more. Yet at the same time, grateful that Solomon's plucked the leadership baton from my fingers.

"That can't be right. How can he expect us to stay here?" Her arms creep around her midsection. I think I see a bump now.

I shrug. "He knows this tunnel. He knows what's going on outside. We have to trust him."

"How can he know? He's at the orphanage!"

I sink to the second cement stair that leads out. "Let's sit down, okay? There's been only one explosion and that was ten minutes ago. For all we know, Skelley and the Enforcers might be leaving."

She plops onto the step too hard and then winces. "Why would they set off a bomb, then?"

It couldn't have been to destroy the house, otherwise we'd have heard lumber snapping and crashing from above as the house collapsed. "My guess is they were trying to get through the projected wall around the house and it didn't work."

"Maybe it *did* work." She yanks the blanket tighter around her shoulders and kicks her pack to the side with her foot. "Maybe they're coming after us right now."

It didn't work. Christian told me that his grandfather had kept the deeper understanding of projections a secret. Only a select number of USE technicians know how to control it. It's like God set up the perfect situation for me to beat this thing. If Erfinder Hawke hid the rest of the invention information somewhere, then I'll be the one to find it.

The wooden door above our heads slides open, and Tawny gives us away with a shriek. I glance up through the projected screen, certain I'm about to see a green fedora and a bored smirk. Instead, Solomon's vivid teal eyes reflect the torchlight. He presses a finger to his lips, then taps a few more buttons. The projected screen goes away. "Come on up."

I take his offered hand and let him help me up the steps. He's fine. He's alive. We're fine. I didn't realize how much I enjoy his presence until I went without it. "Willow . . .?"

"She's a bit deeper in the forest. We'll go there now." He doesn't say how she is. He doesn't look at me. Instead, he reaches down to help Tawny out.

"Is your house still standing?" she asks.

He nods. "From the glimpse I got. Chase and the Enforcers are still there. The projection remains active, though the entrance of the house was hit. The sooner we move on, the better." He closes the entry to the tunnel and it blends in with the forest ground.

Solomon takes Tawny's pack from her and slings it over his own. He doesn't take mine and, despite my irrational twinge of irritation, I understand. She's pregnant. This is all new to her. He does, however, hold out his hand.

When I slip my fingers between his, he lifts our fists up and gives the back of my hand a quick kiss. Then we head through the forest. I reach back with my other arm for Tawny's hand before realizing she'd have nothing to hold.

My left hand has been gone for months. *Months.* And I still sometimes act as though I have it. At least I'm no longer bitter. I've yet to understand fully why God allowed the albinos to take it. Was it to create a relationship with Ash, Black, and Willow? Was it to weaken me so I'd be strong in Him? Was it to draw curious people to me so I could share my story? Yes, yes, and yes.

God works all things for His glory. I just need to keep believing it.

Tawny loops her arm through mine. I squeeze it against my side. I will protect my sister. I will be the sister she needs. After all, she's going to make me an aunt.

We walk for a half-hour through the forest. Tawny's breathing grows steadier the farther we get from the Hawke house. I want to ask Solomon about the rescue, but he's not talking about it. Did something go wrong?

Best to be quiet as we travel anyway.

Then, far ahead of me, I see a glow. She'd be a ghost if I didn't know any better. "Willow."

I run forward, letting go of Solomon and Tawny. She stands beside Elm and looks up when I say her name. Her small doll face doesn't smile. Instead, her jaw clenches and her eyes seem narrowed. She wears a floral jumpsuit and laced boots. A white bandage wraps around her left arm, including her fingers, all the way up to her shoulder—like a mummy arm. She wears a glove on the other. Was she burned? The other portions of her exposed skin are redder than normal—scratched with small scars. Her hair is buzzed to within an inch of her scalp.

So much is different, but I don't care. I pull her into a hug. "We came for you as soon as we could." Her sharp nod bumps against my clavicle. I lean back to get a good look at her face.

Her pursed lips part enough to get words through her teeth. "Parvin, we will stop the Council." Her voice is dark, as though she's swallowed shadows and they tainted her sweetness.

"Yes, we will." Stop them from which thing? I don't know. But we *will* stop their secrets. Their control. Their manipulation.

I look into her light purple eyes, holding her gaze. Let her see. I will keep my word. Let her see my determination. She doesn't blink. Her jaw works furiously, but like a storm blown out of a valley, the fury leaves her eyes. They widen into circles again instead of slits and then her chin quivers.

Tears burst from her eleven-year-old dam of determination. I drop to my knees and she lurches into my arms this time. My throat burns. "We'll stop them, Willow. And we'll get you home."

She sniffs hard and her voice is muffled against my clothing. "Okay." Elm stands a few feet away and watches Willow cry in my arms. He frowns. Has he never seen her sad like this before? His good eye slides his gaze to mine and ferocity replaces the confusion.

"Willow, we *will* stop them." The way he says these words splashes fear into my stomach.

"Let's get going." Christian's voice cuts into our reunion. I release Willow, and Elm hovers near her as though hesitant to let her go more than four inches away from him.

"Where are we going?" I trust him and I'm not too concerned about details, but this gives Willow more time to compose herself.

Christian looks around the grove of trees. Only now do I see the other faces. Kaphtor and Frenchie sit on the ground, leaning against a tree with seven children—all under the age of ten and wearing patterned jumpsuits. Idris and Fight stand a few feet off, whispering in harsh tones that sound like an argument. Another group of about ten children huddle together, some holding babies or toddlers. All of them watch Christian.

He grins at them. "Well, Parvin, if you hadn't noticed, we came out of there with more than just Willow."

My jaw hangs open. "What in time's name are we going to do with all of them?" I throw out a smile when I finish the sentence so the kids don't think I don't want them freed.

"We are together." Willow's resilience is back and she joins Elm at his side. "I can't leave them behind, Christian-man."

"I know," Christian soothes. "And I think yours was a valiant decision."

I stand up and Solomon leans to whisper in my ear. "She wouldn't leave with us unless we took all of them."

I grin at Willow's title for Christian. "Christian-man?"

Solomon smiles. "Thanks to Willow, they're all calling him that now."

Willow tugs me toward the kids. "Parvin, these are new friends. They will come across the Wall with us." The shadows in her voice fade as she points from one head to the next, rattling off names. "Paige, Tanner, Jax, Jaeger, Slade, Beck, Jett, Destany—"

Each child waves when his or her name is called, not that it will do me any good. "Willow . . ."

"—Kenna, Kyla, Josephine, Kannon—"

"Willow, I can't remember them all."

"—Stryker, Adeleide, Levi—"

"Just let her tell them to you," Solomon whispers in my ear.

"—Jayce, Ty, and Aspen." Willow goes forward and hugs a girl her same height, who has long brown hair. "Aspen has a name from trees like I do!"

Well, at least I'll remember *her* name. All the rest have already fled my mind, but Willow puffs with pride as she looks at her little orphans. They are her charge and she's freed them.

"We're going somewhere that guarantees their safety." Christian takes a sleeping toddler from the arms of one of the other orphans and settles her in a piggyback.

"Across the Wall?" Idris asks.

He shakes his head. "Not yet. But eventually. For now, though, I'm taking them to a rather odd friend of mine." He looks at me. I frown. Am I supposed to know who he's talking about? Everyone I know is either in this group or on the other side of the Wall.

"How far?" one boy asks.

"A few hours. We'll take turns with piggybacks."

Solomon shifts his and Tawny's packs to his front and then hoists a little girl onto his back. Fight and Kaphtor do the same—Kaphtor taking one of the smallest children since his shot leg is still healing.

I want to help, but my wrist makes me pause. A little girl climbs onto Frenchie's back. She gives a brief, unladylike grunt, but then adjusts the child. If she can do it with cracked ribs, I can do it with a missing hand.

I kneel in front of a small girl of about five. She has brown curly hair to her shoulders and steel-blue eyes. "Now you'll have to hold tight, I have only one hand." I hold up my left arm.

She gasps and then shoves her arm in my face. "Me too!" Her right arm grows just past the elbow then pinches into a stub with tiny nubbins for fingers. "Did your hand forget to grow when you were born, too?"

I stare at her stub. It's so . . . beautiful. "No," I croak. "But it's happy to find a friend."

She fake-tickles the end of mine with her underdeveloped fingers, then giggles. "I'll hold on tight."

I turn around and she climbs on as if she's done this a hundred times before. She curves her right arm around my neck and then locks onto it with her left hand. It chokes me a little, but I stand and hoist her a bit higher, giving me more breathing space.

"I'm Parvin."

"That's pretty." Her voice is softer, and her head clunks against the back of mine.

"Go ahead and close your eyes. Fall asleep. I won't drop you."

She barely whispers, "I know." Then her head is heavy against mine, sliding down to rest on my shoulder. Her grip loosens, but I've got a good grip of my own.

Maybe this . . . is another reason I lost my hand.

I step toward Willow, with the little girl already snoring in my ear. I don't remember her name, but Willow can remind me if need be.

Willow walks with her bandaged hand in Elm's, staring

straight forward like a marching soldier. After all this time she's finally free, but it doesn't look victorious. She's come out of it angry, distant.

I want our sisterhood back.

It's selfish, but I want to know if Willow missed me. I step forward so I'm next to her and Elm and, just as I reach for Willow's shoulder, Elm snaps his head and gives me the harshest glare I've ever seen from an angry albino.

And I've seen a lot of angry albinos.

He shakes his head once and pulls Willow tighter to his side. I'm not allowed near her. I'm not allowed to touch her. Hopefully there's a *yet* in there.

Willow responds to none of this exchange. A walking statue.

I submit to Elm.

For now.

As morning light shoos away the darkness, we arrive at a cottage—a very tiny, old-fashioned cottage that can't *possibly* hold twenty orphans, let alone us adults. The repainted front door is under a stone arch and a matching A-frame roof. The outer walls are a mixture of stone and wood, moss clinging to parts but in a tasteful way. Christian walks up the two entry steps and knocks.

I guess whoever lives here doesn't mind being woken at daybreak. The curved wooden door swings inward, revealing a woman in her seventies, who's almost as tall as Christian. Her short, nut-brown hair—not quite natural looking—is swept over in a side-part and her warm, indigo eyes scan our sorry-looking group of exhausted travelers.

When she sees Christian, she sticks out her lower lip. "When I told you to visit, Christian, I didn't mean for breakfast." She has a soft and elegant British accent. "You know I don't eat breakfast."

He gives a short bow and the sleeping child on his back sags to one side. "Then we'll do the cooking."

She laughs and steps aside. "Oh, come in. All of you. My carpet makes for *splendid* sleeping."

Who *is* this lady, who doesn't bat an eye at a group of orphans and strangers pouncing on her doorstep?

We walk inside the tiny cottage. There's one couch and a rocking chair around a fake fireplace. A kitchen is off to the right, filled with giant windows that let the morning sun in. Plants and herbs wake in their pots on the wooden sills, soaking up their own breakfast of sunrise.

"Deposit the children wherever there's space." She waves to the living room carpet then heads toward a narrow staircase that leads into a basement. "I'll get some blankets and then we can have tea in the kitchen where you will explain *everything*."

Tea. British accent. Makes sense.

Once we've carpeted the floor with orphans, we congregate around the kitchen table. Thankfully there are two benches we can squeeze on for seating. The floor is made of laid stones, but one wall has an open cooking fireplace.

The woman sets a tray with mismatched mugs and a teapot of hot water in the center of the table. "So, Christian, what's this all about?"

He looks at us. Can he see how tired we all are? I want to sleep more than anything, but my curiosity wins out. Before I can possibly close my eyes, I need to know why this tiny cottage is so much safer than the projection-surrounded Hawke house with the secret tunnel.

He goes around the table, telling her all of our names—our *real* names. I tense when he says mine, but the woman doesn't blink. When finished, he pours hot water over loose-leaf tea in one of the mugs.

"Everyone, let me introduce you to Dalene. This lovely woman is Skelley Chase's mother."

9

Skelley Chase has a mother? I never imagined that being possible. He seemed to just evolve naturally.

From a pile of sludge somewhere.

"You don't have to *define* me like that, Christian." Dalene takes her seat at the head of the table, with the fire to her back. She looks at us. "But that's one way to make things clearer for everyone."

I stare at the smile crinkles at the corners of her eyes. They sweep upward, making her look constantly happy. How could *this* woman be the mother of such a monster? And how in the world does Christian know her?

I glance to Solomon, who sits at my right. Does *he* know this woman?

Christian's right about one thing. Skelley will never think to look for us here. Unless Dalene alerts him. Or unless he decides to drop by since he's in the area. My gut clenches.

"Explain yourself," Tawny says, as though she can't associate with such a person unless a decent excuse is made.

Dalene laughs. "You, dear girl, will learn someday that your child's actions are beyond your control."

Tawny wraps her arms around her stomach as if to protect her baby from the evil vibes that might flow from this interaction. "Your son killed my husband."

"That's not the only person he's killed." How can a mother

speak so flippantly about a murderous son? Dalene scoops a spoon-ful of tea leaves into her mug and adds water, sugar, and cream.

"He is evil!" Willow grinds the words out. Her small fists clench above the table, and Elm matches her fury with narrowed eyes. "He should die! I will kill him!"

Whoa, now, Willow. This probably isn't the time or place to say such things. "Mrs. Chase—"

"Please, Parvin, call me Dalene."

I don't argue. I don't like associating Skelley's name with this woman. She makes me feel at ease. If either of my grandmothers were still alive, I imagine they'd be like her. "Dalene . . . um . . . how do you and Christian know each other? He seems to think we can trust you. I would like to believe that."

"Even Judas Iscariot had a mother, and I'm certain she loved him very much but probably hated what he became." She stirs her tea and then, without my asking, fills a mug with hot water and slides it to me.

I want coffee more than anything, but tea will do. It's been a while since I've had it.

"When I adopted Skelley from the orphanage, he was already fifteen years old."

Beside me, Solomon chokes on his tea. He raises a fist over his mouth, coughs three times, and then rasps, "He was adopted . . . from *my* orphanage?"

She gives a smile, revealing perfectly straight teeth. "From the very same orphanage your father visits monthly, which, inciden-tally, is how Christian and I met."

Solomon looks as though he's about to be sick. What do I do? Should I say something? At a loss, I grab a tiny spoon and scoop some tea leaves into my mug as I saw others do. They float on the top of my hot water, spinning in a sluggish dance.

"It doesn't mean anything, Sol," Christian mutters.

Solomon flings a hand toward Dalene. "*She* kept this from us!"

Christian shakes his head. "Not from me. I've always known."

"You've known that she allowed her son to grow into a monster?"

Christian's face turns hard. "That was beyond her control. If God Himself chooses not to interfere with our free will, why would He give that permission to a parent?"

Dalene's lips tremble as she takes a sip from her mug. "At fifteen, a headstrong boy is already set in his ways. Not even the best mother can train him out of the harm and darkness he's allowed inside his soul during his youth."

Solomon regains control over his choking. Maybe he realizes his barbs were unfounded, because his voice now comes out businesslike. "If Skelley was adopted from that orphanage, why in the world would he allow the Council to do all their Clock-testing on the orphans?"

"Ah, for you, Solomon, the orphanage is a pleasant memory?"

"Of course. I was there before the Council corrupted it." His eyebrows twitch, and the corners of his lips turn down. "I . . . I . . . That's where I clung to hope. I begged God for a family and then . . ." His knuckles whiten around the handle of his mug and he looks at his dad for help.

"Then Jude picked him." Christian smiles at Solomon. "I picked him too, of course, but it was Jude who insisted he wanted an older brother and Sol would be it."

"That's how I found God." Solomon's hoarse whisper fills the kitchen as though it were a shout.

"Oh, Solomon." Idris looks about to cry.

I reach along the table and take Solomon's hand. He found God in an orphanage. I found God through Reid. Such different experiences, yet our God is everywhere.

"That's not Skelley's story." Dalene taps her spoon against the edge of her cup and then sets it on the table. "He was wrenched away from his parents—abusers in every sense of the word—and put in the orphanage."

Tawny straightens at this. She can relate. Does she empathize with him now?

"He tried to escape twice and made enemies fast, both with the children and the caretakers." Dalene smiles at something only she can see. "That's how I found him. He was wrestling in the arms of two Enforcers who were demanding to know who he belonged to. I waltzed up and told them to let go of my boy. Skelley looked at me like I was his savior."

It's hard to imagine Skelley looking at anyone like that. It's hard to imagine him as a boy to begin with. All I picture is a shorter man still wearing his fedora.

"I hadn't married my husband by that point. I wasn't fit to be a mother. I was just a lonely woman who wanted to pour her love into a person instead of plants. I adopted Skelley and we had two grand years before he'd had enough of me. That's when he found his own way, determined to be self-sufficient. He had an obsession with people's stories, so he got into biographying. Only a year later I met my husband."

She gestures to a portrait of a classy gentleman standing in a garden, with shears in one hand and a handful of weeds in the other. "He died last spring."

Almost everyone voices small sympathies. Solomon stares into his tea.

"Now, enough about my son and about me. Inform me, Christian."

No, it's not enough. I have so many more questions. Has she seen Skelley since he left? How did her husband die? What happened to Skelley's parents? Did he kill them, too? What did she mean when she said he had enough of her?

I stir my tea.

Christian gives an efficient rundown of our situation. To my surprise, Dalene has kept up on all the happenings with the Wall, with my biography, with the Clocks, and with the Council, so his story needs very few explanations. "We need a place to bed down for a day so we can plan."

"Well, I don't have much space, but I have plenty of food and specie. Do your sleeping and planning, and we'll go from there. Off to bed with all of you." She gives us a fake glare. "That's chamomile you're drinking, so you ought to be fading by now."

I haven't taken a single sip. The tea leaves have all sunk to the bottom of the cup.

We slink into the living room, grab a blanket from her seemingly endless pile, and find a nook. Mine happens to be near Solomon. We lie on the ground, between the end of the couch and the stair railing, facing each other. My blanket is quilted yellow, and his is a muted green, poofing around his face.

We stare at one another for a moment. He's so close. "Are you okay?"

He breathes out and breaks the visual connection. "I don't know. I'm . . . confused. Sleep will help."

"Okay." Tentative, I stretch out my hand. He responds without hesitation, curling his fingers over mine.

I wake to hushed voices. My muscles lie like hibernating slugs, and my grainy blinks tell me I haven't come close to accumulating the rest I need. Sadly, my brain doesn't seem to compute this. It springs up like a three-year-old on a sugar-high, insisting I investigate.

I crawl from my covers and hover near the kitchen. Frenchie and Dalene sit at the kitchen table, both with mugs of tea. Frenchie sniffs and wipes an eye with the palm of her hand. "But . . . 'ow can I ever repay you? Why would you do zis for *moi?*"

"Because I understand the importance of home." Dalene winks. "Besides, Europe is in our blood. Now go get some sleep."

Frenchie rises and turns before I can duck back behind the doorframe. She spots me and smiles. "Parvin, did you 'ear?"

I shake my head, glad I can be honest, though I'm not sure what she's afraid I heard.

"She eez sending me back to France!"

I look at Dalene, who gestures to Frenchie's chair as if this is a Mentor session. "Come join me, Parvin."

It's creepy how I'm drawn to sit with this woman. I'm unnerved by how comfortable I feel with her. She elicits trust . . . much like a certain man with a green fedora once did.

"That's wonderful, Angelique." I pass through the door and sit in Frenchie's spot. She's going home. That's the whole reason she returned to this side of the Wall with me. And now she gets a piece of shalom back in her life.

Dalene moves Frenchie's mug of cold tea aside and pours me a fresh one. Perhaps this time I'll get to drink it. "Sugar?"

"You're from Europe. Make it your way."

Her thin, sculpted eyebrows pop up. "Sugar and cream, then."

Oh good, I was hoping it'd be sweet. The mug is rough and lumpy ceramic, as though handmade. Once the milk is added, the tea turns light beige, still swirling from her stirs. I'll let it cool for a bit.

"What did you want to talk about?" Despite her friendliness, I still wonder if maybe she's a spy. Maybe Skelley is on his way here right now to find me. Yet . . . that doesn't frighten me. Today I'll rise above my suspicions and doubts.

I will trust You.

Dalene scoots an electrosheet of *The Daily Hemisphere* toward me. "You've been proclaimed dead."

The article is short. The Council doesn't dare give me too much screen time to make me a martyr . . . but they mention my death all the same, so the people of the USE remember who's in charge. What the article doesn't mention is the fact that my death overrode my Clock. That's the important part. There's a picture of me inside the coffin. I'm pale and bruised. Creepy.

I imagine the world reading this. Will they despair or rejoice?

I jolt in my chair. *Father.* If he sees this on his NAB . . . "I need to contact my parents." I move to stand up, but Dalene holds out a hand.

"Wait, Parvin. NAB messages aren't secure. You'll have to let Christian alter your NAB settings before sending anything. This situation is both advantageous and dangerous for you."

"I used my NAB before to contact Solomon and everything was fine."

Dalene refills her cup. "Best not to risk it again, I think. Your parents are safe on the other side of the Wall. Leave them in ignorance of your survival for now."

I haven't had enough time to process the repercussions of this news article, but even *I* know that allowing my parents to grieve over the loss of their last living child will do more damage than good. This was Mother's fear. She didn't want me to return West only to die. Children without parents have orphanages, but what do parents without children have? What if she reads that I'm dead and she gives up on living? On healing?

I shake my head. "How is this advantageous?"

"You can't go anywhere or buy anything without risking being spotted and reported to the Council."

Oh, well, if *that's* all . . .

"*However*, since the Council doesn't seem to know you're alive, the moment you reveal your survival will shock the USE . . . and you will then be their leader because you will have proven that neither the Council nor the Clocks control you."

I didn't think of my survival giving me power. In fact, I didn't consider revealing my survival at all. But at least *that* would set

Mother and Father at ease. "Why are you on my side? Are you anti-Clock, too?"

"I wouldn't call myself anti-anything. I'm pro-freedom. You and I seem to share the same ideas of what freedom looks like."

I hear freedom and think *shalom*. What enters her mind? "So what are you saying I should do?" Not that I'll blindly take her advice.

"You tell me."

She's not here to guide me. Good. I have my leader, and He's the only one I need. So what *should* I do?

Russia.

The word prompts me with a nagging voice, but I'm hesitant because it's not *His* voice. It's simply a place that latched itself onto my brain the moment Christian told me about his Opa Fin, the inventor of the projected Wall.

God, is that where I'm supposed to go?

It's ridiculously far away. How in the world do I even go about getting there?

I CAN DO ANYTHING.

I startle in my chair, then laugh at the irony of Skelley's catch-phrase coming from my God—the One who actually *can* do anything. *Does this mean You want me to go to Russia?*

This happened to me when I was in Ivanhoe the first time. I didn't know what to do, so I made the best decision I could and pursued it through prayer. If God wants it stopped, He has my full permission. Not that He needs it.

All this time, Dalene's watched me, not pressuring me for an answer, simply content waiting as I search my thoughts. "What if . . . what if I wanted . . . to travel overseas?"

"Like Angelique returning to France?"

I grip my mug. "Yes. How do I do that?" And what will Solomon say if I *do* choose that?

"Mentors handle all the travel papers and permissions."

Mentor. Maybe this is a sign that I *shouldn't* pursue Erfinder Hawke's house. My Mentor was Trevor Rain. Whatever happened to him? Was he in Unity when the Enforcers took over and sent half the town to Antarctica to die? Asking him for help is out of the question. I don't even know where to find him.

Maybe Solomon had a Mentor. When he wakes, I'll see if he has any ideas.

I take a sip of my tea. It's still too hot, but the mini mouthful I manage is thin and sweet. The undertaste isn't a punch like coffee. It's subtle, with more flavor. Tasty . . . but it's not coffee.

"I have specie for you, Parvin." Dalene lifts a flap of skin identical to the one Solomon has on his wrist, revealing a scan bar. "I'll give it to Solomon since you don't have a bank chip."

Staring at that fake wrist flap turns my tea into an afterthought. She's nice and everything, but no one's *that* generous. After all, she's already committed to paying Frenchie's way to France. She has an angle. She's Skelley's mother . . . and I haven't seen enough passion in her about my mission to convince me this is a gift.

"Why would you give us specie?"

"Because it's yours." She puts the flap back down, thank goodness. "You realize you're famous, don't you?"

"Famously *dead* at the moment."

"Where do you think all the money from your X-book has been going?"

Need she ask? "To Skelley, of course." But the way she presents this question makes me doubt that. She's about to reveal something. Skelley is already rich—he doesn't need more specie. He doesn't strike me as the type of man who works solely to stack up more coins. Neither does he strike me as a benefactor.

"Indeed. He's kept the profits, but he's sent me a rather large sum every month since my husband died." She gestures to her cottage. "As you can see, I don't need much. My husband left me set up for the rest of my Numbers. In my mind, those sums belong to you."

I can't take her money.

Why not?

Because . . . because . . ."I really don't know what to say." Maybe this is a sign that I *should* go to Russia.

"Seeing as how you don't have a choice, you can just say thank you."

"Um . . . thank you." This is too easy. Or is it? I haven't seen how much she'll give me. I could be blowing this out of proportion. Besides, it solves only one of my problems. I'd need travel papers, documents, permission, transportation. All while remaining undercover. "Now I just need to find a Mentor."

"Done."

"What do you . . .?" But I figure it out before I finish. No wonder it's so easy to sit across from her and talk. No wonder she remains calm and gives advice as though it's her job.

"I'm a Mentor, dear."

"I think I need to go to Russia, and Dalene can get me there."

Solomon's hardly awake before I drop this bombshell on him, but I can't keep it in much longer.

"Russia?" He rolls onto his back, joints popping from sleeping too long in one position. "What's in Russia?"

"Your dad said that's where Erfinder Hawke lived out the rest of his life. And according to him, Jude always believed Erfinder hid the core of his invention somewhere in his house."

Solomon props himself up on his elbows and levels a gaze at me, as though to check if I'm serious. "Jude had a lot of . . . wild ideas."

He doesn't mention how impulsive my decision sounds. I

imagine, for a moment, telling this to Mother. Her greatest enemy has been my impulse bug. "Russia's been on my mind, Solomon. And Dalene is a Mentor—she can get me travel papers *and* she wants to give me the specie earned from my X-book. It's like . . . God set everything up already. Frenchie—I mean . . . Angelique—is traveling back to France. I can go with her and then continue on to Russia—"

"You keep saying *I* and . . . and *me.*"

I halt midsentence. "What's wrong with—?"

"Do you not want me to go with you?"

Oh.

He has on a genuinely curious face, but I still hear the hurt in his voice. I must take too long to answer because he rises from his spot on the floor and heads to the kitchen.

"Wait . . . Solomon." I trot after him, but he reaches the back door and holds it open for me.

"Let's talk outside."

The backyard of Dalene's house is a dormant fairyland. Even without blooms or leaves, the bushes seem happy and filled with life just waiting to appear. The air is frigid and I'm instantly swept back to Antarctica. Only God could have kept us alive there. What a story.

Solomon plops down on the back step, his blanket around his shoulders. He holds one side open for me. At least he doesn't hate me. I join him in the blanket. His arm tightens around me and a gush of body warmth sends my stomach into a spiral. Well . . . that's what I blame it on.

"Of course I want you with me, Solomon." My shoulders tense when I say this. I have to be real with him. "But I don't know where God's going to take me. Think of when we were with the Council. I . . . don't want to do that to you again."

I hate the idea of traveling without him. With him, I feel safe. But I can't force him to keep following my impulse bug. It has to be his desire, too. For the first time, Solomon doesn't speak softly with me. His voice is hard—not accusatory, but serious. "It's time for you to decide, Parvin. Will we be a team, or would you like to continue alone?"

"What do you mean? We've *been* a team this whole time." How can he say this?

"Yes, but things are different now." He sighs. "God's brought you back to me. I have to believe He's giving us another chance at our future. We have the same passions, Parvin. We both want shalom. We both want the Wall taken down. We've been forced to make decisions apart from each other and now we have a chance to do it together." He plops his head in his hand like he's at a loss for words.

That's exactly what I want, but he says it as though I haven't shown this. Maybe I haven't. "Of course I want us to be a team. But I don't want you to feel obligated."

He laughs and shakes his head. I suddenly feel dense, like I'm not getting it.

"Have you forgotten?" He sits straight and takes my hand in his, meeting my gaze full on. "I *love* you. There's no obligation in love. I just want us to start growing together. Build good habits. Practice."

My heart thumps like the feet of a fleeing rabbit, and I speak in a whisper. "Practice?"

"Practice *life* . . . together." He sounds weary, but hopeful. "It's a request. It's my desire." His voice quavers and he looks at his bare feet. "Because someday, Parvin Blackwater, I want you to marry me."

10

Marry him.

Marry him?

The lurch in my gut tempts me to scream, "Let's get married now!" But his statement wasn't a proposal. At least, I don't think it was. It was just . . . a statement.

How unromantic.

My jaw works. What do I say? Oh goodness, what *can* I say? Solomon wants to marry me. I want to marry him. We're both young, but . . . we're older than Reid and Tawny were when they got married.

"Parvin?"

I jerk upright. "Sorry, my . . . thoughts got away from me."

He fidgets with the end of the blanket. "What are you thinking?"

Mere seconds ago, I was perplexed. Now I want to fold into his arms and apologize for whatever confusing ride I've put him through. "I want to marry you, Solomon." I swallow hard. "But I'm afraid that . . . I don't know how to be what you want." He wants us to be a team. I want him to be my leader, yet I also want to follow where I feel God is calling me.

I'm *so* going to mess this up.

Solomon takes my face in his hands and forces me to look at him. Tears spring up. "You *are* what I want, Parvin. Exactly how you are right now. But I want us to grow together, to be one. I want to be *with* you in your pursuits and . . . you with me in mine. Is that too much to ask?"

I shake my head, but I'm not sure. Can I mesh these two things? My love for Solomon and the journey God's placed me on? What if I get distracted from God? "I'll try."

He smiles gently and brushes his thumb along my cheekbone, and I wonder if we're going to remedy the fact that we've had only a good-bye kiss. But he doesn't kiss me, and part of me is disappointed and the other part happy. It's like, by saving our kisses they'll mean more when we actually have them.

And . . . now I'm thinking about kissing.

"So what if nothing's in Russia?" Solomon's question comes with a tone of planning, like we weren't just talking about a future of marriage or almost-kissing. He's not questioning the pursuit of Russia, he's already preparing for it.

He's already on my side.

"Then we try something else. God restarted my heart for a reason. He knows I don't want to waste any time. If we pursue Him in this, He'll direct us where we need to go." I pick at a loose strand on his blanket.

He stills my fingers with his own. "I'm with you, Parvin. I'm on your side."

I close my eyes and whisper, "Thank you." I need him with me. Right now . . . we're a team.

"Give me two days," Dalene tells us once everyone is awake and gathered for food. The children from the orphanage are feasting in the basement and causing kid-trouble—something they never had much chance to do in the orphanage. They are long overdue.

Willow and Elm sit on the ground against the wall by the

fireplace, as still as the stones against their backs. Neither meets my gaze. Neither seems aware I'm even *trying* to catch their eye. There's a gap between the two, like they don't want to be *too* close.

"Two days and I'll have travel papers for those who need them. Now you have to decide who's leaving and who's going to stay and take care of these children."

Two days. I just went from not knowing my next step to mentally preparing myself for a trip to Russia.

"Of course I'm going." Solomon says it for the sake of everyone else.

"And me." Frenchie's eyes flick toward Kaphtor. "I am going back 'ome."

It's not exactly a simple question to throw into a circle of people. Idris and Fight huddle in a corner to talk it out. Elm and Willow discuss through tense lips and mutters. Frenchie and Kaphtor go outside, and I join Christian, Tawny, and Solomon at the top of the stairs.

Christian fiddles with my NAB, making it secure so I can send messages to Mother and Father. Since Solomon and Christian already know my plan, our meeting is mostly for Tawny.

I study her face. "Will you be okay here?"

She glances at Christian. "Well, once Christian sets your NAB, I was thinking we could give you updates on what's happening in the USE—things that don't make it to the news. I'll wait here until the baby comes, and then when you come back . . . we can go through the Wall together, maybe." Her voice fades with a brief tremble.

For a moment, we're actually sisters—and it makes me miss Reid so much I almost lose control. Swallow. Breathe. Refocus. "You're being so strong, Tawny."

I don't want us to separate, not now that we're finally making headway. Will she be okay with Christian? Does she feel safe with him?

SHE IS MINE.

My breath catches. *Is she?* It's been so easy to entrust myself to God, yet not trust Him to care for others. Maybe it's because He let Jude die, and Reid—yet I still trust Him. At least . . . I say I do.

Am I trusting Him with Tawny? Am I trusting Him with *Solomon?* I'm so quick to leave him behind, to use his help and accept his love, then surge forward without a backward glance.

That's not love. That's not shalom.

My eyes drift to Solomon's face. He's focused on his dad, so I allow myself to stare. I take in his scars from resisting the pull of corrupt Enforcing. I take in the weathered eye crinkles from watching his brother die and letting me sacrifice myself. He's a leader. I want him to be my leader in love. Because if he's following God with every ounce of himself, then God stays my leader, too.

"We have to go!" Willow's hiss draws my attention. "To help Parvin and the Hawke stop the Council."

Elm's narrowed gaze reminds me of his older brother, Black. "We must go home, Willow, and help our people fight from *our* side."

"Elm, the Council's bad! I will *kill* them—"

"No." He tears his gaze from her. "Go without me, if you must."

Willow's face wars between sorrow and anger, twitching and contorting until she forces a deep, ragged breath. "Fine. I won't leave. You are mine. My Elm. I'll go with you."

It's so opposite of what I would have done. I would have argued. Insisted. Fought. But Willow's relationship and trust in Elm is more important to her than her own independence or vengeance.

Elm lifts his head and looks at her. Her small lips purse and her purple eyes waver beneath a film of tears. He brushes a hand over her fuzzy scalp, but she flinches away. "Willow . . . we will go with Parvin."

She shakes her head, knocking a tear loose. "I'll follow *you*." Her voice is so small, so delicate and trusting.

"And my mind is different now. We go to Russia."

"Okay."

God is using *children* to show me what it's like to trust and follow. It unnerves me . . . because I'm not sure I can do it right.

Idris steps into my view of Elm and Willow's conversation. "Christian, may Fight and I talk with you a bit?"

"Sure." Christian pushes himself to his feet and follows her to the corner. What will their decision be? The Council discovered the meeting place of the Prime church. Will they go back and defend it? Find the people who scattered?

Willow and Elm are coming with me. It's funny the confidence that surges inside me at the companionship of an eleven-year-old and her teenage grafting partner. They are survivors. Willow's part of my family. I didn't admit it before, but it would have shredded my heart to watch her cross the Wall without me.

Two days—as promised—is all it takes for Dalene to set us up with travel papers, specie, supplies, and encouragement. Then I'm hugging Tawny good-bye. "Will you be okay?"

She bites her lower lip. "I'll be fine. But . . . Parvin?"

"What?"

"Are you going to attack the Council?" Her eyes flick toward Willow and Elm for a moment.

"I'm not sure what we're going to do or where God will take all this." Is she going to ask me to kill Skelley? Is that why she's bringing this up? Is that why she seems nervous?

"If you do, just . . . just deal kindly with Elan."

"Brickbat?" I did *not* expect this. Why in the world does she care about that high-strung, angry beast?

"Do you think God can redeem anyone?"

Her abrupt question takes me aback. "Maybe." What am I doing? I should be saying a firm *Yes,* but with Brickbat on my mind . . .

"See . . . don't be angry, but"—Tawny's eyes plead, but I'm not sure for what—"Brickbat is my . . . my father."

I stare. He *can't* be. But then . . .

The pieces fall into place. He matches what I've learned about Tawny's father. It takes no stretch of the imagination to picture him hitting her. "Are you sure?"

What a stupid thing to ask.

She nods, chewing her bottom lip again. "I probably should have told you earlier, but it's not a big deal. We're not . . . close. He never married my mom. I'm kind of the daughter he ignores . . . unless he's angry."

That man has *kids?* What woman in her right mind would fall in love with that black-and-white creep? "Let me just say, you have *way* better taste in men than your mom did."

Did I really say that?

Tawny grins and relief washes over her face. "I like to think so."

And that's that. Just another bombshell to swallow, but not quite as explosive as I would have expected. "I'll deal kindly with him, Tawny. If I see him again." Let's hope *that* never happens.

She hugs me and whispers, "Thank you."

Who can summarize a whirlwind? When one catches you and spins you around, your jumbled thoughts scatter and you find yourself deposited somewhere new, unsure how you got there. All you remember is chaos and held breath.

I stand on the other side of the whirlwind, leaning against the railing of another cargo ship. Only this time, I'm not a prisoner.

Now we're at sea, headed for France, all equipped with documents bearing our false names.

The frigid January air hikes up and down my bones, stomping the chill deeper and deeper, but I don't want to go inside. Only six weeks ago I was a prisoner in a shipping container. This deck is freedom.

I'm going to *France!* And here I thought visiting Prime was adventurous. My newly constructed NAB rests in my pocket. I'm waiting until we're a bit out to sea before I settle and send Mother and Father a long message.

Frenchie stands at the bow of the ship. I imagine her mind clawing at the wind, trying to draw us faster to her homeland. Kaphtor stands beside her, Mister "I-won't-let-you-travel-alone." Riiight. I saw through *that* excuse in a second.

He leans against the railing thumbing through a book on speaking French.

Elm and Willow crouch together on a deck bench. Willow's smashed against one end of it and Elm's at the other, arms crossed and looking surly. Willow's not quite as fierce of a warrior when she's with him. Then again, she's scarred from being in that orphanage. Something made her hate the Council almost more than I do. They did things to her—mental things. I can only imagine how little it would take to break an eleven-year-old girl.

She wears a turtleneck now with loose pants instead of the orphanage jumper, a hat, gloves, and a scarf over half her face. I hope she's warm enough.

I miss her. She's hardly spoken to me since we rescued her, and I've tried to give her distance to recover. She seems to want it. Does she hate me? Have I ruined this little girl's life?

She seems to think I'm out to destroy the Council when all I'm really doing is traveling to Russia on a whim, hoping to find some clue in Solomon's great-grandfather's house that will help me bring down the projected Wall.

Solomon materializes over my shoulder. "Have you checked the news today?"

The wind ruffles his hair like an affectionate uncle. Here we are, safe for however long it takes to sail to France. Safety. When's the last time I felt safe or relaxed?

"No." I pull the rolled up *Daily Hemisphere* electrosheet from my pocket. We've taken to checking it every morning. Yesterday was the *Mass Kidnapping* headline regarding the orphans. The culprits are "unknown" for now, though the kidnapping was tied to Solomon, Frenchie, Kaphtor, and the others who escaped the Council.

"Have you heard from Fight or Idris?" They took my Brawn suit, planning to sneak the kids through the Wall if they can. Christian and Tawny are helping where they can, but for the most part they'll be staying in the USE, waiting for Tawny's baby to arrive and monitoring things for us until we return.

Solomon shakes his head. "No, but if they'd been caught I think it would be in the *Daily Hemisphere*." He points at the screen and I look at the other headlines.

Two More 'Overridden' Clocks Reported in Prime

That's today's headline. I scan the article. "It's still a requirement for High City citizens to get Clock-matched."

Solomon shakes his head. "The more the Council forces them into that, the more the people will revolt at some point. Even High City people."

The next day, like clockwork, Brickbat undergoes an interview with the *Daily Hemisphere* and explains that, *"There is a glitch in a small percentage of the Clocks. We currently have professionals working out the kinks. For those whose Clocks go* overridden, *please report back for a new Clock-matching."*

Oh sure. So if someone *dies* before their Clock zeroes out, they have permission to ask for a new one. Brilliant, Brickbat. The deception continues. Was my death not enough? It was supposed to prove that the Clocks are faulty, but the Council's not sharing that information. They haven't broadcasted my overridden Clock. Now we know why they're faulty—because Jude harnessed strength of will. So does this mean that the more people who lose faith in the Clocks, the more likely they are to override their Clocks?

I sigh. If only Jude had been more specific.

Solomon looks at his NAB. "It's almost five-thirty. Let's go in and get some dinner."

He heads inside, but I hear a sound from around the corner— a soft girl's cry. As I inch closer, I catch words. Willow's words. "Stop, Elm! Don't touch me!"

"I don't care, Willow!" Elm's shout pierces me with fear. Is he . . . hurting her? "I don't care what they did, I don't care what will happen. You are my grafting partner." His voice breaks.

Willow whimpers. "But I'm . . . I'm rotten."

"You're not!" Her sniffs turn muffled as though being embraced. "You're exactly how you should be. And you're mine."

I suddenly want to be somewhere else. I'm invading something private and, despite my confusion and curiosity, I leave them. What *happened* to Willow? Why would it prompt her to push Elm away? It's so unlike her.

Dinner is served at a round table with six chairs and a white tablecloth. All six of us fit around it comfortably. We are guests. According to Dalene, this is a freighter cruise, and we've occupied the few cabins intended for guests. I almost can't view this vessel as a cargo ship, it's so unlike my last experience. It is larger, more electronic, and referred to as a *container ship*.

Solomon prays over the food and I enter into the prayer with him, jolted by the fact that I hadn't even *thought* to pray. When was the last time I talked to God? I've been reading, but . . .

How can this be? How can it be so easy for me to start taking action and moving forward and living life without considering Him?

Solomon finishes the prayer and I unfold the napkin from atop my plate. "I don't really know what to do."

He twirls a fork between two fingers. "Eat."

A gentleman serves us some sort of thin meat patty—"It is schnitzel, madam."—with a salad and deep-fried potato slices. His gaze holds mine a few seconds longer than what I'd expect from a table server. My tongue curls.

He recognizes me. I'm sure of it.

He clears his throat and then sets a carafe of red wine on the table, to which Kaphtor, Frenchie, and Solomon help themselves.

What do I do? Should I go after the server and ask him not to tell anyone it's me? Surely he's not the only one who recognizes me, or the rest of us misfits at the table. I release a long breath through my nose and focus on the meal. Things will be fine. These sorts of details are out of my control.

Willow, still bundled in all-winter garb, takes one sniff of the wine. "The grapes smell old." She passes it on.

Solomon lets me take a sip from his glass, and my mouth shrivels like a slug under salt. I must make a face because he laughs and takes it back. After a sip or two, he doesn't touch it again.

"What I *meant*, was I don't know what to do while we're on this ship." I wiggle my fork back and forth on the schnitzel. Thankfully, it's tender enough it doesn't need a knife. I didn't want to ask Solomon for help. I'm not in the mood to be humble.

"Maybe eet eez time for us to heal." Frenchie runs a finger around the rim of her wine glass. Nothing can dampen her mood. She's going home.

"And regain strength." Kaphtor's hand disappears under the table and I think he's rubbing the gunshot wound in his leg.

"But what about the fact that I'm proclaimed dead? Don't you think workers on this ship will recognize me?" I say it as if I haven't already noticed one worker staring at my face.

Solomon shrugs and holds a forkful of salad midair. "We'll monitor the Council every day through news reports and through contact with our fathers. Chances are that a shipman will recognize one of us sooner or later. Word will get out. Maybe you should consider revealing that you're alive."

If he's not that worried, then I won't be either. I return to my schnitzel. "I've thought of that, too. But you're right." It's easy to smile at them—my little family of survivors. "This is a time of rest. And Angelique is going home."

Home. Where is *my* home? Unity Village was an old home, but it wouldn't be the same without Mother and Father. Too many negative memories have wiped out the positive ones that lay in that town. Is my house even still there? Did Father sell it? Leave it?

Dinner settles in my stomach. I'm full. I'm rested. I'm safe.

Weird.

Frenchie rises from the table. "I think I will go to sleep now. *Bonne nuit*, everyone."

"Good night." Kaphtor rises, too.

Elm stands. "Willow will go with you, Angelique. She needs sleep."

Willow stares at the tablecloth. The narrowing of her eyes tells me she'll do more than sleep. She's plotting. She's busy hating the Council.

Rest. Rest. Rest. When's the last time I rested? When's the last time I *could* rest? Is this week-long trip across the Atlantic my Sabbath?

Willow joins Frenchie as they leave. Elm walks out. Where is he going? Kaphtor gives Solomon a nod. "I'll see you in the room then."

"Tally-ho." And now it's just us two. Parvin and Solomon. "So this is what it's like."

"What what's like?" I stack my salad plate on top of the empty schnitzel plate.

"Sitting with you without having to plan some sort of escape, rescue, or survival."

"Sorry, this is too normal for me." I give an exaggerated sigh. "Can we go do something dangerous to help me relax?"

He chuckles and slides the NAB toward me. "I got a message from Idris."

Yay! Updates! "What'd she say?"

"Well, they're not through the Wall yet, but she's heard reports about Unity Village. Since it's the nearest town to the gap in the Wall, Radicals have been bunkering down there, defending it. It's like their fortress. They're really putting up a good fight against the Council."

My town. My little, nowhere town is a fortress for Radicals? "It's like . . . it's living up to its name. Finally. Unity Village. People are unified in a fight for freedom."

Shalom.

"And just think, Parvin"—Solomon's voice is intent and low—"you started this."

I want the praise. I want to clutch it tight and keep it to myself because it's from Solomon. But it's not mine. "It was never me. I had a lot of help . . . and pushing . . . and forced growth." Despite the difficulty that comes with the memories in those words, a splash of joy hits me. It may have seemed rough at the time, but when I look at my relationship with God now, compared to when this all started . . .

I wouldn't have it any other way.

We sit in silence. I toy with my silverware. Solomon picks up his wine glass, but then seems to remember he doesn't want to drink its contents. We're alone. I don't think we know how to function alone yet. It's so different than with Jude. I never knew how deep Jude wanted to go. He closed me out. But Solomon?

He encourages openness, transparency. I'm not worried about Solomon judging my words or actions.

Solomon leans back in his chair, draping his elbows over the backrest. "So, adventurer . . . tell me about yourself."

A nervous laugh creeps out. "What do you want to know?" He already knows everything—the darkness, the pain, the prayers.

"At the end of all this . . . what do you want?"

That should be obvious. "I want people to be free. I want the projected Wall to be down for good." *I want God to be proud of me.*

Solomon looks down, a half-grin crinkling the scars on the left side of his face. "I meant, what do *you* want. For yourself." His arms drop down from the chair. "I guess I thought that, since God's allowed us to survive together this far, maybe it's okay to dream a little."

Dream a little . . .

That sounds nice. But I shake my head. "Things are only starting, Solomon. I think it's too early to expect a future."

He quirks his head to the side. "Humor me."

Is it okay to dream? It doesn't change anything. God knows the plans He has for me. Then again, He also knows the desires of my heart. What *would* I want if we succeeded in taking down the projected Wall? Is that such a far-fetched question? "I suppose I'd want . . . to find a new home. A home where my family is with me." Ivanhoe, Lost Angel, albino forest. It doesn't matter.

"I like Ivanhoe."

"Me too, despite the weird Preacher and the fact that I *still* can't walk a tightrope. But where would we live? *How* would we live? I guess I could work for Wilbur Sherrod again if I had to. Father could do woodworking."

The more I think on it, the less I want to live there. Not unless I have a *reason.* I'd rather stay with the albinos and help them figure out the Bible. Well . . . and figure out the Bible for myself, too. "Maybe we could live in the albino village for a while."

Solomon's smile is so wide, the scars on his left temple blend in with normal skin. I've done something to make him happy. "What?"

"You said *we.*"

I guess I did. The idea churns my insides, but I share my vulnerable thoughts anyway. "It's because I want us to be together. Forever. I want to learn to be a team with you, Solomon."

After all this, if we survive, I won't be some famous Radical leading a nation. My calling will be different and, since we're daring to dream, I might as well dream big.

I want to marry you, Solomon. I don't say it aloud. I want him to ask *me.* My first step as a follower and teammate is to trust him. Wait for him.

It feels as natural as blinking when he slides his hand around mine. It's firm. Rough. Safe and consuming.

"I think I'd want to start an orphanage in Ivanhoe . . . if it was needed." His eyes slide to meet mine. "If Fight and Idris make it through the Wall, those kids will need a home."

Okay, so we're moving on. I know he heard me. I'll wait for his timing. Clearly, right now, he wants us to know each other better. I focus on what he just shared. "Didn't Jude want to free all the orphans from life in an orphanage?"

"Jude and I had different ideas about the orphanage. He wasn't there when it was run *right.* He saw only the despair."

My brain searches for ideas. The orphans could stay with Mrs. Newton and Laelynn, but that seems too temporary. Especially because her home is already filled with Radicals. Solomon and I could run an orphanage . . . maybe. "I think that's a fantastic idea, Solomon."

He may not have confirmed it out loud, but we're both thinking it. We'll be pursuing our dreams together.

I return to my room, which is a small cabin with two beds and a couch in it. Frenchie is on the couch and Willow in a bed. Both are asleep, so I leave the lights off. Willow is still fully clothed. She must be freezing to sleep in a turtleneck. I spread another blanket over her and then stumble to my own bunk. Once tucked under the covers, I pull out my NAB and stare at the message bubbles. Father is in the albino village with Mother. I feel so far from them. I balance the NAB against my leg and type with my good hand.

~Dear Father

My throat closes. I long to be his little girl again, sitting on his knee and hugging him so tight his whiskers poke my neck. Not caring about the itch, because he's Father.

~I'm alive. I couldn't tell you before now, in case the Council intercepted the message. But I'm alive. I am well.
~I miss you. Saying so does no good and brings you no new information, but today I am hit with a longing for home. You are my home. Mother is my home. As adventuresome as this big world is, I can't wait to return to you.

I picture his face, thoughtful as I spew impulsive decision after impulsive decision. It makes me smile, though Mother would be giving me a stern reprimand.

~How is Mother? How is her . . . spirit? I hope she knows I'm praying for her every day and that I miss her.

I want to tell him about Solomon and me, about how excited I am for a future together. But it's such a new, fragile thing I decide to keep the treasure to myself a little longer.

~We are successful so far in our journey. I can't tell you more, for safety's sake. I love you.
~Parvin

I rub my fingers down the NAB face as though the warmth of

touch will transcend the space between us. For a moment, I hear his muffled whiskered laugh and imagine the smell of sawdust and soap.

And then, for a longer moment, I imagine Solomon and me surviving all this and returning to Father and Mother. He had the right idea.

It's good to dream.

11

Fame.

I hate that having *my* face say something to the public will enact a type of control, that they'll believe whatever I say just because I'm famous. That's why Skelley and the Council can control people. They're famous. People take their word as law.

That's why the Council wanted me.

But I'm flawed. This understanding smothers me as I stare into the NAB lens, working out what I want to say. I sit on the plush, red couch—Frenchie's bed—with my back to the window.

I decided this morning that it's best to film the reveal-my-survival video as soon as possible, especially while we're safe . . . and alive. Then, when the time seems right, we can send it to Gabbie and she'll spread it like she did the other video we made in the West. She recently sent Solomon a message, informing him of her safety and of Cap's escape back to Unity Village.

Solomon sits across from me on the bolted-down coffee table, holding the NAB steady. He brings a measure of peace. The more I'm with him, the more we figure out this team thing, the more I understand love.

He nods to me. "Whenever you're ready."

I'll never be ready. How about whenever I choose to force words through my lips? "Just tell me."

"Okay, go."

That was too fast. "Hi, USE! This is Parvin Blackwater and"—I run a hand over my face—"and I'm acting like this is a stupid interview. Can we start over?"

"We can start over as many times as you need." He taps a few things on the NAB, then holds it up again.

I take three slow breaths. "Thanks. Okay, I think I'm ready."

"Remember *why* you're doing this."

Why *am* I doing this? "Right."

I focus on the NAB lens and think about the Council's article proclaiming me dead. I think about the Radicals camping out in Unity Village, who are hoping to get through the gap in the Wall while the Council frantically tries to guard it. I think about the people afraid because of the new Clocks, kept in the USE by force.

I narrow my eyes and imagine I'm speaking directly to the people. "The Council lied to you." I breathe in through my nose. "They were too hasty to proclaim me dead, as they are hasty in everything. In that same haste, they are dishing out faulty Clocks to everyone, destroying your old ones."

I hold up my wrist and turn on my Clock. The Numbers blink, but the word *overridden* stands bolder than my proclaimed time. "My Clock is faulty, too. It's not a glitch. Jude Hawke made these Clocks *especially* so they could be overridden . . . by you. Brickbat is lying to you."

Solomon gives me a thumbs-up, but I'm not sure where to go from here. I've established that the Council isn't trustworthy. I can't tell them about my plan to destroy the projection, because chances are Skelley or Brickbat will watch this video. "I see those of you trying to escape to the West. There is freedom on that side that can't be found here. I haven't stopped fighting for you. I will bring down that Wall and bring you freedom. The Council can't kill me. They can't touch me. God will restart my heart as many times as it takes to bring you shalom."

My breathing quickens as my passion builds, but it's time to bring this to a close. "Keep fighting. Stay strong." I level my gaze and pour passion into my voice. "I'm Parvin Blackwater, and I'm very much alive."

Solomon keeps the NAB steady for a few more closing seconds, then lowers it and taps the screen. "Perfect, Parvin."

"Thanks."

He winks. "Welks."

We sit in silence for a while as he prepares the video. And just like that, I'll be back. Maybe the people will find more hope in the fact I'm alive. Maybe it will spur the Radicals on. "Should I share it right now?"

Solomon tucks the NAB away. "I say we wait until we're closer to land. You'd hate for the Council to somehow figure out where you are and meet us in France."

I nod. "Good point."

Solomon moves off the coffee table and sits beside me on the couch. I expect him to say something, to ask a question, to talk more about the video, but he just . . . sits. Maybe I should say something. Instead, I relax into the couch. My arm touches his and neither of us moves. We're just . . . *together*. It is enough.

The silence invites peace. My pounding heart slows as though completing a footrace. I allow my head to plop back onto the headrest and let out a long, very unladylike sigh. "I can't believe everything that's happened since you and I first met on Straight Street."

"Yeah." His voice holds a smile. "I've changed so much since then."

I raise my head. "You? You were handsome, kind, and awesome then, exactly like you are now." I gulp down the word *handsome*. It's weird using it and I half-wish I hadn't. But, if I'm honest, that's the first word that popped in my mind when I initially spotted Solomon Hawke.

"Handsome?" He winks, and his smile widens. "I like that. But

I *was* different when I first escorted the Newtons to Unity Village. The injustice toward Radicals riled me, but I'd never really stood up for them until the day of your hearing. That day was . . . too much. Arguing with Sachem broke the dam that had kept my anger at bay. It finally freed me to take action."

It's hard, thinking of Solomon growing. I've always seen him as a full-grown leader, a man constantly seeking God. "What did I do to catch your eye?" What could I have possibly done? I don't deserve such a friend—such a soul mate. It's still hard to think that he'd want me when the majority of my life was so wasted.

God, you're way too good to me.

"You never caught my eye, Parvin. You caught my heart." His voice is thick and my eyes burn. "It happened the day you sacrificed your life for Reid, when you claimed the Clock to be yours. I knew you were doing that to save him, and you did what I wished *I* was doing—sacrificing myself for the people and things for which I was passionate."

I could argue that he's always been doing that. He sacrificed his Enforcerhood to help get Jude across the Wall safely. He sacrificed his status as an Enforcer because of me. He sacrificed so much for what is right, but my opinions won't change his thinking. He says his heart has changed, and as long as he's now in a place of shalom there's nothing more for me to say.

I sidle closer. His arm goes around me and he plants a kiss on the top of my messy hair. Then, in the softest whisper, "Thank you . . . for shalom."

"Thank you . . . for . . ." My throat closes. Somehow, leaving the sentence unfinished is more powerful than any word I could use to complete it.

I spend the rest of the day at the rail of the ship, staring into the open sea. Solomon and I are more of a team than we've ever been. I know we've barely scratched the surface of who we are. I can't wait to discover him . . . and to be discovered. Someday we'll reveal our warts and we'll realize neither of us is perfect . . . but beneath the leadership of God and the quest for shalom, these things seem trivial.

The waves roll, but I barely feel them through this giant hull. I am small in this vastness. The longer I stare outward or upward, the smaller my worries become. The salt-crusted deck sways beneath my feet, and I grip the rusted railing, remembering boxcar-Radicals having to pound off the rust with a hammer.

The NAB in my pocket releases a small *ding!* I pull it out so fast I almost fling it over the railing. It's a response from Father.

~Sweetheart,
~You are so precious to us. I dared to hope. Even
your mother prayed for your survival, despite the news
announcement. God is power. We can say that now.
It's safe here.

My throat closes. Mother's alive. Mother's okay. And . . . God is power? They've rarely spoken openly about Him.

~Your mother is awake and as beautiful as ever. The burn
on her right leg is infected. If it doesn't get better soon, we may
have to consider amputation.

"No!" My stump spasms. I can't let her go through that. *God, don't let it happen!*

~She's a fighter. She's pulling through. I've been showing
her how to use the NAB. Perhaps you might send her a
message. Think about it. We miss and love you.

A tear trails down my cheek and I sniff. "I miss and love you, too."

A presence comes alongside me and I turn. Willow. She wears a scarf over her shorn head. It's tied tight beneath her chin, making her look like a tiny, pale granny.

She came out to me. Finally, *finally* I can talk to her.

"There is a lot of water." She grips the railing as though to keep from pitching overboard.

I put my arm around her shoulders. "How are you, Willow?"

It's a casual question with a deeper meaning. Willow's a deeper kind of person, so she catches it. "I want to destroy the Council, Parvin."

"That's what we're setting out to do." Well, destroy the *Wall*, which is pretty much the same thing. But then I hear Tawny's voice: *"Be kind to Elan."* I have a feeling I can't let Willow anywhere near Brickbat if I'm to keep that promise. "How's your arm?"

She jerks away. I lift my hands. "I'm sorry. I noticed it was bandaged for a while. Is it better?"

"No! It's not."

I want to cry. Who is this harsh little thing that can't remember how to smile? "What did they do to you?" Perhaps I shouldn't ask, but I need to know.

Her small hands tighten on the railing, until her knuckles press against her thin black gloves. She speaks through clenched teeth. "I don't want to talk about it."

"I'm sorry." I definitely shouldn't have asked.

"Elm knows. You can ask him."

I nod, but she's not looking at me. I don't want to ask Elm, I want to be able to talk to *my* Willow. My fierce young friend. "So you and Elm are . . . okay?"

"Yes."

Sigh. "Willow, do you . . . are you angry with me?"

She rubs her thumb against the railing until it makes a squeaking sound. "Not you, Parvin. But I wish I never came to this side."

My heart wilts. "Yeah." She came to this side to save my life. Without her, I never would have made it through the Wall tunnel. I guess that doesn't feel worth it to her.

I killed our friendship.

I killed her spirit.

"But Elm rescued me. He found me in my room at the orphan place—he came all the way across the Wall for me!" A shadow of a sad smile touches her lips.

I think of Solomon and the things he's done for me—offering guidance on the NAB when I was lost in the West, coming after me onto the cargo ship, rescuing me over and over again, leading the people when I decided to sacrifice myself. "Elm loves you, Willow."

"Yup." Why doesn't she sound happy?

Two deck hands work nearby, muttering under their breath. One glances quickly at me, his gaze traveling to my stump. They catch me looking at them, give a half-smile, and then shuffle away.

"They know." Willow speaks my very thoughts, only her voice is a hollow clipped thing instead of the wind chimes it used to be.

I nod.

"When will you share your video?"

"When we're closer to shore." I'll wait as long as I can, but those deckhands might give me away first.

12

"Land ho!" Frenchie's voice is an excited squeak.

The deck hands laugh. Kaphtor stands by her side, and she launches into his arms. He stumbles back, eyes wide and half-terrified at her joy. I love it.

I see a distant shoreline. My heart lurches and I almost mistake it for seasickness. We're here. The Council could be waiting for me. Or we may never make it to Russia. Or the deckhands won't let me disembark. Being near land frightens me with a prick of surprise. None of these thoughts rested in my head until I saw land. Why have they come now?

One crewmember says we'll reach the loading dock tomorrow by late afternoon. It's hazy, so I can't make out the French countryside. I imagine it lush and green with old houses and cobblestone roads. But I don't stay to watch it grow nearer.

I run into Solomon in the stairwell. His eyes are glued to the NAB. "Solomon, I think we should send the video to Gabbie now." My voice trembles. We should have sent it sooner!

Solomon looks up. His smile, his eyes . . . his features are so gentle they are a blinding distraction from my nerves. "Already loading it into a message."

"Great. Thanks." My heart hasn't slowed any and my body turns of its own accord, propelling me back into the fresh air. I barely catch Solomon's, "Welks."

The video releases to the public only hours later. Gabbie did good.

The following morning, the *Daily Hemisphere* spreads the word to the world with tantalizing headlines like, *Parvin Blackwater is Alive!* and *The Council Lied!* and *Blackwater Says Overridden Clocks Aren't Glitches, They're Permanent*. My prayer is that my message brings hope to the people trying to cross the Wall. Now they know I'm alive and fighting for them. Now they know I still plan to bring down the Wall.

What is Skelley Chase thinking as he sees the articles or as he watches the video? I can't imagine he'll be happy. I'm the problem that won't go away. But he seemed so worn and downtrodden the last time I saw him. Was that . . . because of me?

No. No, of course not.

"Welcome to France!" Frenchie holds her dirty travel shoes in one hand and twirls off the containership walkway and onto French soil (rather, French cement) in her bare feet. The moment they touch the ground, her giddiness melts into tears and she sinks to her knees. "I am 'ome."

And I am in France . . . on my way to Russia.

The dock looks the same as the one in Florida—covered in shipping containers, with cranes overhead. We are loaded onto an open cart with bench seats and driven away from the sea through old-fashioned city streets.

The foreignness of this place carries a different aura than Ivanhoe or Prime. That might have something to do with all the French flying from one mouth to another. Everyone is nicely dressed, but not gaudy like in Prime. Their faces hold hardly any makeup, their hair casual but stylish. A woman in heels, wearing mostly black with a lovely light scarf says, *"Bonjour!"* as our little cart crawls by.

Frenchie returns the greeting with tears in her eyes.

Elm steps into the new world like a soldier, eyeing each new face with scrutiny. Willow clings to his arm with her gloved hands, the opposite of the fierce warrior-girl I came to know in the West. At least they're touching again.

I barely have time to take in this new world. We ride an underground train for an hour, then follow Frenchie back into the light, down several streets, and finally to a long lane with tall, flat-faced apartments. Strings of windows with tiny metal planters hover over us.

Willow and Elm garner a few glances from passersby. I try to hide my face behind Solomon's bulk as we walk, in case I'm recognized. How famous am I in France?

Frenchie walks up three cement steps to a door that has a wintery wreath on it. She tucks her arms around herself and stares at the door for a moment. Trembling, she looks at Kaphtor, who gives her an encouraging nod and places a hand on the small of her back.

Lifting her chin, her fist follows suit and then raps three times on the door.

Why is she knocking? When I returned to Unity Village I wanted to do anything but knock on my own front door. It made me feel like a foreigner. Then again, she's been away for several years.

She chews on her lip, straightens her hair, glances at her clothing, and then looks back at the door.

Nothing.

"Zey are not 'ome."

"Are you sure they still live here?" Kaphtor asks gently.

She nods, then shakes her head. "I do not know. We 'aven't been able to correspond—"

"*Pardonez-moi!*" An older man with a scruffy chin and thick, dark eyebrows strides toward us. He wears a white button-up with the top few buttons undone from the collar, and black suspenders, though he's not pudgy enough to need them. The very depiction of a working man. He gestures to the door and asks something in French. I can't tell if he's angry or not.

Frenchie grips the thin, wobbly railing next to the stairs, pushes Kaphtor aside, and holds herself rigid. She swallows several times. "Papa?"

His eyes snap to hers and he frowns. Then, as though catching a glimpse of recognition, his eyes crinkle so much they're obscured by his eyebrows. His voice comes out hoarse. "Angelique?"

"Papa!" She flies down the stairs and into his arms. There is a lot of crying and French spoken through sobs. She kisses his face in every location a kiss could possibly fit. Kaphtor leans against the doorframe, arms folded and eyes averted. Perhaps the display of emotion is too much for him—too unusual. Or maybe he's nervous about meeting his girlfriend's dad.

I grin.

Elm and Willow wait for the emotion to stop. Solomon catches my eye. We're both smiling. Frenchie's father ushers us inside, speaking not a word of English.

"I will translate." Frenchie *oohs* and *aahs* and weeps, sharing the memories that slam her as she steps into her old home. She runs her hand over pieces of furniture, decorative plates hanging on the wall, a small doll on a shelf. "Zis . . . zis was my childhood toy." She speaks mostly to Kaphtor.

Her father stands afar, watching her, his hands clasped to his chest. There is no darkness in this reunion except the memories of separation.

Solomon surveys the house with a small smile, as though partaking of Frenchie's delight.

"Welcome home, Angelique."

She sweeps me into a hug. "*Merci*, Parvin! *Merci mille fois!*"

The French word for *thank you* sounds quite similar to the English word for *mercy*. It fits this situation—God's mercy abounds. I'm reminded that I am such a small part of His beautiful plan. I am so unimportant . . . yet He sees me.

He sees us.

"Zis is my papa, Alexandre." Frenchie introduces us to him and he nods, clasping each of our hands. He seems to linger with a firmer handshake when she introduces Kaphtor. He gestures to the backward black *E* on Kaphtor's left temple, and then they're off again in French.

There was no unusual response when he shook my hand. No recognition. They don't know who I am!

Anonymity is a wonderful thing.

The flat is narrow, but larger than my Unity house. A staircase in the entry leads to where I assume the bedrooms are. To the left of the stairs through a doorway is a sitting room with a single worn brown couch near the window. Despite the age on the furniture, the house is decorated with fashionable memories.

"Papa says you may sit. Rest. We will talk a little togezzer before joining you." Frenchie sweeps a hand toward the couch. Solomon, Elm, and I all squeeze onto the sofa, but Kaphtor remains standing. Willow sits alone against a wall.

The French chatter is beautiful. Part of me wishes I could understand them, but the other part relishes the musical quality of foreign words on my ears. Solomon once told me he took a Definitions cap when in school. Does he understand any French?

I lean my head back against the couch, smelling the sea on my clothes. Hopefully Alexandre doesn't mind our smell. Sunrays drift through the window, touching my face enough to give warmth but not too much to blind me.

Before I know it I drift off, but a shriek startles me back into consciousness. Solomon is now sitting beside me, but the noise came from the entry. Frenchie's mom has arrived home, and the tears start up again.

What does it look like after this? Frenchie will stay here, but somehow we have to make it to Moscow, Russia. Dalene gave us plenty of specie with a special payment card so Solomon can't be tracked. The only question is, do we go by car, bus, train, or plane?

Travel.

That was one of my dreams back when I thought the Clocks controlled our fate—to travel before I zeroed-out. Now, less than a year later, I've traveled more than I ever dreamed . . . or wanted. I crossed the Wall and went West, then was sent to Antarctica, then escaped and sailed up to the West coast. And now I'm in France.

I'm tired.

I'm tired of discovering. Someday—and I pray it's some-day soon—I will be at the end of this venture and I will settle. Wherever I am allowed to stay indefinitely, I will call that place home. It won't be Unity Village. That place will remain a memory.

"My mother, Gigi"—she pronounces this *Zheezhee*—"would like to cook for you." Frenchie stands in the doorway, her red eyes somehow adding to her glow of shalom. "But she must return to ze market for groceries."

Kaphtor pushes himself off the wall. "I will help carry them back."

Frenchie nods.

"I'll join as well." Solomon rises from the couch and the space beside me turns cold in his absence. "And she must allow us to cover the costs."

"No, no, no—" Frenchie waves her hand.

"Angelique." Solomon raises an eyebrow. "I insist."

"Very well." She ducks out of the room. I'm glad Solomon thought of this. Six extra mouths to feed is a lot.

Both Elm and Willow are asleep—Elm on the couch, with his choppy hair splayed across the back of the couch. Willow is folded up on the floor. I don't volunteer my services. One hand can't carry many groceries. Instead, I act invisible and it seems to work. Frenchie and her father sit in the kitchen catching up on the missed years of Frenchie's life.

I let them have their privacy, but they remind me of my family. Mother. Father. Tawny. Reid. My heart jerks.

I fiddle with my pack and pull the NAB that Solomon and I share from the bag. The contact bubble for Father is still. I never responded to his last message when he prompted me to write Mother.

What do I say? *Dear Mother, I'm sorry I let you get blown up, but I'm glad you're alive?*

I miss her, but I'm not sure she'll really want to talk to me the way Father says she will. Hesitant, vulnerable, I tap the bubble and start.

~*Dear Mother,*

She *is* dear to me. Will she think that when she reads the greeting?

~*I miss you terribly. I feel so far from you and so guilty over what happened with the train. I hate that you weren't awake when I had to leave. So much has happened since I saw you last and there is so much I wish I could tell you.*

The more I type, the more I allow my heart to crawl into the light of vulnerability, crying with the need to be open and honest and raw.

~*I'm afraid that you are angry with me and that you hate me because of the pain I've put you through. Mother, you mean so much to me and my own doubts and fears have kept me from believing you truly love me. But I know you do, my heart is just too afraid to believe.*

*~I'm sorry my actions put you in harm's way. I hope that
you feel safe with the albinos and I'm praying over your leg.
Even if I never make it back to you, I'm glad I was able to
send Father to you. That is my greatest accomplishment in this
entire whirlwind of journeying.*

~Parvin

That was about as easy as stitching up my body after a wolf
fight. My throat is swollen with unshed tears. I take deep breaths
through my nose. Gingerly, I set the NAB beside me on the couch
and then reach for the *Daily Hemisphere*. I'm too nervous to simply
sit and wait for Mother's response. *If* she responds.

The Council has given no response to my video yet.

I like to think I've shut them up, but Skelley and Brickbat
aren't the shutting-up type.

I scan the screen and my eyes light on a headline with *Unity
Village* in it. Why is Unity Village mentioned? Did they discover
the Radicals camping out there? I hold the electrosheet out a bit
and read the entire headline. An ice storm slashes inside my chest.

The Council has given their response:

Unity Village, Bombed. No Survivors.

13

Unity Village is gone—my home. No. Not my home. Well . . . I don't know. It's nothing now.

I am hollow.

The electrosheet trembles in my hand and the words blur. As though to mock me, my mind brings up nostalgic memories of growing up, of searching for purpose amongst those wood-and-thatch houses. Only now, when I envision my house with the lattice kitchen window, it's crumpled in a smoldering heap. *Faveurs* explodes in a shattering of red canvas and dried flowers as a bomb crashes down from the sky. Dogwoods burn.

Not only has my old home been bombed, but so have my memories.

Every beat of my heart pumps another dose of pressure into my veins. Stronger. Stronger. I'm going to explode. The pounding reaches my ears. I can't hear. It invades my vision. Black. I can't see.

I lurch from the couch, stumble into the entryway and out the door, grasping the rickety railing and sucking in a deep breath. Another. Three.

My gasping grows louder, the pounding stronger. I'm a bomb—a bomb from the Council. Falling, plummeting. I think I'm going to scream as the next breath threatens to release the pressure. But instead of a scream, a single sob breaks forth and I press my forehead against my stump.

The pressure flows out of me like a river, washing away my hope and my strength of will.

Unity Village is gone.

It's as though I've found out my family was killed. But they're all safe—Mother and Father in the West, Tawny is with Christian Hawke . . . so why am I so affected?

It's because of the Radicals. The people who chose to be radical in their lives, even if they had a Clock, and planned to cross the Wall. Those who bunkered down in Unity Village for safety, for respite, are dead. Cap. Cap was there with his goats.

No survivors.

No one expected our government to attack its own people. Brickbat. Skelley. The Council.

Terrorists against their own.

How many died? Will they even report it? People must have died. There's no way around it. Somewhere there are grieving families—siblings, mothers, fathers, relatives . . . all on their knees the way I was when Reid died. Mourning and feeling helpless.

I want Solomon. I want him here. Now. I want him feeling what I'm feeling and understanding my despair, providing words of calm. He'd know what to say and what to do.

The *Daily Hemisphere* electrosheet lies at my feet, dropped during my escape from myself. I bend down and lift it from the cement with a challenge to the Council. *Defend yourself.*

I read the article, forcing focus past the red fury interrupting my vision. I comprehend snippets.

Unity Village bombed.

No survivors.

Terrorist attack.

Council is researching the culprit.

141

I'm startled to a halt, like a dog on a short chain. The Council is researching the culprit? For a mere second, I entertain the thought that they didn't do it. But then logic returns.

Of *course* they did it. No one else has motivation to bomb a measly Low City. No one else cares that Radicals and people who are anti-Clock were taking refuge there. No one else would know that this would send a message to *me*—the Radical who keeps on living.

They did this because I called the Council out with my video. Because I survived. I can't feel guilty. My survival gave people hope. I've promised them I'm doing all I can to tear down this Wall.

My determination returns.

I walk back inside the flat. No one notices me enter. They must not have seen me leave, which is hard to believe because my mind was screaming so loudly I'd half expected it came from my mouth, too. How can they not know, or even *feel* that people died today?

Not just any people, but the people living in our old home. Frenchie's old home. How will she take it? She lived there, too, but I can't imagine it will bother her much now that she's back with her real family.

I don't want to break the news. Moments ago, I wanted everyone to know and feel what I felt. But now it's my burden. My secret. My pain that I need to harness, to drive me forward. It will get me to Moscow.

God, please let the answers be in Erfinder Hawke's house.

I will be firm. I will focus *forward*. On defeating the Council and tearing down the Wall. If I let this bombing destroy me, then the Council has won.

The men return with Gigi, loaded down with used burlap sacks of groceries. Solomon catches my eye as he walks in. I must remain calm. Normal. I force a smile—it comes easy and guilt burns. How dare that smile feel natural when my home has just been bombed?

Solomon's return smile lights his whole face like a sunrise.

That's it. Keep focusing on Solomon. The advice seems off, like I should be mourning in a graveyard instead of dwelling on affection. I need to tell Solomon.

After dinner.

Kaphtor tries to help Frenchie and her parents cook. His ineptitude is comical, but Frenchie seems to like it. She gives him coy smiles and shakes a carrot at him in reprimand.

Solomon sits in a wooden chair beside me and leans forward. He keeps his voice low so as not to wake Willow or Elm. "Are you all right?"

Yes. I'm fine. I'm calm. Problem number one: lying to myself. "Mmm-hmm." Problem number two: lying to Solomon. "Actually . . . can we move into the entryway?" I don't see if he follows; I just stand and walk until I'm halfway up the stairs, poised in between the kitchen and the living room.

Solomon sits beside me on a step. I withdraw *The Daily Hemisphere* from my skirt pocket and show him. "Unity Village . . . was . . ." My fake calm snaps like a horsewhip. Tears—the traitorous beasts!—spill out and, once they start, it's like the pathway has been created and I can't stop the others that wish to join the downward stream.

Solomon takes the electrosheet from me and reads the article. "Oh no." His response is low, barely breathed, with just the right amount of anguish. Why did I fear it wouldn't affect him as it did me? This was his home, too, for a year.

"Do you think the Council did it?"

He shakes his head. "I don't know."

"Of *course* it was them!" I snatch the electrosheet back and furl it. "Who else would it be? Who else has bombs?"

"I don't know, Parvin."

That's not right. He's *supposed* to know. He's . . . Solomon. He always has the right answer.

What's wrong with me? Why am I so snappy? I drop the electrosheet to my lap and put my head in my hand. The cold metal of my cross ring against my skin soothes me. The tears stop.

His hand rests on my back, tentative. "We'll figure this out."

"Okay." Then why do I feel so alone?

Dinner is a beautiful array of dishes. French onion soup—or, as Alexandre presented it: "*Soupe à l'oignon.*"—a main meal of something called *ratatouille*, and a diversity of cheeses served with crackers, jams, and different wines. They follow this up with a chocolate soufflé, crispy on the outside with a cherry in the middle and creamy and sweet on the inside.

We are spoiled.

Tonight, with the sorrow that hit me earlier, I deserve to be spoiled. Only Solomon and I know. I didn't ask him to remain silent; he must have his own reasons to avoid breaking the news. That, at least, affirms my decision.

We end up in the living room with a pile of blankets—some purchased today while grocery shopping and some belonging to Frenchie's parents. The wood floors are cold, so Willow and I share the couch. She's small, and snuggling together reminds me of our many days of travel in the West. I've missed the security that comes with being so close to someone. I pull her near, imagining we're back in the West with only adventures chasing us.

"We continue tomorrow?" Elm yanks a blanket up over his shoulders and settles like a brick on the floor.

"I . . . I guess." We have to get to Russia. Moscow. I like the idea of taking a train more because I'm nervous about flying. I've never been in a plane before. I'm not afraid of heights but . . . planes aren't just going into the air. They're at the mercy of a person. A pilot. And *that's* where my fear lies.

But a plane would be so much faster. And we don't have time to spare. "I think we'll fly."

Solomon folds his pillow in half. "I'll talk to Angelique and Alexandre tomorrow to see if they can help us get to the nearest airport. I'll get the tickets."

"Thanks, Solomon."

"Welks."

I don't want to be the leader right now. This is why I need him. Because when I'm weak and having a hard time hearing God's direction, maybe Solomon's the strong one who hears His voice.

Breakfast consists of crepes stuffed with all manner of things— sweet sauces, vegetables, leftover ratatouille. I eat my fill because I don't know what the future will look like. I spent too much time being hungry in the West and in Antarctica. I don't ever want to feel that way again.

Frenchie seems of the same mindset, but I think her appetite is driven by nostalgia—like she has to make up for the last five years of her life by eating her native food. She chatters away with her parents, translating here and there for us. I simply enjoy listening to the smooth language.

It's amazing how quickly I pick up on words by just being immersed in the language. I've never thought of learning another language before, but I think I'd like it.

Solomon does as promised and spends a few hours figuring out plane flights and how to get us to Moscow. The Wall is several hundred miles east of that, but planes don't land any nearer. We find Erfinder's town on a map and discover it's in the same location as Opening One. Alexandre doesn't know how to get us there.

Did Erfinder settle near the Opening for a reason? Did he try crossing the Wall, too?

We stay three more days, waiting for our flight and covering the costs of groceries despite Gigi's protests. Whenever this happens, Solomon just shrugs. "I'm sorry, madame, but I don't speak French." He follows this with a wink.

The food is superb. We don't need to know French to get our praises through to Gigi. Elm grows more and more surly the longer we wait, and Willow paces alongside the windows. But I think it's good to be revived before setting out again.

The morning finally comes where we're all packed up, we're hugging good-byes, and Solomon tries to sneak a download chip of specie into Alexandre's hands. Alexandre refuses, so Solomon sneaks it into Frenchie's dress pocket.

Willow and I fold the blankets in the living room. Solomon and Kaphtor walk in, but Kaphtor doesn't make a move to help. "You must have guessed by now that I'm not coming with."

Solomon nods. "I didn't buy you a ticket anyway."

My head snaps up. "I always wondered how a catch like Angelique wasn't already married." I quirk a smile at Kaphtor. "I think she was simply waiting for the right guy."

Kaphtor's jaw tenses, but I catch the quiver. He takes a few deep breaths through his nose before responding. "Who would have thought I'd change so much? Less than a year ago, I was ready to drag her to a hearing and then condemn her to the Wall."

I hold up the corner of a blanket while Willow folds the rest. "I don't know that you've changed so drastically. I think you've just . . . woken up."

He ducks his head.

I think of myself a year ago—I was writing my biography, obsessed with being remembered, and terrified of the Wall. Change is beautiful.

"What will you do, Kaphtor?" Willow plops on top of the stack of blankets and leans back against the wall. Now that we're actually leaving, her attitude has brightened.

"Find work. Alexandre has connections at the wharf—jobs

that don't require knowing French right off the bat. I think hard labor would be good for me."

"You can always try and find a Language cap," Solomon suggests.

Kaphtor shrugs. "There's a big difference between *learning* something—going through the process—and just knowing it."

Solomon nods, as though approving of Kaphtor's response.

Elm returns from the restroom, Frenchie and her family bid us farewell, and Willow breaks the formality by giving Kaphtor a hug around the middle. On impulse, I hug him, too, and I'm glad that I do.

He saved all our lives in Antarctica, taking a bullet to cut through that rope for me so no one would plummet off the Wall cliff. He's a good man.

I hug Frenchie next.

"Come back to us, Parvin."

"I'll try." This is almost as hard as bidding my family good-bye. These people have become family, too.

Outside is a narrow little taxi car on normal wheels. We pile inside, me squished against the window with Elm and Willow. Solomon up front. Alexandre gives the taxi man directions in French and then we're off.

Next stop: Russia.

14

I hate flying.

Who invented such a thing? The creators of the Wall, of the Clocks, of spiders . . . pale in comparison to the trauma the Wright Brothers have caused to my midsection.

I slide a third white, plastic-lined barf bag under the seat in front of me.

Willow, Elm, and my other former flight neighbors found seats further forward in the plane. Away from me, the girl who's ruined everyone's flight . . . and air supply.

The airplane is only half-full of passengers, so they had several seats to pick from. Solomon stays in my row and I'm mortified. He makes sure I have a thick supply of napkins, a bottle of water, and extra "sick sacks" as he calls them. What a polite name for a bag of vomit.

But this is nothing new to anyone. I lost my stomach contents in front of the entire nation only a few months ago when I returned from the West. They've all seen me throw up before.

It started when the plane took off. My stomach dove into my feet and then sprang back up into my throat. The plane turned, and I ripped the barf bag out of the seat-back pocket.

Things seem to be finally leveling out.

"Take a look out the window." Solomon points past me. I turn my head to look out of the oval, curved window just as we break through the clouds.

Clouds.

A world designed purely for the imagination. My nausea leaves me, probably to go frolic in the cloud cities. Good riddance.

The plane banks right. The nausea beast returns, and I doom another barf bag to a cruel and toxic death. "H-How much . . . longer?"

Solomon digs into a new row of seats for more bags. I'm not sure I'll need them. I'm dryheaving now. "Three hours."

Groan. "I'll never make it." I throw the *Daily Hemisphere* electrosheet at him. "See what's new in the news. I'll just be over here, bidding farewell to all those amazing French meals." Ugh. Reading. The very thought of trying to make my eyes move in a different direction than the plane sends me reeling.

Three hours and four more sick sacks later, we land.

"You'd think after traversing the Atlantic on a cargo ship, I'd be able to handle a little plane ride." My limbs shake, and I can barely hold myself up.

"That was unlike anything sane." Elm is the only other person who vomited during the flight, but all that's visibly different are red eyes and a sheen of sweat on his face.

I catch a reflection of myself in a plastic-encased poster as we walk up an elevated tunnel into the airport. Hollow eyes, raw skin around my mouth.

Zombie-Parvin.

Solomon carries my pack. Willow holds my hand. Her gloved fingers are cool and stiff against mine, yet feel strong. I glance at her—the movement jolting my equilibrium. She stares straight ahead and stomps after the men as though we can't get to wherever we're going fast enough.

She and Elm must still be at odds since that argument I caught. When will she tell me what's going on?

The airport seems deserted except for our small troupe of travelers. It's night, and pull-down walls cover storefronts lining the walking path. Half the signs are in English, the other half in Cyrillic alphabet, angled and harsh.

I wish I could read it. It's more intriguing than French since the language has an entirely different alphabet.

I jerk to a mental halt and take a single breath. I'm in Russia. I'm in *Russia*. For some reason it seems farther and more adventuresome than all the other places I've traveled.

We descend a long set of stairs that must open to the outside at some point, because a gust of frigid air makes me tuck my stump into my coat. "Wow . . . cold."

"Are you sure we're not back in Antarctica?" Solomon grins at me.

No, I'm not. Ice slickens the cement beneath us, and I tuck my arms against my sides. Solomon continues to lead.

I look around. "How do you know where we're going? Have you been here before?"

"There's a saying about Opening One." He holds his hand over his face scar to block it from the cold. "'Take the farthest plane, then the farthest train, and then you find your own way.'"

"How cheery." At least the plane part is over.

"Where is the train?" Willow's voice chimes with new excitement.

We walk onto a concrete platform, with tracks set deep in the ground in a pit. There is no train, but the other people around us walk to several windowed ticket counters and speak low in what I assume is Russian. Lots of *r* sounds are rolled and all the words seem to blend together. It's so different from French, yet both languages carry their own beauty. If I had the opportunity, I'd take a Language cap.

Solomon hops into a line. Elm, Willow, and I hang back. I don't envy him trying to figure out how to get us tickets . . . or to explain our predicament. But when he gets to the counter, he pulls the NAB from his pocket and shows it to the man behind the counter.

No expression. The man mutters a few things, fiddles behind the desk, types a few times looking bored, then has Solomon scan his external specie chip. A few more words are exchanged, though they don't seem to do much good seeing as how Solomon knows no Russian and the ticketer doesn't seem to understand English. He hands Solomon some papers.

Solomon returns to us and gives each of us a paper. I take mine. Everything's in Russian. "How do you know this is going to the right place?"

"I showed him a picture of the Wall with the Russian words *Opening One* in a translation application. It wasn't that hard."

I glance at the ticket man, who's already on to the next customer. "What if he wasn't telling the truth?"

Solomon shrugs. "He has no reason to lie. There are maps on the train. We'll be fine. We have a room to ourselves."

"Room?" I picture the *Ivanhoe Independent* with its individual bunks and curtains over each one.

"These trains are a bit different, I guess. That's all I could gather from the ticket man."

A headlight appears down the track, coming toward us off a curve. It takes me back to when I chased after the *Ivanhoe Independent* the first time and fell across its tracks, almost getting run over.

Ah, sweet memories.

Now the *Ivanhoe Independent* is gone. Blown to smithereens by Skelley and the Council members. Has the Preacher heard of it yet? That *would* give him reason to bomb the USE. But he wouldn't bomb Unity.

I know he wouldn't.

This new train hisses like an aggravated cobra, the sound

151

turning into a windy roar when it passes us. It's so close I could reach out and touch its slick body. It slows to a stop, and Solomon leads us at a jog to the front. Every few cars or so, a ticket checker steps out to admit new passengers.

Old passengers stumble out onto the concrete with sleepy frowns, dragging luggage behind them.

Solomon hands over our tickets as well as the copies of our travel documents that Dalene set us up with. He is the responsible one of the group—I hadn't spared a thought for my documents. I'm glad he thought to keep them.

I grow colder and colder as we stand waiting for approval. The heavyset woman wears a long, button-down uniform coat and a hat. Finally, without a word, she hands us our papers and we go inside.

"I love trains!" Willow hops on the balls of her feet. It's almost like she's normal again. Young, giddy. But even in her train excitement, her eyes don't crinkle right, her mouth doesn't smile fully.

I still grin, but can't help thinking, *God . . . what did they do to her?*

She never got to ride the *Ivanhoe Independent*, and the trains in the USE are quite different from this one. No sleeper bunks, that I noticed. Solomon looks at the papers, then leads us down the train car. How does he know where to go? How can he read those papers?

We reach what must be our room as a woman walks out with a huge armful of used white sheets. I peer inside the room. It's tiny, with two beds folding out from each of the left and right walls. Two are knee height and the other two head height. Between them is a small table jutting out from the base of a wall-sized window. Each bed has a white sheet on it with a pillow at the top and a folded blanket at the foot. Willow scrambles up the bunk on the left and Elm follows suit on the right.

"I guess we'll take the low bunks." Solomon winks at me, then shoves our packs in a hollow above the sliding door.

Each bunk is long and narrow with a small, retracting safety bar to keep us in bed. The space looks cozy. First, I head down the train hallway until I walk through another door into a small bathroom space. There are two doors. Both smell like old sewer, but not bad enough to keep me out.

I glance in the mirror and immediately wish I hadn't. My hair is a creature of static, bunched and hovering over my scalp in a reddish-brown net. My skin is greasy, and I don't dare look at my teeth. If cleanliness is next to godliness, then I'm about as far from godly as one can get.

A knock on the door startles me so badly, I lose my balance and plop onto the toilet seat. "Yes?"

If it's the cleaning lady, I'm doomed. I don't even know how to say hello in Russian.

"Parvin?" Phew! Solomon. "I have toothpaste and things that I purchased for each of us."

I open the door and he wrinkles his nose at the toilet reek. I'd already gotten used to it. He hands me a pouch. "Thanks."

"Welks. See you in the room."

Toothpaste! I hold it and the toothbrush above my head as a victory torch. Good-bye, vomit breath! I plant the toothbrush between my teeth, then realize my mistake. I take it out again, unscrew the toothpaste cap with my teeth, *then* return the toothbrush to my mouth. I squeeze a generous amount of paste on the bristles, put the toothpaste down, and *brush-brush-brush.*

Ironic how I hated brushing my teeth as a child, yet now I crave it. Maybe that makes me an official adult.

Once finished, I strip down to the bare necessities of modesty—my undershirt and leggings—then return to the room. I shove my pile of clothes beneath the low bed on the left, then crawl onto the mattress. The temperature of the room is comfortable, but I unfold the blanket anyway.

Solomon lays on his side, facing me, still fully clothed. Doesn't he want to shed a few layers to be more comfortable? Maybe it's a guy thing.

He looks at me. "I don't think the Preacher bombed Unity Village."

I nod, barely conveying my relief. Solomon knows how much his thoughts mean to me. "Me, neither."

Willow pops her fuzzy head over her bunk. She hasn't shed any layers either. "The Preacher can beat the Council."

"I'm sure he could." But we're not at *that* stage of war yet.

The NAB lets out a *pop* sound. Solomon pulls it out and glances at the screen. "Your father sent a message." He slides the NAB across the table.

Father. Not Mother. She didn't respond.

Before I can grab it, Willow reaches with a gloved hand. "Can I try reading it?"

I want to read that message *now*, but Willow deserves to know what's going on. Besides, when else will she get to practice her reading, seeing as we're in a different country? I pass the NAB up to her. "Of course."

"'Dear Parvin and Solomon, I have n-news. The al-al-albi . . .'" She lets the NAB drop, hanging from her hand in front of my face. "You can do it."

I don't argue.

> *~Dear Parvin and Solomon,*
> *~I have news. The albinos have noticed the struggle of people trying to get over to this side—to freedom. A week ago, they sent a messenger to Ivanhoe to ask for help. Until we hear from Ivanhoe, some of the albinos are going to the gap in the Wall to help Radicals through.*
> *~Please pray.*

I read it out loud to everyone.

"*Our* people? *Our* albinos?" Willow looks at Elm, and I suddenly wonder if he's told her about any of the changes that have taken place in the albino village—Alder's death, the split of the tribe, Ash, and Black's new leadership position. "It is good of Black to do this."

So she does know. Elm nods. "He is a leader."

Albinos, the Preacher . . . I never expected them to gather for the sake of my people. As strange as the Preacher is, I receive a calm assurance at the idea of him coming to fight. He wouldn't come unprepared. He would know what he's up against. He even knows some of the Council members.

Will he come?

"So the Preacher might bring an army . . ." Solomon folds his arms behind his head. His eyes are narrow, scorching the bottom of Elm's bed with his thoughts.

"It's perfect, don't you think, Solomon?" Vengeance will be paid for Unity's destruction. The people who died there will be avenged. Their friends and family who escaped will be set free.

It's confirmation from our God. He is on our side and He *will* send reinforcements.

My optimistic thoughts flicker when I look at Solomon again. His jaw is set. "Solomon? What are you thinking?"

He shakes his head. "This is bad. This will make everything much, much worse."

15

Ta-tam-ta-tam-ta-tam. The staccato of the train wheels brings a sense of comfort as I lie awake in the darkness.

"Worse." That's what Solomon said. He's afraid the appearance of an Ivanhoe army will start a war and that the Council will use that as an excuse to take over the West.

It makes sense. Willow's people would be caught right in the middle. They shouldn't have to die for helping.

Ta-tam-ta-tam-ta-tam.

The train lullaby is a whisper to return to sleep.

Sometimes I can't return. The land of dreams pales when set against the backdrop of snowy Russian hills and trees clouded by night shadows. The train is loud, yet we're cocooned by silence. I can't make sense of it.

So I sleep again, wishing the night to last forever.

Morning comes. The train lights go on, and a voice announces something in Russian over a ceiling speaker. I'm unconcerned. We can't miss our stop. We're riding the rail to the very end.

How many passengers will remain on board once we arrive? And what will we find at that last stop? Is there a town? There must be.

God . . . are You with us?

I crawl from my bed. Willow rolls over, but continues to sleep despite the light. Elm and Solomon are dead logs. Down the hall, there's a line for the bathroom—it's short, but I'd prefer waiting in my room to avoid an awkward conversation. Or, better put, an awkward *non*-conversation, since I don't know Russian.

When I turn around, there's one of the train worker ladies. She says something in Russian. It doesn't sound like a question, but she stares at me as though waiting for a response. She repeats herself, I think. Maybe the Russian inflection doesn't sound like English inflection.

What's she asking? If I slept well? If I'm okay? I nod. "Mmm-hmm."

"Ah, English?"

What? Yes! English. "Yes!" How did she gather from my *mmm-hmm* that I don't speak Russian? Is it that obvious?

"Tea?"

"Uh . . . sure." Coffee would be better. Maybe they don't have coffee. Either way, the idea of a hot drink—even if it tastes like mud—while on a train passing through a winterland sounds glorious. "With sugar, please," I add as she turns away.

By this point, the toilet line has shrunk to only one person. I hop back in line, do my business in the now-stinkier bathroom, and return to our room. My travel-mates are all still asleep.

I'm alone, in a peaceful way. I perch on the edge of my bed and lean my elbows against the small table. I want to write about this, about my feelings and confusion and about where we are. Journal.

The last time I journaled was in my NAB and Skelley Chase took that away. I should invest in a paper one, like Reid had. I still have my writing hand.

The door to our room slides open with barely a sound, and the train woman places a lovely glass cup on my table. It's set in a metal base with a stamp of the train emblem on it. A handle curls away from the base.

The tea bag is already in the hot water, turning it amber. A tiny plastic bag has three cubes of sugar, and a metal spoon rests on top. "Thank you."

"Specie?"

Oh, payment. My eyes drift to Solomon, who sleeps on his back. I can't use his actual wrist chip because it might be tracked. This is embarrassing. I reach across the space and dig in his pocket. Please don't wake!

My fingers brush the small specie chip and I pull it out. The woman raises an eyebrow at me, but scans the chip with a hand-held screen. "*Spasibo.*"

I guess she forgot I don't speak Russian.

She leaves and slides the door closed. I return to my tranquility, this time with tea. Sunrise has barely crested the hills. The intervals between the *ta-tam-ta-tam* lengthen as we approach a station and the silhouettes of people vie for a space in the hallway, ready to disembark.

I just want to watch. People. Nature. Life. God is so creative.

Pop.

I jerk straight and search for the NAB. We have a message. Is it from Father? I find the NAB tucked under Solomon's pillow. Gingerly, I pull it out, flip it open, and tap the message bubble.

Mother.

-Parvin,

The train is not your fault. I'm not angry and will never hate you. Your Father and I prayed very long for your survival. I hope you return to us soon. Keep fighting. I'm here.

-Mother

She's never been one for long messages—I spent hours reading her journal one-liners. Frankly, I figured if she replied to my NAB message, it would be a single line.

This . . . is gold. Especially that part where she says *I'm here.* She's *for* me. That reveals her love more than any other words could. My eyes burn and I stare at her signature. She typed that for me.

I crush the NAB to my chest and imagine I'm hugging her. *God . . . if You're willing, give me another chance with Mother.*

I stare at the message until it's committed to memory, then slide the NAB back under Solomon's pillow. He breathes deep and rolls onto his side.

I need time to process and soak in the words I've sought since being separated from Mother. In these past months of harsh wounds and pain, somehow I've seen her soft side. She *let* me see it, and she's being vulnerable even now in reaching out to me.

We've never been more physically separated than in this last year, yet we've never grown so close than during this time. I'm ready to live together again, growing in new ways and *loving* in the ways I've longed for.

These thoughts make me want to journal again, but there's no paper and I don't want to use our NAB. I search the room as though paper will magically appear. My gaze lands on my pack. Hmm. I may not have a journal. But I *do* have a Bible. It takes me several tries to find *Hebrews*, but once there I turn to chapter eleven and find the verse about Abel.

"And through his faith, though he died, he still speaks."

Those were my last thoughts as I died at the Council's hands. Goosebumps pop up on my arms. I died. My wrist Clock is proof. I activate the Clock, just to see the word *overridden* again. Then I turn it off. God could have spoken through my death if He wanted to, but instead He gave me continued life.

I read the entire chapter, which ends up being all about faith and great people who remained faithful in God—one of whom is Gideon. I like Gideon, but I don't remember his whole story. I need to reread it someday.

People might look at my life and say I've done great things, but they were rarely out of faith. I crossed the Wall the first time because I had to, not because I trusted God. Did these other Bible heroes ever feel like that? That the "faith" part was kind of accidental? Or were they just Bible-time superheroes?

If I ever end up that spiritually buff, it will be because of God's strength in me. Not because of my own. I want to be stronger in Him. How do I do that?

I come across a verse that makes me stop.

"... *but now he*"—Is this talking about Jesus? —"*has promised, 'Yet once more I will shake not only the Earth but also the heavens.'*"

I picture his great hands on either side of the globe, giving it a violent jolt. It's a powerful picture. When? When will God do all this shaking? I read on.

"*This phrase, 'Yet once more,' indicates the removal of things that are shaken—that is, things that have been made . . .*"

Like the Wall. My chills increase, sending their goose bump soldiers up and down my spine. One swipe of God's palm and the entire Wall would be gone. Crumbled. Destroyed.

"*. . . in order that the things that cannot be shaken remain. Therefore, let us be grateful for receiving a kingdom that cannot be shaken . . .*"

Me. I can't be shaken because I'm God's. I like the idea of Him shaking the world to see what's left standing, and all that remains is shalom.

"What are you reading?"

I jolt in my seat and find Solomon's light teal eyes staring at me. I place my hand on the open page so I don't lose my spot. "Oh, you know, God shaking the whole Earth with His bare hands."

"Sounds intense." He stretches, looking particularly attractive with mussed hair and groggy eyes. Nervous he'll read my thoughts, I avoid his gaze and add all three sugar cubes to my tea. The small spoon is just the right height to reach the bottom of the cup and keep my fingers from burning.

He watches me.

I stir. The tea has cooled enough to drink.

"Parvin?"

My, what an interesting spoon. "Yeah?"

His question is barely a whisper. "How are you doing?"

What does he mean? Physically after the plane ride? Spiritually after reading this scripture? Emotionally after discovering Unity Village was destroyed?

I sigh. What does it matter? How am I doing? I try to speed-assess myself but, as with all things when there's pressure, my brain blanks out. I glance up at Elm and Willow's sleeping forms and lower my voice. "I'm nervous, Solomon. But I'm trying not to be."

For a moment, I think he'll reach for me, but he doesn't. "About us?"

I almost laugh. I kind of like that this is the first assumption his mind jumps to. "No. Well . . . I'm nervous I won't be a great teammate, but I'm still learning. Mostly I'm nervous about searching for Erfinder's information. What if there's nothing to be found in his house? What if this is a fool's errand we're on while Radicals just keep dying in the USE? It's so tough to trust God with things that are uncertain."

Before I can continue, he grabs my hand and prays softly for God's guidance. I let his voice wash over me, directing my focus to God. *Our* God.

When he finishes, I breathe easier. "Thank you." I sip my tea. Not bad. Could use another sugar cube, though. "What do you think is at the end of the train line?"

He sits up and the back of his hair splays behind him like little wings. I try not to giggle. "A city of some sort."

"How much specie do we have left from Dalene?" I hand him back the specie chip with a gesture to my tea. I hope he doesn't think about me digging in his pocket.

He raises an eyebrow and slips the chip back into his pocket. "A lot. Enough that we shouldn't have much to worry about."

I think back to when the muggers in Prime chased me down and stole my specie. "Could someone rob us?" Stranded in a foreign-speaking country exactly halfway across the world from my family? No, thank you.

"Someone could steal our specie chip, but I could deactivate it with my NAB if that happens. This is one of the big reasons the global currency went electronic."

A sleepy groan comes from above. Willow's bandaged arm flops over the side of her bunk. "I love trains . . ."

"Good sunrise, Willow." Solomon peers up at her bunk.

Her dangling, bandaged arm gives a limp, half-hearted wave. "Mmm-hmm."

Train food consists mostly of fish—gag—and very dense bread cakes . . . sometimes with fish *in* the bread. But for dinner we receive a red vegetable soup with spices floating on the surface and little bits of pork. It's delightful.

Two days we spend on this train. Willow comes up with a game using sugar cubes like dice. Solomon and I don't have any time alone, but I have to hope that day will come . . . eventually.

I spend a lot of time poring over the *Daily Hemisphere* electro-sheet, and by afternoon a new headline and video have surfaced.

Newly Projected Wall Activated, Celebrating 50 Years

I press the video before I can blink away my shock.

The video shows the Wall gap, guarded by hundreds of Enforcers and challenged by even more Radicals. Then a flash blinds the cameras in white. Static attacks the screens and I stiffen. More static. Then one camera gets going. Another.

Did the people attack? Was there lightning?

The scene clears.

No . . .

The new projected Wall is up, taller, stronger, and never-ending. Just like the projected Wall in Antarctica, only bluish and transparent. It stretches as far as the eye can see, a few feet in front of the stone Wall.

"S-S-Solomon!"

He jerks the electrosheet toward himself, reacting to my cry. I keep watching the video. I want to crumple, to cry, but my mind jousts against the impulse. There is hope. There is still hope. God can rise above this. He already *has* risen above it. He's letting it happen for a reason . . . right?

The projection doesn't put up a picture of stone yet; it's more a film of flickering glass that still allows one to see the other side. It's a trickster—like a polished window that entices a sparrow to slam into it.

"No," Solomon rasps.

The background news narrator is frantic, trying to film and say everything as though the chaos will disappear. The camera flips to show the length of the Wall as it stretches southward into the states, disappearing into fog. The projection runs parallel to the stone Wall, materializing from pillars at the top of the Wall.

I close my eyes, unable to look at the event any longer. Despite the temptation to lose hope, I pray. I pray that God will do what He's promised . . . and complete what He started in me.

We reach the end of the tracks after dinnertime on the third day. The four of us are the only passengers left. We step out onto the platform. It's exposed to the elements and slick from ice. The sun hasn't set yet, but chill sweeps in with every elongated shadow.

The platform is two slabs of elevated concrete on each side of the train, with a few ice-crusted benches. There's a sign, but it's in Russian. Ahead of the train is the Wall, looking oddly similar

NADINE BRANDES

to the one in Antarctica. Icy, but black. Taller than the portion at
home. The train tracks head toward the Wall and then curve to
the right, where I'm assuming the train engine will turn around
somehow.

To the left of the tracks is a small cluster of houses about half
the size of Unity Village. We bustle down the platform, and I try
to gather the folds of my coat in one hand, tightening it around
my body. Elm holds Willow's gloved hand and pulls her after
Solomon so fast she doesn't have time to be cold, or to resist his
touch. She yanks her scarf up over her mouth and nose with her
free hand.

The platform leads us past closed ticket booths, down cement
stairs—"Careful, it's slick."—and then underneath the train tracks
in a cement tunnel. Cement, cement, cement. There's nothing
warm about cement. Just looking at it makes me colder.

We emerge onto the main road of the town. I think there's a
sidewalk, but the ice sits like a paused river, flowing over bumps
and turning the road into a skating rink. All the streets are like
this, and Solomon keeps us walking up them. Many of the houses
have carved gables and beautiful paint jobs. There are tiny cot-
tages with shingled roofs and small fences in front of the ones that
have snow-covered lawns.

The buildings that aren't made of wood are cement. They look
more like eateries and stores. A hunched woman, with a scarf
around her face and a thick black coat, works in front of one
entrance. She uses a long wooden pole with a metal blade on the
tip to pound the ground, chipping two inches of firm ice off the
sidewalk. She stops as we walk by.

Solomon halts for a moment. "Opening One?"

She steps back, as though startled that he's speaking to her.

He holds up a finger. "Opening One? Uh . . . the door in the
Wall?" He points to the Wall.

She shakes her head and shrugs, muttering something in

Russian. I don't need to know the language to figure out she's saying she doesn't understand.

"Where"—he shrugs—"can we"—he points to the four of us—"sleep?" Solomon puts his hands together and uses them as a pillow. So much for finding out how to get to Opening One. But he's right to change tactics. It's almost nighttime, and by the looks of this place we'll be lucky to find a hotel.

She gestures down the road, then returns to chipping ice. I'm still not sure she understood Solomon's question. He leads us away. "Parvin, may I see the NAB please?"

"It's in my shoulder pack, at the top." I turn around and try to keep my footing on the ice as he tugs the straps out of their clasps. Breath clouds burst in front of my eyes as I exhale. Every inhale brings mini daggers into my throat. I yank the zipper of my coat as high as it'll go and pull the collar over my mouth. "I think it was warmer in Antarctica."

I mean it as a joke, but Solomon responds without mirth. "I think you're right." He closes the pack flap and takes the lead again. "Which means we *have* to find a place to sleep. We won't last if we're stuck outside."

"Do you think that could happen?" The tremor in Willow's voice brings a new seriousness to our predicament.

"No." I'm almost angry as I say the word. "It won't happen." I won't let it. And neither will Solomon.

Solomon fiddles with the NAB, and we finally stop walking. The ice is too dangerous for multitasking. "The verbal translator is *still* loading. Cheap Enforcer NAB." He knocks it against his palm. "I'll look up a few words if it'll let me."

Five minutes pass, and no one else is on the street. Empty. Like a ghost town. Nothing looks like an inn or hotel to me. The signs I do see have food items on them, or are slapped on a cold cement outer wall, with no door in sight.

"Okay, I found the word for hotel." Solomon frowns at the

NAB. "Now to get it in English letters." More tapping, more frowning. "Uh . . . *gostuh* . . . *gostuhneetsa*."

"M-Maybe they d-don't have hotels." Willow's teeth are chattering. Elm pulls her against his chest and rubs his hands up and down her arms fast. She yanks away. "Wh-What's the w-word for *sleep?*"

Solomon's bare fingers tremble as he tries to type something in to the NAB. My hand and stump are tucked under my armpits.

"Uh . . . *son*." Solomon purses his lips to one side. "Or *spaht*. I don't know how accurate this translation device is. When the download is complete, all I'll need to do is speak to the NAB and it will translate."

Willow sounds like she's about to cry. "Please, can we find a place?"

"Okay." Solomon slips my NAB into his coat pocket, then offers his arm out to me for balance.

That would mean letting a gap sneak between my arm and my core. I shake my head. "Too c-cold." The tighter I get, the warmer I am.

"I don't want you to fall."

"I won't." As if to show I have no control, my left foot jerks away from me on the icy ground. I throw my arms out for balance, regain it, and then tuck them back against my body. "Well . . . I'll try not to."

Solomon takes tiny steps toward a door. It looks cold. Abandoned. He knocks. We wait. He knocks again.

"N-next." Willow leads the way this time, with Elm keeping a tight arm around her shoulders. They get to the next door and Willow knocks. I barely hear her soft knuckle tap.

Elm grabs her bandaged hand and tucks it back into her coat pocket. Then he lifts a fist and pounds like a maniac. "Open!"

Nothing.

We're like Joseph and Mary, only instead of "no room at the inn," there's no inn.

As we go from door to door, anger builds in my chest. Surely, *surely*, people can see us seeking shelter. Why won't they help? Is it because of me? Because they know who I am?

My mind builds a slow wall of fury against the Russian people of this town. After all, people in the USE always describe Russia as harsh. No one ever really visited, but they said the people don't smile the way Americans do. "Maybe they don't like us because we're from the USE."

It feels good to shift the blame. It's *their* fault we are freezing out here.

"Or maybe we haven't reached the right part of the town yet." Solomon the optimist.

We round a corner and enter another, narrower and more icy street. Each door looks like it leads to a home instead of a hotel or inn. That means people. Maybe Solomon was right. I shouldn't judge too harshly . . . or too quickly.

Control. I need to control my negative thoughts.

There's a flicker from the curtains of a window halfway down the street. Solomon must see it, too, because he breaks into a cautious jog. "I think someone's over there."

"Careful on the ice—"

His tractionless boot jerks away on the ice and, before I can blink, Solomon's flying sideways through the air. His momentum yanks him to the earth with a resounding crack.

"Solomon!" My voice is a windless squeak.

He doesn't move.

That's when I see the pool of blood seeping out from beneath the back of his head.

16

"Solomon!" In my haste to reach his limp body, I lose my own footing and land on my knees, bruising them. I pull myself along the ice with my good hand until I'm beside him and rest my palm on the side of his face. "Solomon."

Elm and Willow reach me. "He needs a bandage."

He needs a *pulse*. I slip my fingers under his chin, searching for a pulse. Maybe I should feel his wrist? I don't know. I don't know where the pulse is!

Thump-thump.

There. He's alive.

Bandages. Warmth. We need help. "Help." It starts as a wavery call. Then I scream it. "Help!"

What were those Russian words? Hotel? Sleep? Why didn't we look up *warmth* and *help?*

But no one will help. They're just like my people from Unity Village when they wouldn't even save me during my hearing. These Russians don't care—

"*Ya zdyes.*" A hand wraps around mine—a very non-albino hand in worn fingerless gloves. I look up into the face of a man in a thick wool hat and blue eyes. His face is grim, but kind. "*Ya pomogoo.*"

I don't need to understand his words. I throw my arms around him.

A helper.

An angel.

He pats my back once, then pushes me gently away and turns to Solomon. When I brush the tears from my eyes, there's a woman kneeling by Solomon's other side. A younger man with wild blond hair rushes out of a house farther down the street, throwing on a coat as he slips and slides across the ice.

They heard me. They're helping. My heart pumps an overflow of warmth and gratitude. Shame on me for assuming these people didn't care. Solomon was right—they just didn't know we were here.

The three toss Russian back and forth, pointing and sliding hands under Solomon's body. Elm jumps in. They're going to lift him.

"*Vas . . . dva . . . tree.*" They lift with a universal grunt.

The first man who arrived jerks his head toward a door somewhere down the road, but a voice calls from behind us on the right side of the road. "*Nyet, nyet, Sergei!*"

Two supermodel Russian girls a few years older than I am stand in the doorway closest to us. One has sunlight blond hair that curls gently past her chin, the other has dark hair. The blond one beckons us toward her and shouts something at the first man, Sergei.

The group changes direction and carries Solomon into the house of these women. They're the first door on the right in this apartment building. I step in behind them and warmth slithers around me, mixing with the icy air. Heat!

Next, I'm slammed in the face by the smell of animal. It enters my lungs upon my first breath. I imagine the stench creeping into Solomon's head wound and contaminating it.

The apartment is narrow everywhere I look. Narrow hall, tiny rooms stacked to the ceiling with furs, blankets, and books. Loose fur clings to every worn chair and the one sofa in what I gather to be the living room. I don't want Solomon in here. I want him in a sterile, clean, healthy hospital with white sheets and bleached bandages.

Solomon groans as they lay him down on the couch. The blond Russian girl presses a folded cloth to the back of his head. His eyes flutter open and his hand curls up to press against his forehead. "Careful . . . it's icy."

I kneel by his side. "Are you okay?"

"Heez head not bad." The blond Russian girl speaks English! Her *h* sounds are rough—a mixture between a *k* and *h*, almost like a cat hiss.

I turn to the group around me. Already, they seem to assess that Solomon will be fine and they're preparing to leave. I reach my hand toward them. "Thank you."

Blond girl translates. *"Spasibo."*

"I . . ." I misjudged them. I labeled them as uncaring before I'd even met anyone. I want to apologize, but it doesn't seem right in this moment. *God, forgive me for . . . being a jerk.*

A couple of them smile or squeeze my shoulder. Then they depart and we're left with the girls.

"Menya zovoot Sasha." The blond girl then gestures to the woman with long dark hair. *"Syestra*—eh . . . sister—Gloria."

I point at each of us. "Parvin, Solomon, Willow, and Elm."

She and her sister exchange a look and seem to be withholding smiles. To them, our names must sound pretty odd.

Our names . . .

For time's sake! I gave them our real names!

Solomon tries to rise from the couch, but Sasha pushes him back down. *"Nyet.* Rest."

He holds up his hands. "I'm fine, really." He meets my gaze. "If I knew finding a place to stay would be as simple as cracking my head open, I would have crashed to the ice much earlier."

But Sasha and Gloria haven't invited us to stay. I look to them.

"Do you . . . have a place we could sleep for the night? We could, uh, pay you."

Sasha's eyebrows jump up. "You sleep here." She says this as though it had already been established.

I'll take the floor if I have to, despite the smell of animal. My fingers are starting to thaw. Willow still shivers. As the nerves settle and I tune in to my surroundings, a new sound reaches my ears.

Barks. Yaps.

I'm brought suddenly back to my time in the cave near Opening Three, after fleeing the wolves and coyotes. Instinctively, I cringe away, but the sound grows. Louder. It's on the other side of the wall. "Do you have . . . pets?"

Sasha checks the bloody cloth beneath Solomon's head. "Ve have . . . em, how you say . . .?" She turns to Gloria and says something in Russian.

Gloria speaks for the first time. "Sled dogs." Her voice is soft, gentle, and shy. Her dark hair hangs over one shoulder in an assortment of mixed braids, curled at the ends.

"*Da.* Sled dogs." Sasha sets aside the bloody cloth and pushes Solomon up into a sitting position.

But of course. Sled dogs. In a tiny apartment.

I so don't understand this indoor pet thing.

The yaps grow more insistent, and one of the dogs bumps the closed door from the other side. By the sounds of it, they have a *lot* of dogs. How many are used for a sled?

"Are they for food?" Elm sits in an armchair in the corner.

"*Nyet!*" Sasha shakes her head and wrinkles her nose. "Zey pull our sleds."

Gloria brings a damp cloth and a gauze pad with bandages. Solomon sits quietly as she cleans and wraps his head. Only a few months ago, he had his head wrapped after being stripped of his Enforcerhood. I know men tend to be injury-prone—they're explorers, after all—but Reid never seemed to get hurt this often. Solomon will have quite the scar collection.

"You need food?" Sasha looks at Willow as she asks—the smallest and thinnest of us four.

Willow shakes her head. "No, thank you." I let her speak for us all. We had plenty of food on the train and, even though most of it was fish, my appetite is quite satisfied. I don't want to take anything else from these women.

"Chai?"

Ha! I know this word from my conversation on the train. *Chai* means *tea*. The power of this knowledge feels like a secret code, letting me into a tiny sliver of the world of Russian. I know a word in Russian. And, if I'm observing correctly, *nyet* means no. If only I could remember what *yes* is.

"Yes, please."

Willow follows my lead and nods.

"What is it?" Elm tugs Willow onto the arm of his chair. She stiffens. Poor Elm.

"Tea." Why yes, I speak Russian.

"I don't want any."

"That sounds very nice." Solomon pats the tied off bandage around his head, then turns to me. "How do I look?"

I try not to think of him unconscious with a halo of blood on the ice. "Dashing." Will he start forgetting our names like Jude did when he was concussed? Hopefully not. After all, that was the pirate chip's fault.

Sasha leaves the room, crosses the small entryway, and walks through a doorless frame into what must be the kitchen. Gloria hovers for a moment, cleaning up some of the blood and cloths, then she joins Sasha.

"Are you really okay?" I perch on the end of the couch across from Solomon.

"I really am." He raps some knuckles against the side of his head, joking, but then winces. "I don't bounce back as quickly as when I was a boy, but it was your typical knock-out. I'll probably have a headache for a few days."

"There was blood."

He shrugs. "Sometimes that happens."

I'm not at ease yet. Willow finally manages to put my feelings into words. "Jude-man hit *his* head and forgot my name. What if you forget things and don't know?"

He reaches across the gap between couch and sofa and squeezes Willow's hand. "Then I'll count on you to remind me."

Sasha and Gloria return with a teapot and a wooden tray with five small, mismatched cups. Gloria unfolds the legs of a tiny table that was leaning against the wall, and Sasha sets down the tray. They don't have anywhere to sit, but when I move to get up from the couch, Sasha waves a hand. "Stay, stay."

Gloria pours hot, dark tea into each cup, but allows us all to put in our own amount of sugar. I balance my cup on my knee so as not to burn my hand.

"Vy you come to Russia?" Gloria helps Solomon put his cup of tea together. I should have thought of that.

I look to Solomon. What will he tell them? They've said nothing about Elm or Willow. Do they know who we are? "We are trying to get to Opening One."

Neither of the girls looks at each other, but they both go still. Sasha sips her tea. "Vy you vant zis?"

How much detail can we give? I don't want to lie, but I don't want to say too much. I jerk my head toward Solomon. "He has family there." Dead family.

Solomon leans forward and peers at Gloria until she meets his eyes. "Do you know how we can get there?"

Timid Gloria darts her gaze to Sasha, though her cheeks turn a deeper shade of pink. Is she . . . flustered by Solomon? Sasha gives a harsh, almost imperceptible nod to Gloria. "Ve can take you."

I jerk upright and spill a scalding splash of tea on my leg. "You can? How? When?"

"*Da.* Tomorrow ve hunt, after zis we leave."

"Will we take another train?" Willow asks.

Sasha shakes her head. "Ve take ze dogs."

As if their ears burned from mention, yapping explodes from the other side of the wall and my nose remembers how heavy their scent is. Yuck. "Wait, so . . . we'll be going there by . . . *dogsled?*"

Both Gloria and Sasha nod. "How much specie you have?"

"Enough." Solomon sets his cup on the foldout table. "What is your price?"

The two talk so quickly in hushed Russian it barely sounds like they take a breath. I keep my ears alert for the words *chai* or *nyet* . . . just in case they say them. Sasha takes a deep breath. "Twenty."

"Twenty?" I'm as surprised as Solomon. Compared to clothes shopping in Prime, that wouldn't even buy a scarf.

Gloria elbows Sasha. "Is too much." Then, louder. "Maybe fifteen? And ve feed you, too."

"How long does it take to get there?" It must be quite close if fifteen specie will cover the costs of feeding their dogs.

Gloria waves a hand back and forth in the air, growing bolder in her conversation. "Em, tree . . . maybe four days."

Three days? Fifteen specie? It doesn't add up—that can't possibly be enough. But maybe they're used to living off little. I glance down at my cup. How much does it cost to get tea way out here? I see their small apartment with new eyes—the peeling wallpaper, the old stained books, and the nasty smell.

"We'll give you fifty specie today, and then fifty when we get to the Opening." Solomon holds a serious face. He speaks so businesslike, it doesn't sound like charity.

I'm glad he said that.

Both girls frown and Sasha leans forward on her elbows. "You vant pay fifty specie?"

Solomon shakes his head, but stops after one movement. "No. *One hundred* specie. Fifty today, and then fifty again when we are done."

Sasha's jaw drops and Gloria's eyes well with tears, but before either of them can protest, Solomon drains his cup and holds it up. "More *chai, spasibo?*"

One day of hunting passes. After the first payment of specie, the two Russian dogsledding huntresses: the epitome of cool—Idris would *love* them—make us a hearty dinner of something they call *pelmeni*. It's a meat-filled dumpling boiled in chicken broth, and we eat it with sour cream.

Thank heaven it's not fish!

They grow chattier, telling us about their dogs and how they work in transportation, bringing supplies between towns. They hunt as they do this, keeping or selling the meat and furs. Gloria opens up, and her English is much better than Sasha's. She directs her questions and comments mostly to Solomon. Each time she does this a little twinge in my gut reminds me how stunningly pretty she is, in a natural way. Solomon is kind to her, but never *too* kind.

I keep an eye on the *Daily Hemisphere*, but there are no more bombings. No mention of the Preacher or an Ivanhoe army. Neither Father nor Mother send NAB updates. The silence instills a deeper urgency, but with that urgency comes this feeling of aloneness. I've been thinking through things too much on my own. Not praying, not sharing much with Solomon.

I'm learning that loneliness doesn't necessarily mean *being* alone.

The morning of our departure dawns bright, but frigid. Gloria is already gone. Sasha almost runs us over, bringing a string of sled dogs through the living room. They pull on her arm so hard, she barely keeps her footing. "Come outside ven you are ready. Ve wait for you at end of road."

Then she's outside, and the barks grow louder. I wouldn't be surprised if she skis her way down the street at the rate those dogs are going.

We gather our belongings, which aren't much, and eat leftover *pelmeni*. Not quite as good cold, but still hearty. The kitchen is half the size of the one in my Unity Village house, but there's no running water. My thoughts pull up short. The kitchen in my Unity Village house is gone. Bombed. Burned.

I look to Solomon, seeking respite from a glimpse of his face. He's adjusting his head bandage before donning travel clothes.

Sasha gave us each a fur coat and gloves from the many stacks in the room. They don't fit any of us completely right, but they're warm. Solomon insisted on paying for them, and she put up a weak fight before accepting the specie transfer.

"Ready?" Solomon stands by the door looking very Russian. Tall, bundled, and topped by a fox-fur shapka hat.

Willow pulls them over her other gloves and clothing. She giggles. "The fur tickles!" She wrinkles her nose before burying her face again in the fur collar of her over-sized, full-length coat.

Elm stands like a regal wolf-lord, unsmiling beneath his black shapka. His eye patch makes him even look more intimidating. "Let's go."

He takes Willow's arm. For the first time, she doesn't resist. Solomon takes mine, though I feel like I should be supporting *him*. We exit the apartment building and, though the light wind burns our cheeks, I feel it nowhere else on my body. No wonder animals can live outside without freezing.

Up the street we trudge, seeing no one except Sergei. "That's the guy who first stopped to help you," I whisper to Solomon, giving a small wave. Sergei nods.

I hear the sled dogs before I see them. They're much louder outside, their cacophony filling the thin morning air. We walk around the corner and see three wooden sleds, the rear runners of which are tied to metal posts in the ground. In front of each are eight dogs, lined up two-by-two with a thick cord between them. Santa's reindeer.

Goods for the journey weigh down the tips of each sled. I go toward the farthest sled with Solomon. Fur blankets coat the bottom, some of which are folded up to go on top. I imagine Solomon and me snuggling in there, covered in blankets and listening to the soft whoosh of snow pass by. Serenity. This will be quite the experience to bring back to Mother and Father. I bet even Reid never went dogsledding.

The dogs leap in the air like rabbits on caffeine. They're not as fluffy as I'd imagined, and the lead dog is bigger than the others, with short blond hair. Out of all of them, he looks the most like a pet. "This is Gumbo." Sasha pats his side. "Strong."

Sasha checks their harnesses, then shouts something in Russian to Gloria. Gloria steers Willow and Elm to a sled. I turn to her. "Who should get in first?"

"Solomon, you sit."

All obedience, Solomon climbs into the sled, shoving his shoulder pack deep into the feet section. There should still be plenty of room for me. I'm small. I put one foot in the sled, but Sasha grabs my arm. "*Nyet*."

I reel back out, not wanting to do anything that might upset the dogs. "Oh, am I going in a different sled?"

"*Nyet*." She shakes her head and points to the back of the sled. "You drive."

17

But of course, have the one-handed girl shout commands in a strange language to eight huge dogs that terrify her.

This is going to be a great trip.

"Why do *I* have to drive?" Are they blind? I have *one hand*.

"He vill drive later, when head is better." Sasha pulls me to the back of the sled, then shouts over her shoulder. "Gloria!"

She comes over and pulls the furs over Solomon's lap. Sasha leaves her with us and returns to the middle sled. Elm is on the back of the first sled, with Willow sitting down—at least I'm not the only one driving/steering/mushing . . . whatever this is called.

"Here is stomp pad." Gloria unhooks a flat, black piece of plastic tied with chains to the back of the sled. "You step on it ven ve start going—it is hard jerk when ve start, so hold tight." She pats the wooden bar at the tall part of the sled. Her English is better and better the more she speaks.

I can't do this. I have one hand! Will I be standing all day? I don't want to admit it, but I'm a weakling.

"Dogs vill follow me." She then gestures to a metal spiked bar on a hinge at the base of the sled. "Step here. Main brake. Stand on it ven I untie sled." She moves to the stake in the ground that's keeping the dogs from taking off. Is she going to untie it right now?

"Wait! Should I get on the brake?"

She grabs a giant set of plastic coated boots and fur gloves from the other side of the sled. "Put zese on. Your boots vill be too cold."

I strip off my boots, my hand shaking. Solomon takes them from me and tucks them deep into the sled. "You'll do fine."

Easy for him to say.

The new boots are much warmer, padded on the inside but heavy and clunky. I pull the fur glove far over my left stump. Already, my fingers are warmer. Trying to appear confident and willing, I step onto the two wooden ends of the sled skis. This will be just like skiing.

Now, if only I'd skied before.

"Step on main brake." Gloria checks the harnesses of the dogs one last time, letting some of them lick her face.

Yuck.

I use my foot to hinge down the metal brake and then hop on it with both feet until it sinks deep into the snow. Gloria returns. "Keep middle line tight. Stop if dogs need toilet. To go forward, say *Hike*. To stop is *Vo*."

Hike and whoa. "English words?"

"English man taught us." She walks to the post, and this time I know she's untying us. Gumbo, the blond dog, keeps looking back at me, like he knows I'm a fraud.

I try hooking my left arm under the arched handle, but then I end up crouching too low. Instead, I settle for pressing my forearm against the wood and gripping with my right hand directly in the middle.

The sled is untied and the dogs leap higher, tugging against their harnesses, like they know we're about to go. Yips startle the very snowflakes in the sky. The sled jerks forward an inch. I swallow a squeal and will my body to weigh more as I rest fully on the brake.

Then, with a harsh shout from Sasha, her sled bursts forward. Elm and Willow follow suit.

Heart pounding, I step off the main brake and yell, *"Hike!"*

The dogs surge forward . . .

. . . and I fly off the back of the sled.

"Ve try again."

Gloria brushes snow off the back of my coat. I think she expected this to happen, because both she and Sasha stood on the back of their single sled. Gloria hopped off, got the wild sled, and steered them back to me.

This time, she's on the back with me as we get going. Her confident presence keeps me calm. The start isn't quite as sudden as before and I don't fall off. It's tough balancing on the stomp pad, but once we get going, Gloria steps onto the wood tracks again and hooks the stomp pad up to the back of the sled.

We reach Sasha's sled.

"Whoa!" I say.

"Good." Gloria steps off and joins her sister.

They both remain on the back of their sled and Sasha yells, "Hike!" My dogs follow without a command from me. I don't mind. The less I have to do, the better.

I balance on the skis and adjust my grip, using my left forearm more than I'd expected. The yapping quiets now that the dogs are getting what they want—permission to run.

And I mean . . . run!

It takes me a full minute before I calm enough to focus on what we're doing, to realize that I'm not only *on* a dog sled, but *driving* one. The hiss of packed snow beneath bids us farewell. I want to tug the collar of my fur coat over my nose, but I don't have an extra hand.

"This is so cool!" Solomon's shout carries to me on the wind.

I'd almost forgotten he was there. Standing on the back, with the Russian winter blowing my hair and chilling my cheeks—I'm glad to be driving. I'm not jealous of Solomon at all, though I do anticipate when I get to experience sledding from that view.

A burst of stench hits my nose, and I immediately hold my breath. When I breathe in again it's gone, but then another one comes. I look at the dogs. A couple are relieving themselves *as they run*. The rest are . . . gassing. I laugh once. I did *not* expect that.

Am I supposed to stop them? Gloria said something about the dogs and a toilet, which I assumed meant relieving themselves. But they seem more anxious to run, so I let them. The main line between the dogs stays taut.

Another minute passes and the dog-gas is mostly gone. I finally look around. We're sledding parallel to the Wall, far enough away that we're still in the sun, where the snow is softer.

I glance behind. The town is already out of view, lost behind a small snow crest. Up ahead is all snow again. It's packed both from the wind and from a faint trail—is this where the sisters usually take the sleds?

Sasha, Gloria, and their dogs are in the lead; Elm and Willow are in the middle; and Solomon and I take up the rear. Sasha and Gloria talk, while each balances on one of the skis.

"How are you doing?" Solomon asks.

"Great!" I can't stop grinning. This isn't work at all. In fact, if I didn't have to busy myself with saving the world, I might consider becoming a wild, Russian dogsledder.

By noon, I've gotten the hang of the main brake and the personality of the dogs pulling us. Gumbo has the most energy. Even though it's frigid outside, the sun warms me and I'm tempted to take my coat off, but don't. My leg starts to itch the more I use the brake to slow us down, as it vibrates against ice chunks. But I haven't grown tired of the standing.

With each twitch of a cold nose or tingle of icy fingers come flash memories of frostbite and death in Antarctica. But this is different. We're with two Russian super-sledders who live in the wild. They wouldn't bring us out here to let us freeze.

Snow builds up around my boots every time I use the stomp pad. Gloria was right—*my* boots would have been too cold. Currently, my feet are toasty warm and I'm not sure how.

Just about when I feel like my poor hand can't grip the sled bar any longer, Sasha calls her dogs to a stop. Elm and I both echo the *"Whoa!"* and step on the main brakes.

"Svitch if you want." Sasha stays standing on the brake. "Ve take rest in five hours." Gloria hops off the sled and curls up in the bed portion. Theirs is packed with piles of tarped items. I'm surprised she even fits.

"Want to switch?" Solomon is already halfway out of the sled.

"Sure." I'm glad he brought it up. I don't want to admit my wrist and elbow ache from balancing my body on the back of this thing for five hours.

I wait until Solomon steps on the brake. "That's the stomp pad, and make sure the line between the dogs is tight enough. Don't get up too much speed on the downhills." Listen to me, little miss professional. "And Gumbo likes to eat snow when we stop. He's the lead dog."

"Got it."

"Is your head okay?"

"As long as I don't fly off the back like you did, I'll be fine."

I laugh and rub Gumbo behind the ears before I crawl into the bed of the sled. The layered fur is warm from Solomon's body heat. I pull the thick stack of furs over my core and nestle down. I didn't think it'd be comfortable, crammed with all the goods at the nose of the sled, but their weight makes me feel like I'm crawling into a bed with a heavy down quilt on it. Okay, maybe about six or seven heavy down quilts. Even better.

I pull a crunched piece of paper from beneath me. I unfold it.

I'm so proud of you. -Solomon

I tuck his note into my pocket and suddenly feel much warmer.

"Hike!" Sasha gives the sled a little push, then hops on.

Solomon copies, but doesn't say his command very loudly. The dogs take off anyway. I think they'd follow Sasha no matter what we say.

Pieces of snow *pink plink* against my coat and face, thrown up from the anxious flurry of dog feet. After about five minutes, the sled dogs settle into their rhythm again and less snow is kicked up.

Sledding is the epitome of peace, despite the occasional reek of dog gas and feces. I don't know how they do it—I could barely relieve myself in the forest, let alone while running and pulling a sled. On occasion, Sasha calls them to a stop when the lead dogs need a moment.

The sun warms my face, but I'm cooler in the sled than when I was driving. Lack of movement causes chills in a winter wasteland. I'm covered in furs, I'll be fine. Before I realize it, I've fallen asleep to the hiss of the passing snowscape and the rhythm of pattering dog feet.

I wake, icy cold, to the scratch of metal on ice. My eyes flutter open to a sunset sky. We've stopped and the sisters are pulling items from the sleds. Metal dog bowls, a tent, furs, wood, and a metal box. They put some of the wood inside this and start a fire, filling a pot with snow.

I crawl out of the sled. "Can I help?"

"More snow." Sasha hands me a bowl without looking up. Good, gathering snow is something I can do with one hand. I half-feared she'd ask me to help pitch the tent.

Elm and Solomon take that role.

The dogs settle down in the snow, panting. The moment the snow is melted, Gloria pours it into the bowls for the dogs. They lap it up, splashing half of it out and back onto the snow. I gather more, it melts, only this time Gloria pulls a plastic-lined crate from Elm and Willow's sled. Inside are cubes of raw meat—the product of whatever they hunted yesterday.

She puts a handful of the meat into each dog's bowl, then covers it in hot water.

"Why the water?"

"Ze dogs vill have more . . . hydration. Is important for energy. And eet keeps ze *vada* from freezing."

There is one tent. Willow and I help layer the bottom of it with furs—fur-side up. "I want a dogsled," she quips.

I laugh, imagining her on the back—a little wild thing covered in wolf furs and zooming back and forth between Ivanhoe and the albino forest. Do they even get enough snow in that portion of the West? "Did you drive it at all?"

"No. Elm did. I'll drive a little tomorrow."

Once the dogs are fed, we all share some fire-smoked meat and a loaf of bread. Gumbo lays near me. I don't pet him, but he keeps nuzzling my leg. When he finally gets the hint that I'm not going to snuggle him, he slouches back to the other dogs. I feel a little bad.

The single tent is so layered with furs, I barely feel the ground beneath me when we all climb inside. Gloria and Sasha aren't shy and lay pressed against whoever's nearest. I make sure to sleep between them and Solomon.

While it looks cozy, it's more awkward than anything else trying to slip under the furs while dressed in full garb and boots. I finally kick off my boots and my toes tingle. I hadn't realized they were numb. Willow does the same between me and the girls and we twine our feet together to keep warm.

Solomon and Elm don't snuggle.

They'll be cold. Part of me wants to scoot nearer to Solomon, to feel secure in his warmth and maybe even his arms. But . . . the idea of physical closeness and intimacy is still too new to me. I like the small steps we're taking.

The wind picks up outside, waving the tent roof back and forth. Sasha and Gloria talk in low Russian. I don't know what

I expected—a campfire with singing and ghost stories? I close my eyes, willing my body to desire sleep. How has a full day of dogsledding not exhausted me?

God, what am I going to do once we reach this town? Up until now, our goal has been to get there, get there, get there. But once we're there, then what? Solomon knows the address of his great-grandfather's house. We'll just . . . search. Perhaps Erfinder Hawke lived in the era where he used pen and paper. Maybe he left a journal behind filled with the information about the Wall.

Please let us find something. The expanse of winter wilderness and thin sky makes my words seem weak, not making it all the way to God's ears. It's an illusion—I *know* He's everywhere. He's present. He's here. I just need to grow spiritually enough to feel it. *Please let us find the information that will help us tear down the Wall.*

I don't remember falling asleep, but waking is that mixture of warm and frigid—warm from the furs, frigid once I pop my head out. My breath brings heat to the rest of my body simply from being confined beneath the blankets.

I'm rested.

Did I oversleep? Why didn't anyone wake me? Willow's still beside me. The only two people missing from the tent are Gloria and Sasha. The dogs yip, refilled with energy. Is that what woke me?

The sun is too bright through the tent canvas. Shouldn't we have left by now? I crawl out, still warm enough to battle the change in temperature. Sasha and Gloria have another fire going and are heating the water for the dogs.

"Good morning." I hover over the fire, holding my hand and stump out, though they're not cold yet.

"Dobroya ootra." Sasha offers me a ladle of the hot water.

I'll assume that's *good morning* in Russian. I accept the ladle. It's not tea, but it's warm. Too warm. It scalds my tongue and I hiss in a breath. "When do we head out?"

"One hour." Gloria shakes a skillet over the fire, cooking shredded potatoes mixed with mushrooms. "Ten hours rest, ten hours sled. Warm snow easier on dog feet."

Elm drifts out of the tent, his long hair even more wild than usual. He straightens his eye patch and rolls his shoulders. Gloria holds a fork out to him. He shakes his head and walks away toward the Wall. Bathroom break, I guess. That reminds me of my own needs. There are no tall trees, but the shadow of the Wall provides cover if I walk far enough. I want to get it over with before Solomon wakes up.

The sisters have no toilet paper, just one cloth per person. Delightful.

I wait until Elm returns, then I go on a *long* walk until I'm content with my distance. It's hard enough relieving myself when I feel rushed, let alone leaning against a towering icy Wall and trying to stay warm.

I remind myself I've done this hundreds of times when traveling with Jude and Willow in the forest. But that was a forest. Trees. Privacy. I'm out of practice.

Once finished, I hurry back to the camp as Solomon, Elm, and Sasha finish breaking down the tent. Gloria hands me a fork and I dig into the fried potatoes. Willow plops beside me with only a slit for sight between her hat and scarf. We share the potatoes. The warmth and salt withdraw an, *"Mmmmm."* I'm half-surprised. I expected my stomach to turn after being forced to eat raw potatoes for almost three weeks when the Council shipped us off to Antarctica.

Amazing what a little oil, salt, and mushrooms will do. I'm cured.

"I get to drive today," Willow says between mouthfuls.

"I'll race you, then."

She smiles and passes me the fork. I take a deep breath and speak words that maybe I shouldn't. "It's good to see you smile again."

Her smile disappears. I shouldn't have spoken. "The Council man burned us if we smiled."

I choke on a mushroom. "What? Why? Which one?"

"Brickbat-man. He said I needed to be serious. For testing. He burned other kids if I smiled too much."

"Oh, Willow." I reach for her, but she moves her arm away. I swallow hard. "What . . . what testing did he do on you?"

She tugs the scarf higher and turns her head away. "Lots of needles with icky liquids. They made me sick. He did this to orphan friends. Some died." She tucks her arms tight against her body.

She's not telling me everything.

"Time to leave." Sasha takes our empty plate and I barely swallow the last bite past the sickened feeling in my stomach. Willow hops up and heads toward her sled. No parting words. No conclusion.

No more smile.

I try to focus on sledding and think about Willow's *future* instead of her past. She's excited to sled. I will be excited with her. The dogs are just as enthusiastic as yesterday, only this time no one falls off the back when we leave. Solomon drives first—he has an advantage with his two hands. I don't mind. I'm keeping busy digesting my potatoes. It's hard work.

This day drags on longer than yesterday. I still enjoy the float over the snow, but the enchantment is weighted by increased cold. Maybe it's because we're heading north, or it's simply a colder day than yesterday, but I prefer staying bundled under the furs instead of driving. I throw snowballs at Willow and manage to get a laugh out of her. This makes Elm grin and he finally graces me with the smile, like he's forgiven me.

Maybe.

I take a nap at some point. We stop midday for more potatoes. At nighttime, I'm the last to crawl into the tent. I take a few minutes by myself out under the stars. The dogs don't bark at me anymore—they're too tired. I finally rub Gumbo's head, and he pants so happily I gag on his dog-breath.

The silence is beautiful, and the stars sweep all around me, stopping only when my gaze encounters the Wall. What an expanse. What glory, those small glitters of light are.

God . . . You are so vast.

Amazing that, amidst such beauty, He would decide to even *look* at me, let alone call me to join Him in a quest for shalom. This journey will not fail. It cannot fail when He is the leader.

Beneath His vastness I suddenly want to be . . . *more.* I want to be better for Him. I want to fight harder to control the dark spirals of my thoughts and to pray harder daily. I've come so far with Him . . . and yet I still remain so far from what I could be.

Day three, the dogs are showing wear. We stop more frequently for them to eat snow or relieve themselves, or simply take an extra breather before going up a hill. I've never been an animal person, but even I find myself stepping off the back of the sled to rub behind the ears of each dog. Especially Gumbo.

"One night more." Sasha lifts the brake off her sled and shouts over her shoulder as the dogs take off, "Ve get there tomorrow!"

Tomorrow. Tomorrow. One more night in the fur-covered tent.

Solomon drives again. He's more anxious than I to reach this town where his great-grandfather hid inventions and eventually died. I've never stopped to think what this might be like for him. Maybe because he hasn't shared much. When he revealed he was adopted, he seemed sensitive about not having the "Hawke gene" of invention. Does he wish Jude were here?

Jude would know what to do and what to look for the moment we step inside Erfinder's house. But Solomon is observant. He'll find whatever we need.

By noon, the snow gets slushy. I grow warm in the sled, but I leave my layers on. We seem to move constantly uphill. The sisters get out and push their sled along sometimes, to help the dogs. The sun has passed over the Wall onto our side, beating down upon us and the canines. They pant, chomp up snow, and pull, their tongues hanging out.

Then we crest a hill and Sasha calls a halt.

"Whoa!" The dogs stop before Solomon's echo disappears.

We are at the top of the hill, looking down into a canyon. The Wall stretches to the floor of the canyon and at its base, filling the valley like pebbles in a riverbed, are houses. Not the cement apartment buildings we saw at the end of the train line. These houses are settled together like a comfortable village, with pathways and roads winding between them. The town itself is bright and thriving. Even from here, I catch the movement of people walking the streets, going from colorful house to colorful house and store to store.

The houses rest right up against the base of the Wall, almost as if it didn't exist. I squint with my head cocked to one side. There's a small space near one section of Wall—like a town square with booths here and there and no houses. But that's not what catches my attention.

I jerk forward in the sled as though the extra six inches will allow me to see clearer. There's Opening One—a huge thick arch at the base of the Wall, four times the width and height of Opening Three in Missouri.

But there's no door.

The Opening is . . . *open.* Masses of people walk in and out as though it's no big deal that they're completely defying the entire reason the Wall was built in the first place.

18

Solomon and I stand before Opening One, staring deep into the long stone tunnel. It's not dark. It's not rough. It doesn't look like a walk of death. Torches in brackets are spaced every twenty feet, their light bouncing off the stone. The carved tunnel seems to have been expanded from an original, smaller opening. The inside is laid with cobblestone flooring and giant, square stones on all the walls and ceiling.

Every footstep and laugh echoes.

"Should we . . . go through?" I instinctively take Solomon's hand. *Why* is it open? What's on the other side? Does the USE Council know about this?

Something in Russian is engraved in the arch stone, curving up one side and then over to the other. I'll have to ask Gloria or Sasha to read it in English.

"We can go home." Willow's voice is a gentle chime from behind me. I turn to smile at her.

Elm squeezes one strong arm around her shoulder. "It's far from home."

"But it is still on home side."

I hear her plea, her longing. We could cross and rejoin Mother, Father, Ash, Black, and everyone else in Ivanhoe or the albino forest. But what would that look like? I've seen how huge *this* side of the world is. To reach Ivanhoe, we'd have to traverse half a globe of mystery.

Frankly, I'm tired of adventure.

"Let's find the great-grandfather's house." Elm turns from the Wall.

I can't. I have to know why it's open. This mystery defies everything I've come to know.

"No." Solomon places a hand on Elm's shoulder, gently enough to ask him to stop, but firm enough to take charge. "Let's go through here first. See what's on the other side."

Elm's eyebrows lower, catching on his eye patch in a frown.

"Please, Elm?" We don't need his okay. He doesn't know where to find Erfinder Hawke's house anyway. He *has* to follow Solomon, but I want us to remain a team. I know Solomon wants that, too.

Elm gives a curt nod and Willow takes his hand, the follower again. I miss the fierce, leading Willow, but maybe it's good she's not a leader while her fury burns against the Council. Elm looks down at their entwined gloved hands and lifts hers against his chest.

Hand-in-hand, Solomon and I walk toward the Opening. Each footstep accelerates my heartbeat. The reaction is unfounded. Then again, I haven't exactly had a normal trip through the Wall yet. Is that why I'm nervous? Because this seems so . . . normal? Like your everyday tunnel that just happens to be placed midway through a valley town.

It's a contradiction of itself. A Wall meant for separation, yet an open and *decorated* pathway through it. We enter the tunnel. The last time I stood inside the Wall, it exploded around me and buried me.

"It's okay," Solomon whispers.

I'd clenched his hand without knowing it. "I know." I'm fine. I am. My body's the one freaking out. There are no guards. No Enforcers. As we walk through the tunnel, the heat of each torch presses a kiss against my cheek. The flow of people sweeps us through on the right-hand side, while others return on the left.

Paper advertisement posters hang between some of the torch brackets with pictures of shapkas, nesting dolls, and ornaments with paintings of this valley town on it.

Then we're out. We're on the other side, stepping into an extension of the town square that's cloaked in shadow from the Wall. The other half of the square stretches out on this side, free of ice and snow. It's almost identical to the town we just walked through. There are a couple of tourist booths, but the rest of the stores sell food, groceries, furs, etc. I don't know what I expected. Something like Ivanhoe, maybe? Something that portrayed the differentness on the other side of the Wall?

This just looks like a town built around an annoying obstruction. It's a secret treasure for committed adventurers to discover.

"The Council can't possibly know about this." Solomon picks up a nesting doll from one of the booths and turns it to see the detail. Then he sets it back down.

"You're probably right. After all, it's not exactly easy to get to." Elm leans back toward the opening. "Now we find your ancestor's house." Is he affected by this at all?

We walk back through the Wall, my head and heart still reeling. On the other side, we meet Sasha and Gloria browsing the goods in the market. Solomon approaches them and Gloria brightens at his presence. How could she not?

I'm surprised that I'm not more jealous. Solomon cares for *me*. That knowledge creates both a comfort and an ache. I ache because I know I don't treat him as well as he treats me.

But I'm working on it.

"Here is the rest of the specie." Solomon holds his chip out and deposits it into Gloria's little wrist scan. "Will you stay here?"

"Ve stay two days." Sasha buys a tasseled scarf wrap from one of the vendors. "Sell furs. No good hunting here. You want come back vis us?"

If they leave without us, we won't have a ride home. We'll be stranded. How long will it take us to find the information hidden in Erfinder's house? I look to Solomon.

"Come find us before you leave."

"Where vill you be?"

"I'll show you." With that, he leads the way through the mystery town, somehow knowing exactly where to go.

We head north out of the square, passing a small restaurant. Now's not the time to grab Solomon's sleeve and give a tug. It's not the time to whisper in his ear, "Are you hungry?" It's not the time to stop for food, but he does . . . for me.

"Let's all grab a bite before we continue." He allows Gloria and Sasha to step up to the ordering window first. "My treat."

I go off of the pictures. There are the meat dumplings the sisters made for us when we were at their house. I point, and Sasha orders it for me. It comes out in a Styrofoam container with a plastic lid and a spoon. There's a tiny container of sour cream.

Walking and eating is hard enough for a two-handed person. I almost spill my pelmeni, so Solomon takes it from me. "We're almost there anyway."

The road between houses is narrow and lumpy from ice. Sasha and Gloria have no problem keeping their balance. We pass two women chatting on a corner, who wear short skirts, stockings, and high heels. How are their ankles still intact?

"Here we are . . . I think." Solomon approaches a cottage-like house on the street and brushes snow off a number *12* on a wooden post.

Shutters are closed over the window. The house is small—about the same size as my Unity home used to be. Blue-painted wood slats cover the outside of the house, interrupted by carved, grey gables and window frames. It's stunningly classic. Straight out of a fairytale. But that's how all the houses are in this town.

Father would love to inspect the woodwork.

Solomon stands on the doorstep, looking at the door, looking at me, then he raises his hand and knocks. Willow giggles and I join her. It seems silly to be knocking on the door of a house that appears abandoned.

No one answers. No surprise. I just want to get inside so I can sit and eat my pelmeni. *Then* we'll set out to discover the secret behind the projected Wall.

My stomach growls.

Solomon rests his hand on the latch. "I guess we can just . . . go in then." He presses down his thumb and pushes. The door doesn't budge. "Locked."

It's too pretty to break down.

He steps to one of the windows, cups his hands, and presses an eye to the crack between the shutters. "I'll go around the back and see if there's another way in."

I want to go with, but I won't be of much help. "I'll take the pelmeni. Free up your hands." I hold out mine, and he places the styrofoam container into it. It's still hot and I hold it close to my chest.

Solomon walks around the back, leaving behind the sound of him crunching snow. Gloria takes a few steps after him and peers around the corner of the house. She shrugs to Sasha. A grunt echoes over the house, carried by the wind to our ears, then the crunch of wood.

"Solomon?" I join Gloria by the corner of the house.

There's a scuffle at the front door and I startle. Then, with a scrape of wood on floor, the door opens. Solomon stands at the threshold with dust in his hair and a grim smile. "Well, I'm in."

I step into the darkness and trip over something lying on the floor. "Watch your step." I hold an arm back to keep Willow from falling, but Elm is already kicking aside whatever was on the ground.

"We vill come find you." Sasha nods once from the doorway, then she and Gloria leave.

The open door allows a beam of light to fall across the interior of the small one-room house. The floors are made of a mixture of wood and brown tile. It's a giant square, with one door on the left wall, which leads, I assume, into a bathroom of sorts. To the right is a small fireplace, in front of which is a wooden rocker.

Across from us, a back door hangs open—Solomon's doing—revealing an old stained porcelain sink with exposed pipes and a wood-burning stove. Card tables decorate the rest of the room, teetering under stacks of papers. A bed to the left sits between the bathroom door and the sink, but a layer of dust hangs over the wrinkled mouse-nibbled blanket.

"Matches, matches, who's got the matches?" Solomon reaches toward my shoulder pack and pulls out the small box of matches.

It doesn't take long to find an old oil lamp squished between books, papers, and random wiring on the center table. There's oil in the bottom and Solomon lights the wick. It gives a belch of smoke and the smell singes my nose hairs, but then there's sufficient light.

"Are you sure your great-grandfather was an inventor?" Elm voices the same question running through my own mind. Where are the electric lights? The gadgets? The booby traps for protection? I pictured us finding a house similar to Christian's, surrounded by projected walls, with passwords at every door. And maybe an underground tunnel. I won't rule out that last one just yet.

"Yes." Solomon's voice is low. Quiet. Disappointed.

I lay a hand on his arm. "It's okay. Let's start by looking around and go from there." But my heart sinks. This doesn't look like a place with answers.

God?

Solomon carries the oil lantern around. The windows are made of thick firm plastic. I open a couple and unlatch the shutters. They release a loud creak that sounds like a screech in this tiny space, but it lets in the light that we need. Dust hangs in the air, crawling into our lungs no matter now thin I purse my lips.

Solomon stands forlorn in the middle of the room, holding the oil lamp aloft, though it's not needed anymore. "Where do we start?"

Looking at the piles and the spilled messes, the loose wires and odd metal gadgets, I don't even *want* to start.

Willow steps forward. "Hawke-man, you start on that table." She points to the corner table by the fireplace. "Look at the papers." She turns to me. "Parvin, you will look at the papers on the floor." Near the window, the piles flutter against the winter breeze. "Elm and me will look at the inventions. We don't read as well as you."

Always thinking. A leader at heart. She and Elm get right to work. I clear a space for the pelmeni on the table, take a few bites, and then join the search. The hot chicken broth and dumplings warm my core.

"We won't be able to stay here long." Solomon lifts the first paper off the heap and a film of soot and dust flows off onto his boots.

"Why not?" I crouch by the stacks beneath the window.

"We'll get frozen out." He sighs and lets the paper drift to the floor. "I don't know what I expected—a decent dwelling where we could sleep, maybe even cook, and plan our next course of action. I was too . . . optimistic. I don't even know where to start."

"Just start with those papers." I try to be commanding, assured like Willow, but it comes out cheap. "We'll work for an hour and then reassess."

An hour of looking through papers of scribbles. The first one I pick up is random. Numbers, letters, lines . . . math. That's worse than fish.

No notes. No explanation, just math scribbles. I go to the next and it's a circular chart with graphs and markings, one corner missing. Not even connected. The stacks are random.

Random.

Random. Mess.

I spread a stack of papers out in front of me. More math, more charts, then finally I find some writing. Real writing. I lift it close to my face. It's in cursive so tight I can barely make out the letters except for the *j*, *y*, *g*, and *t*—the ones that are long and tall enough to stand out amidst the others. The ink has bled and some is washed out. I set it aside. New plan—separate the numbers from the words.

Solomon lights a fire in the hearth. More smoke than heat comes out, but we air it out with an open window. Soon the dirty house warms enough for us to still use our fingers.

I make it through one full stack before the headache hits. So many numbers. I don't know what's important, what's trash. The stack of papers with written words is small—the only encouragement I have after going through a pile of papers.

Another hour passes and the pelmeni's gone, the papers are less dusty, and my stump is numb. Solomon rubs his temples and glances back and forth between piles. I can't bear to tell him we should stop and maybe plan out where to stay for the night.

I rise from the ground and my knees pop from stiffness. I bring my pile of word-papers over to him. "Here, let me take over the search. You see if you can read any of this, because I can't make it out. Why don't you sit in the rocker?"

He doesn't argue. He takes the stack and plops into the rocker, moving back and forth with a squeak on every backward rock.

The stack of papers he was going through is even more intimidating than mine. Drawings of odd objects make me want to study and figure out what they are. Charts look like puzzles but with scribbled notes on the side.

We don't stop for hours. I even search the soot that escaped the hearth. It's the most exciting search of the day. Every so often Willow's hushed voice asks Elm, "What's this?" and he responds with, "Not what we want." I can't imagine what *their* sifting looks like. Willow only barely learned to read and even *I* can't read Erfinder's writing.

Any one of us could pass over the crucial piece of information that we need and not have a clue that we missed it. And once it's missed, once it's been put into the discard pile, there's no finding it again. Panic claws its way through my sternum—a desperate animal out of control.

God please. Let us find what we need! Please!

Another hour passes. It's getting too cold and too dark. The single oil lamp isn't doing anything. I've gone through all the papers on the desk near the fireplace. We've covered only a tenth of the information and paper piles.

Solomon still reads the pages I handed him. "Any luck?"

He shakes his head. "I can barely read it, let alone find a clue."

I walk over to look over his shoulder, as if I'll have a new ability to understand the scribbles. Was Jude's handwriting this bad? Solomon's sure isn—

A gunshot slams against my eardrums. Willow screams. I spin on my heels, but before I can see what shot at us, Solomon's out of the rocker and sweeping me behind him. I slam against the wall and my vision blurs.

"Who are you?" Solomon has his hands raised in the air. I peek over his shoulder to see a bearded man in the doorway, a shotgun aimed at us. A spray of holes lets sunset light in through the ceiling.

"Who are *you*, I might ask?" The man's voice is rough as a tree saw.

"I'm Solomon, this"—he jerks his head toward me for a

moment and in the split second I hear his pause—"is Brielle. Over there are Sasha and Gloria."

I look to where he's pointing and it's at Elm. Okay, I understand code names, but Sasha and Gloria? Those are *girl* names! Though maybe Sasha could be a boy's name.

"What are you doing?" The bearded man punches the air with the shotgun barrel and Solomon flinches back against me.

Don't shoot. Don't shoot. I squeeze my eyes tight against the memory of the assassin shooting Jude. That's when I realize how guilty we look. I also realize . . . he's speaking perfect English. No accent. I open my eyes again. Willow's caught with a metal gadget in each mitten. I'm surrounded by scattered papers.

Solomon pushes his shoulders back. "We have every right to be here. This house belongs to my family. I'd like to know who you are."

"So . . . you're a liar." The man looks up from the shotgun and narrows both eyes at Solomon. "This is my house, and I've got the papers to prove it."

"Did you buy it from Erfinder Hawke?" Solomon asks.

The man quirks an eyebrow. "I *am* Erfinder Hawke."

19

Solomon's knees buckle slightly, and I press a hand to his back. "That's impossible . . . you're dead."

"Smarty-pants, eh?" The man claiming to be Erfinder must realize that we're not going to harm him. He lowers the shotgun so it's propped on his hip and aimed at the floor. "Tell me, boy, what are you really doing here?"

I step out from behind Solomon. "Explain yourself. How can you possibly be Erfinder Hawke? Are you saying you're the same man who invented the projected wall?"

"Ah, you've heard of me, huh?" He drops the shotgun so the butt is on the floor and he leans it against the wall. "Who are you kids?"

"My name is Parvin Brielle Blackwater." That should clear things up.

"Nice name."

I frown. "Have you . . . heard of me?"

He raises one of his wild eyebrows. "Should I have? I don't keep up on much outside of what's going on in this town. That's how I like to keep things." He surveys me. "Hm . . . not pretty enough to be a famous actress."

Ignoring the jibe, I hold out my hand toward Solomon. "This is . . ." Should I say it? For some reason, my gut tells me that Solomon needs to be the one to say it.

Solomon lets out a heavy sigh. "Please tell me how you could possibly be Erfinder."

"Why's it important to you?"

Solomon rests a hand on the back of the rocker, but it sways toward him, so he drops his hand to his side. "Because I'm Solomon Hawke, the son of Christian Hawke. I'm your"—he swallows— "great-grandson." Lighter than a whisper, he adds, "Sort of."

"How can you be my *sort-of* great-grandson? I might be old, but I've still got great hearing." The old man folds his left ear in half—the same habit Jude had, which tells me there's a tune chip in his head.

"You haven't explained how you're alive." I'm not sure I believe this guy. He could be anyone. He could have known this house belonged to Erfinder and then claimed it for himself. But if this tiny house was so important, why is it decrepit and covered in dust? It doesn't make sense—there's nothing here to guard with a shotgun.

"Well, you seem to know who I am, so I figured you'd know I'm an inventor." He grabs a box of matches and lights another oil lamp that we didn't see in the back and darkest corner. "I've still got tricks up my sleeve that will keep me kickin', hearing, and spry for another five good years."

He levels his gaze at Solomon. "So, *sort-of* great-grandson. Explain."

As though a plug is pulled, Solomon gushes out words. "We came here from the USE to see if Opa Fin—you, I guess—left any explanations of your projected Wall invention behind. And the reason I'm *sort-of* your great-grandson is because I'm . . . adopted. Christian Hawke adopted me when I was a kid." His eyes drop to the ground.

"Well, there's no *sort-of* about that, in my book." Erfinder reminds me of Christian—not allowing any fluff behind understanding. "You're not a Hawke."

Never mind. He's nothing like Christian.

Solomon's jaw clenches, and I whip out my verbal boxing gloves.

But Elm stomps forward. "So what are we going to do? I'm Elm and I am strong. Why are you threatening us? You should help us instead."

Erfinder surveys Elm up and down, sending an intimidating appraisal. It doesn't bend Elm one bit. If anything, Elm grows taller, and I'm pretty sure I see him flex.

"Well, this isn't the best place to talk, wouldn't you agree?" Erfinder looks around at the dusty air, wrinkles his nose at the messed piles of paper, and shuts one of the windows. "Let's go to the house I *live* in. This is storage."

We probably shouldn't follow him, but there's something in his voice—a similarity to Jude and Christian. Inflections here and there, an excitement that pops mildly beneath any mention of inventions.

We look to Solomon and he gives a nod. When Erfinder turns around, I sneak a folded piece of his scribble papers into the pocket of my fur coat. It takes true skill to write so horribly, and I plan to put Erfinder's hand to the test. That will ensure he's the man he says he is.

Erfinder hauls a fresh box of papers and gadgets into the house. Then he watches us close the shutters. It's a bit awkward, seeing how messy we left it. "Broke the back door, I see." He locks the front.

"It was necessary." Solomon stands close to Erfinder. Intimidation. It doesn't work, but Solomon seems stronger from the attempt. "Lead on."

I admire him for the strength he shows right now.

"Learn to be a follower, Solomon. It makes you a better leader." Erfinder heads up the dark street. He has no right to tell Solomon anything! This old man has *no* idea what we've gone through to come here, or what rides on us finding the answer. I give my *own* appraisal of the shotgun-wielding great-grandfather and reach my conclusion instantaneously.

Erfinder is a jerk.

Flickering street lamps have been lit with tall candles on the inside. No one is out on the streets anymore, but the city still feels warm-hearted. He leads us to the opposite side of town, where we encounter the same lovely carved houses, only they seem newer. The paint isn't peeling yet and none of the carvings are cracked. He leads us to the biggest house on the street. This is a bit more what I would have expected to find upon entering the famous Erfinder Hawke's neighborhood.

The shutters are a mixture of metal and wood, and there are modern bubbles on the outside of the gables that look like cameras. When Erfinder walks up to the door, he types a code into a panel on the inner frame. A zap in the air changes. He types in another code. Another current runs through my hair. A third code, and then he opens the main door.

We enter a very modern house quite the opposite of the one we just left. The entry is large, with polished wooden floors. Erfinder takes off his boots and the rest of us follow suit, though I feel that in taking them off it makes it harder to flee if needed.

We walk past an entry table. Many of the walls have mirrors, making the house look bigger than it is. The light in the house is more of a glow, and I can't place where it's coming from.

Everything in the living room is wood and leather. Leather couches, wooden coffee table. Leather ottoman, wooden coat rack. Leather and wood, leather and wood, the epitome of a male dwelling, though it's much cleaner than Reid ever kept the room above Father's woodshop. Elm and Willow appraise the décor with narrowed eyes.

"Tea? Coffee?" Erfinder sinks into a leather armchair.

Coffee. It's been forever—about time coffee and I had a reunion.

But before I can say, "Yes, please," Solomon responds. "Not until you explain how you are Erfinder Hawke."

I suppose safety, survival, and information are important, too.

"I don't see how this is so hard for you, boy. I'm an inventor. I've optimized my life and health with a mixture of tech and science. So here I am. I'd say I have about six years left."

Last time, he said five.

"Hawke-man, this is perfect!" Willow bounces on her tiptoes. "We couldn't find answers, but now we have the man." She turns to Erfinder. "How can we turn off the projected Wall forever?"

He reels back. "Turn it off?"

Well, that's one way to get to the point. "That's why we're here. Have you been keeping up on the news at all?" I don't assume so, since he doesn't even know who I am.

"I hate news."

"Clearly you hate family, too." Solomon's arms are tight at his side. "People—my family and *your* family—have been dying because of the projected Wall invention. The Council is taking over the USE, forcing people to obey their will. And you're . . . what?" He throws his arms in the air. "Sitting here and living out the rest of your life? What's the point?"

Erfinder doesn't react to Solomon's accusations. I don't like his passivity. Is Solomon right? That he doesn't care about his family or the death of people?

"I'm here for the sake of inventions. That's always the answer." He leans forward in his chair and tosses a few logs into the fireplace. "My *blood* great-grandson would understand that."

Solomon stiffens. "He did. His name was Jude and he obsessed over you. He studied your inventions and wanted to be like you. If he'd known you were alive—"

"Then I would have had a kid interrupting my work and

thinking space. Why do you think I moved to the middle of nowhere, that still has tech, knowledge, and peace? Don't get all soft on me, boy. I have no regrets."

Before Erfinder and Solomon get too deep into it, I lay a hand on Solomon's arm. "Maybe we should focus on the projected Wall for now."

"I'm not giving up my invention." Erfinder pops his neck.

I realize how well I've come to know Solomon's habits and personality because, though he remains calm, the forward tension in his shoulders and the brief pulse in his neck tell me he's growing angry. "If this is about pride . . ."

"It's about the fact that you're four strangers who *claim* to be related to me and now want the invention that will change the world if you start fiddling with it."

Elm doesn't remain calm. "You are *filth!* My people try to save your people and they are *dying—*"

Erfinder raises an eyebrow. "Who are you calling 'my people'? Inhabitants of the USE? I haven't lived there for years. But if those are your people, then your Council has all the info you need. Why don't you ask *them?*"

"Because they're the enemy," Elm snaps.

Willow stands beside him with her arms folded and red spots brightening her cheeks. Her voice quavers in a mixture of anger and emotion. "You are making people die!"

"I don't argue with children."

Willow looks to me and, in a blink, a tear escapes her eye. I'm the only one who can do this. Solomon's too emotionally involved. Elm is too fiery. And Willow's been written off as a child. I'm reminded of the leader I had to be in Antarctica—and I see I've become lazy. I become a lazy leader when Solomon is around, because I'm confused about how to be part of a team.

It's time for that to stop.

"I have an idea." I rest my elbows on my knees and try to look at Erfinder with compassion, though my heart is sneering at him. "I'd like to speak with you alone, please."

Out of the corner of my eye I catch Solomon opening his mouth, so I surge forward. "Just for a few minutes. I think it will be best for all of us."

"I don't think you should be with him alone," Solomon mutters.

"I won't be alone." I'm not afraid of being with Erfinder. I've been in an empty hut with Brickbat, I've been in an empty coffee shop with Skelley, I've been in a wild forest with the assassin who killed Jude. Erfinder's no threat. God's with me. I'm never alone, and there's nothing these men can do that He won't see.

"Fix him, Parvin." Willow sniffs hard. "Fix his thinking."

Erfinder raises a finger. "If this is an attempt—"

"It's nothing more than a conversation." I step forward. "Now, where can we go for some privacy?"

He lifts a nostril as if I smell of spoiled fish. "Follow me."

We walk through a swinging door, past a spotless porcelain-and-metal kitchen, down a hall, and then through a dark wooden door. We're in an office of sorts. Cabinets with labels line the walls, and books fill floor-to-ceiling shelves on the farthest wall. In front of the shelves is a long desk with a black leather chair. Erfinder sits here.

I take a seat in the upright chair on the other side of the desk. It feels strangely like a Mentor meeting.

"So, what do you have to say to me?"

There's a thin stack of fresh, smooth white paper on his desk and a sleek pen that looks inlaid with gold. "I was actually wondering if you'd write something for me." I gesture to the paper.

"Why would I do that?" He picks up the pen anyway and unscrews the cap. The tip of the pen is a nib, like a dipping pen, only there's no ink to dip it in.

"Because I need to know you're not lying." I gesture to the paper. "Write, *My name is Erfinder Hawke and I am an inventor.*"

He balances the pen in his left hand and scribbles out the sentence as though writing lines as punishment in school. Then he slides the paper over to me. I unfold the paper from my pocket and compare them.

It's the same scribble. The same smooshed consonants and sweeping *y*s. "So you *are* Erfinder Hawke."

"No one but you four said I wasn't."

I rest my forearms on the desk, trying not to shy away from revealing my stump. "My name is Parvin Blackwater and—even though you don't keep up with the news—I want to share my story with you, if you'll take the time to listen."

"Go ahead."

It's been a while since I went back through the whole thing. Where to start? With the new Clock invention? No. I need to go further back than that—somewhere that's personal. "Just under a year ago, I met your great-grandson, Solomon, in Unity Village." I won't let him say Solomon isn't a Hawke. "He was an Enforcer at the time. Do you know what that is?"

"Yes. Go on."

I rush through the details, speaking quickly as though afraid he'll choose to stop listening. But he sits there, impassive, listening to everything and not breaking eye contact. The only time he looks away is when I tell about Jude's death.

It takes at least twenty minutes, and I'm out of breath by the end. Call it nerves or the fact that I spoke too fast. "So now the Council of the USE has replaced the stone Wall with a projection, and that's not something explosives can break through." I lean forward and take his hand. "Opa Fin, we need you."

"The control center to my projection is in the Council center in the USE. I lived there when I created it. Only the Council technician—whom I trained—and I can change it."

That's both good and bad. Good because there's only one other person in the USE who knows how to turn that projected Wall *on*. Bad . . . because there's no way that person—still unknown to me—would possibly divulge that information to us.

"Who is the technician?"

Erfinder laughs. "I've no interest in telling you."

"What *are* your interests? Long life?"

"Legacy, girl. Legacy. Inventions last longer than humans. Why would I let you destroy one of my greatest?"

"Because saving lives can be a legacy, too."

He shrugs.

My pride flares, but I swallow it down. Control. Control. I *must* control my inner flares. "Then what *will* you do? We need your help."

"I'll tell you what I'll do." He stands from the desk. "But I'll tell you in front of the others." He opens the office door for me, and we walk back into the sitting room.

What's it going to be? His lack of emotion sends little assurance.

Solomon, Elm, and Willow look up when we enter. "Did you make him nicer?"

"Niceness is a wasted quality." He stands, regal, in front of the fireplace. "Parvin's told me your story and, while it's certainly the adventure, it's only one side of the thing."

One side? He can't possibly think the Council has any right to do what they're doing. I sink onto the leather sofa next to Solomon. It's cold.

"I'm not going with you back to the USE. I'm too old, lazy, and plain don't want to. I stepped out of that world a long time ago. And I'm not telling you who else knows how to control the projection."

Solomon shakes his head. "I can't believe you're a Hawke."

"Listen, boy, everything you like about the Hawkes came from *me*. I'm the oldest generation of Hawkes still living. Keep that in mind."

"You're the meanest one." Willow raises her eyebrows.

"No matter. If you want to take down that projected Wall, then it's up to you find the answer. I'm not doing it for you."

"Will you teach us, then?" Solomon asks.

"Too much to teach. But I'll give you a clue: *gather your own knowledge.*" He walks to the wooden coat rack and shrugs into a jacket before planting a shapka on his head. "Now . . . I'm going out for a drink. You can stay here if you want."

He walks out before any of us can inform him how stupid and cryptic he's being.

The slam of the front door falls on our ears and Willow turns to Solomon. "You're my favorite Hawke."

"Thanks." He puts his head in his hands.

"How can he *possibly* be related to you and Jude and Christian?" I can't believe it.

"Some children and grandchildren grow to be like their parents. Others strive to be opposite. I think that's what happened with my dad and grandpa." He lifts his head. "What does he mean? Jude was the one good at riddles. He's doing this because he doesn't consider me a Hawke. He's testing me."

"No, he's just being dumb." I tell them about the technician in the USE. At least if all fails here in Russia, we can try and track down this person. "Let's start brainstorming. What's he mean by, *Gather your own knowledge?*" We've barely sifted through the house filled with papers and inventions. Does he expect us to go back and find whatever we missed? The idea of setting foot in that mess again twists my insides.

"It's like Jude's Testimony Log. The thrill of the search is why he does this. Dad did similar things if we wanted to learn something—he made us search and find it. Like a treasure hunt. Only this time, *lives* depend on it, and Opa Fin is being . . . careless. He doesn't see the big picture. It's a game to him."

I hate the doubt Erfinder is sowing into Solomon. He has no idea of all the amazing things Solomon's done! How can this man be related to Christian and Jude? He has none of their kindness, wit, or joy. Though my eyelids droop and my optimism lies like a weight against my neck, I slap my leg. "Well, games have their ends and his has a solution. Let's start playing."

"Do you know the meaning of his clue?" Elm glowers at me.

"It means we need to start looking for answers . . . again."

Willow groans. "Like in that old wood house?"

"Well, this is his main house. How about we start here?" It's different thinking about searching this house. Someone lives in it. I haven't seen any scattered inventions or corners of secrets. Where would we even begin?

"What if two of us return to the old house and the other two look here?" I don't want to split up, but I can't ignore the efficiency. "Willow and I can go to the storage house and Elm and Solomon stay here."

"No, I'll come with you, Parvin." Solomon pushes himself to his feet. "I don't want you girls going alone."

It's nighttime and I see the danger in our traveling alone, but no one in this city knows us. Willow's a fierce fighter. We'll be fine. "I don't think it's a good idea to leave Elm and Willow here alone. This place is part of your heritage, your story. I think you should be here."

"Okay then." He concedes so easily. Where has his joy gone?

"You'll find it, Solomon. I know you'll find whatever it is Erfinder wants you to find. You are a Hawke."

His lips purse to one side. "I'm not sure what that means anymore."

"You're the one who will give that name even more meaning. Remember that." I slip on the rabbit fur gloves, using my teeth to get it over my right hand. "Ready, Willow?"

"Ready."

We head out into the night, me sending up a prayer with every footfall. *God, please let Solomon find the answer. Let him find what we need in order to save Your people.*

"I don't think this will work, Parvin. We need a new plan."

"This will work." It's like finding a needle in a hayfield . . . that's been buried in a snowstorm.

But when we reach the old house my thoughts reiterate what she said. This isn't going to work. We get in with a little tugging on the broken back door. Willow lights the oil lamps, and we return to the despondent state we were in before Erfinder shot holes in the ceiling.

"What did he mean, to gather our own knowledge?" Willow lifts a clockwork gadget to the light.

I shrug. "Find something that's informative? A dictionary maybe?" My eyes stray to the stacks of papers. Ugh. Whatever scribbles are there could teach me a lot if I could read them.

The night drags on and my eyes grow heavy. I give up reading any of the documents and decide to carry them back to the house for Solomon to look over. Willow sits on a rickety stool, her elbow up on the table and her cheek pushed up by her palm, wrinkling her nose at the tickle of her rabbit fur gloves.

She sifts through other small inventions.

"How are you doing?"

She startles and knocks over an old soup can with her elbow. Little marble-like things scatter across the floor. "Oops." In her haste to retrieve the marbles, her glove snags on the corner of one of the inventions. It tears and falls to the ground.

The skin on her exposed hand catches my eye. It's not albino white anymore. It's a dark tan that looks so odd against her pale skin that I can't help but stare. Willow shoves her hand under her armpit, but I already saw. "Is that . . . Willow, what's going on?"

She sighs, like an aged woman might do when she has to deliver deep news, and reveals her hand. "Brickbat said I needed to be fixed. He made them poison me."

"Them?"

"Doctor people." Her voice turns so soft, I barely catch what she says next. "I'm not . . . albino anymore."

"What?" I sputter. "That's ridiculous! Of course you are!"

She shakes her head and lifts her sleeve. The tan color spreads up her arm, still smooth and perfect skin. Then she pulls down the neck of her turtleneck and I see the darkness splayed on her neck, touching her chin. "It goes further every day."

Her definition of *poison* isn't the same as mine. I'm glad she's not *dying*. "It doesn't matter, Willow. It doesn't matter what color you are, or were, or will be. God made you the way He likes you. *That's* who you are. Don't let Brickbat take it from you."

I realize this is the same struggle Solomon is having—debating whether or not he's a Hawke. But labels, names, or skin color don't matter . . . we're children of Christ. Maybe that's what God means every time He tells us to rise up. To rise above the small things, the small struggles that chip away our identity and leave us lost.

"I can't touch any of my people, Parvin! He put a disease in me! It will turn them brown, too! He said so!" She backs against the wall, her arms tight against her chest. "Brickbat said it's a cure for my pigment, but I don't want it. I never felt broken until *now*."

I go to her. "You're *not* broken, Willow. Your color doesn't change who you are, like my missing hand doesn't change or define who I am, or Elm's missing eye, or Solomon's face scars."

She sniffs. "But I can't touch Elm or he'll turn brown too."

I shrug. "So what? Would you love him any less?" She shakes her head. "And does he care?" She shakes her head again. "So let's beat this. Don't let the Council win by breaking you. Rise above this, Willow."

"I will still kill them."

I let out a long sigh. "I don't think that's right. God doesn't want us to murder."

She pushes away. "We should keep working."

Did any of my words get through? I want her to believe that the color of her skin doesn't change how any of us view her, but maybe it feels like when I atoned with my hand—I felt robbed. It took me time to overcome the pain. I pray Willow moves past the things Brickbat did even sooner.

Willow kneels to pick up the marbles.

Now I know why she's so angry. She feels the Council destroyed who she is—*what* she is. Brickbat's a sick, twisted man, and maybe he only "poisoned" Willow to try and break her. Well . . . he succeeded.

I grab the tin and hold it out for Willow. "It doesn't matter, no one will notice the mess." Now that I'm closer, they resemble pills. "What are these?"

"Medicine, I think. There were some papers with drawings on them that looked like the little pills."

I take one from her and hold it above the oil lamp. The light reflects on the viscous orange liquid inside. A foreign, frightening urge tempts me to pop it in my mouth. I thrust it away. It could be anything. It could be *poison*.

"Willow I . . . I think we should maybe take these with us. I don't want to leave them around on the floor."

"Why not? We don't know what it is, Parvin. I don't like them." She continues grabbing them by the handful and thrusting them into the can. Some are different colors. Some are more solid. Some are liquid gel caps. Why would piles of these be sitting in a can?

I gasp. "These could be . . . caps!"

She pauses in her work. "Huh?"

"Um . . . um . . ." I snap my fingers, trying to remember the official word. "You know, caps! They're pills of knowledge. Idris said you swallow one and then you know everything about a certain subject. Solomon took one and knows millions of definitions. That's how they do school in the High Cities."

The possibilities are endless. These could teach me everything

I've ever wanted to know. I pick up another pill. I hold it to the light and squint for a closer look. It's a pleasant color, kind of teal like Solomon's eyes. What knowledge is in here? What will I learn if I slip it between my lips?

A tiny pale hand snatches it from me and plinks it back into the can. "No, Parvin. This isn't good for you. Let's take them to the Hawke."

"Of course." Why didn't I suggest that? "He'll know what to do with them." And it will be a breath of fresh air to return with . . . *something*.

Willow blows out the oil lamp and we step back into the dark cold. I lend her my other glove. I hold her hand so she doesn't fall as we walk. She's steady on her feet. I'm not. It's a good thing she's carrying the tin of caps. It's also a good thing she has a sense of direction in the dark, because I follow her lead to Erfinder's modern house.

I walk up the steps, but a shadowed movement catches my eye. I sweep Willow behind me so she's pressed against the door, then peer into the night. Nothing. The shadow isn't as dark when I'm looking straight into it. "Let's get inside."

"What was it?" Her voice is hushed as she turns the door handle.

I don't say a "trick of the light" because that seems too ominous, too ignorant. "I don't really think anything was there." That's not enough. The door opens and the entryway is dark, but a beam of thinned light squeezes under the door opposite us where the sitting room is. "Solomon?"

Furniture scrapes the floor. Footsteps. The door opens and light floods us.

"You're back." Solomon's eyes are sunken and his voice hoarse. Can a couple of hours of searching really do that to him? Why is this so exhausting?

"Can you come check outside? I . . . feel like something was in the shadows." I sound paranoid, but I don't care. It could be that Erfinder Hawke is slightly insane and has been watching us. Or Gloria and Sash—

I suck in a breath as Solomon steps out the door. "Gloria and Sasha! We have to find them and let them know we've changed our location. Otherwise they'll go to the old house for us. Do you think we'll be able to find them in this city?"

"Just listen for the bark of their sled dogs. No problem." Solomon steps outside and peers left and right. He doesn't mock my nerves or paranoia. Instead, he's alert. Protective. Thorough in his search. "I don't see anything."

I figured. "Thank you for checking."

We close the door and stand facing each other in the entry. Now that Solomon's ensured that it's safe—though I still don't *feel* safe—Willow heads into the next room to join Elm.

Solomon and I are alone. I almost forget why Willow and I returned. I look up into his tired eyes and he stares at mine, seeming to draw fresh life from them. Words string between us, as if we're speaking to each other through silence, but I know it's an illusion. As much as I'd like him to be reading my thoughts, he can't . . . just like I can't read his.

"How are you?" His hand drifts up to lay against my cheek. It's warm, unlike the chilly draft still hovering from our entrance.

He's been asking that a lot lately. I want to tell him I'm good. I want to *be* good. But I'm tired, discouraged, and trying not to be grouchy. "I'm doing okay."

He rests his forehead against mine and I'm brought back to the day, not so long ago, when we bid farewell and I walked to my death with the Council. "You mean the world to me, Parvin. I hope you feel safe with me."

"I do." I feel vulnerable, too, and it's a new feeling. A scary feeling. I lean back, breaking the connection but not abruptly.

"Willow and I found a can of caps in the old house. We don't know what they contain, but we thought we'd bring them to you.

"Caps?" His focus face returns. "Knowledge caps?" He heads toward the sitting room.

"I think that's what they are." I follow, speaking louder. "They're all different colors, but the same shape. I can't imagine why he'd have a can of random pills in that house, can you?"

We burst into the sitting room. The can rests on the coffee table and the room seems untouched from when I saw it last. "Where have you two been searching?"

"Everywhere, in everything. We started with the office. There wasn't anything there." Solomon stops at the table and picks up the can. He dumps a few pills into his hand. "These are knowledge caps all right. But none of them are labeled."

"That's 'cause I made 'em." Erfinder shouts from the entrance. He closes the door behind him. So *he* was the shadow. "Lock the door behind you when you come back in the house, would you?"

"We don't know the codes." I shouldn't snap—he hasn't really done anything wrong, but I don't like the fact that he drains Solomon's optimism so much.

"I meant the deadbolt." He tosses his hat onto the coat rack and ambles toward the seat he held before. He's hiding his age. Sure, he might have tech in his head that keeps him young, but I see the droop in his shoulder, the bend in his spine, the sag of his skin. He's tired. Six more years of life is an optimistic estimate.

He sways on his way to the chair. "Fin' anything?"

His words are slurring. Is he drunk? I've never seen a drunk man. Father would never allow himself to get drunk. I plop the tin of caps in front of him. "Yeah. We found these. What are they?"

He raises an eyebrow. "Whaddaya think they are?"

"Knowledge caps."

"Right. And what'd you found out about 'em?" His inebriation could be to our benefit.

"They're different colors. They're different." And I sound like a preschooler. "Can you tell us what they do?"

He rests his head against the back of the chair and closes his eyes. "One of those caps should be what you're looking for. A few others will benefit you."

"And what about the rest?" Solomon's on the edge of his toes, grasping for the answer, but trying to stay calm. Why won't Erfinder tell us?

"The rest?" Erfinder shrugs and then lets out a sick gruff laugh. "The rest will harm you . . . maybe even kill you. Can't remember. Sorry."

"You can't even remember your own inventions?" I want to take the tin of caps back and start inspecting them. How can we possibly tell the difference by only their color?

"Brilliance does that to you." He rubs his eyes and leans forward again. "Ever heard of an author who can't remember how many books he wrote? Let alone the names of the characters?"

"No. I haven't heard of someone like that." I wrote a book. One book. I remember every word of it. I regret most of them.

"So how do we find the right one?" Willow paws through the caps. I want to snatch her hand away, keep her from accidentally swallowing a dangerous one, but she's the one who snapped me out of my trance earlier. She's more aware of the danger than I am.

"Well, little girl, we're in Russia." Erfinder pours a handful of caps into his palm, then hands one to each of us. I get an orange one.

"Ever heard of Russian roulette?"

20

I drop my cap and it rolls away, across the floor, toward the fire. I'm frozen, but Elm still has his reflexes. He slams his foot on the ground to stop the cap, but accidentally crushes it. An explosion of liquid sprays the ground.

"Sorry." He doesn't sound sorry at all.

"Let's hope that wasn't the one you wanted." Erfinder chuckles while my stomach drops into an icy sea. What if it *was* the one we wanted? There it went. Crushed. Smashed by a boot sole.

FEAR NOT.

My entire body relaxes. *You're here!* He hasn't forgotten me. He hasn't gotten sick of me. His wonderful Words are in my heart and pop up when I need the perfect reminder.

ALWAYS.

"We're not doing this." Solomon sets his cap on the table.

Erfinder shrugs and spills a couple more caps. Elm learned his lesson and instead picks them up with his hand, returning them to the tin. "There's no other way to find out what's in each cap."

Elm's eyes narrow. "You're lying."

Erfinder bursts out in a laugh. Why doesn't God smite this man? "Perhaps. How about this? We do one round of caps. After each round, you get to ask me a question and I'll tell you the truth . . . if you're all still sane by the end of the round, that is."

"No." Solomon's voice grows firmer. "That's sick."

I speak softly. "I'm okay with it Solomon. I'll go first." I pick up a new cap, but Solomon hits it from my hand.

"No! This isn't right. There could be anything in these caps. They could give you false memories, or strip *away* your memories. They could change everything about us. Insert harmful thoughts." I've never heard such panic in his voice.

Erfinder leans back in his chair and watches us with what looks like amusement. He has nothing to lose. He's old. He doesn't care about family. He likes games. Risks. There was so much of this personality in Jude, it's scary. But at least Jude controlled it.

I study Solomon. This isn't about how *I* feel. We must be a team. "God is greater than these caps. He's greater than any man-made invention. He sent me—us—here to find a way to tear down that Wall. I think we should do this."

Solomon's glare produces a laser of fury so visible I expect Erfinder's head to bear scorch marks any moment. "He's making it seem like this is the only option." He grabs the tin and dumps the pills onto the coffee table, cupping his free hand to keep any from rolling off the edge. "If we agree to do this, we need to give it as much thought and deductive logic as possible."

Elm must catch on, because he plops himself on the ground at one end of the table. Willow and I stand still, watching.

Solomon sorts. Blue pill with blue pill. Yellow pill with yellow. Okay, I can take a hint. I kneel next to him and sort all the pills until each is in a pile of matching colors. Erfinder chuckles at our efforts. I don't say anything, even though I want to bark at him . . . or throw something. But he knows he has the upper hand and I don't want to spur him into changing his deal—making it so we can't use any deduction whatsoever.

Once all the pills are sorted, which takes very little time, Solomon studies them. Some oranges aren't the same shade. Same with the blues. He sorts those into separate piles. The largest pile is faded-parchment yellow, with six matching pills.

In the center of the table are five pills, tip to tip, forming a small flower. Black, white, silver, clear, and brown.

Around them are ten piles consisting of other colors.

"These are important." Elm points to the center pills. "We should start with them." He picks up the brown one.

Solomon puts a hand out to stop him. "Don't swallow it yet. You're right, these are important, but they're also probably the most dangerous. We need to think it through."

Erfinder releases a single laugh through his nose, then looks away as though he didn't make a sound.

I purse my lips. "If you know, why don't you tell us?"

He whips his head back around to face me. "I told you, I don't remember. But it's amusing to witness such child's logic."

Elm lurches to his feet. "I'm Autumn-fifteen."

I don't think that's what Erfinder meant. I jerk my chin at the old man. "Fine. You're ready for the roulette. Pick your first pill."

"Parvin . . ." Solomon takes the brown pill from Elm's hand and returns it to the middle of the table.

"I'm not being impulsive." I'm being impatient.

Erfinder leans forward and grabs an icy blue pill from a clump of six. "You're committed, then."

I lean my elbows on the table, knocking aside a little gathering of pink pills. "Do you promise that, no matter what, as long as we all take a pill, you will answer a question honestly when it comes back to you . . . every single time?" Sweat gathers at my temples as I stare him on.

He doesn't catch the seriousness of my question. "Yeah, yeah."

I slam a fist on the table and pills bounce onto the floor, scuttling across the boards, propelled by their fat little bodies. *"Promise?"*

"I said yes, girl."

And I don't trust you, creep. "Okay then. Go ahead."

He pops the light blue pill into his mouth and swallows without water. I clear my throat on his behalf, picturing the thing getting lodged halfway down. Maybe he'll choke. But then he can't give us answers.

Besides, he hasn't caught onto my plan yet.

His eyes roll back in his head for a moment. A hand creeps up to press against his temple. Does it hurt? I didn't imagine that. It doesn't matter. I can handle hurt.

His eyes clear and he looks at me with a grin. "Done."

"And?" Solomon leans forward.

He shrugs. "Find out for yourself."

All four of us spew outrage at the same time. "That's cheating!"

"You have to tell us!"

"You thorn."

"Why won't you share?"

His grin grows wider with each exclamation. "It's no fun that way."

I'm so angry I can barely see the pills in front of me. There goes my plan—he was supposed to tell us and then we could eliminate the whole pile. Fine. "He seems unharmed." I grab the same icy blue pill that he swallowed.

"Parvin, no!" But before Solomon can stop me, I've swallowed it. Someone has to go first. And this conniving *Opa* doesn't count.

At first, nothing happens. I feel the bulgy oval slide down my throat. I try not to gag. For the next pill, I want water. Then a rushing sound fills my ears. I squeeze my eyes tight. Dizziness slams me like a brick fist.

With a splash, words roll into my mind, zipping from one end of my brain to the other. I hear them, see them, feel their taste on my tongue. Words I've never heard. Sounds I've never heard. They spin, spooling on an empty brain bobbin. Faster. Faster.

It's too much.

Breath.

Thought.

Exhaustion.

Words.

Too . . . many . . . words—

"Parvin!" Solomon's voice shakes me harder than his hands. I groan and bat him away. He remains tender. I remain dizzy. Am I upright? Lying down? Curled in a ball?

I force my eyes open.

I'm normal, I'm sane, I'm . . . still sitting in my chair, facing the table of seemingly endless colored pills. Not only that, but . . ."*Ya poneemayo parooskie.*"

"What?"

Whoa. "*Ya poneemayo parooskie.* I understand Russian." I grow giddy. "I can speak Russian!" I think about the flooding feeling as the language gathered on a spool. I imagine my brain's surface covered in endless sewing bobbins, all of which are empty. Waiting to be filled.

My gaze lands on the pills. Oh my, do I want another one.

Erfinder's eyes are bright as he looks at me. "How was it?"

I connect to the question. "It was amazing." Is this why he's having us do this? To introduce us to the awe of knowledge caps? "Is that what was in your cap?"

He nods. "But I already know Russian, so it didn't affect me much."

"The first cap is always hard." Solomon swipes up the blue pills and plops them into the can. "Now we can eliminate these."

"No!" I try to take the can from him, but he holds tight. Is he afraid I might go crazy and swallow them all? Why is he being so . . . possessive? I lean forward and whisper in his ear, though the room is so silent I'm sure anyone can hear. "You three take this pill, too. Then none of us are harmed and he'll have to answer a question."

When I lean back, Solomon's seriousness has fled the scene.

He's almost smiling. Almost. His eyes dart around the table, assessing the pills and the piles, seeing how long we can do this.

"And we'll all know Russian." He holds out the can to Elm and Willow.

Willow takes a pill, but Elm pushes the can away. "I don't want it."

"You have to, Elm. It's not just to learn Russian." I might as well say it out loud. "It's so that we can ask Erfinder a question."

Willow hands him the other one. He takes it and she, Solomon, and Elm all swallow it at once. Now I get to see what they saw.

Willow starts trembling. Elm clenches the table and his eyes snap shut, squeezed so tight they're mere lines. Solomon closes his eyes as though about to take a nap. His jaw clenches a few times, but only a minute passes before he's opening his eyes again and looking at me solemnly. Elm and Willow reel a bit in their chairs, both pressing fingers tightly against their temples. Willow grimaces, then goes limp. Solomon shakes her awake as he did me.

Elm wakes on his own. "I do not like these."

His comment elicits a sneer from Erfinder. "Because you don't understand them."

"Because they're bad!" Willow regains her energy, but doesn't seem to stand fully behind her comment.

"Never mind, never mind." Solomon leans back in his chair. "Let's think about our question."

I have too many things I want to ask Erfinder, starting with which pill provides the information for the projected Wall. But that would be stupid since he's clarified his forgetfulness. However, that could have been a ruse. Next, I'd ask him which pills are harmful, but if he really can't remember, then that's a wasted question, too.

"Solomon, you should ask the question."

He nods. Stares at the pills. Props his chin on one hand like the thinking statue. "What is the name of the USE technician you trained to control the projected Wall?"

Oh. Smart question. I feel particularly dumb for not having thought of it.

Erfinder folds his hands. I remember what it was like to fold my hands. "Her name is Adria Nazarkov."

"Where does she live?" I ask.

Erfinder laughs. "I'll take another round before I'll answer that question."

Solomon growls and turns his gaze back to the pills. I glance at him. "Shall we continue?" Personally, I want to try one of the orange ones. I hope Erfinder picks one of those. Or purple. I like purple. That sounds like a good color for information.

But Erfinder doesn't reach for any of the piles. Instead, he reaches for one of the single pills in the center. The solid white one.

"No!" I lunge for him. "You can't have one of those." If he takes one of the five, we'll never know what was on that pill. If this white pill has the Wall information, then it will be lost. Forever.

He holds the pill out of reach. "You were the smart one who thought you could fool me. This is how the game is played."

Solomon's hand annoys me when it pulls gently on my shoulder. "He's right, Parvin. It's a risk we have to take."

"But what if that's the one?" Willow's timid voice pauses Erfinder's movement. His eyes dart to her. "What if that's the one and we lose it?"

"We have God on our side." Solomon speaks the way I imagine the apostle Paul would. Firm. Resolved. Confident. "And we'll find Adria Nazarkov."

A good reminder for me—the girl who claimed confidence in His will. Why did I shake? How could I forget? Did I allow knowledge to distract me from my faith? "Okay."

Erfinder pops the pill and, this time, he lurches from the chair the moment his Adam's apple bobs. He trembles on the floor. Is he having a seizure? This can't be right! "I . . . I think he's ill." Maybe he's choking. "Solomon?"

"It's the pill." The lines around his eyes darken beneath a squint. "I've seen Jude react like this more than once."

Jude took multiple knowledge caps? Of course he did. Is there a way to take too many? How did he get them if they're so controlled by the government? Did he create some, too?

Erfinder stops writhing. None of us try to shake him awake. Sweat covers his body, pooling in a small line on his chest, seeping through his shirt.

No. Never mind. I don't want to take another pill. Funny how a twitching, choking grandpa can steal away my excitement. "Is . . . is he okay?"

"I'm fine." Erfinder's croak comes through tight lips. His eyes crack open next. Then he pushes himself up to his elbows. "You hoped I'd died, didn't you?"

I shake my head. "No—"

"Don't lie, girl."

"I'm not lying!" The thought hadn't crossed my mind, frankly.

"Take your pill." He crawls back into his chair.

I look back at the pills, my eyes landing on the flower now missing a petal. "Was that the one?"

"You can ask me that as your question when you've all taken a cap."

He wouldn't have told me to continue if that had been the pill, would he? That would be sadistic. I reach for the silver one. My hand trembles.

Solomon's voice is low in my ear. "I think you should try one from one of the piles."

"You and I both know it's going to be one of these center pills. We can't let him take another one." I slip the silver capsule between my lips. Solomon doesn't stop me—an admission that I'm right.

The pill sits on my tongue for a spell, sticking to it. I forgot water again. Drat. I loosen the pill and it takes three tries to swallow it. Even then, it crawls down my throat like a drop of molasses.

The bobbins in my brain start spinning, searching for that thread of knowledge that creeps its way toward them, riding the waves of my blood. Then it's there, threading, winding, a shiny silver thread.

But the knowledge is anything but shiny.

Pictures flash. Silver. Knives. They reflect off the sun before cutting open the gut of another human. They shine with blood—letting Numbers bleed out of a wound. They glisten, flashing back and forth, back and forth on a whetstone.

Knives. Hatchets. Daggers.

I cry out.

But knowledge can't be stopped. Just like accidentally glancing at a raunchy picture or hearing a dirty joke—it's seared. The bobbin spins wildly, gathering every last, sickening detail. Death. Maiming. Pain. Grotesque images spark like mind lightning. Burning. Scorching. Blinding me. All I hear is my scream.

No.

Not this.

Not *this* type of knowledge.

"Parvin?"

Help.

"Parvin!"

"Help me." Stop it! Stop the entrance of this black sludge. Fists. Knives. Bullets. My panting echoes in my ears, deafening.

I . . . don't . . . want . . .

Help me!

. . . to know . . .

"Parvin!"

. . . how . . . to . . . kill.

21

It would take me a single heartbeat to murder every person in this room.

I'm on the couch beside the fireplace—this time a fire roars in the hearth. There's a blanket over me, a damp cloth on my forehead, like a home patient from an old classic novel. Solomon sits on the end of the couch by my feet while Willow and Elm hover by the fireplace.

Willow stares at the logs with narrowed eyes, but says nothing.

"How are you feeling?" Solomon's weary voice weighs my bones down. If *he's* exhausted from all this, there's no way I can recover.

I shake my head. I can't tell him how I feel. When I look at him, the first thing that pops into my head isn't his kindness or the many battles we've been through. No, it's the fact that if I hit him in the face with the heel of my hand at the right angle, it will break his nose in a way that will kill him instantly.

I squeeze my eyes shut, but that doesn't stop the knowledge. I look at Willow and my mind churns through the different ways I could strangle her—

Stop.

What's happened to me? "I'm a . . . I'm . . . a murderer."

That's what the knowledge cap turned me into. Some freak. It zipped through every form of killing—using weapons, using my

227

hand, using trickery, self-defense, military from all eras, martial arts.

"No you're not. The cap planted a lie. You haven't killed anyone."

Oh, yes I have. I can see them. I can visualize someone dying from every form of killing I've learned. Did I do that? If not me, then who did? "Solomon . . . what am I?"

"You're Parvin. And you took a knowledge cap." He doesn't understand. That's *who* I am, not *what* I am.

"She's awake?" Erfinder rounds the couch to look at me. "Shall we keep going?"

He'd be easy to kill. A sweep of his legs and he'd career backward. All I'd have to do is push his shoulder at the right moment and his head would connect with the brick fireplace—

Solomon rises. "We're not doing this anymore."

I sit up, nauseated by my train of thought. "We have to keep going." Not because I'm a saint. Not because the mission is bigger than my suffering, but because I want to take another cap. A *different* cap to get these murderous thoughts out of the forefront of my mind. "Please, Solomon?"

It's easy for me to ask. *He's* the one taking the next cap.

"No, Parvin. We're done."

He can't say no. He can't leave me like this. Solomon doesn't *say* no to me. I lurch from my space on the couch. Angry. He can't tell me no! Does he have any idea how easy it would be for me to jab him in the gut with my elbow and then—

"I will take one." Willow stomps over to the table and snatches up the brown one.

Elm reaches her in three strides, yanks the pill from her hand, and pops it in his mouth. "You are done, Willow." The words barely pass his lips before he goes rigid. His other hand tightens around Willow's arm. She tries to twist away.

"Elm. Elm!" She shakes his shoulder, still pulling against his grip, but he doesn't see her. His glassy eyes see nothing. His knees buckle and they both fall to the ground—him dragging Willow down on top of him. "Elm!"

It lasts longer than the Russian cap did. The twitching, the tightness, but he doesn't scream like I did.

Maybe this one isn't so bad. Maybe this is the pill for the projected Wall.

Elm stops. His grip loosens, but Willow's not concerned about her arm anymore. She slaps his face lightly until his gaze refocuses. It darts around the room, then lands on Willow. He frowns. He pushes her away.

She lands backward on her elbows. "Elm?"

He gets to his feet, but sways. Solomon reaches to steady him, but Elm pushes his hand away. "Don't . . ." Tight lips. Tight eyes.

Willow reaches for him anyway, but he slaps her hand away so hard it flies back and hits the leg of the table. "Elm, stop!" She's angry and clambers after him. He tries to push her away again, but she gets both her hands around his wrists. There's a struggle and, suddenly, I fear for her.

What if Elm's cap was similar to mine? What if he's about to kill her? He's so much stronger than she.

But she keeps her balance and grips his chin with vice-fingers, forcing him to look at her. "Stop, Elm. You are my Elm. You took a bad cap. Calm down."

"Leave me alone, Willow."

"No!" Her glare matches the intensity of her scream. "You remember what's good!" Her voice breaks and, though her eyes glisten she maintains connection with him.

His good eye fills with tears and the fight leaves him. "Oh, Willow . . ."

She pulls him into a hug. "What was it, Elm? What was the cap?"

He shakes his head, his cheek against her hair. "History. War." That's all he says.

I don't realize I'm crying until a tear leaks down my cheek. I think we can safely assume that it wasn't the cap we needed. Who knows what new knowledge rests in Elm's head.

"Well, this is all very exciting." Erfinder brushes past the young couple and plops back at the table. "Who's next?" He levels his gaze at Solomon. "My . . . *sort-of* great-grandson? I know you want to be the one swallowing the right cap. To help make you more of a Hawke."

I've seen Solomon righteously angered. I've seen Solomon desperate. I've seen Solomon broken. But I've never seen such fury take hold of his being. "We're done, old man. You have no answers for us."

He snatches the can of caps and moves toward those laid out on the table. Wait! We're so close. There are only the two main ones left—black and clear. Solomon has a really good chance. "Shouldn't we . . ."

"No, we don't need him. If we're forced to take all these pills, then so be it. We can do it without his sick delight in our suffering."

"Some of those pills *will* kill you, Solomon." A midnight bell clangs from across the village. Erfinder doesn't look bothered at all by the potential death of his great-grandson.

"I'll take my chances."

"But what if he has answers that we need?" Even as I ask it, I wonder if Erfinder's been lying to us this whole time. Toying with us. What if there *is* no Adria Nazarkov?

But if he's *not* lying, we need more information from him. We need to know where Adria lives.

There's a knock on the front door and we all freeze. My first instinct is to answer it—since I'm the group's new bodyguard, even though they don't know it. But this isn't my house.

Who would be stopping by at midnight? Have they heard our

commotion? Do they know what we're doing? Is it Gloria and Sasha? It can't be. They don't know this new location.

Erfinder rises serenely and ambles to the front door. I guess midnight visitors aren't unexpected for him. I follow. Never mind etiquette.

He peeks through a hole in the wall that must give him access to cameras, because the peephole isn't in the front door. He leans back, looks at me, then peers through the hole again. "This will be interesting."

My heart contracts like a squeezed sponge. Who's out there? My mind jumps to the worst conclusion, but . . . there's no way . . .

Erfinder enters a few codes, slides a few bolts, and opens the door. "Mr. Chase, is it?"

Skelley Chase stands on the entry step wearing Wilbur's silver Brawn suit and his green fedora. His bored smile releases the pressure on my sponge-heart and I suck in a shuddering breath. He tips his hat at me. "So you *are* alive."

My old-Parvin instinct is to reel backward, but the new murder-cap instinct sends me into defense mode. In the course of a half second, my brain spins with the threats Skelley's presence brings—he's here to stop us, he's here to steal the caps, he's here to take Willow back, he's here to kill us.

"Run!" Solomon probably won't heed the warning . . . but I can handle myself. I leap toward Skelley, my brain telling my foot where to go—straight into his chest. He careens sideways, but I regain my balance and get him in a headlock, knocking his fedora to the ground. If I could hold him long enough to let the others get away . . .

Two brains scream instructions at me. One brain reminds me I'm a puny nobody who should be fleeing. The other brain tells me I'm a killer—a skilled killer and that I can have him dead in the next ten seconds.

But that murder-brain doesn't calculate the fact that he's wearing a Brawn suit.

Skelley grabs my hair and yanks me off. My limp-noodle arms betray me and set him free. He throws me so hard back into the house that I tumble head over heels into the living room, slamming against the wall.

Ouch.

Solomon's beside me in a flash—rather, in *front* of me, standing like an Enforcer guard.

"Really, now." Skelley picks up his fedora and returns it to his head. "It seems your memories are still intact. Not sure why." He steps into the living room, surveys the caps, and then picks up the clear one. "I'm here for only one thing." His eyes slide from the cap to my crumpled form. "Well . . . two."

My pulse thumps inside my chest as I straighten. What is he doing? He can't *possibly* know what's on that cap. Why—how—is he here?

"One of the greatest benefits of being a Council member,"—Skelley holds the clear cap up to the firelight—"is the advanced technology installed on our NABs." He glances at Solomon. "All it takes is a scan from my NAB to tell you the main contents of each cap. It's pretty accurate even from long distances like . . . through a window." He winks at me. "You were so close. This is the one you want. Too bad there's only one."

My breathing calms. My heart rate slows. My panic dissolves as a whispered voice blows through my consciousness—FEAR NOT.

God sent us here to Russia to find Erfinder. We've found the answer to the Wall problem. It matters not that Skelley has the cap—God is greater than that. We'll get it back from Skelley.

I smile. "It's okay, guys."

Willow launches herself at Skelley so fast, her pale form is a lightning streak. It takes him a minor reflex to deflect her, but in that short amount of time, she snatches the pill from his hand and throws it toward me.

Solomon catches it.

Skelley has Willow by the scruff of her coat. She writhes, kicking and squirming, but the Brawn suit can't be overpowered. Skelley sighs, lifting his bored eyes to me. Elm poises on his toes by the fire, assessing the situation.

"Does it always have to come down to a threat?" Skelley wraps his forearm around Willow's throat and her squirming stops, her small hands clutching at his arm. Her chest still rises and falls, but it would take a mere twitch of his arm to cut off her air. "Mr. Hawke, I'd like that cap please."

How am I supposed to "fear not" in this, God?

Willow sucks in a breath. "No! Swallow it!"

I rise slowly to my feet, not wanting to startle anyone or look like a threat. Skelley looks at me. "Parvin, bring the cap here."

No. Don't put this on me. Solomon still hasn't moved, but Willow's gasps come faster and faster. Elm's gaze darts around the room, searching for something, *anything*—conveying exactly how I feel.

Solomon chews on his cheek, staring at the cap. Is it worth more than Willow's life? Are we, in fact, in the same situation Jude and I were in? Only this time, I'm on the Jude-side, willing to sacrifice anything for Willow's life.

Solomon closes his eyes and passes me the cap.

FEAR NOT.

"It's okay," I whisper, folding my fingers around it. We'll get Willow back and then figure out a new way to retrieve the cap from Skelley. Or find Adria Nazarkov. Skelley has to travel all the way back to the USE, anyway. That's a lot of time in which we can intercept him.

And now . . . we know which cap it is.

With jerky leaden steps, I walk toward him, holding out my

hand. Skelley reaches for it and, when I drop the cap into his palm, he jerks his hand back toward his chest and pushes Willow away. Before I can retreat, he's snatched me by the coat sleeve. "We're leaving."

We? As in me and him?

Solomon takes a single step forward, but Skelley wraps his hand around my throat. I've been here before—suffocating while Solomon looks on.

I can't leave Solomon. Not again. I want to reach for him and fight my way free, but Skelley has the Brawn suit on and God keeps telling me not to fear. *Please, God, let me stay here with Solomon.*

There's no answer. And no freedom. I let out a long sigh, succumbing to the situation. "It's okay." I seem to be saying that a lot in situations where someone's about to die. If I go with Skelley, then at least I'll be able to keep track of the cap. Steal it back at some point.

We take two disjointed steps backward. Willow, Elm, and Solomon stay where they are. Erfinder sits in his chair, napping. Napping!

I glance at Skelley.

He meets my gaze and smiles—the type of smile someone gives when they have a secret. Then, with a backhand to my nerves, he pops the clear knowledge cap into his mouth . . .

. . . and swallows.

22

God couldn't have seen *this* one coming.

Skelley's Adam's apple bobs and his eyes roll back in his head. He shudders. But he keeps his feet . . . and his grip. He swallowed it. He actually swallowed it. Now I *really* can't kill him. *He's* the knowledge cap.

"No!" Solomon lunges forward, but even under the attack of knowledge-overload, Skelley keeps his wits.

He yanks me backward and holds up a small black box. "Detonator!"

Solomon pulls up short.

Skelley rattles the black box and grimaces a moment before giving his head a firm shake. His eyes clear and, after a few deep breaths, his bored smile is back. I guess for a man on the Council, he's grown used to taking knowledge caps.

He takes slow steps backward, letting his words roll out of his mouth. "I've rigged this house. Come after me and go up in flames."

"You wouldn't." Solomon takes a chance, inching forward. "Your own life is at stake."

Oh, yes, he would, Solomon.

"I have plenty of Numbers to survive an explosion." He says this, but I'm not convinced. He saw me die. He knows the

Numbers are fallible. "Besides, it's not your call. Do you really want to kill the kids?" He jerks his chin at Willow and Elm.

God told me not to fear. *Are You sure?* Does he see what I'm seeing?

Skelley wants to take me with him. I don't want to leave. What if Solomon and I can't connect again?

"If any of you step outside this house after me, the house explodes. I have an invisible trip-wire." His grin creeps onto his face like a sinister shadow. "Seeing as how you are all criminals, I'm actually showing you mercy."

Erfinder chuckles from his napping chair, cracking an eye open. "Invisible trip wire? I like this guy."

Psycho.

I force a brave smile. Maybe that will convince Solomon of what I don't yet believe myself—it will all be okay. His wide eyes remind me of a rabbit caught in a corner. I sense the quickness of his heart. *It's okay.*

He'll realize it in the end. Maybe I will, too.

"Let me come with." Solomon loses his ferocity. "Please." His eyes turn to Skelley. "I'll cause no trouble."

Skelley looks at me. "What do you think, Parvin? Will your guy keep his word?"

He's giving me a chance. A chance to decide Solomon's fate and suddenly I don't want us to be together. Not in this moment. Because Solomon will die if I say yes.

Solomon's gaze pleads with me to remember his prayer that we die together. My heart aches. If he comes with me, Willow and Elm are on their own. Skelley might kill him. This is my chance to protect them.

"We should go." My words are barely a whisper, but at their release Solomon's entire posture crumples, Elm shakes his head, and Erfinder bursts out laughing.

I hate myself.

Before another word is said or a kiss is blown, I'm outside the house and Skelley presses the detonator button.

No!

The leap of my stomach suffocates me, but the house doesn't explode. It wasn't the actual detonator, it must have activated the trip wire. Or maybe it simply deactivated for a moment so that *we* could leave.

Down the midnight streets we go. He doesn't drag me quite so forcefully anymore. He knows I'll follow because he knows my weaknesses—people I love.

I'm proud of that weakness. So then, why do I feel so awful? I'm leaving Solomon behind for his own safety. Elm and Willow need him.

THEY HAVE ME.

My breath hitches. All I need is that single sentence to remind me to trust. To remind me of God's power.

"Wait." I pull against Skelley's grip. To my surprise, he pauses. "I've changed my mind. I want Solomon to come."

"It's too late for that." He resumes his stride, yanking me after him.

"No!" I fight, but the Brawn suit does its job. Skelley could restrain me with two fingers if he wanted. I turn away from him and strain for a view of the house. "Solomon!"

We're too far. It's too late. I left him behind. Again. Like I did with Jude, with Willow, with . . . everyone. I hate being alone, so why do I leave people?

Skelley slaps a strip of silvery cloth tape over my mouth. He still doesn't trust me. Good for him.

His balance on the ice is impeccable. What, did he grow up on ice skates? We wind through streets and I resign myself against fighting the tape on my mouth. He looks at me several times, raises an eyebrow, but I remain obedient. That's how he likes his victims anyway.

He yanks me around a corner—I think he's enjoying the strength of the Brawn suit. As we exit the darkened houses with barely a clip of shoes on sidewalk, I realize why he silenced me. Up ahead are Gloria and Sasha, both with tape over their own mouths and tied with their hands behind their backs to the stakes holding a harnessed dogsled.

The dogs—drunk on the excitement of a run—pay little heed to their bound owners. They jump in place, yapping, sure to wake the entire town. Sasha's eyes find mine and widen. She writhes against her bonds, and I pull against Skelley, but it takes a mere jerk of his wrist to yank me back to his side.

I don't know what he said to these girls to get them to harness up their dogs for him. Maybe he claimed he knew us. Maybe he offered them a lot of money. Maybe he blackmailed them. Either way, Gloria's eyes fill with tears and mine follow suit.

How did Skelley even *get* here?

He ties my hand and stump behind my back with more cloth tape. I clench my fist as tight as possible to convey my anger. Once finished, he throws me into the sled and steps onto the back.

I land hard on my wrists and angle my body so I'm not crushing them.

We're leaving. Not just that, but he's ridding the girls of their livelihood. I spin around to see him taking aim with a handgun . . . at Sasha.

"No!" My scream comes out as a muffled shriek against the tape. I writhe in the bed of the sled and knock him off balance. Then I curl in a ball and pull my feet through my tied wrists to get them in front of me.

Skelley tries to shove me back into the sled, aim his gun, and stay on the back of the sled all at the same time. He might be strong, but he's got only the two hands.

The dogs turn rabid for a run. The sled jerks forward an inch.

I roll out of the sled, knowing I can't best him no matter how quick I am. He's too strong with the Brawn suit on. And if I ditch him he'll kill the Russian sisters anyway. I rip the tape from my mouth—*ouch*—and leap onto the back runners of the sled, knocking Skelley's gun arm aside.

I throw my bound arms over his head so we're hugging. My good hand grips the back of the sled and, before he can shoot the girls I do the only thing that makes sense.

I kick Skelley's feet off the brake. *"Hike!"*

The dogs take off, and the tips of my fingernails are the only things keeping us on the back of the sled. Skelley lurches and his gun flies into the snow and darkness. His hat blows off soon after, but he chooses to hold on to the sled instead of trying to catch it.

My gut churns with my arms around him. He's no stick figure. My face is pressed against his back and I can barely breathe, but I don't move. Neither does he, which surprises me. He could take charge in a second—step on the brake, shout the command to stop, throw me off the back—but he doesn't. His white-knuckled grip betrays him.

He's terrified.

I can't imagine what of. The dogs? Sledding? The night? Me? He wears Wilbur's Brawn suit, making him a contender for Superman status, *and* there's nothing out here. We're not even going that fast.

I can't tell where we're headed, but the dogs seem to know the path even in the dark. Either that, or they're following the packed snow.

Ten minutes pass and my arm aches, but I'm not about to let go. If I fall off this sled, he'll come back for me. If I make it back to the village, he'll go after the girls.

I'm not afraid.

"How do you stop this ridiculous thing?" he shouts.

So he can't steer it. I could jump off the back, though it'd be tough with my arms around him. Ick. "Step on the brake!" Skelley obeys and I holler, "Whoa!"

The dogs come to a halt and immediately relieve themselves or start eating snow. With Skelley on the brake, I lift my arms over his head and free myself from that horrible subjection to physical contact.

He opens his mouth—probably to warn me not to try anything—but a distant explosion rents the air. I snap my head around. There, in the center of the far-off village, is a mushroom of fire.

Erfinder's house. I'm sure of it.

"Solomon!" My scream sends the dogs barking again. I spin toward Skelley.

He holds his hands up, eyes wide. "It was his choice."

"Take me back." The panic is coming. The shock. Solomon. No, he's fine. He *has* to be fine. God told me to *fear not.*

Skelley shakes his head. Something like regret is in his voice. "I'm sorry, Parvin. I gave them warning—"

"I'm going back, you snake!" I sprint away from the sled, but he's faster than I am. He gets his arms around my midsection and lifts me from the ground. I'm thrown into the sled and, before I can suck in air for a sob, something strikes my temple and I'm out.

RISE UP.

Hmm?

BE MY LIGHT.

My eyes open to black and a croak slips out. "Solomon." I'm in the dogsled. We're not moving, but the town isn't in view anymore.

Skelley sits on the sled brake eating something. I move to crawl out, but pain explodes in my head. I groan. Skelley turns around. "How's your head?"

I don't respond. Why does *he* care? He knocked me out because . . . because I was trying to run. He blew up Solomon, Willow, and Elm.

They have to be alive. They *have* to be!

RISE UP FOR ME.

I can't forget about them, God!

But He's not asking for that. He's asking for surrender. Can I surrender my fears to Him? "What do you want with me, Skelley?"

His eyes narrow. *What, you don't like me using your first name? Too bad.*

"Stay in the sled."

"Do you even know where you're going?"

He climbs to his feet, a sag to his face and skin. "Be quiet, Parvin."

No need to have a tantrum, Mr. Chase.

"H-Hike!"

A nasty part of me is pleased with the waver in his voice. The dogs don't need much more than a half-hearted command. They're ready to run. Off we go into the night, and my mind finally has the freedom to spin.

Skelley came after the knowledge cap. How did he know where I'd be? Did he get to Christian Hawke somehow? Or did Dalene tell him? And why did *he* come instead of simply sending an army of Enforcers?

I glance back at the black horizon. The only glow is moonlight on the snow. Did I miss my chance with Solomon? My chance to be a team and show him I love him enough to push through my own goals and selfishness?

FEAR NOT.

Ugh. Sometimes I don't like that reminder.

There aren't many furs in the sled and I grow chilly. I tuck my arms against my chest, nestling down in the sled and fighting the automatic burst of Antarctica memories. Frigid chill. Frostbite. Hypothermia. Elusive relief.

How much has Skelley actually planned for our survival?

So many questions, but the most pressing of all isn't for Skelley.

God, where are You going with this? He says *fear not*. I'm not afraid yet, just confused. Was the *fear not* to calm me during the tense moment at Erfinder's house? Or is it to prepare me for future situations? I suppose it doesn't matter. God will never instruct me to be afraid, so I might as well get used to reminding myself to *fear not*.

The stars of an open night lose their shyness, sprinkling the canopy above with their winks.

FEAR NOT.

I know.

FOR I AM WITH YOU.

I will trust You.

Somehow, in some way, God will use this for His glory. I am being obedient, and God has sent me with a lion. Perhaps I'll be dying—for certain—soon, and joining Solomon . . . if he's dead.

Too bad I didn't grab my pack. I'm always without my Bible. Why? If God went through so much trouble to have muggers purchase a copy for me, why does He let me leave it behind?

Was it my fault that I didn't think to grab it?

Hours pass, the dogs slow, and I startle to the loud scrape of metal on ice. We've stopped. "Get up. Your turn to drive."

"No." I'm an ice sculpture. I don't want to move and sacrifice my hoarded body heat resting between my folded arms.

I expect him to pull me out by force—he's so fond of the Brawn suit—but he folds his arms. "Parvin, get up."

"The dogs need a rest." I burrow deeper.

"Then I'll climb in with you." He squeezes a foot into the sled, bringing loose chunks of snow into my heat haven. The very idea of sharing a close space with this man sends me scrambling out of the sled.

"I'm not driving." I will not fear, but I will not help, either . . . even if it *is* the only way to keep warm.

"Then freeze. Good night." He reaches up as if to place his fedora over his face and his hand waves a few times before realizing his hat is gone. With a grunt, he rolls over and pulls the two furs over his head.

The dogs flop down onto the snow. There's no way I'm making them pull us further. Gloria and Sasha treasured their sled dogs, and the best thing I can do for those poor, freezing, tied-up sisters right now is take care of their treasure.

I walk up the line and the dogs glance at me, stretching their heads out for attention. Gumbo pants at the front. I'm not an animal person, never have been. There's not much opportunity in Unity. The only animals people had there weren't for pets—they would provide milk or food or strength. It's hard enough feeding a family. I can't imagine why people would want an animal simply for . . . companionship. Particularly dogs. They're too similar to wolves.

And I've had my fill of wolves.

But the moment my fingers touch Gumbo's head, and he pushes his snout against my palm . . . I drop to my knees and wrap my arms around his neck. He lets out a whine—a pleasant whine. I rub his back. That's what people do, right? Rub animals to make them happy?

The other dogs let loose pitiful whines, wanting their own attention. One even licks my hand as I pass.

Yuck.

They're probably hungry or thirsty. They munch on snow. There are a few bundles in the nose of the sled and I find a small cooler of meat with eight bowls. I dig some more. Skelley's foot kicks at me, but I ignore it.

I could ignore the dogs, let them starve and work themselves until they collapse in order to stop Skelley and his plan, but I'm doing this for Gloria and Sasha.

The fire I build isn't large enough to warm my core, but it melts enough snow for me to feed the dogs the way I saw the girls feed them—a slab of meat with some warm water on top.

Why is Skelley so content to stop? Isn't he afraid someone will catch up? I don't like his confidence in this, but I still allow myself to hope it's an oversight. Until I find out, I need to focus on . . . not freezing.

The dogs, content with their fill of meat and warm water, clump together after a few tussles of rank. If only I had a fur coat like theirs. How odd that God decided to make humans so furless.

I laugh a little to myself. Time to become an animal of my own.

I walk to the sled and remove the top fur off Skelley. He's burrowed down and asleep, so he won't notice until the shivers come. The fur is huge—a bear's, maybe—and I am small. Perfect.

I step between the dogs. A few look up. The rest scoot over as I lie down among them. Then, encouraged by my little, girly-voiced, "Come here, friends!" they wiggle their way up against me.

Their breath stinks, I'm probably lying on trampled poop, and the dog licks hit portions of my face that I never want to touch again, but . . .

I can see now why people might want a pet.

I wake choking on hair. Ugh! I spit and shoot into a sitting position, the bear fur sliding off my shoulders. It's light out, barely, and Skelley stands over me with a half-frown. It's odd to see him without his fedora on. His hair doesn't seem to know what to do with itself—stick up? Lay flat? It's darker than his eyebrows, probably because it never sees the sun, and the cap of his head is balding.

"Get up."

The dogs leap to their feet with throaty growls. I tumble out of their midst, though I know they're not angry with me. They're angry with Skelley. One look at him flares my killing instincts.

My brain spins with ideas on how to defeat a man with super-strength. The goal would be to knock him out—that's easiest since the suit doesn't cover his head.

I can do that when he's sitting in the sled and I'm driving. Disconnect the brake while we're driving, slam it into his skull . . .

I shudder. *This can't be right.* God couldn't possibly want me to kill Skelley.

"We're going." Skelley gets on the back of the sled and gestures to the bed. I don't want to sit where he slept. He probably drooled.

"I'll drive." Standing sounds nice. And it's sunny. The exertion under the clear sky will warm me up. Besides, Skelley doesn't know how to take care of the dogs. He doesn't know to keep the midline tight or to stop if the lead dogs need to relieve themselves.

Skelley shrugs and climbs into the sled. "Okay." He can't possibly trust me, but he seems to know I'm being compliant.

"Where are we going?"

"Follow the Wall."

Ah, duh. Even with my faulty sense of direction I could have remembered how to get back to the train station village. We're quite far off it—the top of the stone behemoth barely peeks a hello over the horizon, enough to keep us out of sight of any followers, but close enough to keep us on track.

I climb on the back of the sled. "Hike!" The dogs leap into obedience. I like thinking I make them happy.

And I like knowing I could kill Skelley if I wanted.

I shake my head. *No. That's not right.* Is this going to be a constant battle? Choosing *not* to kill someone? Why would God allow me to swallow that pill?

My breath hitches. Maybe it's not about Him. Maybe . . . I'm being targeted by the Enemy, and that knowledge cap was one of his tricks. I've never considered being under attack before, but it makes sense.

That must mean I'm doing something right.

The sun is out and the snow softens, eliminating the loud scraping sound the runners made on the ice. It's quiet enough that Skelley and I could talk if we wanted. He probably doesn't want to. In all honesty, I'm not too fond of hearing his bored warble either, but I need answers. And I learned during my trip to Antarctica that I need to be bold and speak. "Why did you come after me?"

I'm met by the rhythmic patter of dog feet and the random pings of snow they fling against the sled. Maybe Skelley didn't hear. I raise my voice as though hollering across a canyon. "Why did you come after me?"

"I have no reason to share this information with you."

I shrug, but he can't see it. "Why not? I'm your captive. I don't have any of my belongings so it's not like I can share your information. I'm controllable, remember?"

"Tasteless sarcasm." He adjusts the furs around his legs. "Just because I can do anything doesn't mean I don't learn. I know you're not controllable anymore, Parvin."

I never was, you snake! Okay . . . maybe I was. I don't want to argue. There's no reason he would reveal anything to me, and he's too smart to tell me things I could use against him. Accursed silence! "If I'm going to be kidnapped, can't you at least make it interesting?"

He chuckles, and part of me likes the fact that I made him laugh. Then I gag. What was that? Why would my heart respond *positively* to his laughter? It should be a screaming ball of fury at everything he says and does.

WHO AM I?

I almost squeal at His communication. As the question echoes in my mind, I see the words on pages of my Bible. Jesus was always asking His followers who they thought He was. All along, He was the Christ . . . but He wanted to know how *they* viewed him.

WHO AM I?

You are God. Jesus. Messiah. Peter was one of the only disciples to get it right when Jesus asked.

WHO ARE YOU?

I am Yours.

WHO AM I?

Okay . . . didn't we just go through this? Maybe I'm getting the answer wrong—no, that can't be it. Maybe I'm not focusing. Who am I? Who is God? If I'm truly God's, then I ought to be imitating Him, like in that Isaiah verse. *Arise, shine, for your light has come.* I'm His light—and the best way to be a light is to become like the candle. God showed us how to be a candle.

WHO AM I?

I don't know! I don't know the right answer! *Please don't go silent on me!*

I AM A STILL, SMALL VOICE.

He didn't leave me. Maybe He never goes silent—maybe I just stop listening or pursuing. Still. Small. Gentle. Kind. A whisper loud enough to rise above the world's roar. That is my God. Working *through* us flawed, impulsive humans.

Is that why I'm here? To be the gentle, kind whisper in Skelley's life? I can't imagine he's received many kind whispers from Brickbat. It's weird thinking of Skelley needing kindness and even weirder imagining myself giving it. But I can rise up.

"Why did you swallow that cap, Skelley? Was it to stop us from having it?" I keep my question relaxed. It's okay if he doesn't answer. If I sound undemanding, maybe he'll open up.

"Every moment in life is a choice to build what you are. I am the man who can do anything." He sure likes his personal motto. "And that cap is another step into cementing that."

"It doesn't matter how much power or knowledge you give yourself. Without God, you can't accomplish anything."

I must be funny today because he laughs out loud this time.

"Loyal, but inaccurate sentiments. Look at me, Parvin. Look at who I am."

He's not going to like this. "I see you, Skelley. I might see you better than anyone else does." I picture him as a troubled teen—*my* age—wanting nothing more than to be accepted by his peers. We're so similar.

My throat closes. "I see that you're famous because you give people what they want. You give them stories. You give them your smile. You give Unity Village's receptionist a wink, to make her day and to build you up a little. You gave me what I wanted—both to gain my trust and to build your fame. You killed Reid to give the people *me*."

I tap the brake as the sled dips down a small hill. "No matter how famous you get, no matter how many people you please . . . or displease . . . you'll never be satisfied. Because you're not pleasing the One who *creates* satisfaction and contentment."

He doesn't respond. I imagine him rolling his eyes, but that doesn't deter me. "Aren't you lonely, Skelley?"

"I think it's time for me to drive." He rises from the sled before I get it to a complete stop. I step off the runners and try to meet his gaze, but he doesn't look at me.

I climb into the sled. It's warm. I'm not disgusted this time. I pull the furs over me and close my eyes beneath the sun. *Soften his heart, God. And . . . if You think I'll be obedient enough . . . use me as the scalpel.*

Later, Skelley threatens me with the silver cloth tape, so I stop talking. This night is similar to the first. I feed the dogs, though Skelley takes a slab of meat and cooks it over the coals for himself. My stomach whines like a needy puppy until I cook my own slab of meat. Now we're out. No more meat for the dogs, no more for us. Hopefully we'll arrive tomorrow.

Skelley comes near to the fire and the dogs growl as one, baring their teeth. He lurches backward.

"Shouldn't have stolen their meat," I joke. Yet they didn't growl at me when *I* ate. I think they have keener memories than I give them credit for . . . and they know Skelley threatened Gloria and Sasha.

I sleep with the dogs again, wrapped in my bear fur. Gumbo snuggles closest. My trust in them grows each day. I don't mind their hair getting stuck on my clothes now. I want them to feel safe with me. We're a team.

Skelley sleeps in the sled—he can't possibly be warm enough. I drift off, unconcerned.

My eyelids lift with the rising of the sun, but the first sounds to reach my ears are the growls. I sit up. Only four dogs rest beside me, but they're awake, watching the other four guard the sled, snarling as Skelley Chase rises.

"*Git.* Go on." He tries to shoo them with a hand, but Gumbo barks. Skelley yelps, despite wearing his Brawn suit.

"C'mere, boys!" I don't know if the dogs are male or female, but my cheerful call is enough to distract them. Their ears perk and they trot over. I rub each of them behind the ears. Skelley may *say* he can do anything, but I'm the only one who's successfully petting and befriending these dogs. I thought I'd fear them, but I've fought hungry wolves. A grouchy sled dog is no comparison.

"Keep your mutts away from me." He shrugs the fur blanket tighter over his shoulders.

"They just trust me and not you." I almost say, "*They know you're the bad guy.*" But amend it to, "You almost shot their masters."

"I wasn't aiming for the girls, I was aiming for the rope." He stands on the brake at the back of the sled, taking up the snow anchors. "Let's go."

I jerk a thumb over my shoulder. "I need to . . ." Dratted bladder. "I'm, uh . . ."

"Hurry up, then."

There aren't many options. Just some scattered sagebrush. The Wall is too far away. I jog toward the biggest looking bush, jarring my bladder with each step. It's farther than I thought, but when I reach it I'm pleased to find that a decent squat will hide me from view.

I'm almost finished when I hear the barking. They're not the excited barks of sled dogs ready to run. They're familiar—the yaps of canines on the attack.

They sound identical to the wolves I fought.

I peer toward the sled as a human's cry splits the air. The dogs are in a giant mass, ripping at the ground next to the sled.

I don't see Skelley.

23

It's not easy to scream when you're out of breath, but I force it out.

"Gumbo, no!" I sprint toward the sled, shouting for the dogs. My thoughts spin with killer-instinct on how I can take down the dogs one by one to force them to stop.

No. I *refuse* to hurt them. Instead, I try calling them by name. I try sounding chipper like I have a treat. Then I yell, "Hike!" and, when they don't desist, I know they're set on their task.

They're killing Skelley.

A dog goes flying.

Then another.

Skelley cries out and it's that call—that terrified break in his voice—that erases any hatred or bitterness my heart ever held for him. He is a man in need. A desperate man, facing his fear alone.

By the time I reach the sled, four of the eight dogs are dead, one is wounded, and the other three have clamped their jaws on some portion of Skelley's body.

I'm angry at the beasts because of my helplessness. I'm angry that some of them are hurt and I've failed Gloria and Sasha. "Go on! Git!" They don't let go, but Gumbo's eyes roll up to meet mine, pleading. *Why? He's not our friend.*

Skelley groans, a hand over his bleeding neck. I drop to my knees and start stroking Gumbo's head. "Shh, it's okay boy. Let him go." His jaw loosens and I move Skelley's arm out from between his teeth. As I'd hoped, the other two sled dogs follow their leader.

"Go lie down."

They walk away, tails between their legs, and sniff at their dead companions. What did Skelley *do?*

I turn to him. Blood is everywhere. His Brawn outfit is shredded. I press the button at his neck and the suit shrinks, though it's larger and lumpier than normal in its torn state. Skelley wears a business suit beneath. Of course he does. Who *wouldn't* wear a suit during a trek across Russia?

His body trembles and he squints at the sky. "G-go away."

"No, sir." I'm firm, but inside I'm scrambling for something, *anything* that will show me what to do. Why did that silver cap teach me how to kill? Couldn't it have shown me how to *heal?*

He pushes at my hand, but the blood on his doesn't allow a decent grip. "Leave me alone!"

"No!" I press my hand against the wound in his neck and lean over until he *has* to look at me. "I'm going to *help* you, Skelley. Not out of pity. Not out of spite. Not because I think you'll suddenly make all the right choices, but because you're a *human.* And because you don't know God yet. I won't allow you to leave this Earth until that's changed."

His jaw clenches and his teeth grate like nails down a chalkboard. He's not crying, but he looks fragile. "And I'm sure the fact that I took that knowledge cap has nothing to do with your . . . i-interest."

I hadn't even thought of it. But now that he brings it up . . . "No."

"Fine. Then stop yabbering and fix this." He goes limp. Shock? Loss of blood? I don't know, but it makes it easier for me to check out his wounds.

This is a disaster. I need Mother. As I fumble with his blood-drenched clothing, trying to expose the wounds, I fight the onslaught of worries. Half the dogs are dead; what will Gloria and Sasha say? How will we get the others to pull the sled? What if they attack again? How far out are we? What do I do with Skelley?

He is fully subjected to my whims right now. Vulnerable. My murder-knowledge flares. It'd be so easy to suffocate him.

Or let him bleed out.

Or desert him.

I shake my head, and it rattles the murderous ideas enough to let healing thoughts in. This new struggle I have—of resisting the pull of dark thoughts—won't go away. Probably not ever. It will be a daily fight and I'm ready with my fists up.

Another glimpse into what it means to *arise* every day.

Part of me—a large part—doesn't want to help this man. I picture Reid next to me. *"What are you doing, little Brielle?"*

I suck in a shuddering gasp. "I'm helping him." *And I'm betraying you!*

"Kill him, Parvin!" Willow's memory screams.

I shake my head, but my throat tightens. "No. I must . . . save . . . him."

Jude's shadow pops up on the other side of my mind. *"Why?"*

"B-Because . . . because . . ."

"Because it is shalom." Solomon's voice is the loudest, bringing out a sob. Yes, it's shalom. *Please don't be dead, Solomon.*

I try making bandages with the Brawn suit, but the material is too slick. It absorbs nothing. Skelley's skin grows paler by the minute. *God, what do I do?*

What would the Bible tell me to do? Jesus said that if I ask anything in His name, He will do it. A spark singes my chest. Oh my . . . could He *heal* Skelley?

I place my hand and stump over the crumpled material I shoved on his neck wound. Not too long ago, I placed my hand on a frozen rope knot and prayed over it. God's power held that rope together.

This could be the moment! The moment to arise and to show God's light *everywhere*. My heart thumps within me, quickening. My hand trembles over his wound.

God, please heal this wound. I should probably say more than that. *Heal all the wounds that are on Skelley's body. Fix it so that he will wake up and see that You are powerful. You are God.*

This is perfect. It's the perfect way to bring Skelley around and, once he's on *our* side he'll be a powerful ally.

I open my eyes, heart fracturing my sternum, and lift away the wadded silver cloth. A pulse of blood washes over my hand. Then another. I stopper the wound again, my excitement crumbling. Why didn't He . . .? No, I'll try again. I'll pray harder.

God, You are mighty! This is for Your glory. Heal him!

More blood.

I try praying the verse from Isaiah 60 about His glory, then I sit in silence in case He wants to say something.

Nothing.

No healing.

So much for *that* idea. It doesn't matter right now. God is God, He can do what He wants. But . . . was my faith not strong enough? Maybe He knows this won't accomplish what I hoped it would, though I can't see how it wouldn't.

I get back to work. I use the metal teeth from the sled brake to cut strips of cloth into bandages. Then I kiss each dead dog on its head and bid it farewell. Such a short-lived friendship we had. I hate good-byes. The other dogs sit by and watch me, licking their own wounds now that they've examined the deaths of their friends. Gumbo whines.

I return to Skelley, stripping what excess clothing I can use for bandages from his body. Every time I'm hit by a wave of disgust, I chant. "Love your enemies. Love your enemies. Love your enemies."

I hate Skelley Chase.

"Love your enemies."

I HATE him!

"Love your enemies."

I'm sweating by the time I finish wrapping his wounds and even then, I'm not sure he'll make it. Why am I so desperate for him to make it? A demon-Parvin pops up on my shoulder and hisses in my ear all the things he's done.

He killed Reid. He turned me in. He blackmailed me. He let the Council torture orphans. He helped the Council kill me. He forced me to get Clock-matched. He sent me and other Radicals to Antarctica. He blew up the *Ivanhoe Independent.* He almost killed Mother. He bombed Unity. He stole our knowledge cap—

STOP!

"I *will* love my enemies." With an ironic twist, I remember a year ago—before the Wall, before Skelley Chase, before . . . anything—when I *had* no enemies. I thought I'd never get to apply that verse. Part of me was disappointed. I wanted enemies so I could practice being more godly.

What a fool I was.

I can't get Skelley into the sled. I try pulling him by his wrist, but my single hand doesn't accomplish much. I put on the scraps of the Brawn suit, but it no longer works. Fine.

I tie the arms of the Brawn suit around Skelley's chest like a sling, then loop a portion of it around my shoulder and manage to drag him parallel to the sled. Instead of trying to lift him, I tilt the sled on its side and scoot him into it, then use my weight to tip the sled back onto its runners. The wood groans and it settles with a few cracks.

By this point I'm sweating and ready for a nap. A trail of blood marks the many steps of my exertion. The only thing to do is to get Skelley to the small train town and see if there's a doctor.

I've seen wounds like his before . . . on myself. And it wasn't pretty.

It takes maneuvering with my hand and teeth to unhook the dead dogs. Blood is everywhere. It gets in my mouth and I spit it out, rubbing my hand and bloodied clothes in the snow. I ought to bury the dogs, but I can't. Besides, if Gloria and Sasha are following me, this will be a sign they won't be able to miss. Blood on snow is a beacon.

The blood of their precious dogs.

I look behind me, in case they are on our tail. They're not. There's nothing. Once the dogs are lined up, with Gumbo taking lead, and I've placed the wounded dog in the sled at Skelley's feet, I hop on the back. "Hike!" Their pulls are half-hearted, accompanied by whines. Gumbo strains the hardest. "Come on, boys."

I hop off the runners and help push the sled along. My arms quiver. I'm so tired. I want to stand on the back of the sled while the dogs do the work and ride them all the way to the town.

But that's not going to happen.

I step off and move to the front. I switch the sled dogs to the back of the line and then loop the extra front harnesses over my shoulders. Time to pull. Everything inside me screams for a rest, but I plant a picture of Jesus carrying his cross in the forefront of my mind. I won't give up. I won't stop.

My Savior didn't, and today . . .

I'm determined to be like Him.

The snow is slush by high noon. My boots slide more than they grip. I don't look up anymore. My head hangs so the sweat drips to the snow instead of my eyes. Gumbo and my other dog companions lag behind, their tongues hanging from their mouths. Maybe they are wounded, too, internally. Who knows how much damage Skelley did with that Brawn suit?

I expect to look up and see the town any moment now, but that doesn't happen. I have to take a break. I have to stop.

Jesus hung on that cross for *hours* and I can't even pull a sled for three. I drop to my knees, the sled dogs sink to the snow, both panting and trying to munch the slush at the same time. I take an hour to melt them some water.

Then we go forward again. I pull in a daze, letting my thoughts bring in the voices of my friends.

"Why are you saving him?" Reid's voice again.

Can't he understand?

"Come back to us!" Willow stomps her foot.

Is she alive?

I can't. I can't abandon Skelley when this might be the only chance to change his heart. Not to mention he has the knowledge about the projected Wall. If I can't convince him to use it for our purposes, then I need to find a way to get it out of him before he dies.

A pirate chip should do the trick.

24

I don't see the town until night falls. The lights bounce on the black snow horizon, small fireflies beckoning me forward. Hope. At last!

One more step. One more step. My chest heaves, pulling in the thin air. If I get pneumonia, I'm sending Skelley the doctor's bill. If *he* gets pneumonia well . . . it'll be easy to stick a pirate chip in his skull. Now I need to find one.

The town is farther than it looks. Everything is farther when you're approaching on foot instead of being pulled by eight hefty dogs. I can't make it with this limited energy. If only the Brawn suit still worked. If only I had my Vitality suit back.

If only, if only.

Shape up! It takes another decision—a *daily* decision—to rise above this moment. For shalom. For my God.

I stop hauling and check Skelley's bandages. They're deep red and frozen, though there's no new blood. He's not as pale. I yank the furs over his face to keep him warmer, then take the bear fur for myself and sleep with the four dogs. They nuzzle closer than usual. Exhausted. Traumatized.

That's the only explanation for why they haven't attacked Skelley again. Or maybe they're just being obedient to me.

Poor dears. What will I do with them once we reach the train town? Who will take care of them? I pull Gumbo closer, finding comfort in his companionship. He barely has the energy to lick my hand.

Uneasy sleep finds me, slapping me awake every half hour with nightmares of wolves, blood, and Skelley shooting Reid. There are also nightmares of me killing people. Friends.

It's too dark inside my mind. I don't want to sleep.

Exhaustion forces me to.

Sunlight is my alarm and relief. I crawl out of the fur, stiff. Every movement shoots aches through my muscles. I groan.

Skelley is in a different position than when I left him. That's good. When I lift the fur from his face, he cracks an eye open. "We're not there yet?"

"Patience is a virtue." He'll be fine.

"I'm hungry."

My stomach churns in response. Why'd he have to remind me?

The dogs wake chipper and needing attention . . . or maybe food. I rub them behind the ears, give them some melted snow, sipping a bit myself, and then check the wounded dog.

It's no longer breathing. I sigh and lift it from the sled, setting it in the snow. "I'm sorry." I want Skelley to see what he's done. To realize and show *remorse* over the death of these dogs. With a lift of my chin, I walk back to the harness line.

Less weight for us to pull.

I head toward the town. The tall buildings rise over the many hills that lead to them. Though my body is stiffer than a mannequin's, I have new energy. We pull together—the dogs doing more of the work than they did yesterday. I start at a jog, but that doesn't last long.

At least I'm arriving during the day.

My knees shoot pain up to my hips with every step. The muscles in there are probably inflamed and surly. I imagine them grumbling amongst each other, complaining that I've never worked them this hard before.

When I reach town, I'm tempted to stop at the very edge, but then what do I do with Skelley or the dogs? Instead, I keep pulling until I'm on the street where Gloria and Sasha live. I pass their house, drop the harness, and walk up the steps to the door of the man who first helped me with Solomon.

Sergei.

After two sharp-knuckled raps, shuffling comes from behind the door. A large bolt is flipped and the door cracks. Blue eyes stare at me, then the door widens. There he is, wearing his same thick wool hat and kindly wrinkled face. "Hello."

Actually, what he says is *"Zdrasvoitye,"* but my brain translates it as soon as he says it. So this is what it's like to speak another language. "Hello. Will you help me?"

He doesn't ask for an explanation. His eyes slide from me to the sled and take in the scene of chaos and injury. "I will help."

He carries Skelley inside. Thank heaven Sergei doesn't seem to recognize him. I suppose that's normal, since Skelley isn't wearing his green fedora. He looks like a different person bandaged and hatless.

"Those are Gloria's dogs, yes?" Sergei doesn't look up from the bandages he unwinds.

"Yes." A lump crawls up my throat. I hope it's not vomit. Where do I start explaining this situation? I can't. It's too much. "Will you take care of them until she returns?"

"You speak Russian, now?"

How do I explain this? *Oh, you know, I pick up foreign languages easily.* Right. I settle for blunt truth. "It was a knowledge cap that I found."

"It is very good."

The Russian words are smooth in my mind, but my tongue is not used to them. The mixture of consonants and new vowel sounds come out jumbled, and I'm surprised Sergei understands me through what I'm sure is a thick accent. "Thanks."

Out of habit, I expect him to respond with *Welks*, but he asks, "Where is Gloria? Sasha?"

"They are at Opening One." Tied to posts and freezing to death if they didn't get free yet.

Sergei nods. "And your friends?"

Dead. I swallow a lump of pressure. "With Gloria and Sasha."

He nods again. I wish I had a fake wrist to give him specie. "I'm sorry, I have no specie."

Sergei peels back Skelley's bandage to reveal clotted blood. "I do not need specie."

It would have been a gift, not charity. A thank you because, despite the fact that we're strangers, I have a great desire to hug this man.

Maybe Skelley has a fake wrist and I can give Sergei some of his money. Sure, it's stealing, but a lot of his money came from the success of my biography. That would be okay, wouldn't it?

As I reach for Skelley's wrist, he wakes—or maybe he's been awake this whole time. He frowns at Sergei, then his gaze slides over to me. "What time is it?"

His speech is in English and Sergei looks to me for the translation. When I give it, Sergei looks at a clock on the wall. "Nine."

Skelley bolts up. "Time for us to go."

I push against his shoulder. "Lie down! You're wounded."

He slaps my hand away. "You've forgotten who I am, Parvin. Don't touch me and don't try to run because I *will* find you. We're leaving. The train is at 9:20."

I'm accosted by his rudeness, his complete lack of gratitude. Sergei has been so kind and now this . . . this *beast* dares to stomp on his generosity. Sergei looks to me for a translation, but I'm too embarrassed to share Skelley's words.

"He . . . he says he's feeling better and that we need to leave."

"That's not exactly what I said." Skelley gets to his feet and rips the bandage off his arm. He pulls another square Brawn suit from his pocket and presses it to his sternum. The material slithers out, empowering him once again. Where was *that* the whole time? I could have used it! Why didn't I *search* him?

"You can speak Russian?" I peer at the wound now exposed to the air. A pink line is all that mars the smoothness of his forearm.

Sergei looks from me to the scratch and back to me again as if asking why I thought Skelley needed care at all.

Of *course* Skelley has a medibot. I'm such a fool. "Were you fine this whole time?"

Skelley lifts a thick fur coat from a hook on the wall, then speaks to Sergei in perfect Russian. "May I purchase this coat from you?"

Sergei shrugs, seeming to move past his confusion. "You may have it if you are in need."

Skelley nods. "Thank you, but I will pay." He holds out his wrist and Sergei pulls back the sleeve on his own. It takes only a second for the transfer, but the process leaves Sergei gaping at his wrist. "*Nyet*, this is too much."

Skelley grabs my arm and pulls me from the apartment. I shout over my shoulder to Sergei, desperate to convey an apology and my thanks in one breath. "*Dasvidanya!* Thank you! Care for Gloria's dogs!"

Good-bye, kind man.

I wrench out of Skelley's grip. He keeps walking, knowing I'll follow. I run my hand over Gumbo's head as we pass. If the dogs knew human speech, I'd pour my apologies onto the ground . . . but there's nothing I can say or do to help them other than entrust them to Sergei.

I stomp after Skelley. Now I follow because he has the knowledge I need. My lips form a scathing insult, but I clamp down on it. Whatever I throw at him will rebound off his skin like a rubber ball. Once I've tamed my tongue, my indignation recedes and I feel only sorrow for the man in front of me.

"Skelley, why . . . why are you so rude to others?" Dalene said he was a people pleaser—and I see that streak in him, but it's only when it suits him. He doesn't really care about people's needs or emotions.

We reach the train platform and he climbs up the steps. "It's not rudeness. It's business."

I snort. "Then why does *business* have to be so rude?"

"Seeing as how you don't know how to be businesslike, I won't insult my intelligence by explaining it to you."

A burst of laughter sends my breath into a cloud. The swarm is coming—the douse of anger that spews through my lips when I've finally had enough. I could stop it right now if I chose to. But I let it loose.

"You act as though I'm an imbecile, the same foolish child who once trusted you with her story. But that's not me anymore. You've seen what I've done. You've seen what *God's* done with my formerly *bland* story. You are trying to tear me down and make me controllable, but it won't work. I have a Master who is stronger than you and I *love* Him. My worth is in *Him* and you can't do anything about that."

Skelley rolls his eyes and purchases tickets from an automated ticket vendor. It's odd not having to present my Clock, but this is Russia. Things are *very* different here.

That reminds me of the village near Opening One. Skelley was there, he saw it, and now my curiosity drowns out my anger. "Hey . . . why is Opening One, um, open? Did you know about that?"

"Of course I knew."

Riiight, because he knows everything. "Isn't that . . . illegal?"

"It's supposed to be, but every country makes its own rules. The United Assembly decided to do things one way, but each country with an opening still has say over how they use it. The only one that must be approved by the Assembly is Opening Four in Antarctica."

Now he's giving me answers. Perhaps my spews of anger are *good* things. I risk another push. "So where are you taking me?"

"Back to the USE of course."

"Why?"

He leads me to the train and hands our tickets to a ticketmaster. She checks them, hands them back, and he mutters, "*Spasibo*." Then we take seats in the dining car. I don't ask where we're sleeping or what the arrangement is. I follow because I want answers, and I haven't come up with any other plan yet.

"I'm not telling you my reasoning behind everything, Parvin. Even *you* know that'd be foolish of me."

"It was worth a try." I wink, which is far too friendly for what I'm feeling, but I have to try and *look* complacent if I want answers.

He pops an eyebrow and surveys me. Did my wink throw him off? It threw *me* off, but as we sit across from each other and he orders two coffees, I'm brought back to a time when I thought we were friends.

Lifetimes ago.

We sat across from each other and even laughed at times. I shared my story. I trusted him. I felt like I was finally connecting with someone and moving forward with my life. A tiny something inside nudges me toward that again.

No. We can't be friends! I'm disgusted by the very consideration. It's betraying Reid's memory. Spitting on his grave. Jude's too. Then verses float into my mind. Verses about rising for God's glory. Verses about loving my enemies. Verses about soft answers turning away wrath and kindness heaping coals on the head of an attacker.

Heaping coals sounds good.

How hard would it be to show Skelley kindness? I guess I answered that question when I decided to save his life after the dogs attacked him. Several weeks ago—when captured by the Council—I told him I forgave him. If that was true, then why do I still cling to bitterness?

"You've been staring off into space for a while." Skelley stirs his coffee.

My own cup of coffee sits before me, untouched. When did these arrive? I couldn't have zoned *that* much. "Well, I've been making some tough mental decisions."

"If they have anything to do with escaping, you can toss those out the window." He sips delicately from the glass cup.

"If I'd wanted to escape, that would have happened a long time ago." It sounds braggy, but it's true.

"If you attack me, I'll win. We both know that."

Uh, not true mister cocky. I could murder you with your own coffee cup if you didn't have on the Brawn suit. "I plan to bring you down a whole different way."

"Oh yes? And what way is that?"

I use one of his lines from earlier. "I'm not telling you my reasoning behind everything, Skelley. Even *you* know that'd be foolish of me."

But rest assured I'll win. Because I'm going to kill you . . .

. . . with kindness.

And it's going to feel *really* weird for both of us.

25

If I have to share a room with the devil, at least it's in first class.

There is an elegantly draped window, a small blue couch, and a wooden table by a bunk bed. The bunk bed is a minor blessing, so I don't have to see Skelley's nasty smirk when trying to fall asleep. I take the top bunk to feel less vulnerable and because it gives the sensation of being in my personal alcove, above this whole situation.

The place smells like lemons.

Skelley acts as though we've hardly been through anything—as though he didn't let loose a tear when he helped kill me, or appear weathered when he thought I was dead. Would it kill him to be *real*?

The window becomes my new best friend. We make faces at each other. It shows me stunning countryside and winks at me with sunrays. I stick out my tongue.

Skelley closes the drapes every time we enter the room. I open them again.

We spend most of our time in the dining car. It's still an enclosed space where we sit across from each other with an elephant in the room, but it's less intimate than the sleeping room.

The entire dining car is open and has sixteen four-person tables back to back—eight on each side of the car. Creamy yellow-patterned cloth covers the chairs. Similar tablecloths drape over the wooden tables, with napkins shaped like flowers and a small fruit basket on each. Overhead are dome lights and clocks hang on the end walls, showing different time zones. Each table has its own window—hello again, friend! —and I spend more time watching the snowscapes zip by than interacting with Skelley.

It's hard to defeat the devil with kindness when I don't speak to him. More than anything, I've stepped into a neutral zone. He's on his NAB almost all the time. I ache for my Bible, my *Daily Hemisphere . . . something* to keep me occupied. To keep me from wondering about Solomon.

Is he alive?

Skelley tosses a news electrosheet toward me without looking up from his NAB. "Better keep up."

Yay! News! I pull the *Daily Hemisphere* near and go over the events of the past week.

With the reading comes the reminder of what the Council's done. They blew up Unity Village. They killed people. They activated a projected Wall to keep people trapped in the USE. The public is furious with the Council—particularly over its lies about my death.

"Skelley, what's the purpose—?"

"We're not familiar enough for you to keep calling me Skelley." He doesn't look up.

"Well, I don't respect you enough to call you Mr. Chase anymore." So much for killing him with kindness. I close my eyes and take a deep breath. "And I feel like we've been through quite a lot together." *Say it nicely, not in accusation.* "You call me Parvin, I call you Skelley."

He taps the screen on his NAB as though our conversation isn't happening. I don't want to call him Mr. Chase—that's what I called him when I admired him. When I thought he was my mini-savior. But I'll do it if it helps me get through his thick skull.

"So, Mr. Chase, what's—"

"Now you're being childish."

Grah! My hand balls into a fist of its own accord, and I stop myself before slamming it on the table. The edges of his lips twitch. The rat! He's *trying* to aggravate me. It's hard enough to swallow my frustration and pretend it doesn't bother me, so I channel it into sarcasm. Hopefully it comes out playful. "Well, what's your middle name then? I'll call you by that."

He chuckles. "You will never be privy to that information."

"Did you *really* just use the word *privy?* In normal conversation?"

"Yes, it's called a developed vocabulary. Do you know what the word means?"

"Well, one version means bathroom, but I don't think that's what you meant." He forgets I was a reader before I became a world changer. "I'll just have to guess your middle name then." I bet it's Snake. Or Viper. Cobra, maybe. Vampire?

"Good luck."

Now, back to my original question, if I can remember it after all his interruptions. "So . . . *Eugene*"—Skelley snorts—"what's the purpose of the Wall?"

That finally drags his gaze up from his NAB. "I thought you knew your history."

I roll my eyes and watch the countryside. "I get that it was built because some people wanted the remains of the government and others wanted to be free. Someone got angry and started the Wall. We didn't have the resources to rebuild the whole Earth after all the destruction, blah blah blah. It's supposedly protecting us from the evils of the other side, but you and I both know that's a lie."

He sighs, but the stiffness of his dismissive expression dissolves. He folds his hands over his NAB screen. "It was never just for protection. The ruined cities and survivors started finding their own leaders. People with different ideals. Those who wanted a more . . . *savage* lifestyle gravitated toward the ruined portions of the Earth."

Hasn't he seen pictures of Ivanhoe? That's not what I'd call *savage*.

"War was brewing. I don't expect you to know what that looks like—"

I flip the *Daily Hemisphere* around and shove it toward him. "I imagine it looks a bit like this." There is a picture of weathered Radicals picketing at the newly projected Wall. Dead Enforcers. Another article with people being led away in cuffs because they refused the new Clocks. Another article about people who died, but their Clocks ticked on.

He waves it off. "Riots are a different world than wars."

"This is much more than a riot." He can't dumb down what's going on. "Even the albinos have gotten involved."

"Charity. They disappeared the moment the projected Wall went up."

Wrong. Black and Ash won't give up so easily. Skelley thinks their departure means surrender, but I know better. I lived among them and they are strong.

"Why are you so obsessed with erecting projected Walls every-where? People *want* to go through!"

"They don't know what they want."

I roll my eyes. "Don't be so superior. It's not up to you to decide what choices they should make."

He twirls a fork between his fingers. "So you're saying we should give people everything they want?" I'm about to nod, but then he says, "Legalize drugs? Get rid of laws? Let murderers run free?"

"O-of course not, but—"

"Your views of freedom are too clear-cut, Parvin. You can't think holistically, and that is why people die from your decisions."

Jude. Reid. Dusten.

No, don't let him get to you.

"If I'm so dangerous, why are you bringing me with you?" I

269

hold back the question of *where*. Oftentimes understanding the *why* reveals breadcrumbs that lead to other answers . . . if I'm lucky enough to hear Skelley's reply.

"You'll see soon enough."

I lean my forearms on the table, crunching the flowered napkin. "I won't run away, Skelley. I'm seeing this through to the end." Even if he thinks my narrowed view will be the death of the people.

He smirks. "Because you have to."

"No, because I'm being obedient. God wants me here with you, so here I am." I used to be embarrassed speaking about God to this high-and-mighty celebrity, but all I feel now is sorrow because he can't relate to my peace. Something inside him *must* be yearning for shalom.

"Then your God must want you to learn patience." Skelley turns back to his NAB, and I quell the flare of irritation inside me.

Fine then.

I can be patient.

By the time the train arrives in Moscow, Skelley's scars and scratches are gone. He doesn't bother to chain me to him or lock my wrists. For some reason he trusts I'll follow. He probably thinks it's because I'm subdued.

I'm anything but.

We take a taxi to the airport, and the only thing that keeps me from getting carsick is the knowledge that I'll be airsick soon. We drive straight out onto the tarmac and park beside the steps of a small jet. A *private* jet. Whoa.

Skelley and I are the only passengers. The interior is larger than my Unity house and smells of leather. I sit in a seat. The leather chills me faster than a snowbed might. "How kind of the Council to provide such stylish transportation. Nice to know all the specie you're stealing from citizens with the Clock scandal is funding your luxuries."

"Buckle up."

Skelley takes a seat on the opposite side of the plane. A lady in heels and a blue pencil-skirt serves him drinks. She offers nothing to me. I don't want anything anyway. I lick my lips and note the dryness of my throat.

Except maybe some sick sacks.

If I can handle being killed by the Council, I can handle a dry throat.

We don't stop in France. The plane continues over countries I can't place and then over the ocean. I vomit only three times! The lady in the pencil skirt learns after the first time to bring me a barf bag . . . and then some bubbly drink that helps settle my stomach.

Now that we're over the ocean, I'm no longer parched and the vomiting has stopped, I stare at the water far below. I imagine an engine failing and being stranded in an icy sea with Skelley Chase.

He'd probably eat me.

I fall asleep to that twisted thought and, thankfully, have no nightmares associated with it. I wake to the jolt of wheels on cement. We're here . . . wherever *here* is. I have no idea what happened with Solomon, Willow, or Elm. Why is this always my situation? I'm called to lead, to speak, to rise, to protect my people . . . but that always takes me away from them. I cross the Wall. I wake in a coffin. And now I'm here with Skelley.

Mother once said that God works in mysterious ways. By *mysterious*, she must mean *weird*.

I'm dizzy as we step off the plane with no sense of time. The sun is high, but my grainy eyes and headache tell me it's midnight. Skelley doesn't look so great either. He's dressed in rumpled Russian furs and his usually pristine five-o'clock shadow now resembles an unkempt lawn.

Being tired makes me think like a five-year-old and I barely manage to restrain myself from pointing and chanting, *"Ha-ha!"*

Ha-ha, the Councilman has scraggly facial hair and lost his hat!

The moment we plop into his sleek green car, I go to sleep. He very well might crash this car on the way to wherever we're going—probably the same prison center I was at when they killed me—but I'm too tired to care.

A day passes in a mixture of sleep, grogginess, and confusion. I can't piece everything together, but I had one correct prediction. I am deposited into a white cell with the projected door that will zap me into ash if I try to walk through it. Not a bad death.

I think I'm in the Council building again. But I'm not here to die.

This cell is nicer than the one I had a month ago. There's a bed with grey blankets and a pillow. On one wall is a toilet seat with a metal sink attached behind it. A shelf is built into the opposite wall, with some folded clothing on it. Sweats and a matching hoodie. Don't mind if I do.

After I clean off Skelley's dried blood with the sulfur-smelling sink water, I change, sit on the bed, and wait. Here I am. Obedient, but confused. Tempted to fear, but reminding myself of God's assurance.

What will they do to me? Or what will they ask me to do? And where is the technician Erfinder told us about?

FEAR NOT.

I'm not afraid. But . . . please give me wisdom to know how to act in the upcoming situations. I'm not afraid to die . . . again . . . but I'd like to know what happened to Solomon. Poor Solomon. He went through so much. He put up with me as I struggled to figure out who I was and how to love.

There's a knock on the wall outside my room. Is that for me? "Come in." The Enforcer I spoke to at my gravesite walks in. "Zeke!"

I don't know Zeke well, but for some reason I'm calmer. He helped Solomon and the others escape—though he hasn't admitted it. He's a friend.

Zeke bows. "Miss Blackwater, the Council requests your presence."

I push myself up off the bed. It's time to find out why they sent Skelley after me. It's time to find out what they're going to do—kill me, free me, or use me. I rub my hand up and down my stump arm.

Zeke holds out an arm and places it on my back to lead me through the door. "I want to tell you everything'll be okay." His words come through pursed lips in a low guarded tone. "But . . ."

I link my stump arm through his. "Everything *will* be okay, Zeke. It will." *Will it?*

MY WILL.

Deep breath. Deep calm. *Okay.*

We're in the Council building—the one that floats over the ground. The one in which I was first Clock-matched and where I discovered Skelley sat on the Council. We enter the same dark room with the circle of chairs and I'm reminded that I'm a little girl, barely an adult, who's trying to save the world.

But I have my God.

I'm set in the center of the room this time, which is far more disconcerting because I have to spin to face whoever is talking. All five Council members are in their seats, forming a circle around me. Zeke takes his place against the curve of the wall, disappearing into the shadows. How many more Enforcers are in here, listening to what's about to take place? It's cliché to think of the villains of this world doing their dirty work and forgetting about the helpers and minions who hear and see all. In this case, the Enforcers.

It is happening here.

Maybe I am here for the Enforcers—for Zeke—not for the Council or even the public.

Skelley sits in his chair examining his fingernails. He has a new hat—still asparagus green, but crisper than his last one. Brickbat is a glowing black-and-white photo with his dyed grey hair, pressed suit, and white shoes. Try as I might, I see no similarities between him and Tawny. Does he know she married *my* brother? Does he know he helped kill his own son-in-law?

President Ethan Garraty gapes at me like a fish out of water. Beside him, the only female on the Council looks at me with an interested expression. That's when I realize that this is their first time seeing me alive after they buried me. It must be odd for them.

"Hi, everyone." I speak first, even though it might not be wise.

Brickbat is the first to respond. "How are you alive?"

"Frankly, I still can't figure it out. I was dead for a while, so I didn't see what happened." A smile slithers onto my face and I let it blossom. "In short, God decided to let me live."

"How?" Brickbat's pale face turns red. "And how do you remember everything?"

"Ask *Him* that." I imagine Brickbat trying to talk to God. There would be a lot of shouting.

"Elan, this isn't why she's here." Skelley's calm, almost bored voice, contrasts with a splash against Brickbat's barely contained rage. The room stills. Why *am* I here? Tell me!

Brickbat chews on his lip so violently, I'm surprised there isn't blood when he finally stops and folds his arms like a pouty child. "Get on with it, then."

"Miss Parvin Blackwater"—Skelley's new level of professionalism blares like a warning beacon—"after much discussion amongst the Citizen Welfare Development Council and input from the public, you are, as of today . . ." He takes a deep breath as though the words are burning his tongue.

" . . . a member of this Council."

26

My guffaw echoes like a taunting ghost in the deathly silent room. *"What?"* I squeak. I catch my breath, glance at Skelley's serious face, and laugh again. "This makes no sense!" It's the last thing I expected and it doesn't fit at all. A trick. Do they honestly think I'll fall for it? "No, thank you."

"You don't have a choice." Brickbat speaks through his teeth.

"Sorry, but you can't force me to be a leader." At least not for the enemy. They have no leverage this time. No one they can threaten to kill. Why didn't Skelley take Willow or Solomon hostage when he came for me? It would have been so easy.

"This is an honor, Parvin. The people want you as their voice." Skelley's not bored this time. Could he really believe I'd want this? And if so, why didn't he at least *prep* me for this offer during our train travels?

"You don't *kidnap* a teenager to make her an equal member on the Council. That's not how this works."

Skelley shakes his head. "You followed of your own free will."

"Yeah, after you almost blew out the brains of two innocent Russian girls and stole the knowledge cap." I should have kept the thought to myself, but there are Enforcers here. They, at least, deserve the truth.

I pop my neck to keep myself from searching for Zeke's eyes. What is he thinking? Does *he* want me on the Council? Are the people truly asking for my leadership? I'm no leader. I'm a survivor who happened to have a thousand people follow her into the West. "Why?"

Brickbat presses a button on the arm of his chair as though expecting this question. A hologram illuminates the room in whitish-blue glow. A scene explodes around me, of miniature people. Everywhere. A protest mob with signs and chanting. One sign reads, *Bring Parvin Blackwater Back!*

I can't tell where the people are, but it was somewhere memorable enough for the Council to take notice. The Wall isn't in view.

"This is what happened one week after your little 'I'm alive' video went viral. Petitions. Picketing. Riots. All thanks to you." Brickbat jams the button on his chair. The hologram disappears.

All thanks to me. It's the highest compliment he could have paid me. "Even if I *did* accept this . . . *honor*"—I snort—"you won't ever see my voice as equal. What's the point? You know you won't listen to me." They want me only to appease the people.

"We'll listen." Brickbat speaks through clenched teeth.

But you won't do anything for us.

"Don't throw away this opportunity, Parvin." Skelley steeples his fingers and rests his elbows on the arms of the chair. "All you have to do is take your seat."

That's when I notice the extra chair situated firmly in between Skelley and Brickbat. I don't know what their plan is—other than it's nothing good—but God brought me here. "If I sit in that chair, then I expect all the same benefits that a Council member gets. I won't be living in a cell."

What am I doing? Can I possibly sit down as a *member* of this Council? It's surely a trick, and I don't want to miss their angles.

"You'll live where we put you."

Will Brickbat never learn? Threats don't control me. "You can't lie to the public. If you want me on your Council, and if you want the people to see me aligned with you—which I assume is your plan—you can't deceive them. All it takes is one slip. One person to notice that you're lying"—like Zeke—"and the news gets out to everyone."

Brickbat stares me down. I don't flinch. He practically snarls at me. "So what's your answer?"

God, what do I do? It was easier making decisions when they were blackmailing me. But this is a decision with two doors—out or in. Well, God took me all the way here . . . He'll get me out if needed.

I nod.

Now, for my terms. I face the female Council member, turning my back on Brickbat. "What's your name again?"

"Adria."

I guess *Adria* doesn't have a last name. Then I gasp. Adria! "Adria Nazarkin?"

She lifts an eyebrow. "Of course."

Yes, yes, *of course.* The lady Erfinder trained. Here she is, practically in my lap. I've found our Wall technician. I swallow several times, trying not to squeal, beg, or allow my *kill-her-now* instincts to get control.

"Well, Adria, we left my belongings in Russia. I want replacements. A *Daily Hemisphere* electrosheet, my Bible, and I'd like a NAB."

"You can't have a NAB." Her voice is calm, unthreatening, and almost kind. "While we are offering you this honor, you are still a threat and a criminal."

"Then why the honor?" I fold my arms. Is the Council truly that influenced by the people's will?

Skelley's sigh bounces off the walls of the small circle room. "Will you take the seat or not?"

I stare at the half-sphere chair with its fluffy cushion armrests. It's just as easy to step out of that chair as it is to sit in it. I'll find out the *whys*, and I'll trust God while I do it. Three strides are all it takes to plop my tush in that chair. It's comfortable. I'd like to burn the thing.

Once I sit, it's like the joke lost its steam. No one speaks. Brickbat still seethes while Skelley picks at his thumbnail.

"Well, since I'm on the Council, I'd like to know what's going on with the public." I might as well ask. The Enforcers are listening, even if the Council members aren't. "Clearly the new Clocks aren't a huge hit. Neither is the newly projected Wall project." I tap my chin. "Is there anything you've done that's working right now?"

Brickbat rises from his seat. "Today's meeting is over. You'll be escorted to your room and we can discuss suggestions, news, and forward steps tomorrow."

Tomorrow. So much can happen in a day. But today I'll play by their rules. Brickbat walks out, followed by Adria, and then President Garraty and the other male Council member.

"It's just you and me again, Leroy." I hope Skelley's middle name is Leroy. That'd be tease-worthy.

He frowns for a second before piecing together that I'm talking to him. "Leroy?" He pushes against the armrests and rises. "Shall we?"

I fold my arms and lean back. "Why? It's so . . . comfortable in here." Now I'm being difficult. The banter isn't fun and I don't have the energy to be defiant, so I stand. Two Enforcers step from the shadows and lead me from the room. One of them is Zeke.

They have me pose for a few photos with the rest of the Council members. It makes me feel dirty, and I probably look a sight in my hoodie and sweats, but I keep my mind focused heavenward. *You are in control, God. You are in control.* Maybe if I chant it enough, the words will latch onto my heart.

I'm given a new room with a window, a comfortable bed, and separate bathing room. The floor is carpeted, and it takes only a few minutes for Zeke to return with a *Daily Hemisphere* electro-sheet and an old worn Bible that's missing half its pages.

"Thank you."

He bows and leaves. Not too friendly, but not too cold.

I sit against the window and look out at the High-City bustle below me. Passersby walk with relaxed shoulders and monotony. Does such mayhem about the Clocks and the Wall really rest beneath their skin? Or is it localized to certain groups and cities?

I expected to look out the window and see a mass of rioting people.

God . . . what am I doing? I'm a nobody. A teenager who can't possibly hold her own against such leaders. They think they have the upper hand, and they're right. I have no leverage.

I AM WITH YOU.

Okay . . . so I do have leverage.

The Council has me here for a reason. What is it?

They want to use my face to lie again to the public. They've done it before, why not again?

They think I have something that they want. I can't imagine what that is, since their pirate chip swallowed my whole brain.

They genuinely want me on the Council. Ha!

They want to kill me. Unsurprisingly, that doesn't scare me. Nobody can touch me unless God wants them to. What they don't realize is that *I* can kill *them.* Easily. At least, I have the knowledge to. For the first time, I let myself contemplate this. Is that the reason God has me here? To kill the Council? Is that why He let me swallow that cap?

No, that's still murder.

But in the Bible God commanded a lot of people to go to war, to kill. King David, King Saul, all those famous guys. Yet Jesus didn't kill anyone as far as I remember. He focused on life, on hope . . . and He is who I want to emulate. So for now, I will swallow the impulse to karate-chop Brickbat's throat.

Instead, I'll focus on getting a pirate chip to steal either Skelley's brain or Adria's.

I lie back on the bed and scan the news in the *Daily Hemisphere.* It has more videos than text now, which I like. I feel more informed when I watch scenes at the Wall. The fighting has increased, but the people make little progress.

Thousands of people form a mob near the broken portion. Enforcers create a human barricade with their rifles, held with firm hands, and their electric shields up. A gap lies between the two enemies until someone rushes forward and shoves the nearest Enforcer. The Radical is brought down with a single bullet in less than a second, but that's not where the focus of the news is.

The camera follows the shoved Enforcer. He stumbles backward, reaches for a friend, but trips and careens through the projected Wall. It happens in a flash. His body falls like a broken statue and lands against the ground blackened and charred, like Dusten Grunt. No one is there to catch him, to bury him, or to help him.

He's dead.

Chaos follows. The other Enforcers flee the projected Wall—their terror sending energy into the mobbers, who then rush forward, shoving and yanking Enforcers toward the projection. Bullets fly, people fall. Enforcers burn.

I don't cheer for either side. While I want freedom for the people of the USE, I don't want it at the cost of their morals. I don't want them to become murderers in their fear.

The Wall *must* come down. And Skelley Chase is my key in.

While my room is nice, the locked door gives away the fact that I'm still a prisoner. A knock rouses me from my spot on the bed. The door opens to reveal Zeke. He shuffles his feet and doesn't meet my eyes. "The Council is meeting."

His nervous stance sets me on edge. Does he know something about this meeting? Are they planning to try killing me again? He steps away from the door and waits. I suppose I ought to follow. I stuff my Bible and the *Daily Hemisphere* into my hoodie pouch and we weave down several hallways, take an elevator, and then he opens the door to the Council room for me.

I hear the chattering voices before my eyes adjust to see the faces. The moment I step inside, the talk stops.

Brickbat leans forward in his chair. "What is she doing here?"

"Um, she is . . . uh . . . a Council member and . . ." Zeke takes a step back.

"Explain yourself, Enforcer!"

Adria rises from her chair. "It's evident he's confused about his duties, Elan. Enforcers serve the Council and its members. It's required of him to have every member present for meetings." She turns to Zeke. "You are dismissed, Enforcer."

Zeke swallows hard and the corridor light reflects off the sheen of sweat on his forehead as he leaves. Poor Zeke. If he wasn't instructed to retrieve me, why did he take the initiative instead of asking? Did he know Elan and the others were going behind my back?

"Take a seat, Parvin." Skelley gestures toward the empty chair.

I sit and look around. Adria fiddles with the NAB on her lap—is she monitoring the projected Wall?—President Garraty looks asleep, and Elan's a red balloon face on the verge of popping.

"What are we talking about?" I'm an actress in a play I'm not supposed to be in. They were talking about me. I pretend I don't notice. They pretend they weren't caught. And now we pretend there's something to talk about.

"Parvin, please prepare a list of things you'd like to discuss with us for the next meeting." Skelley rocks back in his chair. "We'll discuss it this evening. That's all."

The other Council members stare at him, but add nothing to his statement.

Why did I even sit? "All righty." I stride back out of the room and practically run into Zeke in the hall. Let the connivers whisper behind my back. Nothing is as secret as they think it is. The Enforcers hear it all.

"Thank you, Zeke."

He gives a small salute. "Ma'am."

Huh. I've never seen an Enforcer do that before.

As we start to walk away, the Council members resume conversation in lowered voices. The door is still open and I jerk to a halt. Zeke stops beside me. Without a word, I tiptoe back toward the Council room until I'm pressed against the wall near the doorframe.

"This is pointless, Skelley," Brickbat says with a throaty gurgle. "We can't keep pretending she has a voice."

"She *knows* she doesn't have a voice." I can almost hear Skelley's eye-roll. "She's not as easily deceived as you think she is."

Why . . . thank you?

Skelley continues. "The fact is, she's here, she's contained, and when tomorrow's article shows up in *The Daily Hemisphere* the people will think she's on our side. That will cause them to listen to us more. We are boosting *our* voice with her mere presence."

I've heard enough. None of this news surprises me, but when I turn back to Zeke and see his skin paler and his eyes wide, I can't help wondering if this info is new to him.

Back in my room, I find a pad of paper and a pen on a small desk by my bed. The Council doesn't know that *I* know their scheming—well, Skelley knows, but I'm going to keep playing along. Because even if the Council won't hear my voice, the Enforcers will.

Besides, the more I play along, the more chances I have to sneak a pirate chip and get the projection information from Adria or Skelley.

I jot down the first three things that come to mind:

The Clocks—bad for the people

The projected Wall—bad for the people
Selling Radicals as slaves—bad for the people.
I'm seeing a trend here.

As my mind starts zipping, so does the pen. There is so much to fix—the testing of Clocks on orphans, the fact that they charge for the new Clocks, the use of Enforcers to break the law . . .

Evening comes and goes. My list grows longer, but no one fetches me for the meeting. The sky darkens and I allow myself to curl up on my bed, resting my stump over my eyes.

God, I'm starting to see why You have me here. But will I be able to retrieve the projected Wall information from Skelley's mind? Can I change any of this?

WAIT ON ME.

His words are from a verse that reminds me of God's timing. Wait. Wait on Him. Being patient is a lot harder to maintain when people are dying every hour. *Do You see them dying?*

Of course He does. I fall asleep to the mental image of the dying Radicals entering the warmth of His opened arms.

I wake with an itch to open the *Daily Hemisphere*. The moment it unfurls, there's a picture of me standing in the center of the other five, much taller, Council members. My face is serious. My body is . . . disproportioned, like someone tried to touch-up my awkward frame and add curves where there are none.

A fake photo under a very real headline: *Parvin Blackwater— Youngest Council Member in History*

I joined the Council.

Everyone can see it now. It's a different feeling reading a headline that's true. If Solomon reads this . . . will he believe it?

At least he'll know I'm alive. If *he's* alive, that is.

I'm served breakfast in my room. An Enforcer brings it in on a tray. I picture him in a bonnet and apron like an old housemaid and giggle. He catches my eyes as I stifle it, but instead of the cool mask I'm used to in Enforcers, his stone face cracks a smile.

"Good sunrise, Council member."

Is that why he's smiling? Because I'm someone? Or is it because he pictures himself in an apron like I do?

Eggs. Toast. Bacon. Tea. There are even mini shakers of salt and pepper. Don't mind if I do.

I barely finish breakfast before a knock on my door precedes two Enforcer escorts. They take me to the Council room, not forcing me. Not even touching me. Is it because I'm now a Council member? Is it something Skelley said? Or does it have to do with me in general?

I take my seat, *Daily Hemisphere* in hand. My palm is sweaty. I don't know how these meetings are conducted—do they happen every day or did I simply join at the right time? The other members are already seated. My hand slips into my pocket to clutch the folded piece of paper with my list of problems. Where to start? I take a deep breath to bring up the projected Wall incident from yesterday, but Skelley speaks up first.

"The new Clocks are a problem."

Duh.

Brickbat rubs his temple. "The inventors are working day and night to find an answer." The Council doesn't know what's wrong with the Clocks. More importantly . . . they don't know that I have the answer they need.

"We got the newest report yesterday." Skelley taps on his NAB and a light glow illuminates his somber face. "We broke twenty thousand."

Adria gasps.

I look from her to Skelley. President Garraty isn't present. "Twenty thousand what?"

"Twenty thousand people have overridden their new Clocks by either outliving them or zeroing out early." Skelley closes the NAB.

"You already distributed over *twenty thousand Clocks?*" That number is huge, but those are only the Clocks that have been overridden—a tiny percentage in the millions of Clocks already distributed.

"We've put distribution on hold, Skelley. What more can we do?" The grind of Brickbat's teeth reaches my ears from across the room.

"Even with distribution on hold, those who have the new Clocks are the majority of the USE. That's why they want to go through the Wall. They don't trust us anymore." His voice isn't bored. There's no drawl. It's a side of Skelley I've never heard before—all seriousness, and . . . concern?

"Take down the projected Wall and let people through!" My voice bursts like a trumpet, contrasting Skelley's calm solemnity. "Why is that so hard for you?" My thoughts roll toward my lips like a frenzied tumbleweed, but I hold them back and take deep breaths. If they're going to consider my words at all, I mustn't start with accusations. "I'd like to understand why you are opposed to doing this."

The flush on Brickbat's neck prepares me for his outburst. Why is he always so angry? "Not everything is so black and white."

Says the man who wears *only* black and white. "Explain it, then."

I cringe out of habit as he opens his mouth, but Skelley sweeps in with his own unnerving calm. "We can't explain everything to you, Parvin, but replacing the stone Wall with a projected Wall has been a long time in the making. To let down the projection and send people through to the West would contradict all of that. There would be a lot of wasted time, energy, material, and planning."

"So?" That's called *learning*.

"We don't expect you to understand!" Brickbat uncrosses his legs and plants his shining polished shoes on the floor. "The West is outside of our jurisdiction. We don't have the right to simply send people into a different country."

"You've been doing it for years with Radicals! Have you forgotten how *I* went through? Besides, the West is unclaimed. There is no leadership." Even the Preacher, Lemuel, doesn't claim to be the king of the people. "The USE is a free country. How can you keep people trapped here?"

"They're not trapped. They can travel anywhere within this side of the Wall."

"Who decided the other side is off limits?" If he claims to have no jurisdiction in the West then why were Radicals sacrificed through the Wall all the time? The confusion and knotted mess of information clears enough to reveal a single, basic problem. I launch to my feet. "I have a question."

Skelley holds up his hand to silence Brickbat. Perhaps he senses that my question doesn't arise from my arguing. "What is it?"

"Who does the Wall belong to?"

Brickbat's eyes dart to Skelley. Everyone's eyes dart to him. How does this young biographer hold so much leadership over these people?

"It's an agreement between the countries on the United Assembly," he says.

I cock my head to the side. "So basically the portion of Wall going through the USE—projection or otherwise—belongs to us. To the people."

"To the leaders of the USE." Brickbat jerks a thumb toward his chest. "Us. The projection is USE property, since the inventor was a USE citizen."

"So then we *do* have the jurisdiction to let people through." I sink back into my seat. It's the first time I've used the word *we* in reference to the Council instead of *you*. Maybe if I start talking like I've accepted this role, they'll listen. It worked with Solomon.

"Why are we even listening to her?" Brickbat gestures to me with a throw of his hand. "She's not a legitimate member of the Council."

I catch movement to my left and look in time to see two Enforcers exchange a glance. "Then why am I here?"

"The people clearly think you have their best interest at heart—"

"I do."

Skelley rolls his eyes. "As do we. So . . . because they're such fans of yours—"

"Thanks to you." I should probably hold my tongue.

His knuckles pop. "We would like to hear what *you* would do for them. We're not complete tyrants."

But you are at least part *tyrant*.

"Let's get back to the topic at hand," Adria says. "The Clocks have a problem. People need to feel secure. They're losing trust in us, and we need to do something about that."

"Like show them you care about them?" I suggest with an air of innocence.

Adria frowns. "I think we should keep them informed on how the inventors are doing."

"That would be a great idea if they were making any *progress!*" Brickbat folds his arms so tightly a shirt seam pops.

Skelley lifts both hands. "Look . . . people are terrified. They need to see some *action* on our part."

"We *are* taking action!" Spittle flies from Brickbat's mouth, putting watermelon-seed spitters to shame. "We've got inventors going round the clock!"

"The people can't *see* that." If Skelley keeps talking like this, I might actually start to believe he's rooting for the citizens' welfare. "I have a different idea."

"Different?" Brickbat snorts. "I have plenty of *different* ideas. I want a *better* idea."

Skelley raises an eyebrow. "That depends on your point of view."

I want to hear his idea. I want to like it. I want to believe he's on the people's side, but Skelley is so unpredictable, with his ulterior motives, I don't know what optimism I can cling to in regard to him.

"What is it?" My tiny voice barely crawls its way to their ears.

Skelley takes his eyes away from Brickbat and looks at me— holds my gaze. The Enforcers beside me stiffen. I don't look away, neither does Skelley. His gaze is intense, as though his forthcoming words are meant for me.

"I think we should recall the new Clocks."

27

Pride swells inside my chest for the man who murdered my brother. It's not right—the clash of emotions—but Skelley drew out a gasp. The man I hate surprised me . . . in a good way.

"Recall the Clocks?" Adria's breathy voice quavers. "And then what?"

"Then we continue to work for a solution."

Brickbat glares at Skelley. "You can't leave the people without Clocks! They'll panic—"

"People are already panicking, Elan."

I want to shout, "Hear hear!" but if Brickbat sees me supporting Skelley, he'll be even more averse to the suggestion. I can't believe what my mind is doing right now. It's . . . agreeing with Skelley Chase. The traitor.

I'm . . . on his side.

"They're panicking more about the Clocks being faulty than about not having one. I think we should recall them so they stop encountering the overridden Clocks. If worse comes to worst, then we'll have one Clockless generation, but we'll reinstate the original Clocks for their children."

So much for agreeing with him.

"We can't take away people's Clocks," Brickbat repeats like a moping child.

"They don't even *want* them, Elan." Skelley sighs and adjusts his fedora. "Think about it."

"That's a big step." Adria purses her lips. "Recalling the Clocks without an alternative? Doesn't that affirm that we aren't consistent or in control?"

"It affirms that we're on their side."

I feel Brickbat's glare on me before his words come. "You *like* this idea, don't you, Blackwater?"

To say *yes* means I agree with Skelley. To say *no* means I agree with Brickbat. I can't commit to either. "I like most of it." He can take that how he will.

"We need time. Discussion. Go back to your room, Parvin."

"Yes, Dad." That little bit of sarcasm comes out on its own— more of an insult to my dear Father than to Brickbat. Oops. Still . . . I obey.

The announcement goes out one week later. The Clocks are recalled. It's front page of the *Daily Hemisphere*, and I wish I could somehow see everyone's reactions. The only Council members mentioned in the Clock-recall article are Skelley and me— Brickbat's way of protecting his back. If this plan backfires, then he'll look wise and the people will hate me.

However, if it succeeds . . . then Skelley and I become a winning team.

The Council may not be removing the projected Wall like I wanted, but at least they're doing something that I agree is good. No more Clocks . . . for now.

That is the only meeting I've attended, and now I sit again in my room. Locked in and staring at the *Daily Hemisphere*, waiting for some sort of reaction. Instead, the announcement is followed by an article about me. Surprise, surprise.

It's more of a summary than anything new. Parvin Blackwater survived. Parvin Blackwater survived again. Parvin Blackwater saved some Radicals, blew up the Wall, joined the Council . . .

Everyone knows this.

But the person behind these articles is trying to bring the spotlight back on me. Waiting for me to mess up or succeed. Don't they realize it's not about me? Below this article is a question and answer video with random people.

Q: *"What do you think Parvin will bring to the Council?"*
Answer from a random citizen: "I think she'll give us a voice."

Hm. That girl must be a Radical trying to get through the Wall. I can be her voice.

Next answer: *"Nothing. She's a rebel teenager for time's sake! I don't know what the Council is thinking."*

You and me both, mister.

Next answer: *"I hope she'll fix the Clock problem."*

Maybe I will, but not how she thinks I will.

The next answer comes from a face I know—short black hair topping a dark-skinned face. Gabbie Kenard, alive and well. "Parvin is going to save us. She's going to bring new freedom to everyone. If she's on that Council, it's for a reason."

I almost cry. Almost.

Next answer: *"Why is she with the Council? I thought she was on our side."*

I am! I am on your side!

It doesn't matter what these citizens think because a couple of days later the focus shifts. More riots. People don't want to give up their Clocks, at least not to the Council. They don't want to be Radicals. Go figure.

Will they make up their minds already?

Here's proof that we can't please everyone. But I suppose if I'd forked out one-hundred specie for the Clock around my wrist, I wouldn't want to return it without some sort of compensation.

Others—the Radicals at the Wall—have boosted their efforts on defeating the Enforcers guarding the projection. It doesn't take long for the Enforcers to abandon their posts, but the Radical victory is short lived. Even without Enforcers there, no one can get through the projection.

More time passes, but no more meetings take place with the Council. I'm a prisoner again, with no news of my friends. Are Solomon, Willow, and Elm alive? What about Gloria and Sasha? All I have is the *Daily Hemisphere*, and who knows how accurate that is?

One evening, it's not an Enforcer who delivers my dinner. It's Skelley. I try to act cool, but he carries in a tray of fish and I gag on my greeting. "Hey there Maximus"—*cough*—"what are you"—*cough*—"ugh. Is that fish?"

He sets the tray down on my desk. On top of my opened Bible. "Maximus? Not a bad middle name."

"Did I get it right?" Skelley Maximus Chase?

"Nope."

I slide my Bible out from under the tray, nearly upsetting the thing. Skelley catches the wobbling tray and even lifts it a bit to make my extraction of the Bible easier. "So, why are you in here trying to poison me?"

"I take it you don't like fish."

"Putrescence."

He grins. "That's a big word for you. Do you know what it means?"

"It's a synonym for fish." Yeah, I know what the word *synonym* means. I almost laugh, but then a vision pierces my mind like a lightning bolt. Reid. Falling, folding, bloodied, and murdered. Skelley's bored smile.

The laugh dies on my lips. Skelley watches me and his expression, which wasn't necessarily a smile, fades into seriousness. "Funny how forgiveness can disappear in such a short moment."

Is it gone? It certainly feels gone. Right now, I want to hate Skelley. *God?* Sorrow and anger battle for dominance like an evenly weighted seesaw. I grind my teeth, willing myself to remember God's call to arise. *Get me above this negativity!*

My emotions swing to another memory: Skelley watching as I died under the pirate chip. A tear sliding down his face.

We hold each other's gaze. Do the same scenes play through his mind? We're connected. It's scarred, yet pure and hopeful at the same time. I am not without need for forgiveness. *Forgive us our sins as we have forgiven those who sin against us.*

"Skelley . . ." I don't know what to say, but his name creeps out in my vulnerability. Without meaning to, I find myself reaching for him. He stares at me. Doesn't move. Then one of us blinks. The moment's broken, my hand falls, and I'm not sure who I am right now.

"What do you want, Parvin?" His voice is weary again. Vulnerable. He settles himself in the desk chair, leaving me to sit on the bed.

I don't bother mentioning that *he's* the one who entered my room. What does *he* want? I sink onto the stiff mattress with an overwhelming weight of defeat. "I've told you. I've told everyone."

The bored warble returns. "You need to be more reasonable. Be willing to bend. You can't expect us to cave to your will if you're not going to stretch, too."

I lean against the wall. "Why do you care what I want? I'm nothing to any of you."

"That's not true." He avoids my gaze. "You're important to the people."

He must be reading different news articles than I am. "So I'm your key, basically. I'm your key to the public." I'm tempted to tell him I overheard his little chat with Brickbat the other day—about why I'm really here.

Skelley slides the tray of fish further away from himself. "You still don't understand that the people have always been my concern.

I'm not just looking for leverage, Parvin. I want what's *best*. The people want you. I'm willing to listen. So here's your chance."

Our roles have switched. I used to follow Skelley around—his faithful puppy, bending to his blackmail, and succumbing to his demands. Now he follows me, chasing me down in Russia. He stopped being my leader, my controller, a long time ago and I barely saw the shift. I'm no slave to him anymore. My true Master has greater plans that don't deal in the roads to fear, blackmail, or betrayal. Skelley has deceived himself into thinking he is in charge. But he's lost in the dark.

"I don't know how much longer I can argue for my views, Skelley. They won't change."

He waits, one arm draped over the back of the chair. What is the point? Then again, what is the harm?

"I want to break people free. The projected Wall needs to come down and *you* have the power to do that." I don't mention Adria. I don't want him to know I'm aware of her technician training. Maybe even *he's* not aware of that. "The people want freedom, and there's not a fully logical reason why the Council isn't giving it to them. The oppression and control is only growing, but the people of the USE aren't simply submissive followers. They're fighters. They know when someone is trying to control them."

Before he can argue, I continue. "That's why they like me, Skelley. It's not because of anything I can do for them. It's because I represent them. I understand their desires. Those were *my* desires. They've seen me fight *for* them, not for control *of* them."

"It's not possible for us to do this." Even as the words pass his lips, I'm shaking my head.

"Yes it is. It takes sacrifice, as most right choices do." I try to understand from his point of view. "I know a lot of money has probably gone into this project. I know it means relinquishing control. I know it means change for the USE. But you have to choose to be on their side."

He lurches from the chair. It squeaks against the stone flooring. "I've only ever wanted good for the people. But they don't
see it! They don't get that I'm the good guy! I always have been!"

It must be confusing trying to be the good guy when one's
perception of goodness is grounded in the world. "You forced
Clocks on everyone, Skelley. You forced the projected Wall. You
forced Low City citizens to be sold as slaves! How can you call
that good?"

The shadow of his hat passes over his eyes, darkening his coun-
tenance. "A child can't see what's best for itself. It might hurt for
a time, but the parent can see the good ending."

I duck so I can catch his eye. "That's your problem. The people
aren't your children. They're your *peers*. You aren't above them . . .
you are *one* of them. You are equal."

He tips his fedora and walks out of my room without another
word, leaving the reek of fish behind him.

Things seem to get worse from that moment. The Council
doesn't respond to the public's cries. Enforcers in little hovercrafts
are sent to patrol the new bands of rioters. But the people riot even
more. Enforcers die. Radicals die. Meanwhile, the Council sits in
the meeting room, each member sipping coffee while discussing
the people's reactions like an interesting board game move.

Zeke always makes sure I'm there.

What do I do? I ask God this question daily, scouring His Word
for answers in the partially destroyed Bible the Council gave me.
Every verse seems muddled to my eyes. Nothing gets into my
heart. No clarity. No voice. No understanding.

I lie back on my bed with my opened Bible pressed over my
face, willing the ink to seep into my skin and crawl deep into my
heart. *Why am I here?*

I HAVE CALLED YOU.

To what? To lie in this room, passing the time while the world
crumbles around me?

TO RISE.

The Bible slides off my face and instead of picking it back up again, I fiddle with the *Daily Hemisphere* electrosheet. As it unfurls, a blaring siren startles my heart right out of my chest.

Red flashes illuminate my room. Blinking. The door that is kept locked bursts open without anyone on the other side. What's going on? A voice drones over some communal intercom saying "please" and "go to" and "stay calm", but I catch no content words. Please what? Go where? What's happening?

I shove my things into my pockets, leaving behind my old clothing, though I take time to throw Mother's skirt on top of my sweat pants. Enforcers blitz back and forth, up and down the hallway. Is this my angel-moment, when the doors of my prison fly open?

I peek out into the hallway. An Enforcer spots me and skids to a halt. "Council member Blackwater, how can I assist you?"

Oh, well, hello there. "What's going on?"

He glances up and down the hall, then takes my arm. "Please come with me."

I let him lead me away from my room. We pass a screen on the Wall with the latest news reports. The word *LIVE* is stamped on the top right corner. The scene is similar to most I see. A mob of people. Angry shouts. Picket signs.

But this time the rioters have weapons. Guns. Hand bombs. Fire. And they're headed straight toward a black building that floats over the ground.

The Council building.

This building.

Leading this giant mob are three people—two albinos and one handsome ex-Enforcer.

28

"Solomon!" I gasp. The Enforcer keeps me moving, but I point to the screen like an imbecile. "That's my Solomon!"

"Yes ma'am, let's keep going." I hear a smile in his voice.

For a moment, I dare to hope the mob won't come after *me*. Maybe they have orders to leave me alive. But then an explosion shatters the windows at the end of the hallway and I tumble to the floor with a shriek.

Dust and debris pelt my face and arms. I curl into a ball and clap my hand over my exposed ear, preparing to be crushed.

"Miss Blackwater!" The Enforcer's voice cracks and he shields my head as plaster falls from the ceiling. Is the fear in his voice for my safety or for his own?

Things still for a second and I loosen my knotted body. "I'm fine. It's okay. Let's go." *Thank you.* "We need to get out of here."

He's on his feet in a flash, kicking chunks of broken wall out of our way. He holds out a hand for me. I raise my stump to him as I still shield my mouth from the floating dust. Without a flinch, blink, or hesitation, he wraps his firm fingers around my wrist and leads me from the danger at a sprint.

That's when I know . . . the Enforcers are on *my* side. Not loyal just to the Council, but to *me*.

Another explosion. I scream in spite of myself, but keep running, entrusting myself into the hands of this protector. Other

Enforcers show up, forming a small group around me. Two of them have electric shield screens that they hold over our heads.

I stumble blindly, finally using my good hand to clutch a black coat. The seconds are counted off by explosions, shouts, and crashes. With winks of irony, the news screens remain unharmed. We reach a thick metal door that opens outward. One Enforcer— is that Zeke? —rams his body into the door. It opens about a foot, but then scrapes to a stop.

"There's rubble!" Zeke heaves again and another Enforcer joins in. Instead of watching them, I look at the news screen.

I've lost sight of Solomon, Willow, and Elm, but now the camera focuses on a giant black van speeding toward the base of the building. Whoever is filming this chaos is in a helicopter because the scene rotates slowly in a giant circle. Someone tries to commentate, but I can't make out their words. The camera zooms in to reveal ugly splashed red and white paint on the side of the van.

No more Control!

No more Council!

My heart stutters to a halt. What if . . . what if these people take out the Council building? Erfinder said the control center for the projected Wall was *in this building.* If rioters destroy it, we'll never turn off the projection! Or maybe . . . if rioters destroy it, the projection will die.

Suddenly I'm excited to be bombed.

"Let's go!" Zeke reaches for me just as the van bursts through protective rails and screeches to a stop directly centered beneath the hovering building. Its wheels leave skid marks on the smooth metal disc beneath. One man leaps out of the van, leaving the door open. He sprints toward freedom and I'm reminded of when Solomon and I fled from the Wall explosives before detonating them.

"Go!" My voice shreds my throat and jump-starts my legs into action. Zeke holds the door open and we file in, thundering down the metal stairs. I trust them, even though they're taking me *closer* to where the van bomb is.

Someone shouts, but I'm deafened by foot thunder. Hands drag me down, yet keep me from falling. My feet hit every other stair if they're lucky. The gap between the downward spiraling stairs goes deep. How far down do these stairs go? Is underground safer than above?

We've traveled at least ten levels and my legs are jelly. Then an explosion knocks us against the outer walls. We all scream. I lose my footing and tumble down the stairs, dragging the protective Enforcers with me. My fall is cushioned by another tossed body and a few others land on top of me, forcing a gasp out of my lips.

I don't have the equilibrium to figure out which way is up or down. All I know is elbows and knees press into the soft parts of my body and stair edges claw their way into my skin.

The people on top of me scramble off. Explosions continue like the waking growl of a hibernating beast. Louder. Fiercer. Cracks shoot up the walls, and someone cries out as a piece falls. Blood slickens the stairs. Zeke yanks me to my feet, but my knees don't support me.

"Are you okay?" He holds me up.

My brain says *Yes*, but my head only nods. We make it three more steps before the stairwell tips. With my balance already shot, this plays tricks on my mind. It's not a slow tip. The room lurches as though kicked by a giant, and I'm thrown over the stair rail.

I screech as I tumble about, hitting the opposite railing and wondering if I'll end up in the chasm.

Hands claw at me. I *am* in the chasm, but I'm not falling because it's no longer a fall. The building is sideways. Stairs no longer lead down.

"This isn't good," an Enforcer says.

"Thank you for that understatement, Enforcer." Zeke and the

others pull me out of my trap as metal creaks in warning. If this stairwell collapses, we're entombed.

The next ten minutes of my life are a blend of confusion and pandemonium. Somehow the stairwell stays together. Zeke gets all of us crawling and sliding through the twisted stairs until we reach a door that hasn't been shrink-wrapped by the weight of the collapsing walls. It takes four Enforcers to open it and even then, it crumbles off its hinges and falls flat with a slam that shakes loose more cracked plaster.

We're outside, I think. Beneath the building that is collapsing. Rubble everywhere. Zeke shoves aside some debris, revealing a smooth trap door in the cement ground. The building groans above us.

"Hurry . . ." One Enforcer looks up and bounces on the balls of his feet.

Zeke opens the door with the help of two other Enforcers. "Get in!"

We obey and, once it closes after us, more crashing reaches my ears. Guess there's no getting out.

We're in another stairwell. Darker and still crumbling. But the farther down we go, the less destruction we encounter. The floor is a continuous earthquake, shuddering from repeated blows to the Council building.

By this point, I salvage enough awareness to realize I can't breathe. A stitch eats at my side and no amount of air I suck in is enough to clear my head. Darkness blots my vision.

"Just a . . . second." I reach out blindly and encounter another hand. It squeezes mine.

"We're almost there, ma'am."

Almost where? A bunker? The exit door?

Ten more breaths clear my vision and I stumble after the Enforcers. They waited for me. They want *me* to live, not just themselves. Where did this commitment come from?

Deeper and deeper we go until we enter an underground train station of sorts. "Oh good." Zeke's air whooshes out. "There's one subway left."

A decrepit old train rests on sunken tracks. Electric lights buzz from the wall, and I can't imagine this contraption working after all the explosions, but Zeke shoves us all in and then tinkers with some sort of control panel near the front. The subway train inches forward and then gains speed, sliding along the tunnel with a growing metallic moan.

I collapse into a bucket seat and drop my head into my hand. We're okay. We survived. We're free. Did the other Council members feel this type of fear and adrenaline? Are they even alive? Zeke said the other subway trains were gone. How many were there? Who else escaped? And what is happening to the other people in the Council building?

"You did well, men." Zeke pats the shoulder of the nearest Enforcer. Is he a Lead Enforcer or simply a leader-type of person?

"So where are we going?" I'm surprised my voice works at all. I lick my dusty lips and encounter blood. I wipe it away with my sleeve and try to find the wound with my tongue.

There, inside my cheek. Must have bitten it when I fell.

"There's a safe shelter for the Council down this way. We've never had to use it before. Now I'm seeing the flaws in the plan . . . like having the transportation underneath a collapsing building." There's no mirth in his voice. No smile. No chuckle.

I reach for him. "You did well, Zeke. Thank you. You saved all of our lives."

He meets my gaze with moist eyes. "Only because you saved mine."

When? The way he says this implies it happened a while ago—it's been on his mind. Does he mean . . . spiritually? Before I can ask, the subway gives a lurch and slows. It stops at another platform, but the doors don't open. They try, but catch on something.

Zeke slams them with the butt of his rifle and they shatter. "Everyone out."

We pile out, stepping over the broken glass.

Zeke throws out a hand. "Wait." His gaze darts around the darkened tunnel. "This isn't the right stop."

"Then why'd it stop here—?"

A shadow steps from behind a pillar. Whoever it is remains in the black shadows, but not enough to conceal the barrel of a gun pointed at all of us. "No one move." The voice is deep. Focused. Serious, but with an undertone of gentleness.

Instead of freezing, the Enforcers surround me, placing their bodies as shields in front of mine.

But I move toward the voice. "Solomon?"

Zeke's hand on my shoulder stops me from taking another step. "Council member, please."

The gun barrel doesn't flinch, but Solomon's voice registers surprise. "Parvin, come to me. We're leaving."

He's alive. He's here!

Trembling, I take a step, and Zeke's hand slides from my shoulder. Leaving the Enforcers doesn't feel right. "Solomon, you can put the gun down. These men saved me. I trust them."

He doesn't even question me. He tucks the gun back into his belt—and runs to me. I'm wrapped in his arms before anyone can protest. His hug is fierce and almost painful, but I cling to him. "You're alive. Oh, you're alive. Thank you, God."

He steps back in business mode, but the other Enforcers don't give him a chance. The click of six gun hammers makes me spin on my heel. They aim at Solomon.

I step in front of him. "What are you doing?"

Zeke is the only one without a leveled gun, and he shifts his weight. Whose side will he take? "Remember, boys, she's a Council member. She's *our* leader." He holds my gaze the whole time.

As though coming to their senses, the others drop their guns back to their sides. "Thank you." My lip is bleeding again, but I mop it with my torn sleeve, then turn to Solomon.

I want to ask him how he's here, how he knew to come here, or where Willow and Elm are. But he led a mob against the leaders of the USE. We have bigger things to talk about. "What are you doing here?"

"Well . . . I was trying to get you out of here. But I was also trying to get to Skelley Chase."

"I don't know where he is."

Zeke steps forward. "I would expect he's with the other Council members in the bunker."

I slide my arms around Solomon's middle and look up into his face. "I know this won't make sense but . . . I think I need to return to them." In a lower voice, I add, "Skelley and I have had some good talks." Forcing Skelley won't achieve anything. God's not done with him—or me—yet.

Solomon's control slips. His lips tighten and his eyes slant downward. He lifts a finger to wipe a trickle of blood from my temple. "But . . . I came back for you." He rests his forehead against mine. "I'll always come back for you, Parvin. This time I'm staying."

My "No" almost pops out before I register his request. But the echo of his words keeps me still. He mustn't stay with me. It's too dangerous. He can't simply waltz into the Council with me. He's leverage! He's the blackmail they need to make me do what they want.

But I left Solomon last time. And the time before that. And the time before that. I've left Solomon behind every time he's asked to stay. I can't do it again. What right do I have to risk my own life, but not allow him to risk his for his passions?

We are a team. Once and forever.

I press my forehead firmer against his, allowing tears to burn a fire beneath my words. Then I open my eyes and meet his gaze head-on, mere centimeters separating us. "Never again will I leave you by choice, Solomon Christian Hawke."

And then he kisses me. Just like that. In front of six armed Enforcers.

A few chuckles reach my ears and, when I turn, Zeke is blushing. "I can see now why that tattoo isn't on your temple anymore."

My gaze traces the pattern of the scars on the left side of Solomon's face. He doesn't meet my eyes. Is he ashamed? Scars are physical paintings of survived trials. I press my mutilated stump against the webbing on his temple. Scar on scar.

They're beautiful. Our wounds beside each other like that. I don't say it out loud—for some reason I don't imagine Solomon would feel very manly or strong if I called him *beautiful.*

A tremor shakes the cement, and a sprinkling of dust falls from above. Time to go. I face the Enforcers. I need to act like a Council woman. Confident.

Instead, I go transparent. "Solomon is considered an enemy of the other Council members. But he's not *my* enemy."

"Obviously," an Enforcer whispers to his friend.

"I heard that." I grin in an attempt to ease the nerves wrestling in my chest. He laughs, so I continue. "Can I trust you not to tell the Council about Solomon unless . . . unless they ask you directly? I don't want anyone to have to lie."

No one gives a response for a long moment. Zeke chews on the inside of his cheek. He wants to say something, but maybe he's giving the others a chance. When they look to him, he sighs. "You're the Council member. We still obey you."

"And we *like* you," another Enforcer mutters. Apparently they speak only in snippeted undertones.

"I like you, too. And I'm choosing to trust you." Trust them with the man I want to spend my life with. That's all. "So who has an Enforcer coat Solomon can borrow?"

One of the mutterers shrugs his off. It's singed and torn, with a pocket missing completely. "What do we call him?"

Solomon shrugs on the coat and morphs back into the original handsome Enforcer I first spied on Straight Street. "Just call me *Enforcer.*"

And that's the plan. None of us have the energy or mental acuteness to think about deeper consequences. Let's hope the same goes for Skelley and Brickbat. Zeke ushers us back onto the subway through the shattered door, then it rattles farther up the tunnel. This time, I don't sit or cling to the holds above my head. This time I hold Solomon's hand. And he is solid.

29

The shelter for Council members is a concrete tomb. No windows. All voices seem to echo. I guess the Council didn't expect to ever need to use this place, because it's missing the fancy chairs, programmed lighting, and soft carpet the Council building had.

"Ah, she survived." Brickbat peers at me from beneath an ice pack he holds to his head. "Why am I not surprised?"

The Council huddles together in a larger concrete room. Brickbat sits on an overturned bucket, Skelley lounges on a pile of stuffed burlap sacks, and Adria paces against the far wall. A few Enforcers try to stand guard, but their drooped shoulders and dust-coated hair reveal their exhaustion. When they see me, they seem to brighten.

"Where is the president and . . . the other guy?" The other guy. Nice. It wouldn't have hurt to learn the fifth Council member's name.

"President Garraty is in the restroom." Brickbat takes the ice pack away to reveal a giant knob of flesh rising from his forehead. "The *other guy* is dead." His gurgly voice reveals no remorse.

"I'm sorry." Yet I feel nothing. I glance over my shoulder at the open door behind me. The Enforcers who rescued me are all business, organizing belongings and setting up sleeping quarters for us. I don't see Solomon, though he's there somewhere.

"Are the rooms ready yet?" Adria's weary sigh floats through the empty space with the dust.

"I don't think so." I step in further. A projected news screen is on the wall to my left, muted. The smoldering remains of the Council building are the focus of every camera. Only one side of it floats. The rest of it crashed to the ground, cracking the building up the middle. That's where I was.

"Well, you did it, Miss Blackwater. You destroyed our lives and this country." Brickbat glares at me.

I stumble to a portion of blank wall and slip to the ground. "Me? I had no part in this!"

Brickbat rolls his eyes. "Your *boyfriend* led the attack. You think I didn't catch that?"

The mention of Solomon sends a sweep of goose bumps down my body. He can't know Solomon's here, can he? "I almost *died* in there, Brickbat. Solomon would never do that if it risked killing me." Come to think of it, what *was* Solomon's plan in all this?

Brickbat throws his ice pack at me. It hits me square in the face and knocks my head back against the cement, leaving my face wet.

"Throwing a temper tantrum, huh?" I rub the back of my head, then pick up the icepack and use it to soothe my bump. "Do you need a nap?"

The growl that comes from Brickbat reminds me of the giant wolf I once fought. Guttural. Feral. Curse my sarcastic tongue! As he rises from his bucket, Adria holds out a hand while staring at the screen. "Shh. Electroscreen: *Play sound.*"

Noise bursts into our concrete cell. A reporter talks over the chaos, the *thump-a-thump-a-thump-a* of helicopter blades in the background. "It looks like a group of attackers has made it into the Council building. It's not clear what they're searching for. The two albino children have gone inside with them."

Willow and Elm? What in time's name do they think they'll find in there?

My peripheral vision picks up on someone staring at me. Skelley. He's watching my reactions. Hopefully I look shocked and confused.

"They're looking for the control room." His bored warble reminds me how perceptive he is. How nothing shakes him, except maybe the attack of angry sled dogs. "To take down the projected Wall."

My heart backflips. Might they have found another knowledge cap? Then it sinks. This means the projection is still working.

"Can they do that without training or a knowledge cap?" Adria's hand flutters to her chest.

"No." Skelley leans back and pushes his fedora down over his eyes, like some napping cowboy. "Only we have the complete knowledge. It's safe."

Adria's tension slides off her face, but Brickbat jerks a glance at Skelley, eyebrows raised. "How do you have that information?"

"The knowledge cap, remember?" Skelley's voice is muffled beneath the hat brim.

"And when will that be shared with the rest of the Council?"

The static of mobbing and helicopters grows louder. Was Skelley planning on sharing it with everyone? If so, then that gives me another chance of retrieving the information.

"Well, our lab is now destroyed." Skelley shrugs.

"You've been back for weeks."

Skelley doesn't miss a beat. "And all our inventors have been working on the new Clocks. None to spare for new knowledge caps. Even *you* know how long a capping process can take, Brickbat. Besides, if you really wanted the information, we would have capped Adria a long time ago."

What about a pirate chip? I want to scream. Can't those be programmed within seconds to drink up knowledge of the mind? They used one on me without my losing memories—though I think that was more God's doing than the chip's.

Still, pirate chips are possible. And easier. And I want one.

I'll ask Solomon. He may not have inventor blood in him, but he's smart.

A knock on the already opened door brings my head around. Adria silences the news screen. "Yes, Enforcer?"

Zeke nods his head. "Council members, your rooms have been prepared. There is a medic Enforcer in each room to take care of any injuries."

Adria rises and attempts to smooth back her traumatized hair. "Finally. Why wasn't all of this put together beforehand?"

Zeke steps aside, not responding to the rhetorical question. As Brickbat sweeps past me, he says to the room, "We'll reconvene in two hours to discuss how to move forward." He narrows his gaze at me. "And we'll decide what to do with *you*."

My "medic Enforcer" is Solomon. I hardly recognize him when I first walk in. His head is covered in a bloodied bandage that blocks one eye and dirt turns his naturally light skin into a mish-mash of stains.

"What happened to you?"

He taps the bandage. "Not mine. Well . . . the dirt is mine, but the blood isn't."

A bandage of someone else's blood? "Smart. But don't get infected."

"There's a clean bandage beneath this one."

And, of course, he's already thought through those details. I glance around. My door is closed. When I test the handle, I find it locked from the outside. "Just you and me in here . . . again."

He reaches me in two strides, placing his hands on my shoulders. "Parvin . . . how are you?" His eyes search my face, looking for internal wounds beneath the external scratches.

"I'm fine." As the words slip out, so do tears. Why? I *am* fine. I shake my head and sniff. "Really, I . . . there's nothing wrong." I barely escaped an exploding building. I was kidnapped. I don't know how to fix the problems. I'm partnered with our enemies. "I thought you were dead."

But I'm fine.

In a moment of emotional vulnerability the words *I want* creep into my despairing mind. I want to be with Solomon in a place of shalom where all of this is over. I want to return to my family. "I want . . . to rest."

The words jog an old wound—a time when I wanted to *live* because I was sick of resting. One measly year has flipped all that.

Solomon guides me to the bed and we sit. I take a few long deep breaths, expelling the pessimism. "So . . . what happened?"

Solomon scans the ceiling, probably checking for cameras or bugs that I didn't think about. Then he speaks low. "You left and we had to wait until it was clear. Opa Fin could have disabled the booby trap if he wanted . . . but he didn't." His lips curl. "He's dead now."

"The bomb?"

Solomon nods. "He wouldn't disable it, so I fiddled with it and disarmed a part. As we walked out, he set it off. We got some scratches, but I had on the Armor suit."

Solomon *is* a tech guy. His blood picked up the Hawke brilliance—can he see that now? I lower my voice, though it can't possibly drift through these thick walls. "Willow and Elm are okay?"

He shakes his head with a hollow chuckle. "They're more resilient than any suit Wilbur Sherrod could make. But Willow's skin change is . . . spreading. She gets more set on revenge every day."

Oh no. "So where are they?"

He rubs a hand over his face. "They have their own mission. They won't tell me, but I think it has to do with the Council members. They refused to come with me and, since you were my goal, we had to part ways."

I squelch the threat of worry that tries to creep up in my mind. *They're in Your hands.* "What about Gloria and Sasha?"

"It took us a good hour to find them. They were pretty shaken.

The dogs that remained behind had torn away some of Sasha's bindings, but they were harnessed to the sled."

I imagine Gloria with her gag and her tied hands, wondering if her dogs would be okay. "I let them die—the dogs. Only three made it back to the town alive."

"It couldn't have been your fault, Parvin."

"If you were so close behind, why didn't you guys catch up to me?"

"Because there were a lot of us on few sleds. Gloria and Sasha agreed to take us all, but the dogs needed breaks often. We figured Skelley was driving your sled pretty hard. We never could have caught up without injuring the dogs. We tried." His hand strays to mine. "I'm sorry."

"It's okay." I wish I could somehow convey to Gloria and Sasha how much I cared about their dogs—how I fed them and made sure they rested. But it doesn't matter because some still died.

"Once we made it back to the USE, it took a while to figure out where you were. We finally saw the news announcement about you and the Council, as well as the Clock recall. It seemed to incite the Radicals at the Wall even more. They've been demanding freedom through that gap for a long time, and I guess that escalated into planning an attack on the Council building. I was lucky I got on the inside when I did. I was hoping the bomb would decimate the control room for the Wall."

"Me too."

"At least you're alive."

"And you . . . you came for me." Solomon abandoned any opportunity to try disabling the projected Wall. For me.

"Of course I did." He adjusts the bandage on his head. "So . . . how are we moving forward? Any plan yet?"

"I need a pirate chip."

He nods once. "For Skelley?"

"Or Adria—the technician that Erfinder told us about is a Council member."

He shows very little surprise. "I heard."

Maybe I shouldn't ask Solomon to do this. He's already at risk by his mere presence. Zeke would be less noticeable, but would Zeke do something like that for me?

I twist the thin blanket covering the bed in my fingers. "Solomon, I'm nervous for you. I don't know what's going to happen." If Brickbat catches him . . .

"Me neither, Parvin. But God's not nervous."

When the Council reconvenes in our cement shoebox, the news screen is chanting. "Take down the Wall! Take down the Wall! Take down the Wall!"

These shouts come from people outside the Council building *and* by the gap in the Wall. Skelley watches the screen with a tiny crease between his eyes. Focused. Thinking. Brickbat's entrance is quite the opposite—a silver tornado striding in so fast he causes a breeze to blow my hair in my face.

Before he can say a word, Skelley gestures to the screen. "Elan, we have a problem."

Brickbat hunkers by the screen in his Brawn suit. I peer closer. Then the camera zooms and I see what Skelley's referring to. An army marches upon the gap in the Wall, only this isn't an army from our side.

It's a zoomed scene of the Wall. On the other side of that wavery projection film is a face that doesn't belong in our newspaper. It doesn't connect with *this* side of the Wall.

Standing in a red-and-black outfit that screams Wilbur Sherrod's handiwork, with an army of silver-suited people behind him . . .

. . . is the Preacher.

He's brought an army from Ivanhoe.

30

The Preacher came to our defense.

My mind dances around the mental picture of the Preacher crawling off his throne of pillows and deciding to lead an army to the Wall. With the *Ivanhoe Independent* destroyed, does that mean he had to walk to the Wall? That's even harder to imagine

The Preacher walks forward and speaks to the rioters through the projection. Since the Enforcers were called away, there's no one to protest his actions. The reporters scramble to catch what he's saying, but none succeed. The rioting USE people cheer and clamber over the barriers toward the gap. It reminds me of when I first brought down the Wall, but this is bigger.

Much bigger.

Brickbat screams—a holler of fury that would deafen all ears within a mile radius. "Get Enforcers there *now!*" He whips out his NAB and taps furiously.

What will Enforcers do? There's still a projection separating our worlds. But the Preacher's very presence brings comfort. I smirk and lean closer to the screen . . . closer to freedom.

A soldier from Ivanhoe's frontline reaches out and touches the projection.

The fool.

He shrieks and yanks his hand back. It's now charred and

smoking. The Preacher shouts something to his men, but the Ivanhoe army fumbles. Their heads swivel to their leader.

Then Enforcers appear. How did they get there so fast? It's been only ten minutes or so since Brickbat sent orders on his NAB. But they're there—at least a hundred of them. One steps forward to speak with the Preacher, but he has none of it.

Instead, the Preacher advances in his red-and-black outfit, a transparent film of cloth covering his head. With long strides, he walks toward the gap in the Wall, not slowing even when he reaches the projection. Some of the USE Radicals go quiet, some scream a warning, but he waltzes through the projection and emerges on the other side—on *this* side—unharmed.

When he crosses, the Enforcers fall backward like someone struck them. The camera zooms in to show that terror coats their faces like liquid masks. To them, the projection was power. The Council was power. But they never met Wilbur Sherrod—they never glimpsed the wacky brain beneath his afro. The Preacher has, and he came prepared.

I whoop.

Brickbat backhands me.

I tumble and slam against a wall.

"Elan!" Skelley shouts.

My vision is black, and I shake my head to clear it before trying to untangle my limbs from the ground. When the room returns to focus, Skelley crouches in front of me and Zeke stands between Brickbat and us.

Brickbat doesn't seem to care. He glares at the news screen.

Skelley doesn't ask if I'm okay, but I catch concern in his eyes and I'm sure he didn't mean for me to see it. Who *is* this man?

He lifts me by the elbow until I have my feet under me. I slide my arm away—resisting the urge to jerk it from his grasp. "I'm fine. Thanks."

He nods once, then returns to the screen.

That was weird.

I try to focus too, and sense Zeke hovering near me on the chance that Brickbat strikes out again. I spit blood from my mouth. Probably should have found a wastebasket, but the metallic saltiness almost gagged me.

So that's what Tawny had to endure every time her dad came home.

I suddenly want to hug my own father, tighter than ever before, and thank him for who he is. To quell the temptation of these thoughts, I focus on the screen again.

Enforcers are shooting the Preacher.

Bullets ricochet off his suit and he raises his arms as if he welcomes them. Show-off. Radicals rush to him, but I don't know what they expect him to do. He has only the one suit.

But then he's slamming a palm into each person's chest and dull grey suits slither over their bodies, covering their heads like the Armor suit.

"Come!" He turns and leads them back through the Wall, doing a cocky dance-march with his feet like some futuristic pied piper. Some are hesitant and inch a finger through the projected screen before they commit fully. Some walk backward toward the gap, keeping an eye on the Enforcers.

And there he is—the conceited leader of Ivanhoe finally got off his plush couch to rescue my people. Sure, he's pompous, but it's still a glimpse of Jesus to me.

The Enforcers don't seem to know what to do. Do they shoot? Attack? They can't go after the people. Their lines crumble and their hesitance spurs on more Radicals, who swarm toward the Preacher.

"Get our military there, *now!*" Brickbat punches the wall. I flinch.

Zeke steps forward. "But sir, bullets don't—"

"Then *capture* him! And anyone else trying to go through. We stop this *now*. This is a breach of the agreements of the United Assembly!"

"So was blowing up the *Ivanhoe Independent!*" I duck behind Zeke to avoid Brickbat's wrath. My voice bounces off the walls and slaps me in the face. *Don't argue with a fool.*

"Take her to her room." Brickbat jerks his head toward Zeke.

Without missing a beat, Zeke snaps his fingers and another Enforcer comes into the room, snags my arm, and pulls me out. I struggle only once before looking up. The Enforcer is Solomon.

I gasp and then say in an undertone, "Solomon, we have to *do* something."

"I know."

"Have you found the pirate chip yet?"

He shakes his head. "No, but I'm looking." He rushes me into my room, closes the door, and then fiddles with a panel in the wall that's under a metal sheet. A green button turns on a projected screen on the wall.

Solomon presses a few more buttons and the screen is projecting the news. I run to it, pressing my hand against the flickering video. I'm there. I'm with my people as they step to freedom.

Three men from the Ivanhoe army step through the projected Wall in dull grey suits, like the ones the people have. They have limited resources—only a handful of suits per person. I can't imagine how long Wilbur's been slaving away to create these. How did he know to make these suits? Did Solomon contact him?

As time passes, the Enforcers gather to try and stop the Preacher and his men, but the Ivanhoe army is armed, too. At the first wild Enforcer bullet, the Ivanhoans send arrows through the projection. The arrows explode upon impact, letting loose thread-thin weighted nets that yank Enforcers to the ground and keep them there.

In this moment, I know that the USE is no match for Ivanhoe. It never was. The Preacher says there is no leader of Ivanhoe, but

Ivanhoe is united in fighting for good. For freedom. There are even albinos in the army. Did they come from the forest?

Radicals scramble to be next in line to cross as more Enforcers are taken down. Some swarm the Preacher, grabbing for the matchbox outfits. It's in that moment of chaos that Brickbat's military arrives in armored trucks and helicopters. They blast the field with explosives and other tech I can't make out amidst the smoke, attacking civilians, Ivanhoans, and Enforcers alike.

Soldiers and Enforcers swarm toward the wreckage and tussle with some of the Ivanhoe men. They're not trying to subdue them; they're instead wrenching Wilbur's outfits out of their hands.

"Why can't Brickbat let *go* of this?" I grind out to Solomon. "Why is he so set on control?"

Several minutes of this pass until finally the Ivanhoe army retreats back to the West side and out of view. The only problem is . . . now the USE soldiers have Wilbur's suits. Now *Brickbat's* men can walk through the Wall.

Solomon squeezes my hand. "I'm going to keep looking for pirate chips."

I nod, not taking my eyes from the screen. "Okay."

Then he's gone. The confusion and chaos is too much to watch after a while. I flop on my bed, clutch my Bible to my chest and pray. Minutes pass. An hour passes. Solomon doesn't return. Once my praying—which consists of begging more than anything else—ends, I dare to return to the screen.

The Radicals wander around the gap, too afraid to attack the thick wall of Enforcers, yet too brave to give up. The Preacher and his men have retreated out of sight, but I know he's not done. If anything, this has angered him.

There's a knock on my door and a soft call. "Miss Blackwater?"

It's Solomon's voice, so I open, trying to maintain a professional air in case others are watching. The hallway is empty save a few Enforcers, who already know that Solomon's a spy.

Beneath the bloodied bandage and dirt floats a wildness in Solomon's eyes.

"What is it?"

"I've found something, and you're not going to like it."

I prepare myself. The way he presents the information, it doesn't seem serious enough that Father might have died or . . . Mother. "Okay."

"I was searching the different rooms for pirate chips, and in a padded tray in one of the rooms I found these." He pulls his hand from his pocket and shows me three small silver squares.

Small like matchbooks.

"Armor suits."

I gape. "What? How? How did they get these?"

Solomon chews his cheek. "Well . . . down a different hall-way—in a cell—they have Wilbur Sherrod."

31

"What?" My shout echoes loud enough to alert anyone nearby. Like Council members.

Let them come.

I'll kill them. Every last one. "How do you know Wilbur's here? How did they *get* him?"

"I saw Enforcers leading him to his cell after taking him to one of the healers. He looks bad, Parvin. I think they've had him for a while."

The panic builds in my chest. I look at the little Armor suits. "How long have they had him? You and I saw him in Ivanhoe just before the New Year!"

"Long enough to make three suits. I think the Council provided Wilbur with some faster tech."

"But why? Why do they even *want* these?" I know the answer as I ask the question. They've been stealing the Armor suits from the Preacher's soldiers, too. The Council wants an army that can pass through the projected Wall where other armies can't.

I'm growing frantic. The infiltration of the Council into Ivanhoe shakes me more than any other threat. If they can get in there, kidnap Wilbur, and force him to work for them, they have more power than I thought. "No wonder The Preacher came to fight. He's not here to help Radicals. He's here for Wilbur."

My poor, afro-headed Irish employer. "We need to free him."

Solomon nods. "Yes, but not until we have some sort of plan to get out of here."

I hate the idea of Wilbur locked in some stiff, unimaginative cell, forced to use his creativity for a government that will attack his own people.

The night brings new terrors of angry people on the news. They attack the ruins of the Council building with fire and thrown bottles. No purpose this time other than venting their rage at injustice.

They don't like that the Council subdued the Ivanhoe army.

They don't like that the projected Wall is still up.

They don't like a lot of things, and I don't blame them.

The rage spills into other areas of Prime—homes, businesses, news stations. In between flashes of anger, Enforcers try to rescue pedestrians or families from the mob. It's the epitome of disunity. Everyone is against *everyone.* But the majority seem to be against the Council, against the Wall projection.

People gather at the projection. At first, I'm not sure why. Then a few of them whip out guns and start shooting at the projection pillars hanging over the top of the Wall.

"The bullets can't even reach them," the reporter says.

Then a helicopter shows up. And it's not a news copter— Radicals are packed inside with guns at the ready. They shoot at the pillars, but the bullets cause no change. Not even a flicker. What we need are Ivanhoe bombs.

I'm missing the action.

I'm a soldier trapped in a bunker. I need to be with my people, fighting! Instead I have to watch the clash of my two lives on a news screen. The mob of people at the gap in the Wall grows. Congregates. Mills together as though planning how to attack the Enforcers or bring down the projection—not like it's within their control.

That's when my idea comes. I find Solomon and yank him into my room. "First, have you found a pirate chip yet?"

He shakes he head.

I wave my hand. "That's okay. Do you still have your NAB?"

"Of course." He towers over me, watching my face with attentiveness. "What are you thinking?"

"Send Father a message. He's with the albinos. Have him tell the Preacher to use the spider bombs that helped us take down the Wall. If some of the albinos use their camming devices to climb to the top of the Wall like Elm did, they could send the spiders to explode the pillars that control the projection. Maybe it'd work."

Solomon jilts his lips to one side. "I don't know, Parvin. Skelley used a bomb on Dad's house, and even though the house got destroyed, the projection stayed up."

"Yeah, but this is Ivanhoe tech. It's . . . smarter."

He pulls out his NAB and sends the message without another word. I hug him, feeling my first sensation of hope. "Thank you."

The next evening, Brickbat gathers everyone in the meeting room. Solomon still doesn't have a pirate chip, but Father said he'd get a message to the Preacher.

"I've enacted a new plan." Brickbat bounces on his toes. I've never seen him happy. It's more terrifying than when he points a gun in my face. "There are reports of Ivanhoans climbing the Wall on the other side. In fact, they bombed one of the pillars." He directs his sneer at me as my heart petrifies.

It's been only *one day* since we sent the message to Father and already the Council is onto the plan! Brickbat can't possibly stop the attempts so soon can he? He could if he sent an army of Enforcers in Armor-suits.

"In fact, the Ivanhoe army managed to bomb a pillar before we gunned them down." Brickbat directs us to the news screen.

The camera zooms for a better look.

I see movement. On the top of the massive stone Wall are dark shadows, almost so stealthy they blend into the stone.

People.

Ivanhoe soldiers crawling across the top toward the projection pillars. Father got through to them! I want to scream at the news reporters to avert their eyes. Don't reveal the soldiers' plans to the whole world!

I can't take my gaze off the screen. I don't breathe. The soldiers are halfway across the Wall top. Will their explosives work? Will the world be free?

They release little black spider bombs that scuttle toward the pillars. Six of them. With a burst of fire and rubble, the pillar careens over the edge of the Wall and crashes to the ground.

The projected Wall merely flickers and then reseals the projection as if the pillar never mattered in the first place.

It didn't work. How many pillars would they need to bring down to change the projection?

Brickbat mutes the screen. "Adria and I did some experimenting last night."

Oh no. Are Enforcers on their way to destroy the Ivanhoe army? Can they? I watch the screen.

He switches to current time on the news reports. There are more Enforcers. They hang around the perimeters of the mob. Something's going to happen, and I'm not going to like it.

I need Solomon. *We* need to get Wilbur Sherrod and then leave—there's no reason for me to be here anymore.

Brickbat glances at his watch. "It should have happened by now—"

A gasp bursts from the news screen, followed by muted screams. The camera shakes and I step closer to see what happened.

The projected Wall has split into two projections, curving over the stone and the mass of people like a giant tunnel. The entire Ivanhoe army is inside. With a burst of hope, some Radicals sprint through the broken stone gap to the other side, but they can go no further. The projection is their new cage.

The filmy blue threatens to zap everyone in the vicinity into a crisp. The news helicopter careens away from the one on our side and the scene shrinks as we zoom out. Brickbat claps his hands as the chaos takes shape.

All Radicals, rioters, and fighters of the USE are trapped inside the dome. Even some Enforcers. It formed so quickly, a portion of those too close to the walls got fried before realizing what happened. The rebel helicopter is still in the air, trapped inside the dome, and accidentally flies through one of the projections. I don't see the pilot, but when the helicopter crashes into the stone Wall, I conclude he's dead.

Brickbat laughs.

The throaty wetness in his laugh coats me in anger. The desire to kill him bubbles inside me and I spin on my heel. "You . . . *murderer!*"

Brickbat laughs harder. "Oh, just you wait."

The urge to attack him is so strong that I finally let it loose. My body flies across the room before my brain can resist. Hands outstretched, attack moves spinning through my brain, but I don't calculate for the other people in the room.

Because I'm too blind.

Something slams my skull and I'm out.

I wake locked in my room. The news screen is on, and the settling despair of the people trapped in the dome tells me hours have passed. I don't like that I've missed things.

I pound on the door to my room, but no one comes. Where are my faithful Enforcers? Where is Solomon? Does he know I'm trapped in here? "God. *God!* Let me out so I can fix this!"

He tells me to rise up, yet allows me to be trapped in a bunker with the enemy? I rest my head against the cold door. *I don't understand. I don't understand.* Yet as my body and brain panic, my soul reminds me of His presence.

I SEE.

Do you?

I KNOW.

God . . .

I AM.

I breathe in His Words, wishing for a moment that they'd reach my ears in an audible voice, but that's what the Bible is for, right? To *know* His voice. An escaped tear drips onto the door latch.

I straighten, wipe my face, and focus again on the news screen. It's too hard to be strong, but someday . . . *someday* . . . God will let me rest, whether in life or death. And I'm honored to represent Him as long as I can.

The news reporter lady sounds teary. "Why won't the Council speak to the people?"

"Where are they hiding?" another reporter asks.

"Perhaps they've been killed."

A third voice comes off tight and angry. "While in *hiding*, they created this projection trap! This is force, not freedom."

The armies are at a stalemate, and I don't know who to cheer for. I love both sides—*all* the people. My enemy is anti-shalom. And right now, anti-shalom looks a lot like a projected Wall.

I stand at the news screen for hours, aching for my people, desperately wanting to fix their pain. They all huddle in the center of the dome—as far away from the projected walls as possible—not fighting, not shooting. The arc/dome/tunnel—I still don't know what to call it—was extremely wide when it started, but the moment people moved tighter together . . . the West wall and the East wall moved closer together, by a few feet.

I want to hope it's my imagination, but some of the reporters noticed it, too. "Is the tunnel . . . shrinking?"

I need to get to that control room.

Perhaps it's my silence and stillness that allow me to hear voices come nearer to my door. "We can't leave things how they are, Elan." Adria's low voice creeps through the cracks of my door into my foggy mind.

"The people are afraid only because they don't understand." Brickbat still sounds angry when he whispers. "I will write a speech for President Garraty to deliver tomorrow."

"Will that be enough?"

"It will have to be. The people don't make the decisions of this country."

My news screen grows in loudness as the cameras return to the riots. I don't dare turn it off for fear that Brickbat or Adria will catch on that I am eavesdropping.

A speech. A *speech*. Words won't fix this. Brickbat doesn't listen to words, but all he does is *give* them. That's one gift people don't want. You can't wrap words. They're not tangible without action. Even God takes action in our lives to support His words.

Who voted Brickbat onto this Council anyway?

That's all I hear before they pass my location. Pacing in my room, watching the people of the USE subdued and ignored is its own form of torture. I want to be out there! I want to be in the action, fighting and bleeding with them! *God, why am I here?*

WAIT ON ME.

Not my favorite words to hear. I thrive off impulse, remember?

I pound the cement wall, but my fleshy fist makes an ungratifying *slap* against the concrete.

"The projection has narrowed yet again," a shaky reporter says to the screen. She's trapped inside the dome with the others. If this keeps happening, soon everyone will be sandwiched and then burned to crisps, since the Council stole the Armor suits.

I yank on my door handle. It's still locked, but I pull until my shoulders threaten to abandon their sockets. "Let me out! Let me out!"

I scream and shout as loud as my lungs allow, pounding on the door as though my life depends on it. The lives of the Radicals, Enforcers, and everyone in the Ivanhoe army do. No one comes to my door. Not Solomon. Not Zeke.

No one.

The Council must have found Solomon, and maybe Zeke's being questioned right now. That's all that would stop them from answering my call. I run to the news screen, then back to the door, then back to the news screen, as helpless as a goldfish in a dry bowl.

"Stop the Wall," I croak, my voice now barely a rasp. I sink to the ground and clutch my Bible to my chest, rocking back and forth. *God, let me out! Let me rise.*

I'll do anything.

Hours creep by. The Wall keeps inching closer and closer at a turtle's pace. But that turtle's pace sure seems fast when there's nowhere for the people to go. They clump tighter and tighter together.

The Preacher seems to be instructing clumps of his men, but my fear only grows. What can he do?

By nightfall, the city mobs hit a turning point. One moment, they're screaming out against injustice. The next moment, they've become rabid for the blood of the Council . . . including me.

I don't blame them one bit.

"Parvin's betrayed us!" a man screams to the news anchor. "She joined them and *forgot* us. Some of our *friends* are trapped between those two projections! We'll find where the Council is hiding . . . and we'll kill them all!"

"I haven't forgotten you!" The projection plays against the

backdrop of my hand pressed against the wall and my cry ends in a whisper. "I haven't . . ."

They can't hear. The people hold to that man's words and suddenly news coverage shows what's happening in Prime. A real mob that's *not* trapped in a projection starts searching for us. They start at the destroyed Council building. It's only a matter of time . . . hours, even . . . until they find us.

I wish them Godspeed.

32

Light glares through my eyelids, waking and blinding me. Huh? When did I fall asleep? I squeeze my eyes tighter shut and turn my face away, blinking away the spots in my vision and the remnants of despair sticking to my heart.

Wake up!

Clarity sweeps in with a list of reminders. It's nighttime. The projected Wall is closing in on the people. The mob is coming for me. I'm locked in my room.

My eyes shoot open and meet the light head on. Someone is in here, shaking my shoulder. I scramble away, only just realizing I was asleep on the floor. A bloody bandage stands out stark against the darkness as Solomon lowers the penlight away from my face. He's wearing a silver Brawn suit. The lights are off, but my news screen is on with the sound dimmed. My door is open.

"Solomon?" The question turns into a gasp. "Solomon! The people—the Wall—they—"

"I know." He holds up a hand and then talks fast, almost too fast for me to catch. "I have the pirate chip, the Council members are in the meeting room, but Skelley left and he took Wilbur Sherrod with him."

I bolt upright. "Wait, *what?* When?"

"Just now. We need to go."

He holds a finger to his lips. "Skelley told me to get you and meet him at the Council transport station."

I jump to my feet. "He's . . . *leaving?* Where is he going?"

"He sent Zeke and almost all the other Enforcers on a mission earlier. I don't even think the other Council members know he's gone. "

"Should we go after him or stay here and get Adria with the pirate chip?"

I can't bear the idea of remaining here when I have a chance to leave and rejoin my people.

"All the other Council members are wearing the Brawn suits they stole from us when we were captured. Neither of us could overpower her with all three of them in the room."

I nod once, and then Skelley's voice bounces into my room from the back corner. "Well, hello."

I spin on my heel. "This whole sneaking-up-on-us thing is *so* childish, Skelley." I make almost a full 360 before spotting his face, and he's not actually in my room. He's on the news screen.

Wait . . . he's on the news?

The scene is his face, much too close for comfort, with a darkened background. He tips up his fedora so the shadow moves off his eyes, and then speaks directly to me. To every viewer.

"I'm Skelley Chase, from the Citizen Welfare Development Council, and I know you're not happy with me. But let me explain what I'm doing right now. I'm leaving the Council. In fact, I'm already gone. They're probably just noticing my absence, which is why I'm going to speak fast."

He looks over his shoulder, as though nervous he's being followed. Then he pulls another body into view. Wilbur Sherrod. Wilbur's russet afro is wilted and the bags under his already saggy eyes could stop up a flood. He stares at his feet like a beaten puppy.

"This is Wilbur Sherrod," Skelley says. "Council members stole him from the city of Ivanhoe in the West. I am returning him to his people." He levels his gaze at the camera in a way that makes me take a step back. "As for the other Council members. They are in a bunker underground that is accessed through the old Subway near 145th street. Follow the tunnel to the end. You'll find them if you're fast enough."

The camera shuts off and, with a static hiss, the screen returns to coverage of the people trapped between projections.

Brickbat's enraged scream bounces down the concrete hallway.

"Let's go." Solomon yanks me from the room. He grips my hand tight and, even though it's dark, I fear not about where to run. He knows. He's leading me. And we're together again.

We creep down the tunnels but meet no resistance. No Enforcers. They must all be with Skelley. There's a giant metal door that lets us out of the secret bunker. It's too heavy for me to move it, but Solomon reaches forward with his Brawn-clad arm and we're out. It locks automatically, so I leave it propped in case we need to return.

I follow Solomon out, blinking hard and trying to focus on more details, but it's too dark. All the lights are out, probably to keep us from being spotted by any Radicals that make it into the Subway tunnels.

We crouch and Solomon leads me along the wall. My heart thuds. Brickbat could be following us. Maybe we shouldn't have left him and the others. What if the mob finds them and kills them? I will have broken my promise to Tawny.

I'm about to open my mouth and ask Solomon's opinion when the skitter of a pebble echoes ahead. Solomon holds out an arm. I freeze, deafened by my heartbeat. Trying not to make a sound while breathing only makes me need more air. A soft step. Another.

I suck in air as loud as I dare.

The sounds grow nearer, cautiously quiet, but not quiet enough. The person is walking too fast. Too many footsteps. Careless or rushed? Pitter patter. Pitter patter.

White pale skin. Silver suits.

Two bodies—Elm and Willow, slings in hand—speed past us in a blur.

My jaw drops and my gasp is lost amidst the sound of their running. We hurry after them. "Willow!" My hiss is too quiet. They're already out of sight. We run. Faster. Why are they here? I know why.

I call louder, but Willow and Elm have already slid into the bunker and the giant metal door clicks shut before Solomon reaches it. Solomon risks another shout, "Willow! Elm!"

They didn't hear us.

The door is closed. We're locked out. Meanwhile . . .

Willow is going to kill Brickbat—the man I promised Tawny I'd protect.

I abandon caution and pound on the metal door, trying to sound a warning, but no one opens. I sound like a crazed Radical, here to kill Council members. Yet the real attackers are inside.

"What do we do?" My voice is frantic. "Solomon, what do we do? Brickbat is Tawny's father, and I promised to try and keep him safe."

"What?" He digs in his pocket. Then, as though realizing this isn't the time for explanations, he withdraws his fist and slams a little silver square onto my chest.

I anticipate the slither of silver material before I comprehend it.

"Armor suit. Best keep you safe, Parvin. This isn't going to be pretty."

I'm not ready to watch people die. "Where did you get your Brawn suit?"

"Nicked it from Brickbat's coat pocket."

Of course he did.

He slams a fist into the metal. The sound is deafening. I look around at the darkness, anticipating a mob, then bounce on the balls of my feet. "Hurry, hurry, hurry . . ."

Willow could have killed Brickbat by now. I can't let her! For Tawny's sake.

Slam. A break releases muffled shouts from the other side. *Slam.* We're through.

Solomon squeezes himself into the crack and shoves the metal apart. We tumble into the light. I'm on my feet and sprinting down the hall toward the shouting. It's coming from the main meeting room. There are no Enforcers.

"Willow, stop!" I call before I can see what's going on. Solomon hollers for Elm.

I skid to a halt in the doorway of the meeting room just as a rock smashes against the frame, inches from my face. Elm's eyes widen when he sees that he almost hit *me*.

He and Willow both wear Armor suits, but the facemasks are clear so I can see their expressions. They look like the ones the Preacher's men were wearing. The tan color that Brickbat had inserted into her skin has spread to half her face. Willow has Brickbat against the wall, holding him to it with one of her small hands. There must be a Brawn suit beneath her Armor. Brickbat no longer wears his.

Her other hand is what worries me.

In it is a black mechanical spider. An Ivanhoe spider. An explosive. She has it pressed against his chest. Adria and President Garraty are knocked out on the other side of the room.

"Willow, no!"

"Stop, Parvin!" Willow doesn't look at me. As I watch her, the killer-side of my brain informs me how close she is to destroying him. A press of a single button will do the job even with an expensive medibot inside him.

I try to make my voice level. "Don't do this."

Brickbat's eyes flit to mine, a mixture of anger and fear. Even *he* can't hold on to his prideful fury when he's an inch away from dying.

Her little fist beats Brickbat's chest once. He yells and I hear the crack of possibly a rib. "He is evil, Parvin! He took my orphan friends and *killed* them! He killed them for his Clocks! To show me he was strong. He found more albinos and hurt them. He made me not albino anymore!" Her voice cracks.

I want him dead.

No! Think of Tawny!

He *beat* Tawny. He hurt her. It'd be so easy to let Willow kill him.

God, what do I do? "Willow, you don't want to take a life. This will change you forever. Don't do what Brickbat would do. Don't be like him. I can't change what he's done, but you can control what *you* do."

She presses the spider tighter against his chest. Something else cracks—is it bone or the explosive? Brickbat flinches away and shrieks, "Please!"

"I'm not him, Parvin," Willow grinds out. "He has to die."

"But we'll all explode!" I take a step closer, but Elm blocks my way.

"We are in Armor suits," he says.

Solomon enters the doorway. In a low, sad voice he says, "I'm not."

Willow's head whips around. Elm's eyes widen. "Then you should leave."

Solomon shakes his head. "Not if my staying will stop Willow from murdering." His bluntness does him credit.

"Willow, please listen. Your color doesn't matter!"

"Leave her alone." Elm moves toward me, but I'm not about to let him push me out of this room. I thought . . . I thought we were a team. "These people hurt Willow's mind. They hurt her heart. They must atone."

I keep my focus on Willow. She's in one of her zealous moods, like when Elm was trapped in the Wall. Can I even get through to her? Would she really blow up the room when Solomon is so vulnerable? I try a new approach. "Brickbat is Tawny's father."

Willow flinches and looks at me for the first time. That's when I see the tears, the red eyes, the paint of sorrow trapped behind her expression.

Brickbat looks at me, too, with a jerk of his head and a frown. The longer he stares at me, the more I see understanding cross his face. His eyes glaze and dart through information floating on the air in front of him. With a blink, his gaze returns to mine and I know he's figured it out.

He helped kill his daughter's husband.

Willow sniffs hard and wipes her free arm across her nose. "Then I am sorry for Tawny."

With that, she presses the detonator.

33

My killer reflexes launch me into a flying tackle in the splintered second before the explosion. Only I don't kill someone.

I save Solomon.

The explosion blinds me as I collide with his body. Spinning and burning, yet a single thought bellows louder than the real explosion. *Solomon! God, God, protect Solomon!*

Praying is all I *can* do.

I'm wrapped around him in my Armor suit. We tumble. I'm deaf. At some point, it all ends and gravity takes control again. Chunks of stone rest on top of me, their weight presses me down onto Solomon. I need a Brawn suit, but I have only Armor. Beneath me, Solomon isn't moving. I'm not even sure he's breathing.

"Help!" The word is a gasp. My arms tremble.

Moments later, the debris is lifted off my back as Elm digs us out. I untangle myself from Solomon, shaking my mind loose of the visions of the *Ivanhoe Independent* burning all the passengers or the Wall collapsing on me. Dust fills the air and crumbles fall from the cement ceiling.

Elm and Willow are both on their feet .

I take Solomon's head in my arms. "Solomon?" His name comes out in a croak. She blew him up. "Willow . . . you . . ." I can't say it. I can't pour that other guilt on her, though I want to.

"I had to, Parvin!"

I spot a giant stone pinning one of Solomon's legs. "No. No!" I scramble toward it, trying to tear the stone off his body. He's buried. Crushed. "Elm!"

Elm clears the chunk of cement and I brush off the other small rocks.

Solomon coughs.

I scream.

He's alive? He's alive! I protected his core. His life source. My reflexes—my knowledge of death and danger—propelled me to save him. *Thank you, God!*

"Solomon?" I wipe dust off his face, willing his eyes to find mine.

They flutter open and he grimaces. "Argh, my leg."

"Anything else?" My voice trembles so much, I'm surprised he understands me.

He pushes himself onto his elbows and I help him sit up. He sucks in a hiss. "Nothing. Just my left shin." It's sliced open and gushing blood.

"Are you sure?" I sniff hard against the tears.

He gives me a smile and moves wild hair strings from in front of my face. "Yes. I'm okay. I was protected." He's not talking about the Armor suit.

A groan comes from my right. Brickbat.

His body is half buried in rubble and blood—the blood of a man I should have protected. "No!" My screech startles Willow away from him.

She drops the detonator. "I had to, Parvin!" She stares at Brickbat, who's writhing on the floor, his hands fumbling at a giant wound in his crushed chest. "I . . ."

Elm gathers Willow to himself. "We must go, Willow." He looks at Brickbat's broken form in horror.

I move to Brickbat's side. Solomon is right behind me, dragging himself over and then wadding some material over the hole in Brickbat's chest.

Willow, trembling, runs from the place screeching, "I had to! I had to!"

Elm runs after her. "Willow!"

I'm not sure what to feel for her. She blew him up, without even a second thought for Solomon or Tawny or me. If Brickbat dies, Willow's a murderer and she'll have to live with that. It will change her.

It will ruin her.

Elm returns to us and places a hand on my shoulder. "We are going." He gives a stiff nod and avoids looking at the dying man beneath my hand. "I am sorry for this. I . . . should have stopped her." He takes one step away. "We will see you on the other side."

Willow cowers around the corner, staring at us. She doesn't speak a word.

I look at Brickbat's face. It's pale. He's barely moving. How is he even alive? Is his medibot that powerful? Blood is everywhere. *Please, God. Save him.*

Willow steps forward. "Parvin?" For the first time, her voice is vulnerable and young again. "Did I . . . am I . . . bad?"

Elm tugs her away, looking weary. "Willow . . ."

I don't know what to say. As Solomon applies more pressure to Brickbat's chest, he says, "Elm, get her out of here."

For once, Elm obeys and doesn't listen to Willow's protests. "No!" Her voice grows smaller. "I'm sorry, Parvin! I'm sorry to make you sad!"

Elm doesn't need the Brawn suit to hoist her bodily out of the room. Before they're out of sight, he retracts the two suits from around her body and tosses the Armor one to Soloman, who puts it on. Willow's confused wails echo in my mind long after they leave.

She's broken. She broke herself. It took a single choice in a flash of a second and now what will she be? What inner demons will she have to face?

I remember the ones that tormented me when I deserted her and Jude.

This . . . this is so much worse. She's so young. *God, help her.*

There's too much blood. Brickbat's body jerks. Is that the medibot trying to keep his heart going? "This isn't . . . my time."

I jerk away at his voice. Then I glance behind him to where Adria and President Garraty lie dead and half-buried. I bet it wasn't *their* time to zero out either. I don't get a chance to respond. What would I even say?

"Tell Tawny . . ." His voice is a gurgled whisper. " . . . tell her . . . I'm sorry . . . for her loss."

That's it? Sorry about Reid? What about telling *me* sorry? Or apologizing for beating Tawny senseless every time he visited? I open my mouth to spew a reprimand, but other words come out. "She forgives you."

He scoffs, then chokes. "Forgiveness . . . is not for men . . . like . . . me."

My anger is shattered. "It's exactly for men like you." As I say the words, Solomon begins to pray in undertones. Even though his voice is near silent, I feel the power in his words. I focus hard on Brickbat. "Forgiveness is for everyone who sins. The perfect have no need of it and, seeing how none of us is capable of perfection, you're an ideal candidate."

He shakes his head and gives a hoarse cry. "I . . . hate . . . you."

I press my shaking hand onto his forehead. Both are covered in blood and a few of my tears wash clean streaks on his face. I'm crying over this monster, because he's so near the end yet so far from eternity. I shake my head, look into his hate-filled gaze, and release a sad smile. "I don't care, Elan. I don't care that you hate me."

Then I kiss his dusty, torn, rubbled cheek and join Solomon in prayer until Brickbat's shuddering stops. He lets out a last cough and then a last breath.

Brickbat's gone.

Only when I open my eyes again do I see that his own tears left streaks down his temples. I barely had a chance to say . . . anything. About Tawny. About God, not that he would have listened.

Blood speckles Solomon's Brawn suit everywhere. He leans back on his heels, then winces and adjusts his bloodied leg beneath him. "I'm sorry, Parvin." He reaches for my hand, then must realize his is covered in blood. I take his anyway. I need human contact to remind me I'm alive and need to breathe.

"There's redemption up to the last millisecond." I breathe deep through my nose. "I have to hold on to that." I didn't want Brickbat to die. Not like this. Not unfulfilled and consumed with rage and thirst for power.

"We need to go after Skelley Chase."

Oh yeah. Skelley. He has Wilbur. I thought the world had stopped. He's waiting for us.

I push myself to my feet, my hand sliding out of Solomon's. I wipe it on the Armor suit. A quick check shows that Adria and President Garraty are dead. Skelley is now our only chance to stop the projected Wall. What else could I have done?

RISE.

But there's so much darkness.

RISE UP. YOU ARE MY LIGHT.

How? The anti-shalom is spreading into the people I love!

As I release the despair, I think of what Jesus had to endure. He watched his people choose anti-shalom. He watched them suffer. He watched his friends make mistakes and his family reject him.

Yet He rose above it all . . . for the sake of shalom.

If He can do it on His own, then He most certainly can empower *me* to do it. I take a deep breath, brush away the tears, and give Solomon a nod. "I'm ready."

His sorrow is palpable and, oddly, comforting. "I'm proud of you, Parvin."

He leads us, with a severe limp, to the exit of this cement tomb. We return to the subway tracks. With every step Solomon's limp grows, but he says, "I don't think the injury is that deep."

"There was a lot of blood."

He tears off his pant leg and wraps the wound, then puts back on the Brawn and Armor suits. They seem to help.

Skelley is so far ahead that I'm not sure following him will do us any good. He's probably given up on us already. Still, we have to try. We reach the tracks, but there's no train. Solomon's penlight illuminates the way. The tunnel blackens into an ominous mist. "We'll need to go by foot."

I squeeze his arm. "But . . . what if the train comes while we're in there?" I've almost been run over by a train once, and I'm not keen to try it again.

"We're wearing Armor suits. We'll be safe. Besides, if Skelley took the train, it should be gone." He slides his hand into mine.

My head says trust him and trust the suits, but my fluttering, weak heart of fear keeps sending visual pulses of death and smashed Parvin into my mind.

He helps me down onto the tracks. They're more like rails and very different from normal railroad tracks. Easier to walk on, too. But I feel like we're trekking through an elongated coffin, waiting for the grim reaper to show up.

The darkness is thicker, pressing on me like the tunnels inside the Wall. It's no different, except there's no light at the end. Well, I *hope* there's not a light because it'd be a very different sort of light.

"Do you think Brickbat was redeemable?" I picture his pale, lifeless body. I imagine myself having to tell Tawny and watching her react the way she did when Reid died.

She'll blame me. She'll hate me again, and this time there's nothing I can do about it. It was my fault; I should have called out

louder to Willow when I first saw her. I knew from the start what
she was going to do. Why didn't I stop her *then?*

"I think everyone's redeemable," Solomon says. "It's not your
fault if they reject God."

It feels like my fault. Wasn't that the whole reason I stuck with
the Council and let them torture me and control me and threaten
me all during this past year? *To show them Your power, God?*

YOU ARE MY VESSEL.

You always speak in riddles! First it's *shalom*, then it's *speak*, now
it's *rise up.* Haven't I done those things? Is it really possible to fix
any of this?

"Anything is possible with God." Solomon waves his penlight
over the tracks.

"Did you read my thoughts?" Anything is possible. God can
do anything. And one of those anythings was to allow us a choice.
A choice to choose life . . . or choose anti-shalom. *I'm sorry for my
weakness, Lord.*

In a brief gust of wind, I find comfort. He never said this road
would be easy. He sees me trying. Jesus struggled with His calling.

"Think you can jog?" Solomon tugs my hand and I entrust
myself to the darkness, feeling for footing with my mind.

"Can *you?*" It feels better to move faster, like we might actually catch Skelley. But if he meant what he said, he's heading to
the Wall with Wilbur. Does he realize that the Wall is *moving?*
Creeping its way closer and closer to the huddled Radicals trapped
in between?

And the Wall is . . . *far.* Very far away. It takes over eight
hours by train. That's too long. The entire Ivanhoe army and the
Radicals could be dead by then. Maybe we could fly?

"Solomon, did you alert Father about the moving projection?"

"Yes," he pants, and the hint of a whine in his voice reminds
me of his injured leg.

"We should walk."

He doesn't argue, which shows me how painful his wound is. *I'll trust You.*

We walk another ten minutes, and I'm able to leave the trauma behind me and focus on our goal ahead. Why did Skelley ditch the Council? I should know better but . . . I'm surprised he betrayed everyone.

I notice a glow from ahead. "We're almost to the next platform." I look closer. The light is unsteady. "Or . . . is that a subway?" It's growing brighter, though. Is that because we're getting closer?

"Actually . . ." Solomon's hand darts back and grabs mine. "I think it's both."

My heart stumbles and my knees almost buckle. "What?"

"Yeah." The pitch of his voice is a little higher. "Yeah, that's a train. We gotta run."

There's no whistle to warn us of impact. Only a clack and rattle growing louder and louder, the light barreling down on us.

Solomon is right about both things—we are almost to the next station *and* there's a train about to crush us. A stitch in my side has the audacity to still bother me as I sprint for my life. "Are we going to make it?"

Solomon's run is a disjointed gallop and he presses a hand against his wounded leg. All I want is a yes. The platform is closer. So is the train.

"I hope so."

"Yeah, well so do I!" Duh. We run pell-mell toward both lights. Something in me snaps and a laugh bursts forth. This is so silly. Would God really let us die by getting run over by a train? *Now?*

We reach the platform and, as Solomon climbs up, I stand on the tracks like a brick, staring at the approaching subway train. It's slower than the *Ivanhoe Independent*, but still a giant metal beast with no cushion. Louder. Rushing. Louder.

"Parvin, here!" Solomon reaches a hand down. I lift my arm in a daze, my gaze glued to the train. It's so close. Almost here. Then I'm yanked out of the canal like a paper doll.

The train squeals to a stop, blocking the entry onto the tracks and lighting up the platform.

I forgot we were both in Armor suits. I would have been fine, but it wouldn't have been pretty. What was wrong with me in there? Why didn't I help Solomon? Why did I just *stand* there?

I expect Solomon to call me out on it. To shout about my stupidity, but he kneels by me. "Are you okay?"

"Yeah. I'm fine."

"Good." Solomon gets us moving again at a quicker pace, though he's limping severely. I follow. "Let's keep quiet in case we're catching up to Skelley. He might be fast, but Wilbur is weak and slowing him down."

"Okay, should we get on that train? Can you make it go the right way?" I'd much rather ride than walk again. It'd be better for Solomon's leg, too.

"Let's hop on and try." As Solomon and I reach the shattered door, the train starts to move of its own accord. We jump through the hole and he adjusts the control board like Zeke did. It takes him only a minute to make the beast stop midtunnel and then reverse its direction.

"You're brilliant."

Solomon smiles for the first time in days. And I caused it. "Good thing there wasn't anyone *on* this train."

We ride the train up the tunnel, toward the wreckage. "Crouch below the windows so we're not spotted."

I follow Solomon and balance on the balls of my feet below a window. He stretches out his wounded leg, but he keeps his eyes over the edge to see anything that might give us clues. There was another time in my life when I sat with a Hawke man, hiding from an enemy while on a motorcoach.

Oh, Jude. His ending was so sacrificially bittersweet.

The train stops at every platform, but no one ever gets on. My legs turn numb from the crouching, but I don't adjust them until we're moving down the tunnels again.

"I think we get off at this stop." Solomon's whisper matches the hiss of the subway as it slows.

I envision when Zeke led me through the tunnels beneath the Council building. "The very last stop is when I got on."

"Yeah, but the train doesn't go up that tunnel automatically. It was programmed to take the Council members *out* of danger, but no one can ride the train *in*."

"So how do we get in then?" And how does Solomon know all this? Oh wait, let me guess. Jude and Christian. They're the closest things to spies I've ever known.

"There's a door that leads into the tunnel. The tunnel is blocked off by a projection that looks like stone. You can go out of it, but not into it. Zeke told me."

Zeke.

The subway train jerks to a halt and we exit with caution. No one is here, so Solomon goes straight for a portion of wall hidden in shadow. A few beeps reach my ears and then he pushes the wall. It swings inward like your everyday door. "Ready?"

How can anyone be ready? I rotate my shoulders and then nod. Dust whooshes into my lungs as we step through the doorway. I walk through a spider web and stifle a squeak. Everything is pitch black and nearly swallows up Solomon's penlight. But it's a miniature tunnel that leads us to the main subway tunnel. Once inside, we clamber back down onto the tracks and head toward the collapsed Council building.

It feels good to be *doing* something again instead of sitting in my locked room watching the news.

The walk up this tunnel goes faster than the first and I breathe normally, since I know a train can't come barreling down on us. I trip over scattered rock, but the Armor suit keeps my toes from being smashed. Solomon, beside me, lets out a grunt as well and directs the penlight onto the ground. Rubble and pieces of ceiling litter the track.

"Be careful," he mutters. "We don't want to be too loud now that we're so close."

But loudness doesn't matter because the moment the words leave his lips, a burst of human shouts barrel down our tunnel toward us, louder and more intimidating than any train.

Solomon clicks off the penlight and shoves me against the inner wall. The voices grow, matching the public uproars I've listened to on the news screen the past several days.

It's a stupid question, but it escapes my lips all the same in my panic. "Solomon, what is it?"

"The rioters. They've found the tunnels."

34

I'm pressed against the wall, wrapped in Solomon's arms and Enforcer cloak. But the rioters have torches, hand lights, and weapons. They'll be on us in moments.

"Up here." He pushes me along the wall and I squint to see what he's seeing. Nothing. There's nothing. Wait . . . "That walkway. Climb up."

I try, but my missing left hand doesn't do me any favors. Solomon unceremoniously shoves me and my face scrapes against stone, but it's too dark for him to see me at this awkward angle. At least I'm up.

The torches are closer and illuminate his coat. They're going to see him.

With one swift leap, he's up beside me and we're pressed against the wall again. He's trembling, and I catch the grind of his teeth before the mob's shouts deafen us. They run past us. They are on a mission.

We are invisible.

I AM HERE. BE NOT AFRAID.

The wave passes and I push away from the wall. "Let's go."

Solomon gives me space. "There will probably be more people coming."

"Skelley's message didn't do him any good—the members are

already dead." All except me. Will the mob be disappointed and start hunting me down?

"I know, let's go find him. Hopefully it's not too late to turn off the projected Wall."

Be not afraid, He said. I will not fear. "Do you think it's still moving?"

"With Adria dead and Skelley gone, I'm not sure there's anyone to *stop* it." We crouch-run down the walkway, staying as silent as possible. Solomon doesn't turn on his penlight until he collides with the railing at the end of the walkway. He grunts and flips head over heels, toppling down onto the tracks.

I gasp and clamber over after him. "Are you okay?"

I catch a disoriented nod in the dim light. "Why am *I* always the one getting injured?" A smile tilts his voice up. "It's not very manly." I hear the pain in his voice. His leg needs medical attention.

"You're still manly to me." I go to kiss him on the forehead, but miss in the darkness. I don't have the guts to try again. Good thing it's dark so he can't see me blush. "Shall we continue?"

He leads the way, and we make it to the platform in less than ten minutes. Solomon's limp is worse and he grimaces every other step. He's not letting on about the pain. Chunks of rubble and broken ceiling form steps out of the track tunnel. I hope the roof doesn't cave in. Who knows how much pressure is making it crack.

The lighting is dim and Solomon scans the room. For a moment I wonder if he's finally unsure where to go, but then his gaze lands on a location and he swivels toward it. "Here we go."

I grab his arm and stop him. "What if . . . what if *you* tried to shut down the projection? I know you *say* you don't have Hawke blood, but you're smart. You're techy. You could do it, Solomon. We're close to the control room." He could finally prove to himself that he has worth.

"I can't, Parvin."

"You can! I know you can!" Maybe this isn't the time or the situation to push Solomon toward self-confidence. If he *can't* take down the projection, then we've lost precious time to catch up to Skelley.

But if he can . . .

"What if Skelley's trying to distract us? To lure us away from the control room for his own purposes?" The more I think about it, the more it makes sense. Skelley's trying to make us followers again.

Solomon balances on his good leg and looks at me, hard. "Do you really think I can, Parvin?"

I don't know. I don't have the answers, but I can't falter now, not when Solomon has a chance to save the world. I want it to be him who fixes this. *God? Are you with us?*

ALWAYS.

Well, that's not exactly a "Go ahead," or "Don't try," but I'll take it. "Let's try. Be confident in the Lord." *Please help us to rise up for Your glory. Let this moment be Yours.*

Solomon nods once, takes a deep breath, then limps to a door on the opposite side of the room—opposite the one Zeke and I exited through when escaping. The stairs look the same, but we take only five flights before Solomon leads us into a broken corridor. The Brawn suit allows him to push a cracked door open with his shoulder, gently, so as to make little noise.

In the next hallway, new voices come to us. Mutterings, like other people on a search. Solomon beckons me after him and leads us away from the voices, hopping twice on his good leg and once on his bad to propel him into a type of skip. The next door we go through leads to a collapsed passageway. Dirt crumbles from the ceiling in warning. We backpedal from the wreckage as cement and metal groans.

"I think we're a floor too high."

Too high? "Are we even in the Council building?"

"No, we're beneath it. Underground."

Oh. "Is the control room really this easy to get to?"

He laughs under his breath. "You think this is easy?"

"It's certainly easier than what I was picturing." We whip around a corner just as voices enter the hallway. They still for a moment, but we don't. Whoever it is, if they saw us we're in trouble.

I'm not sure I can breathe much longer at the rate of running and breath-holding we're doing. Solomon weaves us through rooms, hallways, and broken building so quickly I'm utterly lost by the time he lets out an "Aha!"

"Are we here?"

It's a black door with signs on it, warning away anyone who's not "approved personnel." The handle doesn't turn when Solomon tries it, but the doorframe is bent like squashed toothpicks. The latch isn't exactly secure.

"Step back." Solomon punches the face of the door. The metal booms like a clap of thunder. The door swings open and allows Solomon a graceful tumble inside. Yay, Brawn suit. *Now* whoever was behind us knows where we are. I want to block my ears as though it will stop the rest of the building from hearing the noise.

I follow Solomon onto a stairwell landing. It takes one push on the door with my good arm and mutilated wrist to tell me it's no use trying to close it. "Let's just go." Solomon skips over the first crumbled step and continues down the next.

It's a relief to be walking again instead of running. "The people who probably heard us . . . don't you think they'll come after us?"

"Eventually." That doesn't stop him, and my chest swells at his determination. His leadership.

Four flights down. Five. Six. This is deeper than even the subway tunnels. That means safer from the weight above . . . I hope. We reach the bottom and stand before another closed door.

Solomon is pale and sweating, but taps the handle. It's not locked. My heart sends a poof of nervousness to my stomach.

He looks at me. "Ready?"

I try to smile. "I'm glad I'm with you, Solomon."

He slides his hand back into mine. I give a weak squeeze—my muscles are shot. He squeezes back. One of us is bleeding and it creeps between our hooked thumbs, but we advance through the door anyway.

It leads into an enormous lab, shrouded in bluish darkness. Screens, NABs, wires, and panels turn the walls and tables into a tech-kid's playground. Jude would have loved this place. The ceiling is high, to accommodate metal poles wrapped in wires and cords. The rest of the tech disappears into darkness ahead.

"Split up?" Why did I even suggest that? I don't want to be alone.

Solomon shakes his head and pulls me into the darkness. My eyes adjust as we tiptoe-crouch around tables and over old abandoned tech. Dull lights illuminate some corners of the darkness, but when we get closer, they're just dormant lights on the panels.

Solomon straightens and releases my hand, speaking in a full voice. "This is it." I shush him, but he shakes his head. "No one's here. This is the control room, Parvin."

How is he so sure? He steps forward, crunching a fallen electroscreen console underfoot. "Here . . . here I go."

I suppress the pounding tick-tock of my heart that reminds me how short time is. "You can do it."

FOR *MY* GLORY.

Of course.

We reach the back wall, which is covered in panels of buttons and an enormous screen with more wires than I can count. The control board looks so . . . old. Does it even run anymore? I guess if Erfinder Hawke made it fifty years ago, it's not like today's high-tech.

Solomon stands in front of it for a full minute, his hands hanging at his sides.

"You can do it, Solomon." This could be the moment the Wall comes down for good. If Solomon can get into the heart of the program and disable it, we can destroy this room and the Wall will never go back up . . . as long as we take care of Skelley.

We are statues in the dark. I breathe so gently even I can't hear it, but Solomon's breaths grow louder and louder as though he's running.

God, empower him for this moment. Show him that blood doesn't matter. He belongs in Your *family and You've built him for great things. Shalom and Your glory.*

God wants this Wall down as badly as I do—He revealed to me the broken shalom brought on by the control in the USE. He showed me the need. He'll take it down, one way or another.

I just really want *this* to be the way He chooses.

In a moment of decision, Solomon breathes deep through his nose and then attacks the panel with flying fingers. I don't move, as though my stillness will allow the aura of tech-knowledge to flow more freely around him.

The giant screen above lights up and, three seconds after it's illuminated this pit of technology, Solomon steps back. He holds his hands up as though burned. "Someone's been here already."

"What do you mean?" I step forward.

"Someone's messed with it. Someone—"

The bored warble comes from behind us. "Hey, kiddos."

35

Skelley wears a Brawn suit and Armor suit. So, he learned about layering, too. He has his fedora on his head, and a gun in his hand. Maybe even the same gun he used to shoot Reid. "I really didn't want to use force. Actually, I thought for sure you'd follow me, but you had to act the heroes, didn't you?" He flicks the gun barrel toward the entry door. "Let's get going."

Wilbur stands beside him, shuffling his feet from side to side and not looking at us.

I don't move. "Why?"

"Because I can't leave you here to mess up what I've done."

My hand inches toward my pocket where the pirate chip rests, but even in the dim lighting Skelley is sharp.

"Come on, Parvin. I know you want the Wall down, I know you want the information in my brain, I know your boyfriend over there is hoping he can break into the program, but I've set it up so he can't. Let's go to the Wall, shall we? The longer we spend talking, the more people die."

He knows me too well. Curse this man. "Why do you care that they're dying?"

He sighs and closes his eyes. "Because, as hard as it is for you to grasp this . . . I'm a *good* guy."

"That doesn't mean anything when you've created your own definition of good." I want to let out my hurt and confusion. I

A TIME TO RISE

want to point out that he not only murdered two men whom I loved with my life, but he just murdered all the members on the Council. "Your idea of good is still anti-shalom, Skelley."

His face darkens.

"We should go," Solomon mutters beside me.

"But he can't hurt us." Solomon has Brawn *and* Armor, and I wear Armor. In fact, if I dart right and then leap left at Skelley, I could land a kick on his skull, which would . . .

No. He's wearing Brawn and Armor, too, silly.

Ugh!

"I can't hurt you"—Skelley redirects the gun to Wilbur's temple—"but I can hurt him."

Wilbur doesn't even flinch, which tells me he's accepted death. He's been through a *lot*. And that makes me want to murder Brickbat all over again. Knowing what Wilbur *was* and what he is *now* after being with the Council for just a few weeks opens my eyes to what Willow might have gone through.

Only she emerged fiery and set on revenge.

"Why are you threatening him when you told the people you're returning him to the Preacher?" My voice increases. "And why did you prompt us to follow you?"

"It didn't do much good, did it? You didn't obey." Skelley smirks. "Is it that hard to believe I didn't want you clubbed to death by mad rioters?"

"Yes. Yes, it is."

"Let's just *go*, Parvin." Solomon takes my hand and I notice his fingers are trembling. I look at him and his jaw clenches and unclenches. Most of his weight is on his right leg.

God?

I AM HERE.

"Okay, we'll cooperate." Solomon doesn't protest—proof he's in agony. "Get that gun away from Wilbur's head." I'm surprised when Skelley complies.

Solomon moves and I follow his lead. "Where are you taking us?"

"To see the adoring public, of course."

If by *adoring public* he means people waiting to kill us, then . . . great. "Where are the other Enforcers?" Did he kill Zeke?

"They're taken care of, don't you fret."

My throat constricts. "You killed them?"

Skelley sighs. "You're always thinking the worst of me. They're following my orders."

Oh yeah, he thinks he's the good guy. Delusional. This man is delusional.

Skelley nudges us in front of him, placing Wilbur between us.

Wilbur's in a daze of sorts and barely gets one foot in front of the other.

I look at him. "Are you okay?"

Stupid question.

He doesn't reply, so Solomon and I hook one of Wilbur's arms over each of our shoulders. Solomon grunts and falls to one knee. I jerk to a halt. He can't do this. He's losing too much blood. "Solomon?"

He pushes himself back to his feet and croaks, "I'm fine." He's *so* not fine, if his legs buckled while wearing a Brawn suit.

Skelley marches us to the front door. We encounter no one on our way out. Multiple explanations spin through my head, none of them pretty. Skelley killed them. Skelley sent them somewhere. Skelley lied to them.

We exit the building through a broken chunk of wall. Skelley keeps low and quiet, which tells me that rioters might still be around looking for the Council. All that is needed is a well-timed scream and they'd be here.

But that won't help me now that Skelley has a gun to Wilbur's back. And not when the people feel like I betrayed them. They're hunting for me, too.

The outside of the Council building is far more intimidating in person than on a news screen. Giant chunks of building lay on the ground, still smoking in places. Rubble is everywhere and dust hovers over the earth like a choking morning fog.

Wilbur grows heavier over my shoulder as he sinks lower and lower. I try to walk tall so I can alleviate more of the weight from Solomon, but I'm short as it is.

Skelley leads us across what used to be the park, his gun concealed by a coat he threw over his Armor suit. We weave through buildings that have been abandoned since the attack on the Council building, until we arrive at an old skyscraper. Advertisements flicker on the exterior, but the apartment windows are all dirty or stained. Skelley uses a key to open the door, glancing over his shoulder at us every few seconds.

"Jumpy?"

"Cautious." He wrenches open the door, then takes his gun fully out again.

I'm not afraid.

We enter the building and none of our footsteps make a sound against the layer of dust on the ground. Skelley directs us to a door that leads down to a basement. "Usually we get to this from the Council building, but the destruction has it blocked off."

Thanks for that bit of info.

Solomon continues to follow. I don't like his compliance or silence. Is it because he failed with the control panel for the Wall? Or maybe he has a plan to take Skelley down so we can use the pirate chip. Or maybe . . . he's dying because of that leg wound and I don't realize it.

Skelley enters codes into a wall beside another door. It slides open and he flips a master switch that groans as it moves. Lights flicker on. There is no dust on the floor of this room.

The ground is smooth cement and a tunnel leads left into darkness—probably the way to the Council building. To my right is a glass chute parallel to the ground with what look like gigantic knowledge cap pills sitting in the chute. Four chairs sit in each capsule.

"Take off your suits."

I clench my hand over the material. "No!"

"Do you really want to bring out the threats, Parvin?" He waves the gun toward Wilbur.

"I thought you were the *good* guy," I say with as much of a sneer as I can muster. Still, Solomon and I comply. I feel so weak without Armor on, especially knowing Skelley has his own Armor on over his own Brawn suit.

I AM STRONGER.

And You are here. I breathe out my worry. He is here. He is stronger.

"Do you realize you murdered your fellow Council members?" Solomon's low voice is like a gauntlet—a challenge thrown at Skelley's feet.

Skelley raises an eyebrow.

"You sold them out!" Can he sink any lower? *God . . . can You reach hearts so encased in sickness?*

Skelley sounds genuinely confused when he responds. "I gave the people what they wanted. In fact, I gave them what *you* wanted. You've hated the Council ever since you learned about it. Your little albino girl hated it, the orphans suffered under it. I thought you wanted this."

"I don't want you to kill people!"

He shrugs. "*I* didn't kill them. I shared their location. I can't control the actions of the people."

The grinding of Solomon's teeth echoes in the cement room. "Elan Brickbat is dead. Because of you."

Well, sort of. Because of Willow. I guess I can see a little of Skelley's point.

"I'm truly sorry to hear that. He brought that upon himself."

"What about me?" I have to ask it. I have to ask because, for a time, I thought Skelley cared about my survival. "I was *there* and the mob could have killed me."

He smirks. "Why do you think I told your boyfriend to get you? It's not my fault you took so long."

Skelley knew Solomon was undercover? I shake my head at my own ignorance. I should have *seen* these things.

He points toward the first capsule lined up in the tube. "Now, climb in."

Crawl into a tiny space with my Solomon and my greatest enemy? This should be interesting. "Where are you taking us?"

"I already told you—your fans await."

"You have the knowledge to stop this!" I throw my arms in the air. "Why are you letting people *die?*"

He shouts in return—the first time I've ever really heard him raise his voice. "Get in the capsule, *now!*"

I don't move. It takes one shove from Skelley in his Brawn suit and I'm sprawled facedown in the capsule. I right myself with a lot of twisting and crawling. Solomon shouts at Skelley, but Skelley treats him no different. This time, I'm a cushion to stop Solomon's face from hitting the plastic footrests.

Skelley's sacrificing us to the mob. That must be it.

Fear not. It's my own reminder now, like a light that comes on at the threat of weakened emotions.

Wilbur is thrust forward next. His head hits the glass on the opposite side and he slumps in the seat, unconscious.

Skelley comes last, punches a few things on the control board and the glass top lowers to lock us in this capsule of doom. I feel nauseous. "Better strap in if you don't want a concussion."

My defiance flares, but Solomon hauls me to the back two seats and clicks the seatbelt in before I can protest. Then he buckles Wilbur in from behind. The seatbelt is different from the ones in the Enforcer cars—this one has two straps over my shoulders, both of which are padded, and it clicks to a buckle between my legs. Also padded.

Solomon yanks the straps so they're tight. He barely gets himself clipped in before the capsule starts forward at a slow slide. We slip into the tunnel and the capsule increases in speed. Faster. Faster. Accelerating with no relief. The seatbelt doesn't feel so tight anymore as I'm pressed against my seat by the pressure of movement.

I suck in a breath and it's like inhaling beneath a chest weight. When is it going to stop? When will we reach the intended speed? I need it to stop. "Solomon?" My word is choked. I can't even turn my head to look at him, but his thumb presses into the top of my hand.

I can't breathe.

Finally, the acceleration slows and my gut lurches in a way that threatens to coat the inside of this capsule with its contents. I groan. Skelley laughs once through his nose, but gives no explanation. Everything outside of the capsule is black, but my body tells me we're moving at incredible speeds. It's confusing and overwhelming.

"Close your eyes," Solomon says.

I obey and breathe deep through my nose, clutching the strap of my seatbelt with my fist. I can hardly think, let alone keep track of passing time. The one moment I open my eyes, I see Skelley browsing his NAB like this is your everyday train ride.

Solomon is a pale green. Is that from loss of blood or nausea?

For a time, I try to form a plan or guess what Skelley's up to, but I'm too lost. At last, I surrender. I surrender to God and trust that He has this under control. He never asked me to fix the world, but I've tried. He asked me to be obedient and be a bringer of shalom. It's hard to see shalom in this situation, but I'll try.

In very little time the pod slows, bit by bit, until it feels like we're crawling. After ten minutes, it rolls to a stop inside an identical mini station.

Skelley gets out first and strolls to the opposite side of the room before Solomon or I have even unbuckled. For a moment, I contemplate trying to get this pod to take us back, but the idea of staying in it any longer and suffocating against the speed gets me out pretty quick.

Both Wilbur and Solomon lie, eyes closed, against their chairs. Solomon's coated in sweat and his breathing sounds shallow. I hiccup a squeak and shake him first. His eyes flash open.

"Time to get out."

Solomon is shaking so hard, he can't even unbuckle his seatbelt. I do it for him, and then help him out of the pod. He gets one leg over the side, then collapses.

"Skelley!" It's the first time I've ever called the man with the fedora out of need instead of fear, hatred, or surprise.

He doesn't hurry back, but he *does* come back.

Blood already stains the station cement from Solomon's soaked bandage. I unwind it and Skelley kneels beside me. "What happened to him?"

"We were trying to save the Council members, but then Willow blew it up and rubble buried him." I shouldn't tell him everything, but he saved my life once with the medibot. Maybe he can help Solomon.

"You'll need to leave him."

"Never." *Never again.* I gingerly lift the rest of the bandage off the wound. It's shriveled and wrinkly like when grapes start turning to raisins. "What do I do?"

"Rewrap it, I guess." To Skelley's everlasting credit, he shrugs off the coat he wore over the Armor suit, tears it into strips (thank you, Brawn suit!) and hands it to me.

I'm so stunned, I don't do anything with the bandages. Skelley avoids my eyes and finally my body remembers to move. The coat is thick and will help stop up the bleeding better than the flimsy pant leg we'd used earlier.

"Maybe you *are* part good guy," I say in a low voice.

"I am." He says it with emphasis, as though he wants it to be true, but knows it's not quite right.

We get Solomon bandaged, give him some water from a small bottle Skelley had in the travel capsule, and when Solomon finally manages to sit up, Skelley slaps a Brawn suit against his chest. "It'll help you walk, so get up."

Now I *know* he's got some goodness in his heart. The partnership we formed when writing my biography returns to me—the feelings of trust, the hopefulness of a brighter future. It's two different lives clashing in one moment.

I help Solomon to his feet, then I try to pull Wilbur from the capsule. He wakes up at my yanking and clambers out—beaten into a follower. "I'm so sorry this happened to you, Wilbur."

He shakes his head and follows Skelley to the other side of the room. I sling Solomon's arm over my shoulder. We follow Skelley through a stone arch hallway into a wide, square space held up by pillars. Skelley pulls a key from his pocket, clicks it, and two lights blink from straight ahead. Headlights.

His sleek green car sits there waiting for him, like a lonesome pup. A few rows behind it are lines of Enforcer beetle-cars. I expect him to climb inside and command that we follow. Instead, he turns and leans his back against it so he's facing us. "We're inside the Wall."

"What?" The word pops out not because I didn't hear him, but because it's such an absurd statement. A garage? Inside the beast that splits the Earth? No, no, no, I've *been* inside the Wall. It's not smooth concrete or nice pillared car garages.

"We're about to go outside. It's a ten-minute drive to the big hole you blew." He levels his gaze at me. "To the war zone."

Solomon adjusts his weight. I'm too busy fixing the hinge in my jaw, trying to get my shocked mouth to close. "Why are you taking us there? What are we to you? A sacrifice?"

My jaw closes and I swallow. So, the Council has a secret passage into the Wall. That explains how they got to the Opening so fast when I tried to save Elm. That explains . . . a lot.

We're going toward the action. Toward my people. This is where I've wanted to be since all of this started.

In full seriousness, Skelley pushes himself off the car so he's standing at his full height. "It's time to end this, Parvin. I did what I had to do to get you here. Now climb in the car."

Well, *I* tried to do what *I* had to, to retrieve that Wall information. The pirate chip is still in my pocket. Is now the time? I'd have to find a way to retract his Armor suit.

Something in me tells me it's not time. Skelley still has the Brawn suit. And Solomon—even in *his* Brawn suit—is too weak. Wilbur's no help at all. "Let's go."

Solomon opens the back door of the car and we slide inside. Wilbur's smashed against the opposite door, Solomon's in the middle, and I'm near the driver's side door. The back is a long bench seat—deep black leather and much nicer than the Enforcer beetle cars or the taxis I've ridden in.

While Skelley is still outside, doing a once-over on the car, I hiss a question to Solomon without making eye contact, so Skelley won't notice. "When should I use the pirate chip?"

Solomon shakes his head, bleary and weak. "I can't explain it, but I feel peace about this whole thing."

"You do?" I shouldn't be surprised. It's been hard for me to be concerned, too.

Skelley gets in and we remain silent. "Seatbelts?" He pulls his over his shoulder. I do the same, helping Solomon with his.

I sit behind Skelley. It'd be so easy for me to reach over, detract the Armor suit, and then strangle him—

Stop. I have to keep resisting the murderous thoughts. The devil's given me power to do things *my* way. But I won't give in to that beast, not now that I can finally recognize him.

Skelley starts the car, but I feel no vibration. I can tell it's on only when we start crawling through the black tar of darkness. The bluish-white headlights illuminate a giant crack in the opposite wall. Skelley presses a button on the visor of his car and the door slides up into the ceiling. A beam of light grows from its base.

It's daytime outside? It doesn't fit with all the sneaking we've been doing. I guess we've been underground this whole time. "What if someone was out there? What if you opened the door and someone saw you?"

The car inches into the sunlight and I shield my eyes. There's something odd about the scene ahead of me—the stretch of Missouri terrain.

Skelley turns right. "It wouldn't open. The door would flash a red light as a warning. There are scanners."

Only as we drive parallel to the Wall, like we did with the dog-sleds, do I figure out the oddity. It's like viewing the world through campfire heat. The landscape is wavery, like a fuzzy photo.

"We're in between the stone and the projection." Solomon points it out before I can. "In the tunnel dome."

"Yes, we are." Skelley accelerates. The ground along the Wall is smoothed out. Not rutted, but groomed. Has it always been this way? Wouldn't I have noticed how easy it would be to drive a car here?

"If we go through the projection"—I swallow—"we'll die." Except for Skelley in his Armor suit. Mere inches separate us from scraping the stone Wall on our right, or sliding into the projection on our left.

"Yup." He accelerates. I peek at the speedometer. One hundred miles per hour. One-ten. One-twenty.

Maybe Skelley's planning a four-person suicide.

Or maybe not. Does he even understand suicide? I only learned about it while in Ivanhoe. I bet he knows. But how would all our deaths help anything? No, that's not his plan. Not without an audience, at least.

In mere minutes, we start passing people on our left. There are little tent villages surrounded by people loaded with weapons and guns strung across their backs. Their everyday mismatched clothing tells me they're Radicals and USE citizens, the few in number who escaped being trapped inside this dome.

They barely have time to swivel their heads before we're past them. I turn to watch their reactions. Some follow a few steps or whisper to their neighbors. We may even be on the news screens already. I search the skies. No helicopters in sight yet. I give them two minutes.

The projection seems closer to the car now. Skelley's side view mirror is going through it as we speed along. "Skelley?"

"Almost there."

Yes, but *then* what? We're trapped in the dome and won't be able to get back to the underground tube!

The landscape becomes familiar. It feels like home—an old home far back in my memory. But then I remember that Unity Village is gone. Blown up. My voice is quiet, and I'm not sure I want the answer to this question. "Skelley, did you bomb Unity Village?"

"Brickbat commands anything having to do with explosives, so not really. But I can't pass all the blame. The Council approved it."

"So he was the one who bombed the *Ivanhoe Independent*?"

"Yes."

"But . . . it smelled like lemon before it exploded."

Skelley's silent for a mile. "Just a part of his humor."

Humor. Right. Sadistic humor.

We reach the rubble and the giant gap in the Wall that's filled with people clumping together. There's a news helicopter now. "Where are all the USE soldiers?"

Skelley's answer is to lay on the horn and drive through the mob of people until we're directly in the middle of the dome. He slams on the brakes. The car slides along the grass, trying to stop. It rotates, then jerks to a stop.

Around us is a mob and the giant hole that I created. Behind and ahead . . . are the walls of the projection dome, coming closer and closer.

Thousands of people gather near the car. Do we get out? I don't want to get out. They're not happy people. That means they know who is in the car. "What are we *doing?*"

Skelley opens his door and unfolds his frame like some necromancer risen from the dead. A bullet comes from the crowd and smacks the glass on the car windshield. Skelley doesn't flinch. The Armor suit will protect him.

Among the people are numerous Enforcers, but they're not in rank. They're with the people.

"It's the Council member, Skelley Chase!" Someone shouts. "Kill him!"

Another bullet pings, but Skelley holds up both his hands. "Listen to me! I want shalom!"

Hey, that's *my* word.

Does he even understand what shalom is?

"Then stop this projection!" someone shouts.

I glance backward. There's no more gap through which to drive. We're trapped in the shrinking projection. At least I'll die with my people.

Skelley steps away from the car toward the people. "That's why I'm here."

Even *I* can hear the production in his voice, like he's speaking to an audience and he's the spotlight actor on stage.

He removes his Armor suit and tosses it to the crowd. They scatter like it's a bomb.

Then one woman, tentative, picks it up. "It's a suit," she tells the others. "Like that general had on the other side."

Skelley tosses the Brawn to them, too, now exposed and fully vulnerable. He glances at a watch on his wrist. "I've seen your struggle, and while the rest of the Council wouldn't heed advice, I've taken it upon myself to see you free."

They're listening. With all my heart, I hope he's telling them the truth. Could he possibly want the best for them? With a startle, I realize that . . . he's without an enhanced suit. And his gun rests on the passenger seat.

This is my chance. It's like he left it there for me. The people would love me if I killed him. Adore me. It's the answer. I sense the urges of my murder cap, but it can't be fully wrong, can it? I think of Willow. Now I understand her urge to kill.

No, not my chance to kill. My chance to stop him.

"But I haven't been on the road alone." He sweeps one arm behind him, toward me. "Parvin Blackwater has fought for you at every Council meeting. She has not stopped pleading your case and being your voice."

I can't stay hidden. I can't stay silent.

These are my people. And Skelley is presenting me as their hero.

I reach across the passenger seat and grab the gun. Then I reach for the door handle with my spare fingers. Solomon stops my arm with a weak grasp of his own. "No, Parvin."

"I need to, Solomon." I pull my arm gently from his hold, open the door, and step out.

The endless sea of people raise their fists and cheer.

Cheer.

And here I thought they wanted me dead. Their cheer is even more disconcerting because that means they think *I* can save them.

I keep the gun hidden and I stare at the back of Skelley's head.

He turns at the cheering to see me. He smiles. A real smile, not a smirk. A smile so filled with freedom and hope that I'm not sure it's him standing there beneath that fedora.

Suddenly, I believe him and the gun feels like a hot coal in my hand. God wants me to be *His* light, and murdering someone who doesn't yet know Him is not the light of God. It's anti-shalom, and I almost gave in to it.

I drop the gun and wave to the people, surrendering to God. Believing that maybe Solomon was right and God can redeem anyone. With a snap, this display of joy and hope hurts my heart like the blow of a hammer. How can I let them hope when I don't know what Skelley is going to do?

The moment the thought enters my mind, the mass of people scream. A tingle rides up my spine and I spin, trying to spot the cause of panic. "What's happening?"

Skelley frowns and glances around, too. "I don't . . . oh."

We see it at the same time. The projected Wall has tripled its speed, closing in on us. The mob scrambles to get away, but the extra space between walls is shrinking. Too fast. There are too many people. I see the Preacher—clad in his safe suit—fighting his way toward me with an Armor suit clenched between his fingers.

"No! Skelley, what's going on? Are you doing that?"

He shakes his head slowly. "Not me. I can only assume it's a pre-programed last hurrah from Brickbat to eradicate the world of Radicals."

My knees buckle.

"Stop the projection! Save us!" a woman screams.

The pleas and shrieks for help deafen me almost as much as my helplessness. The Wall grows closer and people are practically standing on each other, squeezing as tight as possible. I can't think of a way out without having to drive back to the control room at the Council building. If there was ever a time for the pirate chip, it's now.

I let out my killer-instinct and leap toward Skelley, pirate chip in hand. He throws up his arms, and I trap them against his body as we go tumbling to the ground. The people are the background music to my attack, stepping on our bodies, screaming, trampling us.

Somewhere in there, I hear Solomon's yell.

Skelley writhes, but then Solomon's with me, helping me hold him down. I tear the cap off the pirate chip, but then pause. Skelley's eyes stare at the chip.

"Solomon, you programmed it?" I ask.

"Yes." The word is barely a wheeze. He needs medical attention. And I need him. I need *him* to use the Preacher's Armor suit to get back to Prime. Maybe he can stop the projection before it kills everyone. But I know better.

We're going to be too late.

"It's not the terminating type, right?" Even with my mix of hatred, camaraderie, and confusion toward Skelley, I don't want to kill him. I have to chant that to myself so that the knowledge cap instinct doesn't do it for me.

"Nope."

Instead of fighting further, Skelley cranes to get his watch up in front of his face. "You're too late."

I plunge the chip into the back of his head at the base of his skull. He twitches, but Solomon holds his head steady with one of his Brawn-clad hands. Still, Skelley said we're too late and I know he's right.

The encroaching projection has reached the edge of the people. They're screaming, I'm screaming. We've failed.

The pirate chip lets out a beep, and I free Skelley, closing my hand around the chip so he can't take it from me. We're shoved against Skelley's car. There's no space to move. Skelley scrambles to his feet, but instead of coming for me, he glances back to the crowd, lifts his wristwatch to his eyes and smiles.

The last time Skelley looked at his watch like this, as though there was a countdown only he knew about, he shot Reid in the head. My heart flutters.

A massacre is coming. And I'm trapped . . . again.

He climbs onto the top of his car. "People of the USE! Are you ready to be free?" Skelley throws his arms open wide. They're screaming too loudly to hear him, but some look to him with a shine of fading hope in their wild eyes.

Skelley looks at his watch again. I lurch toward him. A kick from his foot sends me reeling back into Solomon's chest. Solomon and I both tumble into the people around us. Skelley wasn't even wearing his Brawn suit!

I scramble back onto all fours in time to see Skelley raise his hand in the air.

Everyone stares in a frozen second of anticipation and terror. He snaps his fingers and the sound echoes even over the din of the crowd. Then . . .

The projections disappear.

36

I'm paralyzed.

There are moments that are too far beyond human flexibility. No matter how prepared my mind might have been, it wasn't expecting to process the disappearance of the projected Wall by the mere snap of my enemy's fingers.

The people fare better than I—or at least they *look* like they're faring better. Most stand with mouths agape. All sound stops.

Skelley is the only human who moves. He steps down onto the car hood and sweeps his arm toward the gap in the Wall. No words are needed.

The spell breaks.

There's no frantic rush. No swarm like when the Wall first came down in pieces. This is different, like the air of freedom has taken hold in the form of hope.

They step forward as one, hesitant and slow. Taking in every moment. The first line of people glance at Skelley, then at the gap, then they quicken their pace. He's really letting them go.

I look to the sky. It's *all* gone.

The pirate chip falls from my hand. "What . . . did you do?"

Skelley turns back to me, looking as though all the world has been lifted from his shoulders. "I finished what you started."

He really freed them. He freed all the Radicals. The USE.

Skelley rocks a bit, and lifts a hand to his head. He frowns, then gives his head a shake. "Seems like you got it all."

Solomon lies panting on the ground beside the dropped pirate chip, still in his Brawn suit. He picks it up and holds it to the light. "For some reason, I believe you, Mr. Chase." And before I can say anything, Solomon crushes the chip between two fingers. There's a spark, a little pop of liquid, and the information behind the projected Wall is officially gone.

Forever.

The masses flow around us and I'm not sure what to do now. This isn't what I expected. I hardly did anything. I didn't do a mighty prayer or walk through the projection suitless, or . . . or . . .

God, this isn't how I expected it to end.

I WILL COMPLETE WHAT I HAVE STARTED IN YOU.

I laugh. *I'll take that to mean this* isn't *the end.* But I didn't start this. *He* did. He simply let me be His tool and now I get the luxury of standing in awe of Him.

A stranger's arms encompass me.

Reflex tells me to fight, but then someone—a woman—sniffs hard and whispers, "Thank you." She steps back. Waist-long red hair, a tattoo of words down her left arm, and running mascara. I don't know her, but she smiles beneath her streaming tears.

Before I can figure out how to respond, she's heading through the gap in the Wall toward the West. Someone else grasps my shoulder—a tall, older man with wrinkles and messy white hair. "You've brought shalom to us. Thank you."

I shake his hand, dumbfounded. *It wasn't me.* I was a passenger. Not even Skelley can take the credit. It was God. My God.

People hug Skelley as they pass. I never get a chance to move with all the thank-yous and tears and hand-shaking going on. When I glance back at Solomon, he's staring at the top of the Wall gap, smiling. Thinking.

I hope he's thinking about how Jude played such a big part in all this. Without Jude's sacrifice and adjustment to the Clocks, people would still be controlled by their Numbers and by the Council.

He pulls out his NAB from his pocket. "I'll let your father know things are safe."

Safe. That word has followed me, spoken flippantly from the lips of onlookers who don't understand all that I've gone through. But for once, it feels appropriate. "Thank you."

"Parvin!"

I spin. A tall albino man, shirtless, with cropped hair, pushes against the flow of people.

"Black!"

He reaches me. "My people will help yours."

"Were you trapped in the dome?" My stomach lurches. "Did anyone from your village . . . die?"

"We were in the forest, waiting."

"Is Ash here?" It's a stupid question. She's pregnant. Black shakes his head. "Is anyone here a healer? Solomon needs help."

Black kneels by Solomon and I retract Solomon's Brawn suit. Black inspects his leg and turns grim. "He needs medicine and sewing."

Without asking, I slap the Brawn suit against Black's chest. He writhes away as it slithers over him, then stills. "It will make you strong and you can run faster. Will you take him to your village? Is your village . . . okay?"

"It is far." He bends to pick up Solomon and lifts him so fast he almost falls backward.

Solomon groans, then laughs a little. "I feel like such a wimp."

I kiss his nasty, dirty forehead and don't mind one bit. "You're not."

Black brightens with every movement in the Brawn suit. "I like this clothing." He meets my gaze. "I will take him to the Ivanhoe camp." He gestures with his head to the many tents behind him that managed to avoid the dome projection.

Even better. Ivanhoe will have the tech Solomon needs. "Thank you, Black."

He moves to leave, but Solomon reaches for me. "Wait, I don't want to leave you." His eyes are determined, despite the pain and hollowness of blood loss behind them.

"I'll be fine." For the first time, I don't fear for his life. I don't fear our separation. I don't fear the Council.

I don't . . . fear.

My smile comes easily. "I know where you are. I'll come for you."

He shakes his head. "Not if I come for you first."

Then Black leaves, taking a large chunk of my heart with him. I monitor Skelley. He pats a woman on the back as she hugs him before she jogs to freedom. He did this. He used the knowledge cap to program the shut-down of the projection. And he did it Skelley Chase style . . . a televised performance.

Helicopters circle us, filming the surge of freedom. May their news screens inspire others to come across. One helicopter comes lower and lower until finally people scatter to let it land. The pilot throws his headset off, leaps from the helicopter, and sprints toward the gap. In the back, a reporter pauses before abandoning her camera and following him.

Enforcer soldiers cross the Wall as well, some clutching their guns to their chests like shields, others abandoning them on the ground.

At the base of the Wall, sun rebounds off glittering piles of trinkets. Bracelets, belts, earrings, wristbands, wooden boxes, high-tech thin wrist wires.

Clocks.

Abandoned Clocks.

The scene blurs. My nose tingles and I don't try to stop the tears. *You've done it, God. You . . . used me for something great.* I may not have destroyed the projection, but He started this adventure when I crossed the Wall the first time.

This—all of this—turned out to be so much bigger than I'd ever dared to think. Bigger than I *wanted*, but now—on this side—I don't mind.

Hours pass as Radicals trickle in from different cities. Skelley delivers Wilbur Sherrod to the Preacher personally. He and the Preacher have a long conversation, while Wilbur sits on the ground, back against the stone Wall and knocking his floppy sneakers together.

Zeke and my other faithful Enforcers show up, towing trailers filled with food, medical supplies, blankets, and tools. He gives me a salute as his little motorbike and trailer pass through the Wall gap and head after the albinos.

So *that's* the mission Skelley sent them on.

Albinos speak to some of the people who have crossed and point toward the distant tree line. I'm ready to run to the albino village and see Mother and Father, but more arms encompass me and I return to the present.

The people are endless.

The shalom is endless.

I can't stand beneath the weight of honor and thankfulness. I sink to my knees. People still press their hands on my shoulder, or into my grasp, whispering thank-yous or giving me hugs.

I simply shake my head. "It wasn't me. It was God's doing." I don't want the glory. *Do they see, God? Do they see You through this?*

I feel the wrap of His arms around me beneath the hugs of others.

The masses thin, but only slightly. I help an old lady over the rubble to the other side and place her in the hands of an albino. When I walk, I search the faces of people. Where is Tawny? Where is Christian? Did Cap come, or Gabbie? Are my friends safe? Alive?

I return to Skelley's green beetle car and lean against it for a moment. A shadow blocks me from the light and I look up. Skelley stands before me, holding the gun I'd dropped in the grass.

I glance at it, then up at his face "I'm not afraid of you, Skelley."

He tosses the gun away from him. "I never wanted you to be afraid."

"Then what did you want?"

He hesitates. "I wanted your story. I just . . . didn't expect it to affect *mine* so much." He reaches into his pocket and withdraws a small brown package tied with string. "Your emotigraphs, from all your travels. And . . . the NAB I took away from you. Your journal entries are still in there."

I gape at him. "I get it all back?" Why would he keep these? How did he know they were important to me? "This isn't so you can keep spying on me, is it?"

Skelley rolls his eyes. "Have Christian Hawke fix it up like you did before. I'm done following your story." He clears his throat and his voice comes out particularly grave. "These past few months, you . . . infiltrated my walls. You"—he gestures to the emotigraphs—"changed me." He doesn't sound happy about it. "I don't know who I am anymore."

My hand tightens around the package. "Then learn who you *should* be." I pull my Bible out from my pocket and hand it to him. "Don't argue. Just take it, and I won't ask what you do with it."

My lot in life seems to be always giving away my Bible.

Skelley hesitates, then accepts. He joins me against the car, leaning back, hands behind his head and eyes closed, breathing this in. "I think I finally see shalom."

The masses thin as people decide whether to go to Ivanhoe or go with the albinos. Skelley and I help direct people, but while I thrive off seeing their joy and freedom, each action of helping seems to drain Skelley.

We've been here for hours. I haven't kept track, but it's been a long time. I suddenly wonder what he's going to do now. He destroyed the leadership of the USE—possibly in an attempt to take over—and then gave the people what they wanted. There's no one else on this world for him to seek to please. He's met his goal and I'm willing to bet he feels pretty empty right now, since he hasn't really figured out that *God* is the one who fulfills our pursuits.

I walk up to him, rubbing the sunburn that's crisped my skin. "You really care about the people, Skelley."

I expect an *I told you so*, but instead, with eyes still closed, he says, "Yes."

The problem was never in his caring. It was in his mindset of what care *looks* like. To him, shooting Reid kept me alive for the people. To him, murdering Jude and stealing his Clock was to help Radicals find a new acceptance in life. To him, sending Radicals or poor citizens away in boxcars showed the High Cities he was cleansing the country.

It's always been about people pleasing, about being the one the people love. That's probably why he became a biographer in the first place—to grow in popularity before leading people in politics.

Sweat sticks his hair to his forehead and stains the crown of his fedora. His face is dirty and weathered. He doesn't look bored anymore. He looks . . . exhausted.

I take his hand. It's callused. "Come with us, Skelley. Come to the West. Start over."

He shakes his head. "There is a lot to do on this side."

He's set it up so he can be the new leader of the USE. Of course he's going to stay. "Why, though? Why are you thirsty for power? There's no Council anymore. Can't you leave it at that?"

"I know you think that completely eradicating any sort of government is the answer because that's how it works in the West. But that's dangerous."

"How?"

He gives his mocking, bored smile. "Think about it, Parvin. The last time there was destruction of the government on this continent, the people built a Wall and the Clocks were invented." He plants both hands on my shoulders. "I know your vision. I know you don't trust me, but I'll do my best for the people."

That will be hard to do if he has no people to lead. I hope they'll all cross the Wall, but I know better. Some will stay. Some will turn to Skelley. And he hasn't changed in the way I'd hoped. But this is a start.

Skelley circles his car and opens the driver's door.

"Wait." I press my hand against the hood of the car. How do I say this? Skelley looks at me, waiting. "Thank you."

His lips quirk to one side. "Good-bye. Thanks for your story."

I guess if I've done my job right, Skelley will see God through me.

His gaze drops to the ground then, in an undertone, "I'm . . . sorry about Reid. And Jude. And . . . many things."

Sorry. It's not a plea for forgiveness but, for Skelley, it's a sacrifice of pride to say these things. In this moment, it's enough. Maybe it won't be tomorrow, but forgiveness is a process of surrender. I'm willing to go through it. "I forgive you, Skelley. I truly do."

He walks forward and retrieves his trampled Brawn suit square from the grass.

"Where will you go?"

Skelley waggles the little matchbox at me. "There are some Radical slaves that need to return to their homes. Or, I guess, find new homes, since their homes are likely destroyed."

The slaves. The shipping containers filled with Radicals who were sold in Panama and who knows what other countries. He's going to save them. "Why would you do that after sending them away?"

"That was Brickbat's doing—always obsessed with 'purifying' our country. That's why he experimented on Willow."

I try not to think about Willow right now, other than concern for her whereabouts. "How will you find the slaves? They could be anywhere."

He winks. "You're forgetting something." He gets in the car, starts the engine, and rolls down the window. "I can do anything."

With a burst of acceleration, he's gone.

37

"Parvin!" A pregnant human bullet slams into me. "Oh Lord, you're alive. You're alive . . ." Tawny hugs me long and tight until my air supply is fully cut off, which is good because I tear up knowing I have to share the news about her father's death.

I've been at the Wall gap for two whole days, directing people and sending them with albinos or connecting them with Ivanhoe soldiers. The Ivanhoe camp provided me with food and sleep. Solomon is much less pale now that he's stitched and healing.

The main reason I've stayed is to wait for Tawny or Christian or Cap or Gabbie or *anyone* I know to show up. I couldn't have lived with myself if I'd returned to the albino village and never seen Tawny again.

Now she's here. Hugging me.

Behind her is Christian Hawke, Solomon's dad. Raw scar wounds mar his neck and arms. They arrived at the Wall in a shabby old Enforcer car. He sprints to me. "Is Sol still with the Ivanhoe camp?"

"Last time I checked." If Christian knows that Solomon is with the camp, then they must have been communicating via NAB.

I return Tawny's hug, pressing my hand and stump tight around her frame. But not *too* tight. She's pregnant, after all. "Tawny . . . I—"

A TIME TO RISE

"No!" She leans back, her face a little pudgier than the last time I saw her and glowing. "Let me say it first. I love you, Parvin."

My throat closes. She . . . does? "I love you, too, Tawny." I didn't have to search for her. She's here. "Are you coming across with us?" *Please, God . . . let my family be unified. Together.*

She glances back at Christian. "Yes. I've been helping Christian at his hospital and, well, he's quite capable of delivering a baby anywhere. I want to be with family." She takes my hand and stump in hers. "I want to be free."

That's when I notice there's no Clock band on her wrist anymore. "How'd you get it off?"

She holds up my stump and digs in her pocket. Out comes a tiny device that looks like Solomon's penlight. She holds it against the wire, presses a button, and I feel a single sharp shock. Then the band is cut in two. "Like that." One look at my face draws a laugh from her. "Christian whipped it up. The Hawke boys are quite inventive." She nudges me. "As if you didn't know."

It's strange standing here, in this place that's been a battleground, a refuge, a place of rebellion, and now the gateway toward shalom.

God said fear not.

Here I am safe.

God said to follow Him.

Now we are free.

God said to rise.

And I found my purpose.

"Dad!" That's . . . Solomon's voice.

I spin as Christian starts running. Across the gap of the Wall, standing with a cane in one hand and wearing a Brawn suit, is my Solomon Hawke. Christian collides with him on the other side, both with new scars and wounds the other hasn't seen yet.

Over his dad's shoulder, Solomon spots me and smiles. *"I told you I'd come back for you."*

It's been only two days, but he looks fantastic. I reach out my hand toward Tawny. "Shall we?"

She tosses my broken Clock band in the pile at the base of the Wall. "Let's go."

Arm-in-arm, we cross the Wall. Unified with my people. Solomon waits on the other side, a beacon of hope for me. Arms wide. In this moment, the pain and loss of the past, the pain and loss that may come in the future . . . don't matter. God renews. God redeems. And we are unified in Him. That is enough reason for me to love Solomon, to join Solomon as a teammate, and . . . to *marry* Solomon.

We're halfway to the tree line before I break off and find the Preacher at the edge of his war camp. We've both been so busy that I haven't had a chance to thank him or check on Wilbur. The camp is made of thousands of tents, all shimmery and probably created by Wilbur. I give a brief bow from the waist.

The Preacher stands firm, still dressed in the red-and-black outfit he used to cross the projection. "Well, Parvin, you caused quite a bit of chaos. But in the end, you achieved your goal."

"Thank you for coming to help my people. And thank you for helping Solomon." I think back to the first time I met him.

He shrugs and holds his hand out toward one of his men, who places a goblet of wine in it. "I did what I had to. They stole my couturier and destroyed our train, after all." He gestures behind him, and that's when I see the newly created yellow locomotive.

The *Ivanhoe Independent*. "You extended its track."

He shrugged. "It seemed necessary. It will leave in an hour, taking some of your refugees to Ivanhoe. Are you returning?"

I look back at Solomon, who waits with Tawny and Christian by the trees. "Not yet. But . . . someday."

This time *he* bows. "You are welcome." Then he grins. "It's a lovely place for weddings, you know."

My face warms and a giggle bursts out before I can catch it. Little traitor. I turn sober. "How's Wilbur?"

"He will be fine." The Preacher says it with such flippancy, that I wonder if he truly understands the change that came over Wilbur after being held captive by the Council.

"Is someone going to help him?"

"We have excellent mental healers who use simulations—like what you went through—for trauma patients. Wilbur will be back to his glorious creations within weeks, I assure you."

I'm not reassured. "I'll come visit him soon." To check on him.

The Preacher nods and then turns with a flourish.

And that's that.

I return to my family. Solomon wraps me in a long hug, feeling solid and strong again. Tawny holds out an arm for me and I take it. My family—my, how it grows so quickly. "Let's go find some albinos, shall we?"

Solomon nods his head toward the trees. There's already a trodden path through the forest from the USE refugees. Good thing Black's albino village doesn't make people atone anymore.

Tawny keeps her arm linked with mine as we walk back to the trees. Once we're in the shadows she asks what I've been dreading. "Did . . . my father make it out?"

I shake my head before she's finished. The tears ride the wave of high emotions. "I'm so sorry."

Solomon keeps walking, possibly to give us some privacy. To my chagrin, Tawny hugs me again. "Oh, Parvin, it's not your fault. I would have been surprised if he made it."

"You don't . . . blame me?"

She lets out a long sigh. "Of course not."

I see reflections of Mother's strength in her. "He said to tell you he's sorry about Reid."

She's silent for a long time, then nods. "Thank you."

"Are you . . . sad that Brickbat—uh, your father—is gone?"

What sort of question is that? Why do all my inappropriate questions come out around *her*?

This time, she doesn't get angry. "I'm sad for him, but I'm also . . . freed from him. I hope that's not wrong to say."

I shake my head, picturing *my* father. What a good, calm, and kind man he is. I can't imagine growing up with a father who never married my mother and visited only to beat me.

I kiss Tawny on the cheek, then trot to catch up with Solomon to give Tawny some time alone.

"Are you okay?" he asks the moment I join him.

I nod. "I'm more than okay. What about *you?*"

He hardly uses the cane as he walks. It was either made from dropped branches or the albinos have truly overcome the captivity of their old beliefs. "I'm doing great. The Ivanhoans have some intense healing techniques, but I opted for . . . *primitive*. You know I don't like tech in my body." He winks. "I watched the news on the NAB while there. Your face was blasted on every video every day."

"It was?" Great. More fame. It doesn't matter. I'm in the West now and no one is watching the news screens *here*. "So, I wanted to tell you"—I smile despite my attempts to be serious—"I love you, Solomon Hawke. And I want to live life with you, as a team. I want to marry you . . . even though you technically haven't asked yet."

He doesn't react with a whoop or a shout. But the smile is all I need, and he looks ready to burst with joy. "All right, then, Miss Parvin. And don't you worry; I'll get on one knee."

"I better be your bridesmaid!" Tawny shouts from behind us. When I look over my shoulder, she winks, even though she's still crying.

What a weird day.

Christian breaks from the side trees and joins us on the path. He has a giant pack, probably filled with medical tools.

I look ahead of us. "How much longer until the albino village?" Mother is there. Father is there. I *hope* Willow and Elm are there. By now they've probably realized what happened, what with all the USE people swarming the village.

I need to see Mother with my own eyes.

"It is a few hours' walk," Christian says.

"Well, for once in my life, I'm not pressed for time." Everyone laughs, though it's not very funny. I think we're just relieved to be *free*. I try to ignore the nagging haunt of the open Wall behind me. *Anyone* can come through now, even enemies.

But then I remember God's promises. I will fear not. He's broken down the walls that interrupt shalom. He can—no, He *will*—stop those who come against us. *He* will rise for *us*. And we'll join Him.

As we walk—me holding Solomon's hand and looping an arm through Tawny's—Tawny chatters about the adventures I missed out on. "Did you know that Fight and Idris broke the door to the tunnel?"

I duck under a branch and hold it up for her. "You mean Opening Three?"

"Yes! They broke it down a few days before the projected Wall went up, because Fight had the Brawn suit. Then when the others from the orphanage went through, he put the door back up. The bridge that Elm built saved everyone's lives."

Solomon jumps in. "I told Dad. He and Tawny helped sneak Radicals through at nighttime until the Wall projection went up. The Enforcer guards were on your side, Parvin. Instead of guarding people from going through, they guarded the door so people *could* get through."

Tawny shushes him with a flap of her hand. "*Anyway*, Christian and I went through, only to find that the Preacher was already sending everybody to Mrs. Newton's house! He gave us a bag of Armor suits and fought at the broken part of the Wall to *distract*

the soldiers so that people could keep going through the Opening."
She laughs in victory. "We fooled them!"

"You are amazing." *I am amazed by You, God.* "What made
you come back to this side?"

Tawny shrugs. "Well, we started spending time with the
Radicals here, telling people who could keep it quiet that we had
a way through. I just . . . didn't want to miss the action."

"Tawny, you're *pregnant.*" I add a wink so she knows I don't
blame her. *I* wanted to join the action, no matter the risks, too.

"Yes, well, the baby will like these stories when he's born."

I gasp. "It's a boy?"

She laughs. "I don't know. I've decided not to find out, but I'll
switch back and forth to keep myself amused."

The walk through the forest is the nearest thing to magic.
Moss glints under late morning dew. We continue on a downward
slope and my steps grow faster and faster. Mother is ahead.

I need to apologize for what happened to her. Are her burns
healing? No matter what her disposition is, I need to be with her
again. I need to spend the rest of my life showing her how much
I love her and how much life God has given me.

And then there's Father, and Ash, and Mrs. Newton . . .

This time, when I see them, I won't have to say good-bye.

After a couple of hours, my feet start a familiar ache—the type
I first experienced when walking for a long period of time. I sat
in my little Council member room for far too long. My feet have
grown lazy.

I welcome the ache. It means I'm heading home again.

"Almost there!" Solomon grows lighter with each step. Those
Ivanhoe healers work magic.

The bird chirps lessen and distant voices take their place. It's
like when I approached the market in Unity Village—the sounds
of talking, trading, and cordiality thickens the air with welcomed
warmth.

My heart quickens, sending bursts of nervousness to my stomach. My arrival will be a surprise. Finally, a blessing instead of a curse.

We come into the clearing of Ash and Black's albino village, though now the other skin colors outweigh the albino. People lounge on the grass surrounding the brook that cuts through the middle of the village. Black skin, albino skin, Caucasian skin, brown skin . . . all sorts. And all of them seem to be smiling.

But my eyes don't linger on any of them too long. My gaze searches out one face in particular, and when I see it my heart weeps. She sits on the bank with her bare feet in the water and a skirt hiked up to her knees. One leg is so mottled and scarred, I'm not sure it's even functional.

Mother's face is a mixture of all the skin colors. Her left cheek sags, a polished shine of scars. Red blotches cover the rest of her face and one eye is droopy. Her lips are thinner and a little more twisted than before.

Oh Mother . . . what did I do to you?

Her gaze drifts over to where our group steps into the village. It lands on me.

I don't need her original face to recognize the joy that blooms beneath her tightened skin. She scrambles to her feet and hobble-runs to me with a jilted gait, using a gnarled stick as support. I stumble toward her, too, my arms outstretched.

"Parvin!" Her raspy breath is a golden gift.

"Mother." I'm wrapped in her arms before I can even finish speaking her name. She doesn't sway, doesn't falter in her embrace.

I am hers. I am her daughter and her joy.

I am full.

Tucked in her arms like this, I don't bother to wonder about the future. There are answers I will never have—like what happens to Skelley, what the future of the USE holds, or whether the Clocks will ever be reinvented. All that matters is that I opened the gateway to choice. I found shalom and I brought the doorway to others.

That was my job.

WELL DONE, GOOD AND FAITHFUL SERVANT.

"I think He's proud of me, Mother," I sob into her shoulder.

She runs her hand over my hair. "So am I, dear one."

We stay like this for a long time while everyone else mingles with the crowd, meeting and hugging and crying. Father finds us and joins in the weepy reunion. I kiss his whiskery cheek, and he hugs me tighter than ever before.

They both whisper, "I love you." And I hear God's voice in theirs.

Father leaves to fetch us some food. Mother and I walk back to the pond where there's still an open spot, but it feels like *our* spot. Our spot of solitude to just be mother and daughter.

"Oh Mother, I'm . . . so sorry about the train. I should never have let you—"

"Hush." She smacks my leg. "It may not be pretty, but God used it to reveal Himself to me."

My jaw opens and closes twice before I get words out. "H-He did?" She's talking about God. She's talking about Him *confidently*.

"I used to fear Him, Parvin."

I shake my head. "Isn't that what we're supposed to do?" It says to fear the Lord in the Bible, but I'm still not sure what that means, especially with God constantly reminding me to fear not.

"Not the way *I* feared Him. You know the story of Job?"

"He lost everything, didn't he?" I'm glad that's not my story.

"Yes. I was afraid that was the lot God gave me. I was afraid of His tests and the fact that He's, well, *God*, and He'll do whatever He wants for His glory."

The way she says it makes God sound like a power-hungry control freak. "But His glory is *beautiful*, Mother. It's not the way you make it sound."

She smiles and it's crooked and deformed, but so stunning. "I know, Parvin. I know that, now. It's funny how God sent you to this side, you met Ash and introduced her to Him, and then she cared for me and renewed *my* view of Him." Tears stream out of only one of her eyes.

I brush them away with my thumb. I made Mother cry. But these tears are so lovely I can't bring myself to feel guilty.

"God has given me a new life, a new family, and a new understanding." She hugs me and I lean into her until I'm enveloped by her love. "And He used *you.*"

The reunions that take place after this moment only add to my awe. Who knew a human could feel such elation? Such hope? Such . . . shalom?

Ash kisses my cheek and Black pats my shoulder with a firm hand. Father gives Tawny a whiskery kiss on the forehead and hugs both Tawny and me at once. Tawny and Mother seem to be on a new leaf and spend the day talking about the baby.

But the best part is when Solomon sneaks me behind a hut and finally kisses me in a situation that doesn't involve our near-death. He rests his forehead on mine and stares into my eyes.

I could stay like this for days, just like this. In his presence, enjoying his company.

"I'm ready to explore the world with you." He grins. "What do you think?"

He doesn't say *get married*, and I'm glad. Because someday we will get married. Someday soon, I hope. I'm not sure when, but that's okay for now. Marriage isn't the end, just like my ticking Clock wasn't the end. God has created adventure for every single day and I'm ready to share it.

"No way, Solomon Hawke. No more traveling for me for a *long* time."

"But someday . . ."

I wrap my arms around his waist and pull him into a hug. "Tally ho."

He laughs, giving away our hiding spot. Willow rounds the corner, sees us, and pulls up short. She's fully brown-skinned now, with a fluff of white hair. She's never been more lovely.

"Willow!" I jerk out of Solomon's arms.

She looks between us, then her gaze stays on me. Her chin quivers and, after a brief hesitation, she bursts into tears.

"Willow! What's wrong?" I kneel down and she falls into my arms.

"I'm rotten, Parvin! I'm *rotten!*"

I brush my hand over her fuzzy hair. "Shh . . . no, you're not. No."

She takes a shuddering gasp. "Yes, I am. I knew it was bad to kill the angry man even *before* Ash showed me in your Bible book. I knew it." Her sobs are so young, yet so broken. "And now my skin is spoiled like a rotten tree."

What can I do? Solomon kneels beside us and wraps his long arms around us both. "You are forgiven, Willow. And you're *not* rotten."

She shakes her head. "He died, didn't he?"

I nod. I won't lie to her. "But Solomon's right. God can forgive anything. You are repentant. It will hurt, and it will take you a long time to heal but"—I hold her an arms' length away—"You *will* heal. And God will grow you."

"But I hate myself," she whispers. "I touched Elm's skin and now he's turning brown, too."

"Because he loves you. Because he knows your color doesn't matter."

"But other friends won't touch me. They don't want to be brown. They hate it." Innocent and carefree Willow is gone. My heart aches for the journey she's led, but I already see God opening her eyes to His embrace in all of this.

"But God does not hate you." I try a smile. "You and I will pray together every day. We will learn more about Him together. And we'll heal together, okay?"

She glances to Solomon, then back to me. *"Can I?"*

"Yes," I say fiercely.

I think of all the ways I've had to heal and Solomon has had to heal. I think of Mother and how she's healing from her own long-lived fear of a loving God. "We are all healing. You are not alone. You will *never* be alone."

She nods. The tears continue for a while and neither Solomon nor I let her go. After ten long minutes, she leans back and wipes her nose. "I'm okay. I'm okay for now."

I nod.

She attempts a mischievous grin, but even I can tell it's forced. "You two are going to graft, aren't you?"

"Where should we have the grafting ceremony?" Solomon asks her, joining in with mirth.

His reaction helps her along and she throws her arms wide. "Here, silly!"

Solomon winks at me. We leave our little secret space. After all, there will be plenty of time for kissing another day. For now, we twine fingers and just . . . breathe.

The next several days are spent building huts and guiding Radicals and people from the USE. Some are afraid from what they read in my X-book about the albinos, but Ash and Black set them at ease with long talks about how they changed.

A lot of the time those talks involve my Bible.

Things start to settle, and the feeling of *home* is born among those of us staying in the village for a while. On April second, I turn nineteen and feel three lifetimes older than when I met with Trevor Rain on my One-Year Assessment Day—the day I allowed my impulse to throw me into a tornado.

On my birthday, with a wreath of herbs in my messy, loose

hair, I stand in the center of the village and look around me. The dogwood trees are turning greener, budding a little. Their presence sparks the desire to go adventuring. Not too far. Something close and simple like . . . learning how to walk a tightrope.

I have time to learn that, now. And Willow's ready to teach me. Solomon's already tried it a few times, and I don't want him to beat me to it.

It's so strange to think that I once walked through these woods, forced by Skelley's traitorous plan, lost my hand, lost my brother, lost Jude, lost so many hours of freedom.

But I gained shalom.

Was it all worth it? Was this wild adventure that changed my nation, my heart, and my faith *worth* it?

Oh my, yes. All because, after a desperate prayer on a hospital floor so long ago, God showed me that—with Him . . .

. . . it's *always* time to *live*.

Epilogue

December 25, 2150

Merry Christmas to me—I now have a journal! It can't be hacked, but it can get waterlogged like Reid's did . . . because it's made of paper! I learned today that Solomon spent the past several months trading traveling Ivanhoans for paper and binding this journal as a Christmas gift to me.

Fear not, little journal. I've been learning to tightrope walk, so there's little chance you'll fall into the Dregs.

I'm unsure where to start writing, but I want to tell my story. It's daunting imagining all that must be written, but I've promised myself not to write one-sentence entries like Mother and Reid did.

Before I step back in time to my One-Year Assessment, here's my update since moving to the albino village. Mother, Father, and I built our own stone hut, with Solomon's help. It's very cozy. Solomon and Elm share a hut because they're both bachelors.

Solomon brought the tin of knowledge caps back from Russia. He finally told me about them. He's spent the past several months identifying their contents. The green caps contain survival knowledge. Now that he's taken one, he's been teaching others various survival techniques and about plants. Even the albinos are learning new things from him.

I finally figured out a way to put my knowledge cap to use. I've been teaching self-defense. Some people want to reach out to the other albino clans and share the message of Christ. I am helping prepare them so they can protect themselves from attacks. I don't feel dirty from that cap knowledge anymore.

Solomon and I will be leaving for Ivanhoe soon to visit Mrs. Newton, Laelynn, Wilbur, and check on the other Radicals who recently moved there. Like Cap, the milkman! Can you believe his goats survived? They were still in Unity Village after the bombings happened. He and his goats came through the village and then hopped on the Ivanhoe Independent. *But he informed me that Gabbie Kenard decided to stay in the USE for now.*

Gabbie said she ran across Trevor Rain in Prime. He's quit being a Mentor. I'm glad he's alive. Meanwhile, Zeke and the other Enforcers are staying with Mrs. Newton, helping settle the Radicals into jobs.

Frenchie and Kaphtor have kept in touch via Solomon's NAB. They're married! Already! That happened fast.

Fight and Idris have stayed with the albinos. Fight took a liking to hands-on work—gathering dead standing, gardening, building huts, hunting. His previous life in Prime kept him pretty stationary. This is good for him. Idris spends a lot of time with the women, teaching them more about the Bible. I like listening in on those meetings because I'm still ignorant about so many of the lessons and stories in there.

The two of them help Christian Hawke care for the orphans we rescued in Prime. He outlived his old Clock. I'm so thankful because he was scheduled to zero-out last April. Now, Solomon doesn't have to lose his father.

I feel so close to God, but in a different way. A calmer way. I'm realizing that growth in Him can come through the crazy trials of trying to save the world (and not get killed along the way) as well as during the calm, quiet moments of life. That's when I hear His whispering. It's beautiful.

Mother doesn't have to use a walking stick anymore. I've never seen her so happy, which in turn, brings out Father's more vocal and goofy side. We are a unified family and my heart is full. She spends most of her time gardening. Solomon helps her with his new plant and survival knowledge. She's grown quite fond of her future son-in-law. Father has started building bridges over the Dregs, with Black and Ash's permission. He still tries to use fallen logs so as to not upset other albino villagers.

Willow is still struggling with what she did, but Tawny's taken her on as a little sister of sorts. They do everything together, and I think it helps show Willow the power of forgiveness. She's still tough and strong, but not as confident or filled with light as before. I think she'll come out of this okay. It will just take some time.

She seems to have accepted the change in her skin. There are no mirrors in the village, and we're a melting pot of color anyway. It doesn't bother me—or anyone else, really—but it's been a tough transition. To distract herself, she's spent the past year helping with the orphans. It always seems to bring out the bright, original Willow I first met. She has demanded to come to Ivanhoe with Solomon and me. It will almost be like rectifying the trip she, Jude, and I tried to take when I left them behind. Except Elm is coming, too. He's her greatest encouragement and supporter.

Oh, Gloria and Sasha are alive! They didn't blame me for the death of their sled dogs; instead they thanked me for saving those I could. Solomon and I sent them some compensation. And . . . they sent me a pup! Gumbo's the daddy. I named the pup Gumbo Junior. Not very original, but I'm allowed that luxury. He's coming to Ivanhoe with us.

My favorite update: Tawny had her baby on June 8, 2150, and named him Antony Reid Blackwater. I love it—it's Reid's name, but flipped. Antony's the fattest mini-human I've ever laid eyes on. Ash also had her baby—a girl named Magnolia, and she's the perfect playmate for Antony. I declared that they should be grafting partners when they're older. Tawny just pursed her lips.

Last, and possibly the least expected, is Skelley Chase. He's been sending me photos via my NAB. Just photos, not emotigraphs. Every photo has a group of slaves freed from their masters. It's been nine months since I saw him last. He really can do anything. In fact, he's back in the USE now and stepping back into a political role. People are running for president and he's a candidate, though not doing so great the last I heard. I think he ought to stick to biographying.

Oh, and I learned something from the news reports that were talking about presidential candidates . . . Skelley has no middle name! The sneak!

Solomon and I have spent nice, calm time together, learning more Scripture and rising above the trials of each day. Yesterday he took me on a walk down the river and he finally got on one knee! We're planning the wedding for April. That's four months away! I keep rolling the name Parvin Brielle Hawke over in my mind. Doesn't it sound perfect? Mrs. Newton is going to help me sew my dress.

Those are my updates.

Inside this journal, I'm going to write my story. I'm rewriting my autobiography, but I'm starting it at the part when I really started living. In fact, I thought up a rather brilliant first line.

There was once a time when only God knew the day you'd die . . .

Dear Reader,

Are you crying right now? Because I'm totally crying. Can you believe the journey is over? I've put you through a lot, and you stuck with me. I put *Parvin* through a lot, but she came out of it stronger and fiercer and mighty in the Lord.

Thank you for reading her story. Thank you for hurting with her, for growing with her, for questioning life with her. Thank you for being SO AWESOME that I don't even know how to handle your fan-ness! I couldn't have completed this long road of writing the *Out of Time Series* without your constant encouragement, fan art, love, squealing, tolerance, and His grace. You helped me persevere and not give up. THANK YOU. *giant hugs*

Whether or not you liked the story, would you consider writing a brief, honest review of my books on Amazon and/or Goodreads? Reviews help get my books into the hands of new readers! It's one of the greatest gifts a reader can give an author. (And if you're feeling self-conscious, I promise that I don't mind negative reviews! I just like honesty. ☺)

Be sure to hunt me down on social media because I'm slightly addicted to connecting with readers. (Not in a creepy way. Only because I love you all. *wink*) You can find me on:

> My website: *http://nadinebrandes.com*
> Facebook: *@NadineBrandesAuthor*
> Instagram: *@NadineBrandes*
> Goodreads: *@NadineBrandes*
> Twitter: *@NadineBrandes*

Thank you for who you are. I pray daily that you grow more and more to be a bringer of shalom. Arise in Christ!

—Nadine

Discussion Questions

- What do you think it means to *arise* for God's glory? What does that mean in your life?

- How has Parvin's character and view of life changed since the beginning of the first book, *A Time to Die?*

- After Willow was rescued, Parvin tried to reach and comfort her to little avail. Are there hurting people in your life who you feel you can't reach? What are some ways you can help/reach hurting friends?

- Parvin blamed herself for what happened to Willow. Are there things that have happened to loved ones that you blame yourself for? How can you give them over to God?

- Parvin and Solomon strive to be honest with each other, and they rely on each other for advice and support. How important do you think honesty—even when it is scary or awkward—is to friendships and other relationships?

- When Skelley Chase is injured by the dogs, Parvin tries to heal him through a prayer. God doesn't perform a miracle of healing. Have you ever experienced something similar, where you asked God for something and it didn't happen even when you thought it would be good? How can you be patient and trust in God's sovereignty even when He doesn't answer prayers the way we want Him to?

- When saving Skelley Chase's life, Parvin was determined not to give up pulling the dogsled because Christ didn't give up carrying His cross. While most won't find themselves pulling a dogsled, what are some ways to daily pick up your cross (or pull your dogsled) to follow/be like Christ? What makes you want to give up?

- How did Willow's self-image change when her skin color changed? What if you were a different race/background/gender/ etc.? How would your self-image or life change?

- The knowledge caps were tempting and slightly addictive to the taker. What lengths do we go to, to get the things we want? Do we act selflessly or selfishly? What boundaries can we set in our lives to avoid/withstand peer pressure in these situations?

- Parvin wonders "Can anyone be redeemed?" a few times throughout the story in regards to Brickbat and Skelley. What do you think?

Acknowledgments

So many people gave me kicks in the rear or chocolate to help me finish this series. I'm so thankful for the family that can be found in others. So in an attempt to show my gratitude on paper, I'd like to say thank you . . .

To Daylen—Everyone thinks Jude and Solomon are swoon-worthy, but they're *nothing* compared to you. Thank you for being the most encouraging and godly husband I could have ever dared to dream of. You are the greatest bringer of shalom to my life.

To Steve Laube—The most hard-working, brilliant, and witty publisher I have the honor of writing for. I'm so very honored to be one of your authors. To Jeff Gerke—for dropping everything to edit the nasty sludge-filled first drafts so I could make my deadlines. To Karen Ball—my amazing agent and editor. I'm so thankful and blessed by your friendship, your hard work, and your endless godly attitude. *hugs* To Kirk DouPonce—for signing my own book for me because I'm still starstruck over these covers. They're incredible. You're incredible.

To Mom and Dad—thank you will never be enough. Your lives shaped me into the writer I am. I love you. To Angie Brashear—for being calm while I freaked out on the phone and claimed this was the worst thing I've ever written. Thank you for your pep talks. *wink*

To Al Russo—for getting me a dogsled ride. I still don't know how you did it, but I owe you a lifetime of memories and thanks. To Aunt Angela and Uncle Frank—you'll totally be in the movie. *grin* To Lauren Cole—for your French background and help with cuisine. Thank your mom for letting me steal her name.

To Mary Weber—not sure you know this, but your class at the 2015 ACFW Conference totally revamped my passion for this book. Thank you for reminding me of God's calling! To Katie Grace—my word war buddy, fellow cocoa drinker, friend, and Owl Ninja. You, girl, have made this past year one of great joy. *hugs* Thanks for being you. God's going to use you to shake up this world. I know it.

To My Camp NaNo cabinmates—Katie Grace, Alea Harper, Natasha Roxby, Athelas, FaithSong, Rebel Rider, Mickayla, Ana Ideline . . . I never *never* would have finished the first draft without your word wars! For realz. To my beta readers who were forced to read this book in all its ugliness in less than a week because of my deadlines: Lisa, Angie, Josh, Binsk, Rosalie, & Megan. *hugs and hearts* Thank you.

To My Street Team, Launch Teams, and Ninjas—YOU ROCK! Your support, your excitement, your fangirling/fanboying and memes keep me laughing and remind me that God *is* using these books. Gold ninja stars for all of you. *wink*

Last and most important, my Savior Jesus Christ. Again and again, You showed me that the words are from You, even when I feel like they're sludge. You are my everything. You are my shalom. Thank you for dousing my life in purpose and allowing me to spend it doing something I love—not just writing, but glorifying You.

ISAIAH 60:1-2

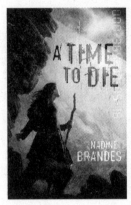